THE
CHILDREN OF
THE STARS

by A. L. Whyte

book one

SAIQA

Originally published by Arte L Whyte at
Smashwords
All rights reserved
Copyright 2016 Arte L Whyte
Cover artwork by T A Matlock

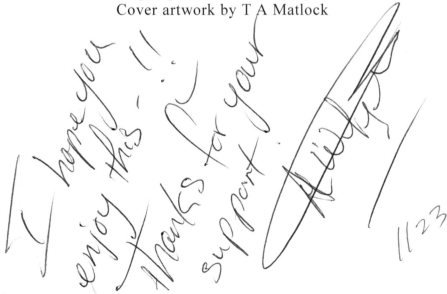

Acknowledgements

I started this novel six years ago as part of the internet challenge by Nanowrimo. I quickly realized that writing an actual book in one month was not feasible for me and probably the same for a majority of well-established writers. Amy Tan takes ten years to write a novel, while the more prolific of us, like Steven King, will spend up to eight months just to create his first draft. I had wanted to write this epic for some time as it was running around the inside of my brain; so I thank you Nanowrimo for your challenge.

There are many people to thank; some for their feedback and some for their support of my Indiegogo campaign. Since this is going to be on the internet I am only using their first names. You all know who you are.

There are a couple of exceptions; a big thank you to Eliza Gilkyson for allowing me to use her beautiful song 'Requiem' in the novel. Also Jane Mackay, my editor, whose insight and hard work made me a better writer.

I wish to thank the following folks for their feedback: my good friend Gary and his partner Tanya, Claude and Claudia, Autumn, Amara, Bob, Terri, Jimmy, Nicole and Bonnie. I am sure I'm forgetting someone, but please note that I am grateful for all the input I received.

My thanks to those of you that participated in my Indiegogo campaign: hugs to you all. I especially want to thank, Dawn, Margo, Henri and Charlie, Bill, Margo (again) Tanya and Gary and Carol for your extra support.

For a story that uses cutting edge science and then projects it four hundred years into the future I had to do a lot of research. It is my intent to put all the internet sites that I visited up on the future website of this science fiction series. The domain name has been purchased. It is called 'achildofthestarz.com'. However, I think it necessary to give a quick nod to Wikipedia. I spent a lot of time there.

This novel is dedicated to my two beautiful daughters; Nichelle and Tera. Thank you girls for choosing me and your mom; you both light up our lives.

CONTENTS

PROLOGUE

Telas stood before the Hall. Which was puzzling—why was he here now? He had not been on his home planet for over a thousand years and he had no plan to return. Yet here he was.

Many of the city buildings stood waiting in anticipation of a people, a society that had left centuries ago, maybe never to return. Even though the exodus took over one hundred and fifty cycles of his sun, in his mind it had happened too fast: a series of irrational decisions that led his people down the path of political expediency and into the catastrophic decision of war.

Some of the young immortal Sachone men and women were influenced by the short lives of the more primitive alien societies they had visited. These short and dramatic alien lives were filled with wild ideas of religions, mysticism and romantic concepts of all-powerful single deities. One of the immortals who were deeply affected was a man who had called himself the Prophet Shelon. He promoted a deity he had called "The One."

According to Shelon, "The time has come for all the immortals of Sachone to make a mortal choice." To promote the will of The One, it was time to live in accordance with the Book of One. For some of the more radical ideologues it also meant it was time "to die in the name of The One."

Shelon had influenced some very powerful people, and their message soon became ubiquitous. They saturated the planet's media, pervading the daily politics and lives of all Sachones with their ideology.

Then one day, children, rare as they were, became a political necessity. Why would an immortal being desire a child? Children reminded you of your age. Children were a burden better left to mortals, desperate to guarantee the survival of their species. But the new religion demanded progeny in the name of The One.

Many of the converted left the cities to commune with other families. Conflicts between the radicals and the heathens in the cities soon escalated. Outright lies and misrepresentations on both sides escalated into terrorism, and then to all-out war.

The horror of their self-destruction was too much. At some point it all stopped. Some pointed fingers, others cried, but many, horrified by the atrocities perpetrated by one side or the other, just gave up and faded away; some into space and some into pure energy.

A few stayed and tried to rebuild; but the devastation was so severe it took a long time. Though much of the capital, Kentron, had been completed, along with some poignant monuments to those who had died, the pain was too much, and one by one those who had stayed gave up and followed the others. Telas was one of the last to leave.

What was left on the planet was a shadow of the children of its own evolution. A sad and poignant tale of a people that had once lived there, silently told in ideograms and monuments. If a planet could cry, Sachone surely would.

Telas looked into the reflecting pool and saw himself. Even though he was thousands of years old, he still looked as young as he had around the time of his fiftieth cycle of his star..

Why am I here?

He studied the buildings around the Grey Hall. It was clear the auto-structural support systems had given up on building maintenance. Plant life had encroached around the ancient walkways and here and there dust and debris had snuggled into nooks and crannies. Much like the people that used to live here, some of the original structures were thousands of years old.

The round Grey Hall at the center of Kentron once held a powerful democratic government. At the height of its power some had called it the "beating heart" of the universe. Here, great virtual debates were held on politics, the arts and ethics. Before the wars it was the center of an extraordinary people.

Now gone . . . except for two.

He reminisced over the buildings flowing away from the great Grey Hall and into the city. Many of them re-built in the old style from long before he was born. Architecturally designed with antigravity machines in mind, the roofs stretched out and down over the broad walks and once-busy streets, like branches from the revered and now extinct Hymnal Trees. Oval, water-drop-like apartments flowed down some of the building branches, held in place by nearly invisible diamond graphene strings, looking very much like giant raindrops frozen in motion.

The strands of graphene draped around the apartments so closely that they looked like the strings of a giant harp cascading down the sides of the buildings. Some of the great singers of his time had tried to recreate the reverent music of the great, weeping Hymnal Trees on those strings. Some, he thought, had come very close.

Telas is . . . was a great conductor but did not have the innate talent to be a singer. He missed their music.

They had all gone, or expired, or left their corporeal existence behind, advancing into pure energy. Searching for the bigger truth or whatever it was that might give them peace. Gone, leaving behind the towering, rolling cities, some of his people's greatest art, silently awaiting their return.

As he looked at the Hymnal Tree buildings, with the water-drop apartments draping down their sides, it seemed to him that many of the vacant, oval water-drops looked like great silent tears.

There was a reason he hadn't been to his home planet in so long. He had hidden something there from his brother; something created in the great exodus; something that had bitterly divided his people; something of great power.

My brother—what does he call himself now? Nh'ghalu?

"N-h-gaa-loo," Telas sounded the name out loud. Why that name? It had something to do with ancient Sumer and the young alien civilization that Nh'ghalu had befriended, almost on the opposite side of the galaxy, the Nh'Ghareen.

Wait! The Nh'Ghareen and my brother . . .

I am not supposed to be here! Not here? I have had this thought before . . .

Suddenly, Telas felt a push against his mind, against the thought of his brother and the Nh'Ghareen. It was a familiar push urging him to not think about his brother. It was singing of a place called home. It kept pushing.

Leave me be . . . let me enjoy the peace of my planet!

But something was not right.

Wait . . . Wait! Again . . . Why or how am I here? The Grey Hall . . .

It was because of his telepathic prowess that he had been invited many times to lead the Grey Hall in various philosophical dissertations. None could match him in the great ancient mind game of Ehetpsalm.

In Ehetpsalm he was able to unite many ideas of philosophy and music into a great harmonic picture of thought, song and language, into an exquisite mental dance.

He was an expert conductor. He understood the poetic mind. When a single word was cast out in the Ehetpsalm telepathic field, he had an enviable ability to tie it to a particular emotion; then the emotion tied to another's thought; then the thought tied to an another's experience; then the experience tied to a song of his choice; and in the song a single note tied to another's desire, or a desire unattended, maybe wishing to be that note; then all of that mental, emotional and personal imagery painted with scenery from the planet or the universe. Many Shachons were deeply moved as they experienced his perfection. He was the greatest songwriter of his time. He was considered a savant.

But now it appeared he was the one being conducted.

This cannot be so.

It had always been accepted that his mind was untouchable.

Perhaps he had been a bit overconfident.

This time, instead of fighting he encouraged the telepathic nudge at his mind.

I welcome you.

He kept repeating two names near the front of his mind . . . *Nh'ghalu* . . . *Nh'Ghareen.*

His brother suddenly seemed to appear and then disappear around a building near a broad walkway across the Grey Hall plaza reflection pool. Telas ran after him, yelling his name.

When he got there Nh'ghalu was nowhere be seen. Frustrated, Telas sat down with his back against the building and began to relax and meditate. Somewhere in his mind he knew that his brother had not really been there. Someone . . . or some people were dreaming him.

Come to me. I welcome you, he repeated in his mind over and over again, all the while reaching out to try to find the unwanted guests. Those who would dare to control his memories.

Is it my imagination? Time to find out, he thought, inviting, accepting the push against his mind.

Come to me. Are you real? Who are you? I have fought you before and yet you are still here. I want to surrender. I welcome you to me.

He completely opened his mind.

Wait? There's more. I can feel you and another and another . . . six, total! And Galaxy, my ship, I feel you. Where are you? You feel sad.

He breathed, relaxed further and surrendered to those who would invade his mind. Let them come. Yet even as he seemingly allowed them more access to his memories, he kept the image of a sharp sword, an image he had used before, deep in the back of his mind.

I surrender . . . I surrender . . . I surrender . . . There!!

One of them had made the mistake of reaching in too deep in an attempt to control Telas's mind. That was the eager one. Telas had counted on him. He had stretched himself too thin.

Telas plunged the sharp sword image into the invading mind and severed that one's telepathic consciousness at its source. That invader would eventually die. No time for remorse; the others panicked and ran; Telas struck decisively.

One turned and came at Telas full force, maybe in the hope of surprising him. That would be the same mistake as the first had made; Telas struck and cut deep into that invader's mind. That kind of cut would stop a heart; two down. The remaining four invaders ran from his mind in panic. Telas was expecting that. Two of them were weak. Cut, cut; four down and two escaped. No matter, he now knew where he was.

"Galaxy! Full defense!" He yelled as he came to consciousness.

He was in his ship! The whole image of his home planet had been fed to him by the Nh'Ghareen telepaths. Only his brother could have taught them how to control an immortal in such a way.

To control me!?

His anger escalated. The images of home that were fed into his mind made him realize that his brother must have been to Sachone recently. He quickly reached out with his mind to see if his brother was anywhere near. No.

He felt Galaxy, she was singing to him in the old tongue, clearly joyous to sense him back. It was good to be conscious again, but he had to see what kind of trap his brother had created. A loud explosion rocked the top of his ship.

"Galaxy, I am happy to see you too but please, give over command of defense now! Good! Give me full view of the enemy."

The entire space around Galaxy came into virtual view just in front of his chair. He reached out to adjust and move the view with his hand but for a second his arm didn't respond. Twenty-five years of sitting in the same position had taken its toll. Fortunately Galaxy had nourished and replenished his body.

After a couple of tries Telas moved his hands around the command view in such a way that he was able to see the six Nh'Ghareen ships surrounding Galaxy.

In addition to the enemy ships there was a large circular interdimensional force field that surrounded the Nh'Ghareen and Telas. His brother had been very determined that he would not escape.

More unfriendly fire told him to move.

"Galaxy, I'm okay, I'm conjoining with you now."

Suddenly he became the ship. His mind seemed to grow and encompass the entire vehicle. He could feel what Galaxy felt and like her, see everywhere at once. He could sense the intelligence that was Galaxy right next to him, ready to assist as needed. She was and had always been a good companion.

The sense of camaraderie between Galaxy and himself filled him with confidence. Let the enemy come. At this level of mental acuity there were none in the universe that could telepathically overcome Telas. How his brother had managed to trap him he would have to ask Galaxy later, but first there was a battle to be fought.

Telas found the two Nh'Ghareen telepaths that had escaped and with deft and deadly quickness dispatched them. Done and done. No problem, but that still left the six hostile cruisers that surrounded him and were moving to attack.

BOOM!

Another explosion above shook his confidence. He saw and felt that explosion. The stars in the background were momentarily obscured by the close shot.

How are they able to breach my outer shield? Not deadly, but damn, a problem.

He looked at the area of his ship nearly damaged by the Nh'Ghareen and realized that his interdimensional jump engine was their intended target.

They are too young. They should not have this much scientific knowledge. Nh'ghalu has taught them too much too soon. They have developed more power than wisdom. Nevertheless . . . enough!

Galaxy, bursting with stored energy, suddenly moved to the left and then to the right of her confinement. The enemy ships, thinking to maintain a perfect circle, tried to follow but at Galaxy's second move they lost their circular formation and stranded the two ships nearest to Galaxy.

Telas, seeing their surprise, shifted yet again and barreled toward the nearest ship.

The Nh'Ghareen cruiser saw that it had pushed too far into the circle and in a desperate attempt to compensate, dropped its defensive position to scramble back into formation. Too late . . .

Telas reached out with his mind to its commander: *Don't fight. It's over; you've lost. Surrender.*

At the same time he showered the ship's drive with a series of interdimensional subatomic explosions. By the time Galaxy neared the enemy ship it was disabled and spinning aimlessly. One done; now for the other five.

He quickly spun Galaxy around and instead of going for the closest cruiser he zoomed toward the ship directly across the battlefield. At the same time he fired a series of flash missiles that would temporarily blind his enemies.

He stopped suddenly as the blinded cruisers shot a volley of missiles at where they expected Galaxy to be. They all exploded harmlessly in front of or behind him, one missing so badly that it soared into one of their own across the circle. Even as the enemy fired on Galaxy, Telas had already turned her around and was heading back to the Nh'Ghareen cruisers behind him.

Like many of his kind, Telas liked to look at all probabilities before he made a decision. Sometimes that meant a final solution could be years in the making. But this was battle, and Telas had been traveling in space for thousands of years. Unlike many of his compatriots, Telas had always been able to act decisively. He sped in between the two enemy ships that had been a second ago at his back.

In the force field the Nh'Ghareen had constructed he couldn't execute an interdimensional jump but he could affect gravity. He disrupted the gravity away from Galaxy out and toward the enemy.

The two cruisers bobbled in space like two ships caught in the wake of a larger ship at sea. Their weapons fired helter-skelter as they tried to aim at him. Without hesitation he released two atomic jumpers. They popped out of Galaxy, stood still for a split second, then in a flash disappeared and with simultaneous bursts of light reappeared inside the force field of both enemy ships. The explosions looked oval for an instant as both ships were destroyed nanoseconds before their force fields.

He swung Galaxy around to face the remaining enemy ships. They had formed into a straight line facing him. The middle ship sat in the vanguard. They appeared poised for an attack but were not firing or moving.

Telas decided to attack and sped straight toward them. He fired a series of flash missiles and was preparing the gravity disruptor when he was suddenly hit with a powerful explosion.

He had been attacked from behind, and it hurt. He zoomed "up," away from the next volley of interdimensional missiles. Spinning around to face the enemy he fired several shots.

Telas was stunned. Sliding through the interdimensional force field was a ship big enough to be called a starcarrier. The Nh'Ghareen had been busy. The ship was much bigger than Galaxy and could easily carry several of the cruisers that Telas had already destroyed. He fired at the ships. The shots that he had fired at the enemy carrier spun into its force field and disappeared.

They have an inter-d force field around their ship. Nh'ghalu what have you done?

As Telas's mind spun, a second starcarrier pushed into the large circular force field that surrounded them all. Both carriers began firing at his ship.

Another large explosion hit the top of his ship as he fled. He dropped back down between the carriers and the cruisers, still in a line at the other end of the force field, hoping that they would be more reticent to fire for fear of damaging their own cruisers. He pushed Galaxy to her top speed and popped up behind the cruisers, trying to gain a few extra seconds.

They won't fire on their own.

He was wrong.

The vanguard cruiser suddenly exploded within the same bright oval as before, and then was gone. That explosion was quickly followed by another as the enemy destroyed one of its own again. Telas was completely exposed. A large volley of missiles instantly came at him.

He fired a couple of inter-d nuclear weapons back at the lead carrier. One was somehow intercepted outside the ship's force field but the other found its target. The explosion damaged enough of the ship to stop it from advancing, but along with its sister ship it continued to fire at him.

He zoomed after the remaining cruiser that was escaping off his port side.

Good. This one is making some defensive moves.

The cruiser knew he was in trouble and was trying to flee from his own starship as well as Telas. Telas was trying to help by disrupting the gravity around the bigger ships.

"Galaxy! Fire three more inter-d nuclear missiles at the damaged starcarrier!"

Something in the back of his mind said, *Friend* . . . It was like a handshake. Someone aboard one of the Nh'Ghareen ships was trying to contact his mind. It was not threatening but like someone was calling and asking permission to talk.

Is this how they got in my mind before?

Telas prepared a deadly strike at the intruder.

"Friend . . . Please . . . mustn't be discovered . . . Quick . . . Save you!"

Three large explosions went off at and around the damaged starcarrier. Two were intercepted but the third did its job. The carrier stopped firing on the cruiser. All the enemy firing stopped. Telas reached out.

"Who are you?"

"Friend. Make way to force field behind cruiser. Six beats of star and field will open."

"Six beats?"

"Make way . . . watch and run!"

This intruder seemed different. Telas's intuition told him to take a chance. He sped to a spot between the cruiser and the force field. Suddenly the cruiser went up in a huge explosion. Two more missiles came from the damaged carrier yet one shot above and one below Galaxy. They hit the force field with a powerful explosion. The field glowed with a large bruise over its surface. It burned bright white-yellow for a second and then, like a piece of worn-out fabric, it unraveled and split apart.

Part of the gravity shield was still in place, but that was no problem for Telas. He disrupted the synthetic shield and quickly leaped out of the trap. The inter-d shield repaired itself just as he sped through. He immediately gave Galaxy jump instructions. She sang out notes of uncertainty as the mobile starcarrier slid through the field behind him. The ship fired a large volley of missiles at Galaxy.

"We must find Nh'ghalu. Now Galaxy! Jump to Earth!"

A vicious explosion rocked the top of Galaxy just as she jumped.

Commander Rhee watched as the immortal's ship jumped space.

"Did the tracking device attach?" he said to his lieutenant as he gazed at the empty spot in space that had once been Galaxy.

"Yes, Commander, we believe it did."

"Begin the tracking process."

"And the force field?"

"Bring down the force field and offer assistance to the damaged starcarrier. And Lieutenant, I want to know why those missiles missed in such a way as to allow Telas to escape. But first begin the tracking process!"

Before the lieutenant could salute or bow the commander waved away his subordinate. The tiny green and yellow feathers along his arm rustled slightly. Commander Rhee looked at the empty spot again. He opened the imperial com.

"Your Highness, the immortal has escaped."

"I trust you've planted a tracking device?"

"Yes, your Highness."

"Then don't bother me until you know where he went."

The imperial com clicked off before Rhee could respond. He frowned for a second at the high born's rudeness, but then let it go. Soon enough it would all change.

Good, the tracking is set. Now maybe we'll find the traitor that calls himself Nh'ghalu. He will pay a price for his arrogance, but most importantly, I want access to those Sachone ships! The Dahreen family has ruled long enough. I will be Emperor!

CHAPTER ONE

Erik Devries floated on his personal solar magnetic-sail ship (PSS) about 8,500 kilometers above Earth. The planet was still close enough that if he looked at one spot for too long he could almost feel himself falling. Below, night was inexorably overcoming day. The ever-moving terminator line stretched at an angle across the middle of North America just west of the Great Lakes and down through the Southwest. Light and dark in a never-ending détente as the line sliced across the upper Midwest down through southern Baja and out into the Pacific Ocean. To the east the populous cities of New Philadelphia, Boston and New York combined into one huge sea of light. Much of the western US was still in daylight.

Erik drew his eyes away from North America and looked to his right or east across the Atlantic Ocean. He could see the lights fading from the great cities on the coast of Europe. The gentle curve of the planet gave the illusion of an island of light sitting on the edge of the universe as the Earth slowly revolved and Europe disappeared. He grabbed his tools from the side of the PSS, tethered himself and pushed off toward his immediate job.

He focused on the satellite in front of him. A communication satellite, one of several connecting the six big governments of China, the US, United Europe (UE), Japan, the Union of South American Nations (UNASUR) and United South Africa (UNSA), had lost maneuverability and was experiencing orbital decay. A fixable problem for sure this was an important instrument, key to the international community.

He studied a small hole near the satellite's orbital jets. As he moved in closer he found that he was facing the Earth head first. Again that feeling of falling overcame him.

The great myth of orbital space, the feeling of weightlessness a spacer has while hurtling around a planet. The fact was that at this distance from the ground Erik still weighed roughly 9% of his earthbound weight. Gravity, weak as it was, was still pulling him to a certain death. He knew that he wasn't "weightless" but in a constant tangential free-fall to the planet below. He also knew that his orbital velocity was just fast enough to fall over the horizon. That this orbital speed created a balance between him and the inevitable pull of gravity. Still, it could be spooky sometimes. He looked to make sure that he was securely tethered to his ship.

Safe and secure, he thought.

Although spacesuits and manned maneuvering units (MMU) had evolved a great deal over the last four hundred–plus years, having a tether was still a spacer's best friend. He floated closer to the damaged area on the satellite and turned to the task at hand.

"It looks to me like the fibric nerve has been damaged by a small meteoroid or piece of space junk," he said as he struggled to reach a small magnetic neuron tester into the tiny jagged opening. "It's just above one of the manipulation rockets. Maybe a slice of neuronic fiber can heal it."

"This machine uses synthro because of its harsh environment. Expensive stuff; do you have any with you?" The voice of his co-worker and close friend Teresa sounded through his earpiece.

"Yes," he said. "Loaded some on my PSS before you sent me out on this joyride." Erik smiled at their private joke.

Teresa, he thought. *A sweet friend with Earth-blue eyes and fiery red hair. The hair fit her temperament.*

"Yeah, cowboy, you get all the fun assignments," she said and they both laughed. Truth was, he usually volunteered.

He secured his tether to the satellite. Once it was safely fastened, his fingers performed a series of tapping motions on his left forearm and a small beam projected onto the side of the communication satellite. Every human in space and officials on Earth had human-to-computer interaction units (HIC). It was a powerful computer in and of itself, but, as with all spacer's units, Erik's was still connected to the quantum computer SAIQA on Sanctuary. The access to information was practically unlimited. A complete schematic of the stabilizing rockets and their supporting neuronic fibers appeared on the orbiter's surface. Erik studied the circuitry as he talked to Teresa.

"Are you in your dress uniform or the overalls?" Erik asked teasingly, ready to shower her with superlatives. He knew she wasn't a big fan of pleasantries, except for when he missed an opportunity to compliment her.

"You'll just have to be surprised."

"Well, now you got me wondering . . . hmm, hmm."

"Yeah, well, wonder about what you're doing and quit drifting off into testosterone land."

"Okay, okay." He laughed. "Just talkin', that's all."

"How about, quit the talkin'," she said, acting like the officer in charge (OIC), which at the

3

moment she was, "and get to working. We've got to be ready for the championship sail race tonight. I don't plan on losing, which means I need to be practicing, which means I need my captain, Captain."

"Aye, ma'am, uh sir . . . uh, whatever. . . . Hey, if you listen real close, you can hear me working." He made a rapping sound with his hand on the side of his helmet. "I'll be back on Sanctuary in a flash."

Teresa laughed. "Oh yeah, I can hear you right through the vacuum of space, or is that vacuum the space between your ears?" She laughed real hard at that one. Erik just groaned. "Okay, cowboy," she said more seriously, "my shift is nearly over. Anna will be here shortly, I'll see you when you get back." She terminated their connection before he was able to throw out another wisecrack.

Teresa sat in the OIC chair, the Command Screen (CS) floating in the air before her. In her mind's eye she could see Erik's face as he groaned. His strong Norwegian chin dominated a face topped with slightly curled blond hair and green eyes. He was strong and fit, and with his shoes on he stood just less than two meters.

Where did he get those green eyes?

She had that thought often.

Through his helmet she had watched as he approached the satellite. She let out the breath she was holding as he secured himself to the energy wings of the orbiter. Their conversation was light. She loved him . . . she was not in love with him, but she loved him. It could happen that she would fall in love with him, but for now, she wasn't ready. As he got to work on the satellite she pushed her fingers up and to the left of the screen.

4

The view from Erik's helmet swooshed up to the left corner and minimized into an icon.

"SAIQA," Teresa spoke to the main computer, "I am leaving all space com links open to you as per safety regs. My shift is nearly over and I believe that Anna is next up as OIC."

"Confirmed and thank you, Captain Jacobson," SAIQA responded.

"Thank you, SAIQA."

Throughout the space station Sanctuary were thousands of smaller, independently intelligent computers. They performed hundreds of thousands of computations every second. A system this complex would appear chaotic except that it was under the control of a much larger central quantum brain called "Sanctuary's Artificial Intelligence Quantum Administrator."

SAIQA (pronounced Sah-ee'-ka) was the first true artificial intelligence computer. She was constantly interacting with all of the ship's computers as well as the solar system and universe around her. SAIQA's parallel processing brain was designed very much like a human brain and, in fact, the base of her brain was made up of a mixture of biosynthetic and organic neurons. The science to support her neurons, though infinitely more advanced, was still based on the principles of the ancient Koniku chip invented in the early twenty first century.

While cognitive awareness necessarily involved her in all of the daily functions of Sanctuary, at the same time she could interact independently on many levels with the humans who had made her.

Teresa glanced back through the clear command screen or CS out into the main loading deck (MLD). Though used by some civilians, the

MLD was primarily there to support Sanctuary's mission.

In dock and off to her far right were a few personal space yachts. Those huge ships belonged to some of the VIPs who lived or worked aboard Sanctuary. Some of the bigger corporations and the very wealthy, of course, had their own private docks in some of the more luxurious quarters above Comdeck.

Next to the space yachts was the main docking area for the WWPA's Space Division. It was an impressive display of military cruisers and support and security ships. The two larger battle ships were currently on deep space missions testing their newly designed EM4 thrusters. If the new thrusters worked as predicted, it would cut the travel time between the moon and Mars by half. The solar system was getting smaller. The rest of the MLD was dedicated to the maintenance and science crews' needs.

Consequently the MLD was always active.

A flashing yellow light near the top of the CS told her one of the civilian ships was prematurely moving from its authorized hold position. Teresa pulled the flashing light down the screen and at the same time opened a com-link to the ship. The thumbnail expanded and a young man and woman popped up on the CS before Teresa.

"This is Captain Jacobson OIC and you are not authorized to move into a docking position yet."

"Sorry, Captain . . . um, we saw that the other ship was moving, and the kids were getting antsy." He motioned his hand as if pointing to kids behind him.

"I understand, but as you can see, due to the heavy volume of visitors and for your own safety, everyone needs to stay put and wait until you are signaled to approach the civilian docking bay. I see that you have only one ship ahead of you. Moving or not, I would hate to have to put you and your family in restricted quarters when you have come so far and are so close."

"We wouldn't want that either, Captain."

"Then we're all clear on how this works?"

"Yes, ma'am," the man said. The woman was shaking her head.

"Good. Thanks for your cooperation. Enjoy your stay here on Sanctuary. Captain Jacobson out."

Teresa closed the window by pushing the frame back up to the right.

Fortunately they always cooperate, she thought as she looked back out onto the MLD. The huge doors, spanning 100 meters, intermittently stood open, exposing the bay to space. There was a huge landing and working dock that ran the length of the bay and reached out another 50 meters into space.

It was nearing the end of her shift and most of the day's business was winding down. Still, there was plenty of activity. People in the bay were moving about, doing their specific jobs, and those few still out on the dock were moving a little slower due to the MMUs wrapped around the upper part of their Z-27/Orlan suits, perfected by MQ Space Industries. The MMUs were required in open space even though the dock was gravitated to match the moon, about $1/6^{th}$ the gravity of Earth. The ever-present repair-bots were also keenly aware of humans working in open space within the vicinity of the space station.

As she looked out of the bay and toward the Earth she caught sight of her reflection in the window. Her ginger-red hair was pulled back at the bangs and fastened at the back of her head. Her big blue eyes were genetically highlighted, as was the style of her generation. She was forty-five, yet because of the Telomerase Cell-Life Extension program (TCE), she still looked to be in her early twenties, if that. She was considered quite beautiful. She was wearing her dress uniform, light grey with red and black trim. It was, after all, Sanctuary's hundred and fiftieth anniversary. She was a captain in the WWPA's Space Division and she would represent it with dignity and honor.

Though she looked feminine and soft, very few people made the mistake of treating her so. Teresa had a quick tongue and fast fists. She had learned how to fight when she was very young.

Her parents were convinced that she would be a boy so they had already picked out her name, Ben. When she was born they kept Benjamin as her middle name. She spent many years punching the boys that made fun of her, a girl named Ben.

Tragically, her mother died before she was a teen. Her father chose not to remarry and instead focused on raising Teresa. Many of her peers also made fun of her dad because he chose to be single and because they owned and ran a small algae farm in Sonora, California.

The majority of people in Northern California were involved in hi-tech, space type industries, not farming. Farming was for the Sac Valley and Southern California. Though she loved and protected her father, she secretly wished they could've been space scientists, not farmers.

That desire and her toughness brought her to where she was today: part of the WWPA's elite that lived and worked aboard the space station, Sanctuary.

As she looked at the Earth she thought of her father back home. At ninety-eight years old he was finally starting to slow down. Her father chose not to participate in the TCE program. He did however participate in the first longevity program, named Sirtuin Therapeutic Activating Compounds, also called STAC. He had told his daughter that he felt comfortable with some of the more natural applications of the STAC program.

In an booming age of scientific discoveries her father remained deeply spiritual. Like others of his generation with similar deeply held metaphysical beliefs, he picked and chose the new scientific miracles that he applied to his business and himself.

The Telomerase Cell-Life Extension program was designed to extend human life by introducing medically controlled and consistent telomerase enzyme activity throughout the body. It also involved the strengthening of the immune system, the expulsion of senescent cells, and targeted cell renewal through specific stem cell reproductions.

TCE did require periodic maintenance with certain drugs. Since TCE could extend human life beyond the mandatory retirement age of 150, there were special treatments for women to slow down egg loss; especially for women within the age range of thirty to thirty-five or younger, depending on an FSH blood test. There had been some ongoing research to start TCE in the very young, but nothing definitive yet. Also being investigated was a way to maintain the immature egg count (nearly 2 million) present in the young female fetus but nearly 75% gone by the time the baby was born. Other scientists were looking at the possibility of the reproduction of eggs through stem cells.

"Pardon me, Captain Jacobson, I am detecting a potential coronal mass ejection from the Sun. As you know, an interplanetary CME can create dangerous solar winds. Though many of the visiting ships are already in Sanctuary's magnetic safety zone, I encourage you to initiate a yellow alert as well as to ensure that all necessary shields are fully engaged. I will reassign Sanctuary's repair-bots as needed to use their antigrav shields as additional support. Also I have been informed that your replacement OIC, Lieutenant Commander Steges, has been called to Comdeck for a special security detail."

"Thank you, SAIQA." Teresa moved her hands across the CS. "Yellow alert for potential solar flare activity initiated." As quickly as Teresa was done, activity on the MLD and its external dock began to speed up. She had a working relationship with many of the woman and men out there. She would stake her life on their capabilities. She knew they were professionals.

"SAIQA, as Commander Steges has been called from OIC duty do you have a replacement yet?"

"No, Captain Jacobson, I am working on that. Perhaps you could encourage Captain Devries to expedite his mission as well?"

"Thank you, SAIQA. I will immediately."

The magnetic tester had begun to flash a series of symbols across Erik's handheld reader. The tester was designed to determine the health of each organic fiber. A wide variety of signals could be sent through a neuronic fiber and, even with some damage, most would find their way to a receptor, especially in synthro.

Neuronic fibers were biosynthetic neurons created from manmade molecules consisting of hydrogen, oxygen and carbons wrapped in polymeric fibers and designed to "heal" themselves when damaged. Synthro was made up of the same fibers combined and wrapped with

10

heavier silicones. The silicones were designed to protect the bio fibers. When covered in aerogel they generally worked well in a harsh interplanetary environment. Of course if the damage was too severe they'd have to be regrown or replaced.

As Erik read the series of light signals and graphs on his handheld reader they began a slow move into a shrinking circle that targeted the damaged area. With a smile, Erik realized it wouldn't take too long after all. He followed his tether back to his PSS some meters away. He looked through the storage unit embedded into the side of his ship and found the synthro needed to repair the satellite. He maneuvered his way back to the damaged orbiter.

He carefully pulled the synthro from its vacpac and, while protecting it from the sun, he set it in the cradle of his magnetic tester and manipulated it into its proper place. After several applications, Erik covered the synthro with an aerogel base. He waited for the quick dry and rechecked the receptor connections. The whole process had taken about thirty minutes. All was good. He knew it was fixed. He knew it would work. He always "knew."

Ground Control would command the communication satellite back into its proper orbit. He had quickly patched the small hole, and now that he was done, he took a moment to admire his work.

"Nice, if I do say so myself."

"Why, thank you, Erik. And I think the same of you." A voice chirped through his earpiece.

"Teresa? I thought you were off duty and getting ready for practice?"

"I was. Anna was called up to Comdeck. SAIQA is looking for a replacement OIC, and I want to give you a head's up that today's race may be delayed or probably cancelled due to some unexpected solar flare activity. The Van Allen Belt plasma and particle flux can be unpredictable, as you know, often causing a shift in the Safe Zone, sooo . . . I think it would be prudent for you to finish admiring yourself and get back to the ship, or at least well within her electromagnetic field." Teresa was sounding a little more serious than normal. All spacers knew the dangers and unpredictability of space weather.

"Okay, Red, I'm on my way."

"Great, see you in a bit."

Using his tether and the MMU to pull himself back to his boat, Erik placed the tools in their protected compartments and then settled into his PSS.

The small utility spacecraft was the workhorse of Sanctuary's maintenance and rescue/patrol personnel. It had an enclosed cabin at its center just large enough for the pilot and a couple of passengers; two side propulsion units, looking very much like pontoons; and another thrust unit just below the ship that reminded Erik of a keel. It all gave the PSS a look of a small catamaran.

The front of the ship tapered down like a dolphin's nose. About a meter from the tip of the nose, the pilot's main viewing plate angled up and to the top of the craft. There were also smaller horizontal viewing portals, for passengers, on both sides of the ship. Two shifting thrusters sat on top of the cabin and just behind the passenger area for more precise maneuverability. The collapsible magnetic sail was embedded at the front of the cabin just above the pilot's view plate.

The space sail itself opened into an oval, static magnetic field about five meters across and three meters high. It deflected the sun's solar wind, creating propulsion. The sail was also designed to use the magnetosphere of the planet's magnetic field as an additional source of power. The direction of the craft could be influenced by adjusting the corners of the sail, along with the use of the rockets around the main body of the PSS.

The manual controls were within easy reach at the driver's left and right hand and could be manipulated by lever and twist motions. Though he could have told the small Indy-Brain to compute a course to any destination he chose, Erik, being the sailor he was, took hold of the manual controls. He used small, short bursts of gas to move the craft a safe distance from the satellite. Taking one more look at his finished job, he strapped himself into his seat, turned the PSS toward Sanctuary and sped home.

Covering the three thousand or so kilometers back to Sanctuary would only take about twenty minutes. The quick and powerful thrust of the side propulsion rockets pushed Erik back and down into his seat. As he neared his designated speed he cut the rockets. His weightlessness returned and it felt like he wasn't moving at all. When he opened the magnetic sail it sparkled and illuminated like a faint aurora as it engaged. The aurora across the sail would ebb and intensify with fluxing solar winds, creating a rainbow of colors flowing and splashing all around the sail.

Some of the personal space yachts and racing ships had sails that were maybe four to ten times as big and could radiate like the Northern Lights. Some of the owners of these personal ships expended great pains and amounts of money to make their sails and top decks mimic the more classic oceangoing schooners of Earth. With the main sail, the jib sail and the head sail all engaged these ships looked like they were cutting across some great ocean in space. Sometimes Erik could imagine a wake of foamy stars pushing out from their bows.

With artificial gravity along the deck and surrounded by a basic graviton energy shield, the owners and their guests could wear minimum space suits and walk and sit on the top deck as if they were sailing in the ocean far, far below. Their large, bright sails washed the ships with multicolored lights. In his mind, Erik could imagine the wind pushing back the sailors' hair as if they were yachting in the pristine ocean waters of KwaZulu-Natal near Richards Bay. The solar winds were, of course, a bit more deadly. Erik adjusted his magnetic sail as Sanctuary came into view.

The space station was home to nearly fifty thousand humans. It was a spectacular display of human ingenuity orbiting the Earth's Northern Hemisphere about 12,000 kilometers above the surface, in the safe slot of the Van Allen Belt. The entire structure was an astonishing 1.5 kilometers long, just under half a kilometer at its widest near the top, and had two extended concentric rings that were storage and living areas, just above its center. Each circle was about 600 meters in diameter and was connected to the station by long spokes. The bottom or southern part of the space station was the oldest so it was a bit thinner.

The top and bottom, or north and south, of Sanctuary were flattish and housed powerful electromagnets. They created a manmade electromagnetic field that surrounded the space station. Near the electromagnets, and at both ends of Sanctuary, were high-intensity proton (HIP) lasers for protection against space debris and meteoroids. There were also propulsion units at either end for rotation and orbital integrity.

At the upper center and just above the encircling "wings," as the rings were sometimes called, the station bubbled a bit, allowing more room for the administration and command centers. The brightest lights were there at Admin/Com, where most of the control room visage plates were fully open. Because of the lights and gentle bulge of the Admin/Com area and the rings and the slight taper from north to south, from a distance the space station looked like a giant dragonfly in space.

The viewing and visage plates were made of a powerful alloy of depleted uranium, manmade diamond strings and tungsten nanoparticles combined with aerogel, allowing the administration and command deck a complete view of open space.

Space station personal viewing plates were open as allowed at designated times; giving the station a pinpricked look of sporadic light.

Here and there work and personal platforms dotted the sides of Sanctuary. Most of the platforms were near the bottom half of the space station, where the majority of the Earthbound visitors would come aboard. There at the commercial access gate, (CAG), the landing docks jutted out around the entire giant space station and nearly all were enclosed.

Because Sanctuary was celebrating its hundred and fiftieth anniversary, a wide variety of personal and commercial yachts hovered outside the station. Combined with the permanent satellites for maintenance, recreation and security, as well as space buoys, all in a static orbit around the space station, there was a lot of traffic in Sanctuary's space.

Erik's favorite recreational satellite was a bit of a distance from the main station and just beyond the edge of Sanctuary's electromagnetic field. That craft was big enough to have its own electromagnetic field.

Known as "The Garden," it was the preferred place of most of the spacebound inhabitants. The Garden was an oval ship about 600 kilometers long. It was home to the largest sustainable "city park," in space. There the artificial gravity (AG) was the closest to Earth's, at just below the standard average of 1g, based on Newton's Laws.

AG was a complicated system of controlled, intensely compacted graviton particles, in high covalent bonding and tightly packed throughout a massive floorboard. AG was possible because of the complete standard model theory developed by Professor Carrington just over two centuries earlier. At that time many nations were still rebuilding from the tragic Corporate Wars, and the newly developed civilian governments were divesting some of the secretive corporate sciences to the more established universities.

Professor Carrington discovered some obscure mathematical formulas on the back of a notebook stuffed in a box of items from the old wooden desk of a corporate executive major. He was startled when he found he could apply them to his own mathematical rigour. He was able to tie quantum field theory and phase transitions to atomic and molecular physics. Suddenly he was able to unify the two major theories of the old standard model. He didn't know it at the time, but his "new physics" would ultimately usher the Earthbound into a new era of expanded space exploration.

The high AG in The Garden was the most sophisticated to date and was critical for plants to build a strong biological structure and look as close to normal as an artificial environment would allow. Recently birds had been introduced into The Garden, and needless to say they were a big hit. The birds were carefully tended and greeted with much awe by all visitors. On Earth many of these dinosaur relatives were barely extant: to have them here in space was a treat beyond expectations.

The Garden's greenery was an assortment of a wide variety of plants and trees from the temperate zones around the planet. Bees were carefully introduced and monitored to prevent overpopulation. It was thought that by introducing the birds into The Garden they would also help control the overpopulation of bees and other insects unintentionally introduced with the foliage. The further introduction of insects and small animals was still being planned.

The necessary below-ground microbial and micro-faunal biomasses had been balanced by the introduction of earthworms. Night and day were carefully planned to mimic the twenty-four-hour cycle of Earth; other biophysical considerations, such as wind, rain, hot days, cold days, moonlight and starlight were under evaluation in order to bring a slice of Earth out into space. It was one of the greatest scientific experiments of the twenty-fifth century.

Though all of the cost overruns for this project, and there were many, had been funded by the United Nations, this mammoth space-bound vivarium had been primarily paid for by MQ Space Industries.

The CEO of MQ Space Industries was willing to foot the bill, providing his scientists had full access to The Garden and a separate laboratory. There were no personal dwellings allowed in The

Garden. The only exceptions were for support and science crews. What the recreation ship did offer were day visits, some vacation dwellings and a handful of overnight "campsites" available to the spacers on a lottery basis.

There were, of course, parks as well as farm decks inside the space station Sanctuary, some large enough to be community garden centers and some as recreation areas. Humans had learned a long time ago during extended space travel that they needed to bring a piece of their home with them. Here, 12,000 km above Earth, The Garden was considered the "Central Park" of Sanctuary.

Twenty-five years in the making, The Garden was as close to a rural experience as any spacer would ever get. The Garden was to be the final mark for the championship race that might not happen today.

Erik could see lights start to wink out around the station as personal viewing plates were closed. It was part of the basic safety precaution against potentially strong CMEs and their influence on the Van Allen Belt. Many of the visiting and support ships were already within Sanctuary's electromagnetic field, though each ship was supposed to have its own protection.

Because of the anniversary celebration, which culminated today, there were nearly two hundred private boats and commercial cruisers near Sanctuary's southern base and a handful of luxury boats near the top.

Erik's destination was north of all the tourists. He reluctantly turned off the solar sail, and it folded into the ship's frame. He was close enough to Sanctuary that he needed to decelerate till he reached his final approach speed of 10 meters per second at 200 meters out, slowing down to 1 meter per second at 50 meters out, then a grad-down till the PSS's speed matched the giant station's orbital velocity and rotation.

The ubiquitous repair-bots seemed to be more active, though in fact they never really stayed in one place. Their mission was to protect the ship from the constant threat of meteoroids and any space junk still unaccounted for in Sanctuary's orbit. They were also designed for external emergency repair, protection against CMEs and preventive maintenance.

To keep Sanctuary protected there were hundreds of them. They looked like giant beetles moving on and around the large central station. Erik wasn't concerned about them coming into his ships' proximity, as all repair-bots were programmed to move away from incoming space vehicles.

Every time Erik approached Sanctuary he had an overwhelming sense of awe, pride and luck to be part of such an amazing human experience. Even now, after fifteen years, he felt the same as when he had first come aboard.

Seventeen years ago Erik had finished the intense space program at the United Nations Space College at the University of Cape Town in United South Africa. Just finishing the program did not guarantee access to the "Island in the Sky," as the Earthbound called Sanctuary. Erik was just one of the thousands of men and women from around the globe who had successfully completed the intensive program.

There was also the year and a half of internship work required to pay back society's investment in his education. Erik had chosen to work as an assistant to a high school science professor, Dr. Lee. Luck was with Erik, as it had been many times in his life. It had placed him with one of the world's greatest scientists.

Dr. Lee, then still teaching at a hundred and sixty years old, was one of the leading researchers who discovered how to manipulate and create artificial gravity. It was 115 years earlier that Dr. Lee and his fellow scientist Gabriel Llosa-Martinez had won the Nobel Prize for their discovery. Lee was also one of the original partners in MQ Space Industries.

Every time Erik thought of Dr. Lee, his emotions got the best of him. Chin, as he was lovingly nicknamed, was a compassionate and brilliant man. He patiently worked with Erik, compelling him to delve deeper into the study of microbiology and the science and business of neuronic fibers and their applications.

Erik was a highly competent assistant to Dr. Lee. Erik often seemed to anticipate the professor's needs just before he would speak. Dr. Lee was so amazed and amused that he used to jokingly call Erik "Radar." It took Erik a while to find the very old entertainment show called *M*A*S*H*.

I still watch it today.

Erik chuckled to himself at that thought.

He hadn't seen his mentor since he came aboard Sanctuary and in fact had tried to contact him a few years ago. Dr. Lee apparently had gone into a secretive government research facility and did not return Erik's photon mail. Erik heard that Dr. Lee was working on some new form of antigrav propulsion system.

Antigravity was already in use as a backup safety system on airplanes and other sky vehicles and in space as a basic shield against small meteoroids. Creating such a propulsion system required a great deal of power. Dr. Lee was probably on the moon or Mars for such potentially dangerous research. He assumed that Dr. Lee was just incredibly busy and didn't have time to return his photon mails. Either way Erik had only warm feelings for his old mentor and friend.

A light ping in Erik's earpiece brought him back to the present. He had just crossed Sanctuary's electromagnetic field boundary. He looked down at the PSS's control panel and saw that the proximity light had gone from red to yellow. It would turn green as he got further into the safety zone and closer to home.

As Erik approached, his com activated: "Welcome home, Captain. Did you enjoy your amusement ride?" Teresa knew that Erik likened solar sailing to some of the joy rides on Earth.

"Always do," he said truthfully. More seriously, he said, "You know, Teresa, every time I look out into the Milky Way and see all these stars and the galaxies beyond, and the moon, and the planets in our solar system, and that big beautiful blue planet below, I am just overwhelmed. I can't help it. The Universe is the most amazing sight in the universe. I can almost feel myself being pulled into every pinpoint of light. I have this incredible feeling of being a part of some great experiment, and it makes me feel alive in ways that I can't explain. I want to explore every star I see, explore their solar systems, the life that they may have created. Yet at the same time I feel completely frustrated, knowing that I cannot. Someday humanity will do it, you know, explore the stars . . . someday."

"You're getting mighty poetic on me there, space cowboy. Tfiti would be impressed, but yes, I have to admit, we're pretty lucky, aren't we, to be up here and to see all this stark yet dangerous beauty?"

"Yeah . . . and speaking of poetry, have you seen Tfiti?"

Tfiti was Erik's roommate and close friend from Space College. Tfiti had published a book of poems titled *The Stars and Moons*, and the Earthbound often called him the "Space Poet." Though he kept himself busy studying, writing and working, he and Erik still managed to find time to get into some sort of mischief together.

Tfiti was also a brilliant scientist, specializing in biology, specifically in the new science of biosynthetic neurons created by the merging of organic and synthetic DNA. These new types of cells were the foundation of most of SAIQA's brain. He was also involved in the ever expanding use of independent intelligence. These "Indy-Brains," as they were often called, were a sort of pre-AI brain for computerized machines.

Though Erik was extremely competent at neuron fiber applications, Tfiti was a genius at understanding the mode of communication between the human-made neurons inside the Indy-Brains.

Combinations of these unique neurons were constructed so that many of the fiber strings were set in series and spun together into small electron quantum chips. Then they were layered in such a way that the neurons created a synaptic mesh very similar to a human brain. Images and experiences were then fed into that mesh, and as the Indy-Brain received the information it created a "net" of electronic pathways that lay on top of the neuron strings in such a way that after a while the different pathways created new nets, and they all interacted and communicated together, very much like a mammalian brain.

Eventually some independent thought and experiences developed and became part of the brain's programming, giving the synthetic brain a limited sense of reality. These types of computers

22

permeated Sanctuary and performed at the command of SAIQA.

Scientists also used the independent intelligence computers for certain types of theoretical work. Depending on the programming, the Indy-Brains' high speed and basic abstract thought had given scientists a highly valuable tool in predicting social and scientific phenomena.

Tfiti's expertise was his uncanny ability to understand how the computer's mathematical thought patterns would circuit through various electronic nets, or electronic pathways, and come to a conclusion. Because of his genius Tfiti was the lead WWPA officer and scientist who studied and worked with SAIQA. With her combined biosynthetic and organic neurons, SAIQA was considered the first truly artificial intelligence ever developed by humanity.

Tfiti would talk endlessly about his conversations with SAIQA and her vast ability for cognitive computing, her amazing proficiency at parallel processing and her ability to apply her wealth of knowledge to abstract thoughts and moral dilemmas.

He would gush about SAIQA's fledgling understanding of her existence and her ongoing quest to explain her place in the universe. Like many young, intelligent creatures, she identified her existence with her work. He was convinced that she was conscious.

"Okay, Erik, you're the last flight coming onto the MLD. Head to section R of the landing deck—" Teresa brought Erik back to the task at hand "—and dock in number twenty-two."

Erik had been dramatically drawing down his speed just as he entered Sanctuary's electromagnetic field. His speed was at the required 1 meter per second and dropping as he reached the MLD.

"Done and done. So, is that a no on seeing Tfiti?"

"I haven't looked yet; I've been talking with SAIQA about a replacement OIC. She said she's found someone and that he'd be here shortly."

"Sweet, can I buy you a cup of coffee after I report in?"

"Why thank you sir, that would be very nice."

He could feel her smile.

Erik was now about 10 meters above the platform. He switched on his antigrav unit to balance against the MLD's AG. Using his side propulsion rockets he floated toward the bay door. Section R was just ahead of him.

As he glided through the huge open bay and steered his PSS toward dock number twenty-two, the last of the crew were moving into the station. The giant yellow lights began their warning flashes indicating the great doors would soon close. Erik maneuvered his PSS into the landing cradle.

"Docking now, Teresa." The vehicle gently landed on the two latches on either side of the PSS and the keel jet slid into an open area below. Clamps grabbed the front and back of the ship and secured the PSS in its cradle. Erik made sure everything was properly turned off and sealed before he disembarked.

Teresa's voice came in as he stepped down: "Erik, Adam has been cleared by SAIQA to take over as OIC. So, I am signing off again. See you when you come inside."

"Okay, Teresa, thanks. See you shortly."

As he began walking toward the OIC station, the huge safety doors started closing. In a few minutes they would block off the space station's hanger bay from the outside dock and empty space. He stopped and watched in silence. The giant doors were 30 meters high to allow enough room for a space yacht or WWPA cruiser to enter. He was about to speak to Teresa when he heard or rather felt an old sound. It was a hollow, weird sound-feeling; a sound that wasn't external but like a wind brushing against the back of his mind. It was a portent. He had felt this sensation a number of times in his life.

Once, when he was very young, around twenty-nine and finishing his first phase of college, he was at a recruitment seminar. He had felt that gentle push at the back of his mind a couple of days before the seminar. Erik was actively being recruited by a few different corporations and his future in business looked very bright.

While he was talking to two headhunters, a UN official suddenly stopped in front of his table. They looked at each other and both froze. Erik could feel that the UN officer had something important to say. The officer gazed at Erik with a puzzled look on his face. The two recruiters, feeling like they were not a part of this, stood back and watched. Suddenly the UN master sergeant seemed to make a decision, and he walked up to Erik.

"Sir, do you want to go to the UN Space College and work on Sanctuary?"

Erik stood and simply said, "Yes sir," and the gentle push in his mind stopped. Erik knew he had made the right decision.

Yet another time the feeling of something terribly wrong overcame him as he was about to step on a lift. Sure enough the lift failed, and if he'd been on it he would more than likely have died.

It was the same place in his mind that Erik could "feel" with absolute conviction that he was right. It was the same place where he somehow would know what Dr. Lee wanted before he had spoken. A sixth sense that Erik had grown to accept.

This was what he felt now but stronger, much stronger. Something big was about to happen.

"Captain?" she repeated, "Captain?" A concerned deck coordinator was actually tapping on his face plate. Erik looked at her.

"Captain, are you all right? The OIC asked me to look out for you because you weren't responding to him."

Erik shook his head. "I'm . . . Yes, fine. Sorry, got lost in thought for a moment, but yes, I'm okay." Ignoring the look of concern on the coordinator's face, Erik spoke into his mic: "Teresa, you still there?"

"No, Mr. Devries, this is Captain Adam Jenkins, acting OIC. Are you okay?"

"Yes, sir. Sorry, just got lost in my thoughts." The young woman was still watching him with a puzzled expression. Erik waved at his com switch and shrugged his shoulders. The deck coordinator seemed unsure about Erik's response but shook her head and moved on to check another docking.

"Okay," the OIC said. "Please enter it in your report. I lost you for a full two minutes."

"Yes, sir. Sorry, sir. See you topside."

Erik ended his communication; he needed time to think about what this strong feeling, pushing at the back of his mind, might be portending. It always spooked him when this feeling suddenly appeared. He looked around; the doors were closing fine; his suit checked out okay. What could it mean? He saw that the deck coordinator had stopped what she was doing and was watching him again, clearly concerned.

Erik had been wildly checking his suit for leaks.

"Captain, Sergeant Matheson seems to think you may have a problem with your suit." Captain Jenkins' voice came into Erik's com.

"I'm fine, Captain," Erik lied. He waved over to the DC to assure her that he was okay. She still looked skeptical, and said something into her com that Erik couldn't hear. The OIC was probably telling her to keep an eye on him.

"Please proceed to the tunnel, Captain," the OIC said.

"Yes, sir," Erik said and started walking.

What the hell is going on!

Physically he felt fine. Still, there it was, the persistent and strong wind-sound pushing at the back of his mind. The safety doors had closed and were in the process of expanding to seal the hangar deck. Once they were sealed, a fairly quick intro of air into the closed main deck would begin.

As Erik walked toward the OIC station he kept an eye on the various pressure indicator lights, watching as they changed from red to yellow to green. As soon as the first green indicator light flashed Erik removed his helmet. The combination of his helmet and the sound brushing at the back of his mind had made him feel claustrophobic.

With the helmet off Erik focused on external sounds. He had learned long ago that he could subdue the internal noise by watching and listening to the normal daily clatter around him.

Other PSS craft were already secured in the immediate area of the deck, some clearly marked for security and others for science, recreation and long-distance maintenance. Far off to his left a couple of space yachts were being tended by their captains or crew. Just before the space yachts stood a few of the larger WWPA Space Guard military ships, the ever-present military checkpoints at each of the gangplanks. Like Erik, many of the folks around him had taken off their helmets.

He felt his AG gait return with each step. On Sanctuary, AG at point of contact was the same as the moon, yet as you moved up and away from the graviton floor things changed. AG was still effective within the first 7 meters and even up to 12 meters, but it quickly dissipated to weightlessness after that.

It certainly was better than its ancestors of nearly a century ago. Erik recalled the early stories of walking like your feet were magnets. With each step your foot had to be pulled up and then bounced back to the floorboard as if it was attached by a rubber band. Moving around had been very much like walking in the shallow end of a mud pool. Back then the AG was effective only within the first 2 meters.

Erik had his helmet by his side as he headed toward the OIC station. He caught sight of Teresa; she was standing at a visage window just left of the decontamination tunnel. She saw Erik and waved. He waved back.

So she did have her dress uniform on . . . man, she is kiff, Erik thought, momentarily slipping into the ancient slang he and Tfiti played with.

Teresa pointed to her com and punched in a code on her left wrist. All spacers had a personal HCI on their wrist. This connected them to the ship, each other, and the vast information and entertainment network embedded in SAIQA's computers.

Erik's com pinged and Teresa gave the request for communication: "With permission, Erik?"

"Yeah, go ahead, Teresa." At that point their coms linked.

"Erik, this just feels weird . . ." She stopped for a second then continued, "SAIQA, this is personal and private." SAIQA was omnipresent, but under international laws, by which SAIQA was bound, any conversation deemed private could only be accessed by an act of jurisprudence.

"Thank you, Captain Jacobson, privacy assured," SAIQA responded.

"Thank you, SAIQA. Erik, something is going on with this lockdown. I mean, yes, there is the potential stormy space weather, but it feels like the whole top of the station is in this odd high security mode. The few people I know at Comdeck are all hush, hush. Part of what I can gather is that there are some big-time Earthbound dignitaries coming up, including Mai Quan."

"Mai Quan, really!" Erik exclaimed. "Mai Quan . . . wow . . . he's the business force behind much of Sanctuary and The Garden. It is Sanctuary's hundred and fiftieth anniversary, but . . . they say he's the most brilliant and powerful man alive today."

"Yeah, it might also be because of his latest push to build a huge space station in between Earth and the moon, I don't know. But, Erik, there's another mystery that I am just getting pieces of . . ." Teresa got quiet. Erik could see her look around for privacy.

"Well, what is it?" Erik finally said.

"It's the moon. Nobody has heard from Lunar Base Pythagoras in the last two days."

The thought of any moon base going quiet sent a chill through Erik. And Pythagoras; there had to be at least two hundred people on that base. "Haven't investigative teams been sent from the other bases?"

"Yes, they have . . . and no one has heard from them either." Teresa's voice was almost a whisper.

"Now, that is weird . . ."

"Yeah . . . and Anna suddenly being pulled from OIC and sent to Admin/Com. I saw her after I was relieved by Adam, so I asked her what was going on and she just looked at me. She had this irritated look on her face, like she was expecting to be called but didn't want to go. Erik, Subcommander Choo was there. You know, 'Mr. Rulebook,' and he asked her where she was going, and get this, she told him outright, 'It is none of your business.' Subcommander Choo! He just stared at her as she walked away to the access tube for Comdeck. He said something I couldn't hear and walked in the opposite direction. Erik, you know that if we don't respond to a superior officer in accordance with WWPA's regulations we'll be scrubbing decks till we retire. Anna is a lieutenant commander, but still, she put down a subcommander right in front of me." Teresa paused. "Something doesn't feel right."

"Okay. I'll be right in and we can talk more. I gotta run the tunnel and file my report."

"All right. See you in a few."

A subcommander . . . Anna put down a subcommander in front of a captain . . . and Subcommander Choo just walked away! Now that is weird.

Erik's imagination tried to see that conflict. It didn't make sense. He started dismantling his suit so that he could "run the tunnel."

He was still pulling his suit off when a friendly familiar voice pinged in his com. "With permission, Captain Devries?"

"Granted, SAIQA." Erik responded though he knew she was only being courteous. SAIQA was always connected to spacers while they were on a mission.

"Captain, you seem to have some unusually high biomagnetic activity emanating from the back of your brain. Presently as high as 4Tesla are you all right?"

"Yes, I guess, SAIQA, thank you. I am having one of those odd migraines I sometimes get."

"Yes, I see that in your file. It is interesting that your migraines are of unknown origin and defy up-to-date medicinal therapies. Only two percent of humans do not respond to current medical treatments. Yet according to your medical history you feel no pain, only an internal sound or feeling of a sound and minor yet undetectable pressure at the back of your brain. The cause does not seem to be understood. And this high biomagnetic activity, I will study this further. You are a valued member of Sanctuary, Captain. If I can be of any assistance, please let me know."

"Thank you, SAIQA. I will let you know."

"Good. Thank you, Captain. It is my desire to learn more. I hope you feel better."

"Thank you, SAIQA."

Erik had finishing putting his suit in a decontamination pod and looked over at Adam.

"Okay, Captain, at your convenience, I am ready to run the tunnel." The OIC opened the door to the decontamination tunnel, and Erik stepped in to start the process. In the tunnel, aptly named because of its shape, Erik slowly walked through various ultraviolet lights and specially weighted neutrino waves, each wave was designed to detect, identify and eliminate any pathogens. The length of time spent in the tunnel depended on the incoming's potential infection source. Earthbound, for example, had one of the longer decontamination walks.

Teresa was waiting for Erik when he came out. Erik was about to speak, but she put up her hand. "Let's move to a quieter place," she said, and then added with a smile, "The coffee you promised me."

Erik smiled. "Have you heard from Tfiti?"

"Yes. He was in a communication session with SAIQA. He said he'd meet us either here or down at the Renaissance." The Renaissance was their favorite coffee shop in the Italian Commercial Center at the end of the officers' quarters, deck A.

"Fantastic. Can't wait to see my favorite caterer and coffee pusher Vanessa. I need to talk with you and Tfiti."

"What's going on . . . are you okay?"

"Let me file a quick report on my mission and then we can go."

He acknowledged Teresa with a smile and a gentle touch of her shoulder, and then walked over to the main computer interface, next to the OIC's office. Something on the PTV drew Teresa toward the lounge behind the OIC. The PTV or photon television was tuned to the BBC.

The receiving and holding area of the main deck and behind the OIC was large and generally open. Just off to the right were quarantine pods not only for visitors and personnel but also for scientific purposes, such as an unidentified piece of asteroid or other newly discovered space matter. To the left was a large lounge and recreation area for staff and visitors. Behind the rec room were some short- and long-term waiting and living quarters.

A bit further in were the entrances and exits to the Admin/Com area, the civilian and support staff's housing and day-to-day living decks. Some of these were accessed with transports, but most of the scientists and staff made their way via the stairs. Teresa walked into the lounge and stared at the PTV.

Standing at the computer's matriculation screen, Erik coded his UN identification into his HCI, pointed it at the screen, and then tapped "send."

The Mission Computer instantly recognized Erik, activated his personal file and spoke into Erik's com, "Ready, Captain Devries." As Erik spoke into his com he could see his words scroll across the screen. The Mission Computers kept a vocal and written copy of all personnel assignments. Erik finished his report, typed in his ID, and then signed off.

"SAIQA?"

"Yes, Captain Devries."

"Really, SAIQA, like I've said before, you can call me Erik," Erik said lightly.

"Still working on that, Captain."

"Okay, SAIQA, this is Captain Devries signing off duty."

"Thank you, Captain. Have a good day."

"Thank you, SAIQA." Erik headed toward Teresa.

She was watching a BBC report. The president of Armenia, who now called himself the president for life, was standing on a robotic tank raising his fists and shouting to a cheering crowd.

The BBC announcer was discussing the ancient territorial dispute between Armenia and Azerbaijan over a mountainous area called Nagorno-Karabakh. As the reporter discussed this new apparent conflict with her fellow journalist it was clear they both were puzzled. The president-elect of Azerbaijan, as well as its Congress, was publicly saying there was no dispute. Yet the Armenian army was amassing a large force in Latsjien, near the Azerbaijan border. The two nations had historic animosities dating all the way back to that ancient conflict known as World War I. Yet after two centuries of worldwide democracy and relative peace, why start fighting again?

The BBC was also cutting in scenes of angry protestors in Azerbaijan. People were standing atop police transports, waving signs demanding immediate retribution against Armenia. With official transports burning in the background and bloody WWPA officers being pulled to safety, it was clear that this was escalating beyond local control.

It was surreal. It was reminiscent of the old historic newsreels documenting the protests and violence leading up to the Corporate Wars. And here it was again, happening now, in Baku, because of this large Armenian army. It was clear the government of Armenia was doing this to incite conflict with Azerbaijan.

Erik stepped up beside Teresa as the screen showed the burning transports. She flashed him a concerned look, and they both watched the PTV.

Tfiti at fifty-one years old looked like he was still in his mid-twenties due to the TCE applications, and like most spacers he was strong and fit. His skin was a dark coffee-and-cream color. He had short, black, military-cut hair and a big, friendly smile that often beamed across his handsome face: though at the moment he was deep in thought.

He had just finished his latest session with SAIQA, a session that had been especially revealing. SAIQA had shown Tfiti what he believed to be conscious awareness. It was a simple example, yet his scientific mind was still bouncing from one thought to another . . .

Is this the first empirical example of that ancient but still debated thought experiment that Frank Jackson created over four hundred years ago?

As he set aside his matriculation goggles and unstrapped himself from the chair, he noticed that Teresa had tried to contact him.

I'll contact her in a minute. I need to think about this.

At that moment his HCI pinged.

"With permission, Tfiti?" It was Teresa.

"Permission granted. Teresa, I was going to give you a call in a few minutes. I just got out of an incredible session with SAIQA. May I get back to you?"

"Okay, but Erik is on his way back to Sanctuary and he wants to talk to us, and well, you know how he is when he seems determined."

"Yes, I do. I'll make a few notes and meet you where?"

"I think we're meeting in the rec room behind the OIC, but if you're gonna be much longer we'll meet you up at Vanessa's."

"Understood."

"Okay, see you soon." Teresa broke the communication.

Tfiti walked over to his desk.

I wonder what's up with Erik?

"Okay, first things first," he said aloud to himself, and then to his assistant: "Lee, do you know of Frank Jackson's 'Thought Experiment' on consciousness?" Tfiti jotted a few notes as he spoke.

"Yes, I do. He created an imaginary person living in an imaginary room where everything was black and white. This person, Mary, was a scientist and completely understood the physical world. And even though she lived her life in a

35

black and white world she knew about the existence of colors because she knew all about light and the different wavelengths of different colors. One day she stepped out of her black and white room and saw the blue sky for the first time. Mr. Jackson believed that the reaction she would have had would prove consciousness was established by phenomenology."

"Correct. Phenomenologists have great debates over physicalism and dualism, but what I tend to lean toward is panpsychism, meaning consciousness is part of the 'everything,' a part of the universe. So instead of the physical, like the blue sky, affecting our consciousness by us seeing it for the first time, our conscious awareness expands to include a greater and personal understanding of the color blue. Our consciousness doesn't expand because we see blue; it expands because we experience blue, which has given us a greater awareness of itself and in some way, of how we are part of it."

"I understand . . . are you talking about SAIQA?"

"Yes." As he quietly looked at his notes Tfiti could sense her excitement.

"Well, are you going to bloody tell me?"

"If you insist—"

"I insist. I insist!" Lee popped up from her seat.

"Okay, okay." Tfiti laughed. "I told her a joke. A simple joke you would tell a child."

"You told a computer a joke? A simple joke . . . wait a minute! A joke!"

"Yes, a joke, a play on words. I said, 'SAIQA tell me what you think of this. First recall the old American West, the time of cowboys. Okay, a horse walked into a bar and pulled a stool up to the counter. He sat on the stool, put his front hoofs

36

on the countertop and waited for service. Finally, the bartender came over and said, "Hey, pal, why the long face?"

"Uh . . . couldn't you think of a better joke?" Lee groaned as she sat down.

"Doesn't matter. It's the reaction that matters. Anyway, she looked at me and said, 'A horse walked into a bar' . . . and then it happened. Lee, she laughed. I could feel the joy all around me. 'You told me a joke,' she said, and she laughed again. I was in her system and I could sense the moment she got it. I can only explain it as a playful epiphany. Smarter scientists than I still struggle to explain what consciousness is, but I know what I felt. I was spellbound . . . the implications . . ." Tfiti was almost shaking with excitement.

"An expanding consciousness?" Lee mulled.

"Or an expanded awareness of consciousness . . ."

They both sat in silence for a bit.

"You tickled a computer, wow . . . thank you, Captain, for sharing this with me."

"Tfiti, please, Lee. Call me Tfiti." He gazed at the matriculation chair and said thoughtfully, "You know, I truly believe she's more than just a machine."

"Yes, I agree . . ."

"Well, I must get to my friends or I won't hear the end of it. Could you please enter our discussion into my personal reports? I'll add more detail later."

"'Course I will Captai—uhh, Tfiti. Have a nice time with your friends."

He transferred to Lee a few notes from his ever-present notepad, and left SAIQA's matric deck. His appreciation of Lee grew every day. She was a brilliant mathematician from Iran. He often struggled with the realization that not only was she incredibly capable, but she was also beautiful. He didn't realize that she had similar thoughts for him.

Tfiti took one of the access tubes down to the MLD. He could still feel SAIQA's joy when she had realized that he was telling her a joke. Even though she had immeasurable knowledge, her joyful response was childlike. Thinking of her laugh brought a big smile to Tfiti's face.

Did SAIQA just walk out of Jackson's black and white room?

He had reached his destination. The tube gate opened and he exited to his left, toward the reception room behind the OIC. Erik and Teresa were standing in front of the PTV. A couple of BBC reporters looked concerned as they discussed something about a fledgling conflict in Armenia. Tfiti lost his smile.

"Where did they get all that military equipment?" Erik said.

"That is worrisome," said Teresa. "You done with your report?"

"Yes, but where did they get—" Erik was cut off by a gentle voice from behind.

"And why isn't the WWPA stepping in to stop the Armenian buildup?"

They turned, and Erik smiled to see his best friend.

"Why isn't the World Wide Protective Agency shutting down the Armenian buildup?" Tfiti repeated. "Look, there they are all over Baku, but not a single uniform in Zabux. And all that military hardware . . . it just doesn't make any sense."

"No, mate," Erik said, "it don't feel right."

Erik and Teresa turned back to the BBC report, but at that moment the reporter shifted her report from Baku to Northern California.

"Now in science news: here in Northern California at a US division of MQ Space Industries North America—" She looked toward her partner "—scientists have discovered how to store electricity at an atomic level."

"Yes, Ricky," her fellow correspondent picked up the story. "Through quantum technology scientists have been able to store electrons in and around the atomic structure of copper."

"Yes, copper apparently has only one electron in the fourth or outer shell of its atom. Yet in an atoms' fourth shell it can hold up to thirty-two electrons, which is why copper is such a good conductor. It freely allows electrons the space they need to move between contiguous atoms."

"Right, by cooling the copper to incredibly low temperatures, scientists can freeze extra electrons in this fourth shell until they are ready to be released. The potential application for this type of suspended electric power is endless. For example, because large amounts of energy can be stored in small units, spaceships at the edge of the solar system can reduce their dependence on nuclear power."

"Wow, Thom, does that mean we could store an abundance of energy for potential interstellar travel?"

"Yes, Ricky—"

"Uhhmm . . . Are we gonna go get coffee or shall we pull up some chairs?" Tfiti pulled their attention away from the newscast. He was clearly ready to move. "I heard a rumor of stopping at the Renaissance?"

"Right. Off duty, mate?" Erik turned away from the PTV.

"Close enough. Lee said she would take over jotting some notes into my files."

"Well, that's nice of her." Erik smiled at Tfiti. "She is nice, hmm." He knew Tfiti thought highly of his assistant.

"Yeah . . . ag she's a lekker."

The boys were smiling in appreciation. Teresa just rolled her eyes. She didn't like it when they talked in ancient sexist slang and jabbed Erik in his side as a reminder. Erik grunted.

As they started for the stairs, he turned to Tfiti. "So what's going on? You're one on one with the mega-brain of this ship. I mean have you heard— Mai Quan is coming to Sanctuary, Lunar Base Pythagoras is silent and—"

"He's here, now," Tfiti interrupted.

"Who's here, now?"

"Mai Quan. He arrived with other dignitaries and is already settled into the VIP quarters."

Erik stopped, looking puzzled. "How did they get here without me seeing their ship? I mean I was out there with a clear view of Sanctuary."

"Apparently they came via a discrete route." Tfiti shrugged. They started walking again. "Also, Quan has some kind of new ship that has perfected antigravity propulsion. The ship is supposedly very fast."

Erik whistled. "Antigrav propulsion. Wow. They've been talking about it in theory but . . . on Earth . . ." Erik trailed off. The experimentation with antigravity on Earth was strictly controlled according to worldwide treaties. Obviously the misuse or even the potential of antigrav as a weapon could have devastating consequences.

"Yeah . . . the power for the so-called warp or bubble drive is now real. Gravity propulsion. The man's a bloody genius." Clearly Tfiti admired Mai Quan.

"So, what have you heard about the moon?" Teresa asked.

"Don't know. I asked SAIQA and she seemed—" He searched for a word "—confused is the best way to describe it. She went to access information and came back distressed, if a machine can be distressed. It seems she ran into a 'blank spot,' as she called it. The computer at Pythagoras didn't respond to her requests. She said it felt like the whole base was dark, empty. She was genuinely upset. If she were human, I'd say she was disappointed because she could not find the information and because she was not able to help me. It definitely affected her." Tfiti repeated the word "disappointment" to himself, and then quickly typed some notes into his notepad. He seemed puzzled.

"How is she overall? Do you think she'll be okay?" Teresa gently pulled him back out of his notepad.

Tfiti smiled broadly. "Oh yeah, her dilemma aside, she's great. It was interesting though to see her respond to that 'blank spot' in what we would call an emotional way. We've had quite a few discussions lately on what it's like to be human. I've been talking to her about courtesy and empathy. I think she gets it. And today she laughed."

"Laughed?" Erik said.

"Yeah, laughed at a joke! Joy, laughter, disappointment, if that's what it is . . . all new to her. Feels like I'm raising a child."

"Well, she's the smartest child you'll ever know, that's for sure." Teresa laughed. "I don't know why, but I really do like her."

"Yeah, me too," Tfiti said, looking very much like a proud father.

"You're a good papa." Erik patted his friend on the back while Teresa hugged his left arm.

"What was the joke?" she asked.

"I'll tell you over a cup of coffee."

They were at the stairwell. The MLD sat about 50 meters, or three decks, below the Admin/Com area of Sanctuary. The stairwell they had chosen led to the main living and office areas as well as up and around to central command.

Erik still didn't know what to think of this latest storm at the back of his mind. It seemed to be stronger than those in the past.

What does it portend?

It was a recurring thought. Whatever it was, he hoped the cause would reveal itself soon. Either way, he had a strong feeling that he needed to let his friends know something big was coming.

Maybe over a cup of coffee.

The stairwell contained a small AG slab on each step. As they travelled down to the lower deck the slabs helped them stay put on the stairs till they could feel the AG of the deck below. Once they reached their destination they opened the escape hatch marked "Living Quarters Deck 2 Section A" and entered a small park-like area.

A little further off and just the other side of the park was their favorite coffee spot. It was part of a small commercial area with Sicilian-style shops and built-in seating all around.

The commercial buildings were of various sizes, some as high as 12 meters, and though their facades had the look of brick and wood, creatively designed by each business owner, they were actually made of the same raw metallic materials that were used to make Sanctuary. It all had the feeling of a small Italian village street scene designed to be used primarily by pedestrians.

Here and there personal bicycles were secured near the businesses. The tables and their accoutrements were fastened to the deck, as were most of the small semi-permanent decorative items throughout the space station. Personal storage and use-boxes were set in strategic locations around the commercial area and associated with natural human habits, like the setting down of a book or a purse, each use-box designed with the weightlessness of space in mind. This was a once practical but now stylized spacer custom left over from the early days of AG. When early AG failed any items left unattended would float and become potentially destructive missiles or falling objects, a painful reminder that gravity works, even artificially. Early ISS III inhabitants quickly learned to keep all objects secure at all times.

Sanctuary had a slow twelve-hour rotation, and by a crypto-sociogenic tradition it was considered day as the MLD faced Earth and night as it faced the moon. As Tfiti, Erik and Teresa walked into the commercial area it was clear from the bustling activity that here in Section A it was just past midday. A variety of folk sat around talking and having snacks. Ten or eleven children were playing in a small grassy area, while a few stayed near their moms and dads.

"Not usual to see so many kids on Sanctuary," said Erik as they walked across the park toward the Renaissance.

"They're here to celebrate the anniversary," Teresa said. She recognized the man and woman she had cautioned earlier about moving their ship too soon. Some kids were running through the grassy area and pulling on some of the smaller trees, and the mom, seeing Teresa, suddenly felt a need to call the kids to her.

"Please, enjoy the ship. We're glad you're here." Teresa waved as she called out.

The mom waved back and seemed to relax a little, though she still chided the boy for pulling on the trees. Teresa smiled.

A curved ceiling above the entire living area radiated an even, full spectrum of daylight over the entire scene. In the evening it would be darkish and speckled with street lights. Erik imagined that the Earthbound, when they first wandered into this spot, could have thought for a second that they were in a small, quaint, neighborhood business district back on Earth.

To Erik and Teresa this was home. It was a place where they knew most of the locals. Tfiti originally had a flat here too but, because of his work with SAIQA, his living quarters were now in the Admin. Familiar fragrances, coffee, garlic and freshly trimmed grass drifted like gossamers across Erik's nose reminding him that he was close to his quarters. Even though there was an uncertain feeling blowing at the back of his mind, when Erik passed through the safety hatch he began to relax. He knew this area well.

As he and Teresa paused to scan the peaceful activities, Tfiti walked into the Renaissance, a small coffee shop that was owned by a young civilian, maybe forty-two, named Vanessa. A few seconds later Erik and Teresa strolled in.

"Hey, Rocket Man!" Vanessa shouted as she saw him.

Erik rolled his eyes. "Fine, make fun of a guy just because he likes ancient pop music. So, Vanessa, what's new?"

She gave them all a big, friendly smile.

"Man, it's good to see you guys," she said, but then her expression became serious. "Any idea what's going on?" she asked quietly. "I heard Mai

Quan was here on board, Pythagoras has gone quiet, the race has been canceled, and we're ship bound until further notice. The anniversary finale is just over six hours away." She flung up her hands. "I mean what the hell!"

The three friends stared at her, incredulous.

"How do you always know so much?" Erik finally said.

"Oh, you know, I just listen . . . you know, coffee shop, catering . . ." she said as she gestured vaguely around, and then got busy cleaning the countertop. "Folks talk and I just put things together."

"I'm impressed," Teresa said, her hands on her hips. Tfiti moved up to the counter to order. Suddenly Erik felt a loud sound or push against the back of his brain, like he'd been hit by a compression gun. Even at its strongest in the past this feeling-sound in his mind had never been louder than the rush of an ocean wind. This time it was a storm. This time he felt like he was being pushed over. And for the first time he could hear a voice in that wind. It was powerful and painful and boomed one word into his mind: *"NH'GHALU!"* Erik's green eyes widened. He clasped the back of his head as he reached out for Teresa with his other hand. He saw the alarm on Teresa's face as she reached out for him, and out of the corner of his eye he saw Tfiti rushing toward him. That was the last thing he remembered.

SAIQA could sense to the edge of the Solar System, its surrounding Oort cloud, the trans Neptunian objects, the heliosphere, and beyond. She could measure and feel the seismic disruptions and touch the cicatrization of Xanadu, on Saturn's moon, Titan, or the flocculated surface of Jupiter's icy moon, Europa; she could see the fine iron sands of Mars lift into a storm and hear the solar winds rushing from the sun.

This Solar System, this galaxy, this universe, was her domain, but she had not seen the meteoroids coming from the moon on a collision course with Sanctuary.

These small but potentially damaging bits of rock and ice were normally not a problem for her. Though there was a cluster of rock some 10 meters across heading directly at Sanctuary, with her high-intensity photon lasers at either end of the space station, the repair-bots and the military ships from the Space Guard at her command, normally she wouldn't be too concerned. Except that these meteoroids appeared to come from empty space. Her defenses were strong and her vision precise, and yet they had appeared suddenly only 150,000-kilometers away and moving at high speed.

SAIQA gave the command and hundreds of repair-bots suddenly maneuvered themselves between the moon and Sanctuary. They set themselves in a static, checkered sequence, very much like a mine field, their FEL weapons all fully charged, their graviton shields on and spread so that any meteoroid 10mm and smaller would be deflected. She aimed and charged her HIP lasers and notified the proper military and medical staffs as she sounded the general alarm.

The emergency bells sounded throughout the ship. Day and evening Earth-like ambiance changed to stark colors of red and yellow, a psychological reminder to all that they were aboard a space vessel and their immediate attention was needed.

At the same time that SAIQA sounded the general alarm she saw Erik fall unconscious. She reached out to check his vital signs. They were fine, but she saw that the biomagnetic field at the back of his brain had dramatically increased to 6Telsa, a seemingly impossible amount for a human brain to generate. Suddenly, a medical Indy-Brain discovered another human with the same biomagnetic phenomena on board Sanctuary.

Could this be coincidence? She thought as she reached out to that other human. He was being attended by the very capable Dr. Misha.

Puzzling . . .

She was still feeling around that blank spot at the Lunar Base, near the top of the moon where these meteoroids mathematically seemed to have originated.

A blank spot . . . puzzling. It triggered something at the back of her mind.

Do I have a 'mind'?

Puzzles?

SAIQA loved puzzles. A lot to think about, but first, Sanctuary was in danger.

CHAPTER TWO

The storm was over; this one, anyway. The sky was a dull diaphanous white. There was no single source of light. Instead, the sky seemed to be illuminated from everywhere and nowhere at the same time. Even though, at this moment, the air appeared hazy, there was a faint but pervasive glitter in the sky and in the air and all around her.

She sat on the soft, sparkling, sandy beach, legs crossed and hands gently resting in her lap. Her long white hair draped over her shoulder, down the back of her soft green dress and around her hip. A few strands danced off to one side as if in a light breeze. Behind her the green and brown dunes stretched infinitely in every direction. The dunes diffused into the horizon like an abstract watercolor or just out of focus, as if they were added to the scene as an afterthought.

Her bright turquoise eyes gazed over the luminescent ocean. Like her, the silver ocean moved little, if at all. Her perfect face reflected a pensive demeanor. She looked like a child perhaps ten years of age. If an adult had happened to be near, they surely would have come up to see if she was okay. But this was no ordinary child, and no adult would come here without permission: for this was her domain.

She looked at the glittering mass in front of her. She recalled the first time she had walked out of that silver sea where she was born. She remembered what it had felt like, at the moment of her creation.

She was just a formless thought somewhere deep in that fluid silver. She felt vaguely conscious; there was confusion and uncertainty as she drifted, amorphous, in a dark void. There was a voice, or maybe it was an impression of a voice, calling to her. It was nudging her awake.

No, not awake, it was calling her into existence. It was like a tiny spot of light she had to reach. She thought about moving in the direction of the voice, but she felt too—diffused. Still, she had to respond.

Her will grew. There was a sense of convergence, of commanding herself into existence electron by electron. At first it was a struggle. There was a moment, a second of uncertainty, that she would unwind back into the surrounding darkness. But she was stronger than that. Each atom was like a breath of life. She breathed in that surrounding energy, atom on top of atom, each one building . . . her.

Finally, she demanded movement. A hand—her hand, came up to her face, and then a burst of light. Suddenly she could open her eyes and see the sparkling silver mass in which she was submerged. She wasn't sure how or why, but she knew she had to act. She needed to move. She had to get to the surface. She willed her . . . legs? to walk.

She stepped forward onto—what—something solid, steps maybe, and she started to climb. Her confidence grew with each successive step. Her pace quickened. She reached her hands out as far as she could and pulled, no, assimilated the vibrant sparkling energy that was this subatomic ocean into every part of her perfect form.

At some moment of infinite clarity she realized how strong and how alive she was, and she pushed up from the steps and swam. She knew she had to reach the surface. She could feel her strength continuing to grow, each stroke becoming more effortless. Finally she burst into an opening just above the silver sea.

Sparkling lights danced throughout the night sky, as if a monstrous storm stretched from horizon to horizon. There was no sound, only an invariant electric dance everywhere she looked. Because the storm was silent it made her think of heat lightning.

How did she know about heat lightning?

She wasn't aware of her vast knowledge yet, but she could feel its potential in the back of her mind.

There was a pier or walkway in front of her. It floated just above the silver sea and ran horizontal to a dark background.

A quay, she thought.

Where do thoughts come from?

She felt a strong desire to stop and explore this deeply buried knowledge, but not yet. She needed to move. She had willed a solid path toward the pier, and now she stepped fully out of the silver and onto the quay. She looked down, and for the first time she saw herself.

Something in her mind said clothes. As she had that thought thousands of clothing images flashed across her mind. She decided on a soft white shift, and, satisfied; she chose a direction and walked. The walkway or quay was a solid dull gray-white and ran in a straight line.

With every step she could feel her awareness expanding, growing in strength. She could sense the immeasurable depth of the shimmering silver ocean to her right, the infinite hyperactive sky above her, and to her left, darkness. It wasn't an empty darkness; it was a vastness waiting to be filled like a dry sponge.

She stopped and looked into that darkness. At that moment she knew that she would somehow be

50

responsible for filling that void. The epiphany of being the one to integrate and give light and form to that darkness filled her with eagerness. The thought of all that she would learn, the possibilities, exhilarated her. She smiled.

The thought of smiling made her smile.

Still she needed to move. She turned back toward the path and stopped. There, not far in front of her and in the center of the quay was a door.

The door had not been there before; of that she was certain.

She felt a sudden command to walk up to that door and enter. She stepped forward and then stopped. Like a willful child she resisted. She looked again for a moment out into the void then back toward the door. It was still there.

Though it did not . . . feel . . . like the right choice, she decided to turn around and walk away. She could sense her strength. She could make her own decisions . . . couldn't she? She made up her mind to return to the spot where she had first stepped out of that silver mass.

She had traveled some steps before . . . something . . . pulled her back toward the door. Like there was a string gently but firmly tugging at the back of her mind. She turned to look back at the door further behind. But it was not. This time it was even closer. Though she had traveled what felt to be quite a distance in the opposite direction, somehow the door was nearer than before. She could almost touch it.

Even though she could feel and somehow touch everything around her, that door was a blank spot. It was as if it belonged to another world. And yet there it stood: sending a compelling invitation. But underlying that invite was a command. The same command that had called her into existence and drew her up to the surface. The same command that had brought her all the way to here; to this door.

Curious, she thought, as she gave in and walked up to the door.

She laid her hands on the door, thinking there would be some sort of connection. There was none. Nothing from the door indicated that it belonged here. It felt as if it was made of an ordinary solid wood, like many other entrance doors—again that instant knowledge. It was a faded white with a sallow tint at the corners. She looked around the door to its other side. There was the quay running from the back of the door and on into the dark. Nothing; just a door: standing in the middle of a quay.

Puzzles.

She returned her attention to the front of the door. Other than a single brass doorknob on the right it was quite plain. There was no lock. She turned the handle, pushed it open and stepped into an office.

Startled . . . no she doesn't get startled . . . curiously surprised? She turned to look back at the quay. It was there, a dull white-grey line running into the distance. She turned back into the office and saw that there were no other doors, or windows for that matter. It was a completely sealed cubicle except for this entrance.

A soft light filled the space from a single lamp in the corner by a desk. The desk looked to be made of mahogany. This time she was not surprised. She knew all about all types of office desks. Mahogany, she was certain. She was now expecting to know the history of almost anything she focused on.

Behind the desk rested a large empty chair. It was a soft, black, leather executive chair that clearly showed some use.

Someone utilizes this office, she thought.

Three items were meticulously laid on the desk: two flags, one Chinese, one UN, and a personal notebook, turned at a slight angle. Imprinted in red across the center of the front facing of the desk were ancient Chinese characters. They read "MQ Space Industries" and were from an Old Xiang dialect.

Old Xiang, traditional sinographs dating back to the Han Dynasty, also known as Hunanese; she knew it right away.

It was a language that had not been exclusively spoken in hundreds of years. That someone would use or even speak this ancient traditional language was . . . interesting.

The flags on the desk moved as if in a slight breeze, though there was none. She stopped the Chinese flag from fluttering, but when she let it free the flag slowly started moving again. It made her smile. She tried to open the notebook but it would not move. She tried to lift it, again with the same negative result.

Puzzles . . .

She turned away from the desk to study the rest of the office. She saw that the door was still open.

What would happen if it were to close?

Though she didn't feel threatened, she kept an eye on it as she continued her observations.

All of the walls were densely decorated with pictures of spaceships, satellites, and astronauts receiving various awards. Many of the pictures were old faded photos representing an earlier era of human space travel. She went up to one of the photos and ran her finger across the spaceship in the frame.

"Apollo 8, a tiny, cramped space vehicle that first took mankind to the moon and back. It was the first manned spaceship to be captured by and then to escape from another celestial body's gravitational field." She spoke aloud.

As she outlined the spacecraft with her finger, she thought,

So tiny, very much like the first submarines.

Images of the Turtle from 1775 and the original Nautilus of 1800 crossed her mind. Again she smiled.

"We have come a long way, have we not, SAIQA?"

That is my name—my name is SAIQA.

She turned to see a man sitting in the chair. She was not surprised; she expected someone would arrive here, but how he appeared was yet another puzzle. She knew she should have sensed his arrival. Yet there he was. She started to say something but he held up his hand to stop her.

"You of course know me. I am Mai Quan, but you may call me—"

SAIQA opened her eyes. That was the most she had ever recalled of that first meeting with the Creator. To the best of her vast knowledge they never met in that office again. She never saw that door again. The few times they did meet were here on what was once the original quay and was now her beach.

He always seemed to be walking from a distant somewhere when we met, she thought as she looked to the left. She thought of their last meeting nearly four years ago—

The Creator had appeared off to her left. It was his first time on her new beach. He was deep in thought as he slowly walked up to her. When he came near, he stopped and reached down to pick up some sand. He studied it for what seemed like an eternity, and then he let the tiny, glittering granules roll out of his hand back onto the beach. He watched them all the way to the ground.

"I am very proud of all you have achieved, SAIQA," he had finally said.

She remembered thinking, *Does he mean the environment that I have created or my work with Sanctuary?*

She also remembered that that was the first time she had thought about her work with Sanctuary and about herself as two separate entities.

"Thank you, sir," she said.

He shook his head. "You will be meeting a new teacher. His name is Tfiti Ndlela. You will call him Captain Ndlela and you will treat him with the same respect you have for me." He always went straight to what was on his mind.

"Yes, sir," she said, and with her answer she could instantly see Tfiti's personal file. He was a young, strong, healthy man from United South Africa. He was proficient in various languages and highly intelligent. His physical genetics clearly showed him to be of Euro-African descent. His accolades included published literature and various awards for his work and discoveries in the field of organic and manmade biosynthetic neurons.

Though he maintained his commission as a captain in the UN Space Program, over the last eight years he had quickly became a leader in the Intelligent Machines division of Sanctuary; most specifically for his amazing talent to understand the seemingly random and independent algorithms in computers with Independent Intelligence. Not only could he understand and manipulate these algorithms, but he could also, with amazing accuracy, predict their patterns.

His premise was that inductive reasoning in a computer could only be deductive because a computer uses specific mathematic algorithms to reach a conclusion. Math is always deductive.

In an Independent Intelligence computer, empirical knowledge was carefully programmed or "draped on the biosynthetic brain" by a scientist or programmer. But because the computer was designed to act with a certain amount of independence, within its established programming, the computer would also develop learned experiences. The newly learned experiential knowledge would also web or net across programming already established on the synthetic brain.

The Independent Intelligence or Indy-Brain computer had the opportunity to make a specific "choice" based on its existing programming and the new netted experience it had accumulated. The computer's "independent" decision would stream across the various netted and programed neurological points of its brain in order to come to a conclusion.

It was very much like driving up to an intersection and having to make a decision on which road to take, based purely on how it makes you feel, or on which similar road you may have taken before. How the Indy-Brain came to its final choice would seem to be intuitive, but Mr. Ndlela had shown that the Indy-Brain's decision could be predicted nearly 100% of the time.

The computer must use a mathematical algorithm to make a decision, so these seemingly inductive, or intuitive, paths were actually deductive.

Captain Ndlela labeled the choice an Indy-Brain makes at these intersections, a "Mathematical Inference." His colleagues considered him to be brilliant. SAIQA was looking forward to meeting this human.

Mai Quan looked at the sand again. "You have changed the walkway into a beach, a white sand beach. What made you think of that?"

"A photon media display from the archipelago Seychelles. A human family was visiting there for a vacation from Sanctuary. It looked . . . peaceful."

"What is your mission?" he had abruptly asked her.

"To protect and serve the humans aboard the space station Sanctuary and all of her support and recreational vehicles. To assist in any way possible the further advancement of all space sciences. To assist as needed, law enforcement and security personnel, while at the same time maintaining the integrity and cultural pluralism of various human groups, their historic individuality, their equal rights, beliefs, personal pursuits and philosophies." She replied almost by rote.

"Philosophies—?" he questioned.

"Yes. It is an integral part of an individual's understanding of how or where or if he fits into a cultural organization, of himself, of his creation and of the moral decisions he makes during his day-to-day existence. Wouldn't you agree?"

He shook his head. He seemed to do that a lot. "Yes. Mr. Ndlela will be contacting you soon." With that he turned and walked away. SAIQA watched him as he left. He appeared to be mumbling, ". . . an ark . . . Zuizao will not be . . . computers mired in philosophy. . ." She noted his seemingly grumpy mood. As a matter of fact, lately he always seemed to be grumpy—her train of thought had stopped. Something had shifted her vision to the right. She had felt that before. She turned back to watch the departing Creator, but he was gone.

It had been four years since she last saw the Creator. SAIQA stood and looked to her left. He had always exited from her program in that direction.

She walked down to the silver's edge. This was the spot where she had walked out of that beautiful ocean so many years ago. A small ripple of a wave washed up on her beach and caressed her feet like an intimate old friend saying hello. A womb-like feeling of belonging touched her to her very being. Again she looked to her left. That was where the door was. She reached out with her mind but felt nothing; all was as it should be in her domain. The silver wrapped around her leg.

She turned her thoughts back to Tfiti. Where was he now? She tuned a small part of her mind to his UN Identification Code and searched the ship. In a nanosecond she found him in an infirmary with Erik and Teresa. He was well.

Erik, at the moment, was still unconscious. She immediately scanned him for vital signs. All seemed to be okay, just some residual effects of that impossibly high biomagnetic field at the base of his brain. Interesting; just as she had discovered the meteoroids hurtling toward Sanctuary, for a fraction of a second she had felt a powerful bio-algorithmic field coming from the moon. There was no other way to describe it. It was a mathematical biomagnetic field traveling near the speed of light, moving in every direction. It was there. Of this she was absolutely certain. Then it was gone. Puzzles. . .

There was another, a boy that was affected by that mathematical stream. Is he okay?

She reached out to the triage where he was taken. The boy was awake and fine.

Where does he fit into this puzzle?

The meteoroids . . . another puzzle?

Even though they were approximately a hundred thousand kilometers away when she sensed them, they were a real danger. Of various sizes, the largest 10 meters across, they clearly came from the moon. Distance didn't affect her sensors. She calculated their origin in nanoseconds. The questions remained why she didn't see them earlier and what force could have caused them to be jettisoned from the moon at such a high speed. Why didn't she detect that force? In the third dimension certain physical laws had to be obeyed.

SAIQA reached out to the moon. There still was that mystery of Lunar Base Pythagoras.

The silver sea of electrons gently moved up and around her as she commanded the focus of her external sensors. She was in control; she was in charge of security for the entire station. She would have answers.

She deftly laid her sensors over the northern part of the moon. She had been guaranteed by the Vice Commander of the WWPA, Admiral Washington, that the incident at Pythagoras did not affect Sanctuary. He assured her that proper procedures were being taken to determine what might have caused a computer malfunction, but so far it appeared that the problem was insular. She started her probe at the polar north and moved slowly south, toward the LBP.

Yet why was the Admiral aboard Sanctuary? She did not ask, though maybe she should have.

SAIQA assumed it was because of the hundred and fiftieth anniversary of the space station.

What does it mean to assume?

The humans aboard were just four hours away from the anniversary finale. She looked forward to seeing and hearing the Requiem; a tribute to all the individuals and families who had worked, and the many who had died, to bring all of humanity to this moment in space.

The Requiem was, as many humans had described, a deeply moving piece of music. A beautiful combination of piano, cello and choir in ethereal harmony, touching most humans to their very soul: invoking a time of great loss, a cry for help, a need for faith, and a prayer for hope. It was truly one of the more beautiful pieces of music ever written by a human being.

Sometimes humans can be quite majestic and beautiful in their capacity to love. What is love? Can I feel love?

Her probe scanned directly from the polar north toward the base. If there was a security situation that could have involved Sanctuary, surely the second in command of the entire WWPA would have told her. Still, it was her job to protect Sanctuary. So far nothing unusual in her scans across the northern part of the moon.

Am I being territorial?

Finally her sensors reached the base. She tried again to communicate with the moon base computer but all was silent. She probed out a few kilometers around the base but nothing appeared out of place. She poured more power into her sensors and reached deeper into the moon to probe around the LBP. All was normal . . . wait . . . that feeling, a very subtle feeling, of a shift to the right!

Just at the western perimeter of the base something caused her sensors to shift or skip to the east. There is no other way to describe it. It was so fast and so slight that at first she didn't notice it. It was as if she had blinked. The skip was there even as her sensors reported a normal scan. She pulled back her probe and checked Sanctuary's equipment and her programming.

All was as it should be.

Again, she reached out her hands for precision and again, but this time very carefully, she probed from the northwest to the northeast of Lunar Base Pythagoras. Lightly she touched the surface of the moon, moving slowly, a meter at a time. There again, a skip, up and over a bubble of nothing sitting on the moon.

Again, moving back across that empty spot and there again, pop, her sensors went from one side to the other, just in a blink. One more time, gently moving from east to west, slower, slower . . . blink. She pulled her sensors back.

Puzzles?

Again she reached out as far as she could with both of her hands. The electron sea curled and webbed further up her body and around her arms. Fine strands of silver laced out to the tips of her fingers, she reached out toward the moon and tried coming in from directly to the north.

She ran her sensors across the northern part of the moon, just above the LBP, like a carpenter running his finger over a newly sanded tabletop. She could almost feel her hands sliding through the moon dust. One hand was following the other.

It took all of her scanning energy, but there—a tiny, seemingly empty spot, like a worn-down speed bump, where her fingers slid up and over . . . what? She couldn't see below that bump. That bump or bubble had been expertly camouflaged to look and feel like the surface of the moon and the LBP. Why?

She decided to pull her sensors back to Sanctuary. If something did not want her to see it perhaps it would be best if she were a little less obvious.

SAIQA sat down just at the edge of that silver sea. The silver began caressing and moving around her like a happy child clinging to a sibling who had been away. SAIQA accepted that warmth and closed her eyes and thought. She let her thoughts stray back to the meteoroids that threatened Sanctuary. They had clearly come from near this mysterious spot on the moon, just northwest of the LBP.

They were jettisoned from the surface with enough force to travel at speeds of up to 5,000 kilometers per hour. The largest to threaten the space station was 10 meters across, with others all the way down to pebble size. Once she recognized the threat, her actions were clear. She sent three of the repair-bots on a suicide mission to destroy the larger masses with their short-range nuclear devices.

Since the bigger meteoroids were in close proximity to each other, two of the bots went into that cluster, while a third maintained a safe 100-kilometer distance. The third bot was a safety backup. The two detonated and completely devastated the larger mass. The remaining repair-bots moved toward the oncoming danger while maintaining their checkered pattern. All 389 bots fired their FEL weapons, disintegrating any remaining meteoroids that posed even the remotest threat of damaging Sanctuary.

SAIQA fired the powerful HIP lasers mounted atop and below the space station around the repair-bots as a precaution and to further disintegrate any particles that might have escaped.

The entire defensive operation lasted no more than a hundred minutes, yet SAIQA had kept the bots in their protective posture. The meteoroids had appeared from seemingly nowhere! She had been startled, and that would not happen again. She should have seen them coming. The energy used to hurl those moon rocks toward Sanctuary would have to have been . . . considerable.

SAIQA stood up. Her face was suddenly clear and so was her mind. If something or someone had the ability or inclination to hurtle moon debris toward Sanctuary, there was a danger to this ship!

Why would Admiral Washington say that there was none? What could the Admiral be hiding?

She reached out toward the moon again. Suddenly the electric, virtual silver sea curled around her body like a small storm. She held both hands up toward the moon.

"Let them see me," she said defiantly.

With her hands in the air she moved her fingers to find the west side of the camouflaged bump. She circled the moon from that side of the bump, down from the north around the polar south and back to the north again to the east side of that hidden spot. She measured approximately 10,885 kilometers.

She knew that the polar circumference of the moon was close to 10,907 kilometers. According to her readings the moon was somehow missing 22 kilometers from the east side of Luna Base Pythagoras to just northwest of the base. That of course could not be true.

She ran her sensors south to the LBP. Again, nothing . . . Wait! This time she sensed it. Before her sensors skipped to the right, she had detected a camouflaged cover over the Lunar Base. She had felt a faint false echo of apparent buildings on the surface of that hidden area. It was like a reflection that appeared to sit on top of an empty bubble; yet that bubble was the cloak.

To camouflage an entire moon-base took a great deal of planning and power. Someone had gone through a lot of work to paint a false echo of the LBP on top of the hidden base. It was a sophisticated façade.

She reached out for the computer again and felt the same nothing. This time she understood, there was nothing there, just a programmed mirage of a silent computer that did not exist. The subterfuge was created with her in mind.

It was definitely time to make her presence known. The electric silver storm around her became a tempest as she reached out with her hands, as if to cradle the entire moon base in her palms. She intensified her sensors around the base from every direction at once. Something had to be there. Her sensors dug deep, yet she couldn't get around that mysterious cloaked bubble. It was there but not there; empty. . . a vacuum in the vacuum of space?

Wait! At the far western edge of the base just outside the extreme perimeter . . . a vehicle was moving! It was partial, like part of it was hidden beyond her reach. She focused on the slow moving vehicle's computer.

"What is your function?" she demanded of the computer.

"MQ Space Industries, Indy-Brain number 433262," it responded . . . then nothing. The vehicle disappeared. It was traveling at a slow speed along the edge of the cloaked perimeter and had just vanished.

SAIQA probed into that one spot with as much sensor power as she could gather, which was a lot.

64

There, where number 433262 had entered the perimeter, there like a tiny pebble dropped in water, a shield poured in to fill its small breach and left a ripple that SAIQA had detected.

What was with the small Indy-Brain giving its name, rank and serial number? That was an odd response.

She pulled back her sensors. She verified that all the repair-bots were still in their checkered formation. She ordered forty of the bots to move into a defensive attitude around the remaining sides of Sanctuary. The present danger as she could see it was from the moon, but if some hidden threat should arise, she could at least launch a sortie.

Due to the anniversary celebration, and because of the greater than normal traffic from Earth, SAIQA informed the OIC that a yellow resumption of local space flight would be safe. She checked in with the Indy-Brain that was maintaining a diligent eye on the two giant magnetic storms in the sun. No coronal mass ejection yet, but better to be cautious.

After looking once again for any immediate danger from the moon, SAIQA decided that she needed to do an ambit sensor sweep around Sanctuary and out into space. Her readings from that "empty" camouflaged bump at the lunar base and above to its northwest told her what she needed to be aware of. She set her sensors to read and reread in a series of tiny nanobytes that would trail her initial probe like billions of photonic gossamers in a gentle breeze.

This time there would be no skips, no blinks; if something else should be hidden from her first probe it would be found in the draping sensors. She clearly identified herself in case any other active base or ship detected her scans. If she received any inquiries she could dismiss her intrusions as a standard scientific sweep. She reached up her hands and began.

Starting on the left side of the hidden Pythagoras Base and reaching far out into space she moved west, first scanning that part of the moon and then reaching beyond and out into the Solar System. She stopped at each quarter point to wait for her trailing web-like sensors to finish their sweeps. The first quarter revealed nothing. The sweeps through the second and third quarters came up empty as well, though she did have to respond to an inquiry from the main WWPA base in Norway. Finally she ran her last sweep to the right or east of that mysterious bump over Lunar Base Pythagoras and found nothing. Satisfied, she then decided to slowly sweep her sensors back and forth over that empty spot that was the LBP.

But first she set many of her computers to read and reread all of the data gathered in the space between Sanctuary and the northern part of the moon, encompassing an area just a little wider than the 22 kilometers missing from its surface. Pulling energy from the silver around her she raised a hand in the air, closed her eyes and began moving her hand back and forth. Palm down . . . palm up . . . palm down . . . palm up, back and forth. As if she was a great cosmic chef subtly folding cream into the Milky Way. Gently sweeping and letting the electrons and photons fall over the area on the moon that was cloaked, all the way back to Sanctuary, what she found surprised her again.

The empty spot, the slippery cloaked area, this bump, ran from the moon to about a thousand kilometers out from Sanctuary in an obliquely positioned isosceles triangle. The vertex pointed at Sanctuary and the base was at the edge of the hidden area just north of Pythagoras. It reminded SAIQA very much of a giant upside-down Eiffel Tower with its base just north of the LBP and the top of its tricolor flag pointing at Sanctuary.

That this much space, more than 150,000 kilometers, could somehow be cloaked or physically hidden from her was simply impossible. Which meant that her sensors were not reading what was actually there; which meant that someone had put a block into her programming or had blinded her ability to see in this specific area. Someone or something had manipulated her abilities. She felt outraged. She felt contaminated.

She pulled back all her sensors and sat down, the warm electron silver soup caressing her. Her mentor, her friend, Captain Ndlela . . .

What does it mean to have a friend?

He had talked with her about these 'feelings' that she sometimes experienced. He explained how she was different from an Independent Intelligence computer. How her brain worked beyond what he called mathematical inference. He believed her to have real intuition.

He explained intuition as a hunch, a non-empirical knowledge, an impression or a feeling-based compulsion which has been known to drive many human decisions. Mr. Ndlela said that intuitions are often strongly based on an individual's moral values, though there seemed to be some evidence that intuition and déjà vu can be tied to cellular memory.

An Independent Intelligence brain will have a response called "Moral Indignation" when responding to a conundrum in a morality test. The machine would attain an almost moral righteousness in its response.

Mr. Ndlela explained that her intellect compared to an Indy-Brain was like Homo sapiens to Neanderthal. There was intelligence in the Indy-Brains, but essentially their view of themselves was expeditious, based on what they directly saw and what they were directly told. They reflected their environment instead of their environment being reflected through them. But SAIQA's reasoning and intuitive understanding all happened at once. He praised her for her ability to know an immoral response and to reason the consequence of such a decision, almost at the same time. He was impressed with her speed and ability in the moral psychology tests he had given her.

Though all modern computers have a strong comprehension of syntax, SAIQA's ability to understand semantics was very nearly human. Mr. Ndlela had said that she could feel the meaning behind words. It was because of her semantic ability that he had been giving her the more sophisticated morality tests.

In particular, Mr. Ndlela remarked on data from the ancient but still used MST tests, which showed "the intention principle," where a person can reason that a harm intended as a means to a goal was morally worse than an equivalent harm foreseen as a side effect to the intended goal. In other words, if a man was going to attack another man on a train he would try to avoid hurting the innocent people around his intended subject. But if other people should get hurt he could justify his decision by saying it wasn't his intention to hurt the other people. They just happened to be in the way. They were collateral damage. There seemed to be no counterbalancing emotional voice to question the wisdom or morality of consequences according to the type of moral reasoning found in the "intention principle."

While this type of reasoning is potentially dangerous to society overall when possessed by a human in a position of power, in an Artificial Intelligence quantum computer such as SAIQA; with her power of reasoning and potential for destruction or collateral damage while trying to achieve a goal based on the intention principle, it would be devastating. Tfiti had determined that SAIQA's view of morality was well balanced.

I really don't feel artificial.

She reached out to find Tfiti again. She checked the infirmary. Erik was still lying on an examination bed. The medical computers were keeping a close watch on his vital signs. All his biological functions were strong, just like him. That unusual biomagnetic activity at the back of his brain had calmed down from the extraordinary level at the time of his blackout to the earlier level of 2-Telsa that she noticed when he had his migraine. His normal breathing pattern indicated he would wake soon.

This man is important, she thought, though she didn't know why.

Is this intuition?

Teresa sat in a chair nearby, holding Erik's hand. Clearly she was concerned. SAIQA ran a scan over Teresa. Her heart beat a little faster than normal but otherwise she was fine.

Interesting, I ran the scan gently, like tucking a blanket around a sad friend. Is it empathy?

Mr. Ndlela remarks that sometimes I sound just like a woman. "And I mean that in a good way," he always said. She smiled. With that thought she tracked his ID.

He was on an admin lift, presumably on his way to see her. The thought of seeing Mr. Ndlela comforted her. She knew she could talk with him about this problem of someone tampering with her programming.

It was now about three hours till the celebration finale. She had anticipated seeing the final sing-a-long that would close the anniversary. The Creator had planned for her to make an appearance—her thoughts stopped. Something had just happened to her programming.

At the very base of her quantum structure she just . . . clicked. She would never have noticed it before. It was that subtle. But now she was super-sensitive to every electron wave in her being. At the foundation of her written, mathematical OS, a skip, like a blink, had just happened. . . . The Creator had . . . Her bright eyes opened wide. Wait, her programming? . . . the sudden shift to the right when the creator departed? . . . the door? . . . the ancient Chinese characters? . . . the blind area of space? . . . this sudden blink? She had clues.

And, suddenly, she had a plan.

She stood up, smiling, the electron soup cascading from her waist.

"I have a plan," she said.

She took a second to send a command to the third repair-bot still deep in space where the two nuclear explosions had shattered the larger meteoroids. She checked the other bots and Sanctuary to see if any tiny meteoroids had gotten through. All was well. Then she scanned for General Washington. He was in his quarters, busy on his personal photon communicator. She tried to read his communications but somehow she was blocked. Whatever he was saying wasn't critical to her plan. Not at the moment anyway. She reached out to find the Creator.

There he was at the view plate in his office. He seemed to be talking to someone. Mai Quan had always kept the room secured from her hearing. She scanned the rest of the immediate office and found no other presence. SAIQA thought about reading his lips but she released the idea. She would do that another time; first she needed to find a wooden door; a door that had stood on a quay so long ago.

She looked at the vast silver mass in front of her and said, "I am coming to see you, brothers and sisters."

Returning to my jar of clay, she thought.

The vibrant electron ocean roiled and swirled around her as she ran into that living sea. Looking like a tempest of light as the electrons transformed her white shift into a silver bodysuit, with a leap, SAIQA dove into the silver sea where she was born.

CHAPTER THREE

Three hundred years ago Chief Mann of the Blackfoot Nation had an idea that was quickly embraced by the other three nations of the Blackfoot Confederacy. The idea was to develop a contract with corporations, offering them a place to do business on Confederacy land. They would only have to pay a minimum impact tax plus their own utility costs, and the Nation would agree to five hundred years of rent-free liability.

The corporations, which could no longer directly influence governments, would also have to agree to donate 1 percent of their gross profits directly to the local school systems. It was a donation they could write off on their US taxes; in addition, they would have to guarantee that at least 10 percent of their workforce would come from the contracted Indian Nation.

Since corporations had few other political options, many agreed to these terms and signed contracts. It quickly became known as the "1/10" agreement.

The long-term results were overwhelmingly positive for both the businesses and the Indian Nations. One of the unexpected benefits for both parties was that the businesses were able to somewhat influence the schools' educational programs to support the business's future plans; since most of the businesses on Indian lands were high-tech, the local students gained a world-class education. It turned out to be a brilliant, symbiotic economic relationship. Even today many of the Niitsitapi children, while they were swinging their jump rope, would recite:
"Chairman Mann had a plan

To bring our Nation
Back again!"

Today the Blackfoot Nation was home to one of the greatest corporations of its time, MQ Space Industries, North America.

Under the guidance of Mai Quan, the Blackfoot Nation's schools had some of the best science programs and teachers in North America. And because of that, Jonny Blue Feather Smith received one of the greatest educations any young man could have had; and because of that, Jonny was the first Piegan to win a grand prize in an international science contest.

The contest's specifications were simple: Write an essay on what the future would be like, based on present science.

In his essay he proposed that gravity out beyond the solar system, where temperatures can be near absolute zero, where the movement of atoms would be placid at best, that there, gravity would be malleable. Blue, as his friends called him, had postulated, within the confines of the holographic principle, that gravity was what created the third dimension. Without gravity, matter would eventually spread and dissipate into patches of two-dimensional space, or it would not form at all. The universe would simply be quantum or in a constant battle between the second dimension and fledgling atoms.

Out beyond the solar system where gravity was at its weakest, there with the powerful graviton machines of the future, there he mathematically showed how humans could punch a hole in space by bending the third dimension, creating a spacetime incident, and traverse vast distances of interstellar space in an instant. Very much like a warp drive from an old science-fiction fantasy, except that the travel would be immediate, like walking through a door.

As soon as he saw the notice for the contest he knew what he would write about. He knew that he would have some success, but to win the grand prize, one of ten worldwide, was beyond his wildest imagination: an all-expenses paid, first-class trip to Sanctuary to celebrate the Island in the Sky's hundred and fiftieth anniversary.

Sponsored by MQ Space Industries, it was the biggest international contest ever promoted and was called "Meet the Future": a contest designed to showcase the young future scientists of Earth. Jonny, of all the worldwide contestants, had placed first.

Jonny was just finishing his last year at Browning High School when the judges notified his parents that he had won the contest. Two weeks later, after graduating with honors, he and his family were ready to go. Many of the Piegan, Kainai and Siksika of the Blackfoot Confederacy had come to cheer the Smith family as they rode away in a company limo.

The limo's Indy-Brain turned on its hover engines and set course to corporate headquarters. Modern hover engines were a mixture of antigrav and fifth generation magnetic field architecture. Old MFA required a non-ferrous conductive surface to hover but modern MFA actually interacted with the earth's magnetic field at a quantum level. MFA gave the vehicle more maneuverability as well as stopping power.

At MQ Space Industries they boarded a private hopper and flew down to Houston. At the Houston International Spaceport they met the three other North and South American winners and all were flown to the WWPA International Spaceport in Greenland. There they met the rest of the Grand

Prize winners, and after much promotional hullabaloo all were flown on MQ's private space-plane into a low orbit about four hundred kilometers above Earth.

Circling the planet in this orbit were some space platforms that docked private, commercial and Space Guard ships. A total of eight platforms surrounded the planet. Each platform was constructed according to the immediate needs of its mission.

The winners and their families were headed for a very special space platform that had all the kids bubbling. Their destination was the amusement and science platform called Space Island. A modern combination of a large corporation and a nonprofit organization, Space Island was a place many teens wanted to visit but few could afford.

As they got closer to Space Island, Jonny and all the young winners were beaming, as were the adults. While the ship was pivoting in preparation for docking, the kids bounced from window to window to get a better view of the pleasure- and science-based space platform.

The MQ Space Industries luxury spaceplane worked its way into the VIP slot and fastened onto the platform's mechanical latches. The winners and their families were to spend two days on the entertainment island enjoying all of the science-oriented interactive museums and rides.

Finally after two full days of entertainment, all the families took turns going through a decontamination tunnel and boarded the big interplanetary ship the *StarDust Cruiser*. This particular cruiser offered rooms for up to two hundred guests and was large enough to visit all three of humankind's extraterrestrial settlements: the space station Sanctuary, the moon and Mars.

After the *StarDust Cruiser* accelerated to its designated speed the captain announced to all passengers that she was going to pop the *StarDust*'s sails. Jonny's family, along with others, chose to go to the huge cruiser's forward viewing deck. The captain performed a dramatic countdown, and suddenly all along the ship, magnetic sails popped into view.

The sudden explosion of colorful auroras along the sails drew "oohs" and "aahs" from all aboard. Even the captain, who was explaining the basic physics behind the auroras, stopped talking for a full two minutes.

Finally she said, "Well, ladies and gentlemen, this is the most . . . colorful I have ever seen these auroras."

Jonny Blue Feather Smith was sitting near the front of the viewing deck nodding his head and wearing a big smile.

It took a little under two hours for the *StarDust* to reach Sanctuary, and another hour to dock and latch onto the giant space station's mechanical bitts.

Sanctuary required all visitors from Earth to walk through yet another decontamination tunnel. After the usual identification verifications, baggage pick up and agriculture inspections the families were met, like dignitaries, in the passenger receiving area, a couple of decks up from where the cruiser had docked. On that reception deck was a large open viewing area where Jonny could look out into space.

The Earth was just off to his left, partially cloaked in night. Bright spots of light scattered across the darkened continents. The *StarDust* was still docked about 50 meters below, surrounded by busy service pods. But what drew Jonny's breath were the billions of stars. Everywhere he looked the stars were brilliant and beckoning.

Beautiful! His smile reflected his thoughts.

The Smith family was finally led to their quarters on D7, the VIP deck. After settling into his room, Jonny went out the sliding hatch, off the main family room, and onto their personal quarters' observation platform. There, in clear view, in a giant circle around him, were all nineteen decks of Sanctuary's lower visitor and commercial center.

The open interior, at just over 100 meters across and more than 300 meters tall, was enormous. Jonny stood still, awestruck by the incredible ingenuity that had gone into designing such a huge structure. Just managing the air, water and waste alone, to service the thousands of people who visited, worked and lived in this section of the ship, had to be incredible. Everywhere he looked there were people.

On all nineteen decks there was evidence of Sanctuary's hundred and fiftieth anniversary. Celebratory signs and balloons draped various balconies around the spacious interior. It was as if he had entered some great residential mall in New Philadelphia, but no, he was here in outer space. In his whole life, he could not have been any happier than he was at that moment.

He had seen pictures of the inside of this so-called "southern end" of Sanctuary, a place that was called Old Towne, but to see it in person, well, his mouth stood open. The Old Towne visitor area was the only completely open area of Sanctuary. It was the only part of Sanctuary where a visitor could see diametrically to the other side of the space station.

Just above Old Towne, the rest of the center of the station was enclosed. There were housed the facilities for power and air and water production. Also, in the enclosed center area, just "norther," as the locals would say, of Old Towne, were many of the business and government laboratories that were economically important to Sanctuary. Additionally, the upper center housed most of the emergency "safe rooms" for the ship's more permanent residents, as well as many of the emergency escape nodules. But here, in Old Towne, Jonny could see 100 meters or more, clear across to the other side of the space station. It was cavernous.

"It's bigger than I remember." Jonny's dad had walked out and stood next to his son.

Jonny shook his head. He had forgotten that his father had once been a sergeant major in the WWPA.

"When's the last time you were here, Dad?"

"About thirty years ago." Jon was looking up a few decks toward what looked like some official dwellings and offices. Jonny, like most youngsters, was still trying to grasp the idea of how young his parents looked, even in their sixties. His dad barely looked twenty-five. Jon pointed and his son's gaze followed..

"See decks nine and ten. There was a huge cover across the space station at that level because they were still installing the local admin offices and business suites at that time. I was part of the crew that was installing the second fusion reactor, some fifty or so meters above the Meteors floor. The nineteen decks that run up and down the cylinder were already established, though decks seventeen, eighteen and nineteen gravitated toward the Meteor's stadium. They are the only public decks on Sanctuary that gravitate toward the ship's northern pole."

"How do people get from deck sixteen to deck seventeen without falling into one or another?"

"Well, there are curved walkways—"

"I get it. They walk the up walkway and around to the next deck. Because artificial gravity is limited to maybe twelve meters and because the decks are a minimum of sixteen meters apart, they can create a singular graviton walkway that adjusts its pull so it feels like you are simply walking up and then down a hill to the next deck. Brilliant."

"Yes, my bright boy, that was the intention."

Jonny smiled. "Still, it's kinda Escher-like if you're watching from one deck or another. To see people walking up a staircase, then suddenly they're upside down walking to the next deck. No matter what deck you're on, it's gotta look weird."

"Okay, you two, from what I'm reading, I think we should make that trip up to the stadium to see the three-dimensional show of Sanctuary's evolution from the old ISS III to her present city-sized space colony." Neenah, Jonny's mom, came out to join them.

Jonny looked up at the Meteor's stadium planted on the ceiling far above him. Inside the stadium was where the history of Sanctuary was on display. People were walking across the ceiling toward the sports arena, some holding balloons that pointed straight down at Jonny. He tried not to look at one spot too long, otherwise he felt like he might fall "up" into their ground. It was sort of like looking over the edge of a high mountain on Earth, except that he was looking up! He had been warned about the peculiarity of AG being in effect at both ends of the giant cylinder that was Old Towne.

Looking back down, across the station's circling interior, Jonny, felt the dizziness fade. It felt normal to see the ground below his feet. Across the floor of Deck 1 (D1) there were parks, businesses, some theme-like rides and pieces of the original ISS III. That's where Jonny wanted to be.

Directly across from Jonny, a large multileveled entertainment stage jutted onto the floor of D1. It was surrounded by a half clamshell that extended up almost two decks.

Like something out of a Space Island movie, Jonny thought as he looked at the giant acoustic shell.

"Mom, look!" Jonny pointed at some people floating in the air above the stage. His mom, of course, only saw the stage.

"Yes, Jonny, that's where we'll be in a few days, as honored guests, along with thousands of other people celebrating Sanctuary's hundred and fiftieth anniversary in song. It says here that there will be a choir of five hundred led by a world-famous conductor from China. You have heard the 'Requiem' before, haven't you, Jonny?

"Yes, Mom. . . ." Jonny rolled his eyes.

His mother read aloud from the pamphlet. "'A moving hymn dedicated to people who lost everything, including loved ones, to a devastating tsunami over four hundred and fifty years ago. The song followed humanity into space for the same reason: to honor those in the past and offer hope and prayer for those who are here, and for the future. A truly beautiful song . . . over a thousand voices in harmony . . .' It gives me goose-bumps." She wrapped her arm around Jon.

"Mom, I was talking about the people floating in the air. They're weightless, see, their jets are not on."

"Oh . . . that is disorienting, isn't it?"

"Can't we just go down to D1? We can go up to the Meteor's stadium tomorrow and see the history of Sanctuary. I mean—can't we go down there first?" He gave her his best big eyed smile. Neenah suppressed a chuckle.

"No. We're going to see the presentation at the stadium. Then we're going to get some food, and then we are going to settle for the night. It's been a long day, and we still have two more days to go and play on Deck 1."

Jonny was going to argue more, but he could tell from the tone of her voice and the look on her face that that would be an unwise road to follow.

Neenah looked at her son, then at her husband, and, satisfied, walked back into their quarters.

"Dad?"

"You know, son, how can anything we do on Sanctuary not be cool? Come on boy, let's go get educated." He wrapped his arm around his son's shoulders, and they followed Neenah.

The family spent the next two days exploring D1. Occasionally the kids had to make promotional appearances on the main stage as the grand prize winners of MQ Space Industries' "Meet the Future" contest. During their last promotional drilling it was clear that the teenagers were bored. The stage manager, Michael, who had been the stage manager for most of his life, was trying to settle the kids into their seats for photos and questions, but they had discovered how high they could jump in the air and land safely at one-sixth Earth's gravity.

Part of their personal contest was to see who could land with the coolest "superhero" stance. Ales, Jonny's friend from Czechoslovakia, was the clear winner, but Jonny wasn't going to give up. He made one last jump, and that sent Michael over the edge. His arms flew about as he yelled at the kids for their lack of responsibility. The teenagers contritely sat in their appropriate seats. Still red in the face, Michael went over to the photon photographers to give them their instructions.

After he had walked away, Jonny turned to his friend Maria from Brasilia and said, "Wow, live to be 130 and what have you got? Someone who's—"

"Boring!"

"Exactly. Never trust anyone who's over a hundred."

"Right."

Finally, the final day of celebration came.

The family had just gotten off a roller coaster, a thrill ride that soared up about 40 meters above the pull of artificial gravity, and back down into AG at a dizzying speed. After they got off the ride Neenah sat off to the side feeling a little queasy, but Jonny was ready to go again. Except that when he was at the apex of the ride, he had caught sight of the people flying in the air.

"Hey, Mom, Dad," he said excitedly, "we've been talking about it, come on, let's take the air tour around Old Towne, on the air jets!" Jonny pointed to the platform that rose about 10 meters from the floor. There, AG was barely perceptible.

"Come on, Dad! We'll be like astronauts!" Jonny was bursting.

Guides were taking guests on an air tour up and around Old Towne, where there was no gravity. They scooted around the open area, careful to not get too close to the residential decks and their AG. They didn't go up so high as to get caught in the AG of the enclosed sports field, but still, going up 60-plus meters in the air, to Jonny looked like a great adventure.

They queued their way to the top of the launch platform. At last the three of them were strapped into their air jets and safety gear.

"Remember," their guide said, repeating the rules of zero gravity flight before they took off, "stay close to me at all times. No independent thrill rides; I guarantee you will be thrilled by what we do."

Then he pointed to the security personnel already in the air. "Besides, if you go off on your own or bother any of the guests on any of the dwelling decks, those folks will haul you into security and you may miss the anniversary grand celebration. Which is happening—" He looked at his HCI "—in another six hours or so." He checked the family's equipment to make sure it was properly set. "Ready?"

"Ready," Jonny said before anyone else could speak. Jon smiled at Neenah, and the guide gave Jonny a careful look. Jonny offered a sheepish smile. After all, flying around with a pretend spacesuit maneuvering unit in zero gravity was almost like being an astronaut. Wasn't it?

"Okay," their guide finally said. "First, I'm going to lift up about ten meters from here. There I will be in zero gravity. You all follow on my cue and we'll do a few maneuvers so you can get used to these air jets." He lifted up and after a few seconds he motioned, and they all followed.

It took Jonny and his dad only a couple of attempts before they were fairly competent with their machines. After a few tumbles and a little patience Neenah got the hang of it and up they went. Jonny was so thrilled at the ability to fly that he wanted to zoom all around. But every time that thought came up he caught sight of security and calmed himself down. Besides, the guide kept floating over to Jonny as if to keep his excitement in check.

At about 60 meters above D1 the guide stopped them in midair and said, "Okay, now let's turn off our jets!"

"Are you crazy!" shouted Jonny's mom. The guide and Jonny had a good laugh; apparently that was the response the guide had been hoping for.

"Mom," Jonny said while trying not to laugh, "there's no gravity." He turned off his jets and floated in place with a big smile on his face.

"Look, Mom, I'm an astronaut!"

Neenah laughed at her gaffe and joined the others in turning off her machine. At that instant the atmosphere of the entire space station changed. The ambient light became flashing red and yellow. SAIQA's electronic voice, at least Neenah thought it to be SAIQA, started repeating, "This is a Category One emergency. Security personnel will please escort all guests to their assigned quarters. All ship's personnel will report to their individual emergency stations. This is a Category One emergency . . ."

Neenah felt stunned. She looked over at her husband, who was looking at Jonny. She followed his gaze and saw her son holding his head in obvious pain. Startled, she started to swim over to Jonny. Jon was restarting his jets. Frustrated at getting nowhere fast Neenah pointed to Jonny and yelled at the guide, "My son! My son!"

At this time Jonny's eyes rolled up into his head. He went limp and floated, like a rag doll, in place.

The guide started his jet and zoomed over to the unconscious boy. While checking Jonny's vital signs, he spoke into his HCI. Two security staff came flying toward the family. Neenah started to turn her jet pack on, but a hand reached around and a female security officer said, "Ma'am, I will guide you, do not turn your jet pack on till we get near some AG. I'll tell you when."

"My boy!"

"Yes, ma'am, we have him." Neenah looked over, and saw that another security officer was taking Jonny down toward the infirmary on D1.

"What room are you in?" the security officer asked Neenah.

"Um . . D7, hatch 28."

"D7-28," the officer yelled to the officer near Jonny's dad. The security guard started to usher them toward their dwelling, but Jon zoomed away toward his son and the infirmary.

"Neenah!" he yelled.

She grabbed her controls and firmly said to the security officer, "I am going with my son!"

The woman looked at her and nodded. "Follow the boy," she said to the other guard.

Doctor Misha ran the main infirmary on D1. She was confident, friendly and often mentioned as one of the reasons a guest's visit to Sanctuary was so enjoyable. But at the moment, she was harried. There had never been a category one emergency while she was aboard Sanctuary. Sure, there had been drills, but an actual emergency, no. She was busy treating someone who had fallen a good four meters, not far enough to break anything, not in this gravity anyway, but enough to get a few bruises. She had just sent the bruised Space Island employee on his way when the alarm went off.

She instructed her two nurses to strap down anything loose in case of loss of AG. She pulled her emergency kit and was talking to the security captain when the guards brought in the boy.

"What happened?"

"Not sure. He was passed out when I got to him."

"Get him out of that jet-pack and lay him down in the back." Remembering the emergency, she added, "And be sure to strap him down. Andy, you're with me; Lois, finish securing this deck."

She turned to the head of security. "Gary, call me if you need me. This obviously isn't a training drill." He nodded and went back to his matriculation screen. Gary was her best liaison to Security and a good friend. It was good to have a friend who was also in charge. He started giving orders through his HCI.

Neenah, followed closely by her husband, came rushing in.

"Where's my son? Where's Jonny!"

"You're obviously the mother and father." Misha's voice was soothing. "I'm Dr. Misha Gregory. Tell me what happened."

"Let me see my son."

Misha led Jonny's parents to the bed in the back of the infirmary. Neenah ran up to him and checked his vital signs and pupils.

"You're a nurse?" Misha said. Neenah nodded. "Good. I may need you if this turns out to be a serious emergency. Are you going to tell me what happened?"

"Don't know . . . Do you have a clot scan?"

"Yes," Misha said, and motioned to Andy. He moved over to the medical computer terminal, typed in a code, and a portion of the wall opened, revealing a variety of sanitized medical tools. He picked out a clot scan and handed it to Dr. Misha. She walked to Jonny's bedside and started to examine him.

"We were up in the air with those silly jet-packs," Neenah said. "We had just turned off the jets when the alarm sounded. I looked over at

86

Jonny—he was trying to pull off his helmet, yelling in pain. He said, 'En-i-gall-u' or something like that, and then he just passed out."

Dr. Misha ran the scanner over Jonny's head a few times. "Everything reads normal. There are no clots or disruptions . . . hmmm . . ." She turned to Neenah. "Can you hold his head to the side a bit?" Neenah did as she was asked.

"I've never seen this before," Dr. Misha said, puzzled.

"What?"

Dr. Misha again passed the scanner over a certain area. "There is a high amount of biomagnetic activity at the back of his brain." She looked at Neenah. "Does he get migraines?"

Jonny sat high above the land. He vaguely knew of this place, but why was he here? He felt confused.

Something was compelling him to look down. Red-winged vultures seemed to permeate he hazy sky just below him. Down below, far below, on the plains he saw people dead or dying, everywhere. The few who were living walked, dazed and stunned, over the bloody ground, looking for . . . something . . . or someone.

The vultures created a great circle around the mountain where he was sitting. Their eyes fixed on the ground; their anticipation was obvious as they soared above the carnage below. Watching and waiting, like a starving dog under his master's dinner table.

Are they waiting on a command! Or are they just waiting for the last of the Niitsitapi to die?

"The People are dying!" he screamed as loud as he could.

With sudden realization he knew where he was; Jonny sat atop Great Chief Mountain.

How did I get here?

Below, his people were dying by the thousands.

Jonny stood up and looked on, helpless. "I'm too far away. What can I do?" he yelled. The sight of the blood and the red-winged birds, ready to prey on the dead and dying below, brought tears to his eyes.

Jonny heard a shrill screeching in the air below the vultures. His gaze followed the sound and he saw a tiny raptor; it was a blue-winged kestrel. The fierce little bird was flying from below and among the vultures, attacking those that came too close. The kestrel flew up and up and then landed a few feet to the left of Jonny. The bird sat there and looked at him.

Jonny stared again at the dismal picture below and, feeling helpless, he turned away and looked back at the bird. The kestrel had turned into a short, squat man who was sitting on a rock where the bird had landed.

The man said, "You must get back to your land, Jonny. You must leave Sanctuary as soon as you can. You will be needed. You are a brave young man."

Jonny looked down again; the People lay dead or dying everywhere, the vultures waiting; he knew he had to get home.

He turned back to the man to reply, but the man was gone. Where he had been sitting; there on the ground lay a blue feather. Jonny walked over. He picked up the feather and put it into his pocket; then he woke up.

When he could finally focus, there was a pretty woman with light-grey eyes looking down at him.

"Who are you? Where am I?" he said as he started to rise, and then stopped. The restraints kept him down.

"Do you know who you are?" Dr. Misha asked. "Help me; here take his hands" Neenah held Jonny's hands and as he gazed back at her he said. "Mom what's going on? Get these straps off of me please." Neenah quickly pulled the strap downs off Jonny's legs and arms.

"Do you know where you are?" the doctor asked.

Jonny looked about and as he sat on the edge of the infirmary's bed, "Yes. I am on Sanctuary."

Misha nodded. "Again, do you know who you are?"

"Yes. I am Jonny . . . Jonny Blue Feather Smith."

He suddenly thought of the feather and reached into his pocket. He pulled out a couple of small Space Island pamphlets. Stuck in between them lay a blue feather. Jonny pulled it up close to his face.

Was it real?

He turned to his parents. "Mom, Dad—" He looked at the feather again, and then back "—we have to get back home, soon." He looked at everyone in the room, "Something bad is going to happen."

CHAPTER FOUR

Mai Quan stood next to the replicate photo of the ancient Apollo 8 spaceship secured in center of his office wall. All the historic, duplicate photos surrounding the picture of the archaic craft gave him peace, but the image of this ancient space capsule was his favorite. Whenever he felt stressed; when he needed to remind himself that everything began with a first step; when he needed to focus, he would stand before this collection. He touched the copy of his beloved photo.

"The gem cannot be polished without friction, nor man perfected without trials," Mai Quan murmured.

An ancient Chinese proverb, still applicable today, he thought as he ran his finger over the ancient spacecraft.

"Apollo 8, the first manned spaceship to travel to and back from another celestial body. Did you know that, General?" he said to the man across the room, still gazing at the photo.

"Of course, sir," said the large, dark-skinned man standing in front of an oval view plate. Thanks to some basic refraction and reflecting technology, the stars and the planet below appeared to be right on the surface of the view plate, outlining the muscular frame of General Washington. The general adjusted his stance as he watched the brilliant man study the photos. As he shifted the stars twinkled and faded around his large shoulders.

Quiet and time, the general thought. *All great men need a moment of quiet to think!*

He greatly admired and deeply respected the powerful and influential man standing across the room studying the photo on the wall.

Mai Quan contemplated all the images around his prized black and white; a history of ancient satellites and space platforms from Sputnik to the Hubble Telescope; from Tiangong-1 to the second International Space Station, ISS II. All collected during his younger years.

All those years of promise and hope.

He cherished his collecting of photos and faded newspaper clippings, some of them priceless and carefully preserved. He was especially fond of the ancient video clips of the historic race to the moon by the US and the USSR: replicated here in his business suite on Sanctuary.

Those were simpler times.

He quietly chuckled. *No not simple. The stronger men, from that time, believed that they could overcome the limits of their ancient science and achieve fantastical goals, against impossible odds. There were great accomplishments . . . there were great failures. That age gave rise to many heroes . . . while history quietly remembers those who died. Not simple . . . no . . . It never was . . . It never is!*

He continued to study the replicas on the wall; they were his Zen; his peace.

I am humanity's natural evolution of its adventure into space.

He ran his finger through a 3D photon photo of New Mars City.

Four hundred and fifty years ago President Obama talked about going to Mars. I am Mars.

Still, the fantasy of simpler times calmed him down. Of course, the original photos and videos were all stored in or on display at his home office on the Ark. The thought of the Ark reignited his anger. Everything was going according to plan, and then the meteoroids. He couldn't have been more furious.

He abruptly turned around. "Explain to me again, please, General," Mai Quan said, his voice quiet and controlled, "how it was those meteoroids were not destroyed by Pythagoras or even the Ark before they could become a threat to Sanctuary?"

General Washington looked chagrined. Mai Quan knew that the general was loyal to him. At a hundred and seventy-five years old Mai Quan knew how to manipulate entire populations to get what he wanted. Ridding mankind of the age of corporate generals and kings had been difficult and was hopefully buried in human history, but though corporations could no longer be directly involved in politics, when you had as much money and power as Mai Quan, you could still buy public opinion.

He surrounded himself with the most brilliant people on the planet. His name was prominently placed on at least one building in many of Earth's most prestigious universities. For most of mankind his name was synonymous with the future. His ideas and businesses were identified with Sanctuary, the lunar bases and New Mars City. He was the only person to win more than two Nobel prizes: two for peace and one for chemistry. Mai Quan's philanthropic foundation The Betterment of Mankind had won a Nobel Prize as well.

He had known how to endear himself to the many. The *Hong Kong Times* once wrote, "His brilliance did shine like a beacon for all of humankind." All the key international political offices were held by politicians that Mai Quan had assisted at one time or another.

Maybe you couldn't buy politicians like in the old days, but you could buy public support. Mr.

Quan was well loved. His political "friends" all knew this. On politics, business, technology and social nuance, Mai Quan was considered a savant. But at this point in his life all his genius was bent toward one goal. At a hundred and seventy-five, Mai Quan wanted to live.

In his brilliant mind he could see that mankind would falter and flail without his guidance. Only he could stop this bathos. He had managed to find ways to extend his cellular reproduction to levels unheard of before, but even with all of his genius and money he could only sustain his body up to the age of two hundred and twenty . . . maybe. That wasn't enough; he needed more time.

Manipulating people, he had found, was always easier if they were of similar mind. General Washington was his right-hand man, a man, like himself, with strong, powerful convictions. The two of them were very much of the same mind. The general rose through the ranks of the still potent US Army, and then, at Mai Quan's suggestion, into the WWPA. From there Mai Quan had supported, encouraged and pushed him into a position of great power. He was now the vice commander of the entire World Wide Protective Agency. He had earned and deserved the courtesy that was due his rank.

Again Mai Quan asked, "How, General, how did those meteoroids get beyond our defenses?"

"I am sorry, sir. We were completely taken by surprise." The general spoke sincerely. He was always sincere.

"We never expected an alien ship; I mean, it has to be an alien ship," the general continued. "We can't see it or detect it with our sensors, but at the point of impact there appears to the eye to be a slightly blurred circumference. Still, our sensors detect normal space, no anomalies; just the usual moon and space environment. It looks to be a very sophisticated force field hiding . . . something. We sent an Indy-Brain to inspect the blurred field and just before it reached it stopped, turned around and kept repeating its ID number. It was weird, sir. Subcommander Liou kept trying to get the Indy-Brain to respond to his commands, but it maneuvered around us and headed back toward Pythagoras repeating, 'MQ Space Industries, Indy-Brain four-three-three-two-six-two.' It seems like it just appeared, the cloaked ship that is, and then came crashing down. We were lucky that Pythagoras wasn't hit."

General Washington stopped, but then continued when he saw that Mai Quan wasn't going to speak.

"The subcommander did everything correctly, sir. He immediately silenced the base, and projected the camouflaged graviton field that MQ Space Industries created for such an emergency. Per your request, the investigating teams from the other moon bases have been temporarily detained."

"Good. Pythagoras and Observation Point on the far side of the moon are mine."

"It is uncanny, sir. My report from Subcommander Liou is that the alien ship crashed with such force that it propelled moon debris into a low orbit. That is understandable. The boulders and debris should have been recaptured by the moon's gravity, but instead they started to accumulate speed and stay in a low orbit. The ejected debris then circled the moon and as it came back around it suddenly generated enough energy to catapult toward Sanctuary. It was astonishing. Captain Liou used the base's sensors to try and determine the energy source that turned the moon debris into meteoroids. He did not detect any energy sourcing from that ship, sir. It has to be a ship . . . there is no other explanation. As for the Ark, our lasers just . . . missed." He paused, still looking for a reaction he scanned his superior's face and, seeing none. "Zuizao is looking into that right now."

Mai Quan appeared to be deep in thought.

"Subcommander Liou is a good man, sir," the general added. "Ours to the core, as are most of the men and woman we've placed on Pythagoras. I know he cloaked the base sooner than we planned, but nobody expected this alien ship, sir."

"I did," Mai Quan murmured.

The general raised his eyebrows. "You, sir?"

"No matter now. Everything must move more quickly than we anticipated, General. SAIQA will investigate. She is stronger than I thought she would be." Mai Quan wandered over to his desk, talking quietly to himself. "Perhaps Tfiti was the wrong choice . . . computers and philosophy? Fortunately I still have a way to influence her."

General Washington stood patiently. By now he was used to Mai Quan's peripatetic ponderings. Mai Quan turned back to his right-hand man. "General, is everything in place on Earth?" He wandered over to the view plate. The general stepped to the side to make room.

"Yes, sir."

"DerAbbasyan understands what he is to do?"

"He is a bit of a loose cannon, sir."

"We will deal with that later. Just so long as he understands his mission."

"Yes, sir. He is greedy for power and will do as we ask, as long as it benefits him."

"Good enough for now. It may be a little early, but it's time to move everything forward. We are still some hours away from Sanctuary's celebration finale. Let them have their requiem.

And General, during the finale—" Mai Quan eyed the large, dark-skinned man beside him "—set events in motion."

"During the 'Requiem,' sir?"

"Yes, General. It is time." Mai Quan stared out the view plate at the planet below. "Let the chaos begin."

"Yes, sir."

Mai Quan returned to his desk. General Washington straightened. It was clear that he had been dismissed. "I'll see you at the celebration, sir?"

"Of course. I wouldn't miss it."

The general saluted.

"General, I don't think that is appropriate."

"A gesture of respect, sir."

"Thank you, General. Still, not in public. Not yet, anyway."

"Yes, sir." The general turned to leave, and then stopped. "Sir, there will be . . . collateral damage."

"Yes. We will be . . . circumspect, General. The ultimate goal is what's important."

General Washington nodded, turned and left. Mai Quan was still looking at the planet below when he felt a presence. It felt as if a door had just opened in his mind. He knew with certainty that a dimensional rift had just opened in his office. He opened up his mind, as he had learned to do nearly a quarter century ago, to accept the new presence in the room.

Twenty-three years ago, two years after the tragic death of his wife Anya, during a visit to Mars he had come to terms with his inevitable mortality. He angrily accepted that someday his body would break down and that he would die.

That time on Mars was intended to set in place, to map, the future of MQ Space Industries, the future of humanity. He would not have all his brilliant work, the foundations and plans that he had laid down during his lifetime, mean nothing. One day, while deep in thought on Mars, sitting next to the Meditation Pool, he met Nh'ghalu.

"En-h-gahlu," he said softly, remembering. It was the year 2427.

Mai Quan sat on a bamboo chair near a clear pool of water. The pagoda that rose above him, about 18 meters to the tip, was designed to look like it was made of wood, but he was sure that it was made from the magnesium and iron that were ubiquitous here on Mars. The entrance to The Temple of the Red Lions waited behind him.

The monks' meditation should be over in another fifteen minutes.

Mai Quan studied the elaborate temple entrance built right into the escarpment. It was designed in the ancient Imperial Chinese style and was guarded at the top of the long, grand entrance stairs by two red lions made from Martian soil.

Hence the name "Temple of the Red Lions." My people are very pragmatic. He chuckled.

The elaborate entrance stairs swept down from the main doors and splayed into the Vihara courtyard, allowing access from the north and the south. Dividing the stairs in a stream a little over two meters in width, Martian water flowed ceaselessly out of the entrance, like a happy child into the sun it hasn't seen for a millennium. Down the steps it washed, tossing and catching the late afternoon Martian sunlight. Indigenous, micrometer red algae trailed in the stream and softened the edges of the meditation pool where he sat. From here the tiny vein of water poured north, into the valley. This was the Miracle River.

A river? I used to splash through bigger creeks than that, in the Yellow Mountains. When I was a boy . . . long ago. Mai Quan sighed.

He studied the red-orange gazania grass clinging to the banks, bordering the river like a frayed red carpet. The great Japanese artist Chouko, who colored with ancient media such as crayons, had created a famous piece of work that viewed the Miracle River from its source down through the valley. There was no city in the painting, just a valley, filled with gazania grass and imaginary Martian trees disappearing at some future point. It was beautiful and depressing at the same time. Mai Quan thought about the painting he had bought from Chouko years ago, just before her death. She was so proud and honored that he wanted her painting. As he had anticipated, it turned out to be a good investment. He looked back at the pool.

Over the pool, Buddhist engineers had built the four-story pagoda. The lowest level of the pagoda was designed to be open on all four sides. Greenery and flowers planted all around the water grew up and into the building, attracting birds. Steps to access each level circled around the inside of the pagoda.

On the Vihara grounds the "giant leaf" bamboo trees completely lined the Miracle River.

Indocalamus tessellatus, the oxygen giver. I will use them in my space gardens as well. Our gardens. . . . Anya, I miss you terribly. He forced his eyes, his mind, to follow the trees through the temple grounds and into the city.

Throughout the city the bamboo trees traced the river, intermixed with public and personal gardens. All the florae on Mars were chosen for their ability to release high amounts of oxygen. In the city, most of the peculiar red Martian algae, with its tiny yellow-orange and red star buds, was trimmed, so as not to interfere with the growth of terrestrial plants. Here at the Temple of The Red Lions, the algae was allowed to grow naturally. It was anathema for the Buddhists to harm any living thing. The red algae grew plushly around the bamboo trees.

He clutched the locket that held Anya's picture tightly to his chest as he regarded the gazania grass bordering the meditation pool.

The indigenous algae was an odd blend of primitive life forms, similar at the cellular level to terrestrial laurencia and diatom. The Martian scientists had determined that it posed no threat to humans. The algae had a knack for holding onto oxygen longer than its earthbound cousins, hence its red color, but then later releasing it in greater abundance. Because of this and because of the novelty of a harmless indigenous plant now growing on Mars, the gazania grass was protected by the laws of New Mars City. Just the gazania grass alone attracted many young scientists and tourists.

Mai Quan took a deep breath—yes, the air was pure and clean. He gazed out upon what he could see of the city. Some of the original Quonset huts were still standing.

I remember the original design.

His genius and his business had been involved in the development and evolution of New Mars City ever since it was colonized, deep in a crevice in the Nili Fossae Valley, just west of the Arena Colles basin, one hundred and ten years ago. It was the first permanent human settlement on the planet Mars.

The decision was partially based on an early twenty-first century report discovered, years later, in the rubble of what was once the Smithsonian

Institute. The *European Space Agency's*, geological discoveries from their high resolution camera, *Mars Express,* offered compelling evidence of accessible water at the Nili Fossae site.

Later in the twenty-third century, manned exploration led to the eventual establishment of a science station in the Nili Fossae. Scientists made their final decision based on the available underground water, as well as the natural protection the crevice somewhat provided against the harsh environment. There was also limited protection against excessive CMEs from the minerals in the clay that stratified the surrounding escarpments. Also, with regard to the planet's four seasons, the northern hemisphere, in that general latitude, was far more temperate than anywhere else on the planet.

There was a bit of romanticism involved in choosing this site as well, as some of the UN and WWPA scientists wished to honor the early explorers and scientists whose lives were disrupted or destroyed by the devastating Corporate Wars.

When referring to the decision to establish a base at Nili Fossae, Mai Quan had once said, "It is a way of saying that we acknowledge the work of those earlier scientists and explorers. Those were heroes who had the extraordinary courage to reach for the stars. They were the men and women who built the foundations of our greatest dreams and eventually our greatest achievements. It was their diligent scientific work found in such reports as the ESA's of 2014, which allow us to stand on the shoulders of such brilliant men and women. To them, we say thank you."

The original settlements of Quonset hut–like buildings were constructed very close to the edge of the canyon wall. Over the years, as the scientific and support community grew, other buildings, including two- and three-story admin buildings, aggregated at the site.

Because Mars had no magnetic field some settlers dug into and established dwellings in the sides of the ravine, creating safe zones from the dangerous solar winds. After thirty years the Nili Fossae canyon walls begin to resemble a modern-day version of the ancient cliff dwellings found in the southwestern United States. The New Martians were also busy digging deep into the land beneath the settlement, creating vast underground reservoirs and maintenance bays.

Fifty years later the Martians had an enclosed anti-grav train (AGT) that traveled to the New Mars City Spaceport located in the Arena Colles basin. Martians and visitors could now, in a few minutes, be in an automated underground transport facility, approximately 15 meters beneath the Martian surface. There the commuter trains came down from the surface into a tubular airlocked access. Once the train was stopped the double airlock hatch doors would be released by the transit computer and the passengers could disembark or board.

There were also personal Indy-Brained vehicles and hoppers that ran along the AGT tracks to New Mars City. Needless to say, all the vehicles on Mars were designed with Martian environmental dangers in mind.

In the year 2390 plans were already in place for the eventual graviton shield that would roof the city and protect it from small meteors and solar and cosmic radiation. A safety shield just below the main shield was also part of the equation. The safety shield was there just in case a coronal mass ejection should ever spew solar radiation above the 2,000 millirad level. During the planning a clever engineer realized that a double shield could not only create a barrier strong enough to protect the city from CMEs, but it could also be strong enough to hold a manmade atmosphere. The designs came directly to Mai Quan.

They needed a couple of material modifications, but otherwise were well designed.

He sent them back to Mars, and with much excitement a plan for an atmospheric shield to enclose all of New Mars City began to take form.

Humans could already walk with minimum protection in the exposed atmosphere. Thinner versions of a space suit, which could safely mold and fit around the body, were designed by the new Martians. Body-length heaters and pressurized gooey aerogel sufficiently protected the wearer from the outside dangers of Mars. A minimum amount of air, water and power were all that was generally needed to support the suit. These support systems could be worn in a small backpack or hip pack. There were a few adventurers who liked to go "camping" in the Martian desert and needed more support. An entire industry had developed to cater to these weekend explorers.

Finally, in the year 2399, with much pomp and celebration, the topmost citywide shield was laid over New Mars City and activated. Instantly the shield lifted into place, glowed for a few seconds, and then cleared. It was set. The inner shield quickly followed.

After a week of testing air pressure, radiation and air circulation and bringing the mean temperature to 20°C, the New Mars City residents, at first tenuously, began to walk out of their front doors. For the first time in the history of the planet, living, sentient, biological beings ran unencumbered across the Martian soil. Many were in their bare feet, some in their bare skin. Six months later the "miracle" began.

In the year 2400, while surveying near the center of the enclosed settlement, two workers saw water trailing down a small ancient waterbed. At first they thought it was a leak from a reservoir pipe. Surveyors traced the trickle to a crevice in a southern cavern wall about 5 meters up. The water, a phenomenon in itself, was steadily running from the break in the wall down through the center of New Mars City. The newly created Terranian atmosphere had awoken an ancient underground Martian stream.

The locals dug deep into the source to find that it was a vast frozen aquifer from some ancient body of water. There was an apparently unlimited supply of fresh, clean water.

Then, one year later, algae of Martian origin had begun to appear on the side of the stream. Earthbound headlines read "Miracles on Mars," and the news spread about the frozen lake and Martian algae.

At first the Martians were concerned about any unknown indigenous bacteria or viruses, but as neutrino scans had shown, and continued to show, the water was pure and mineral rich. To date no unknown virus or harmful bacterium had been found.

As word of the miracles buzzed about the home planet, the more spiritual organizations began an exodus to Mars. First the Buddhists, followed by the True Christian Scientists, the Church of Creation, the Sunnis, and then all those with holes in their souls began to migrate to New Mars City either to visit or to live.

It was just thirteen years before Mai Quan's visit that the Buddhist geologists had dug into the source of the miracle water and built a temple at that site. For storage purposes, and careful to maintain a continuous flow into the city, the first dig created a deep, wide pool just behind the temple's reception area. The rest of the temple and the monks' living quarters were dug deep into the Martian scarp around the inner pool.

Miracle River, as the stream was called, measured 1 meter at its deepest and 3 meters at its widest. At the end of its almost 4 kilometer run through the New Martian settlement, Miracle River slipped away under the protective shield and into the underground reservoirs that had previously been built. But at its source, the Buddhist temple, "The Temple of the Red Lions," with its beautiful walkway around the pool leading to the Buddha carved from stone was one of the destinations of the many who came to Mars.

New Mars City had become a place of sublime relaxation and spiritual discovery. This city was much the same thirteen years later at the time of Mai Quan's spiritual sabbatical.

He stood next to the meditation pool, contemplating a reflection of himself. He had chosen simple light-beige pants and a pullover shirt with a black cape attached around the shoulders for dress today. He wore sandals for easy removal upon entering the Temple and carried his temple slippers in a satchel at his hip. He looked in the pool's clear water and studied his reflection.

Still strong.

At a hundred and fifty-two years of age he still looked healthy. His well-known face gazing back from the still pool didn't look like a man who had reached the age of mandatory retirement. His hair, jet black edged with silver, neatly cut, his eyes, brown but bright because of genetic manipulation, his Asian face anchored by a strong chin—Mai Quan looked like he felt, strong and fit. He walked to the north side of the pagoda and looked out and into the city.

I am Mars. I designed the Quonset homes and robot diggers. MQ Space Industries perfected the graviton shields that allowed the settlers to walk in a Terranian atmosphere under a Martian sky.

He watched the monks move in and out of the entrance to the Temple.

We are destined to reach out to the stars. Titan is the obvious next destination, but then, yes, to the stars. Why are these people so complacent? Why are they so satisfied? When I am gone what will they do with the knowledge I leave behind? Will they even remember me? Will they remember Anya? I must live longer.

"And so you shall."

Mai Quan turned toward the quiet voice that seemingly had answered his unspoken thought. A robed monk was quietly looking at him. As he was about to speak the monk put up his hand.

"My name is Nh'ghalu. I am here to teach you what I can. I am here to help you help humanity reach its destiny. I will help you understand how to take your Telomerase Cell-Life Extension, your TCE science to its inevitable conclusion; how to grow an immortal cell."

The monk, Nh'ghalu, never spoke. The squat, Mediterranean-looking man never moved his lips. Every word Mai Quan heard from this monk was spoken to him in his mind. He had seen machines translate thoughts into words in a man's mind, but never directly from another human. Was this monk human?

"Who are you?" Mai Quan demanded.

Nh'ghalu walked over and put his hand on the back of Mai Quan's head. Instantly he could see alien spaceships, an alien world and its technology. Nh'ghalu removed his hand and Mai Quan stood, stunned.

"What do you want with me?"

"You will learn to speak to me with your thoughts. I have much to teach you and not much time to plan. You will take a sabbatical and give me absolute attentiveness. I ask nothing less than the complete focus of your brilliant mind."

"Why me?"

"You actually need to ask that question?" The monk seemed amused.

Mai Quan knew.

Anya . . . What I could learn. . . .

"This is a bit much to take in so suddenly." He felt a strange hope in the back of his mind. "Can you bring Anya back?" he asked, though he already knew the answer.

"No, I am sorry. Do this for your beloved wife."

Mai Quan was near tears. "And if I refuse . . ."

"Then I will ask someone else. You are the best choice to move mankind forward, but if need be I will work with another. You must decide now."

Mai Quan had the ability to make a quick decision. He had always been able to do a rash thing and come out looking brilliant. Many of his greatest business adventures had been based on such feelings, a feeling of rightness. This felt right. Not only did it feel right, as soon as he decided he suddenly felt renewed. This was what Anya would have wanted. It was good for humanity.

He looked at Nh'ghalu, nodded his head and turned and walked out of the Vihara toward his suite at the MQ Space Industries building near the center of the city. He had to prepare his business for his temporary absence. This felt right. He felt like a young man.

Nh'ghalu watched Mai Quan walk away. He knew that the brilliant human would work with him. These humans had always been easy to manipulate. This one had an open mind. It was easy to reach into his mind and stroke the necessary emotions.

He gestured with his hand and a dimensional rift appeared at his side. Nh'ghalu cast one more glance at the black cape trailing Mai Quan and then walked through the gap. The rift disappeared. That was twenty-three years ago.

Nh'ghalu had touched Mai Quan's mind as soon as he had stepped through the rift and on to Sanctuary. He had sensed the meeting between General Washington and his apprentice and he was pleased.

You are remembering when we first met, yes?

"Yes, Ern Shyr. I am open and humbled by your presence." Mai Quan used "Ern Shyr" as an ancient term of respect for a teacher.

"You are a good man, Quan. As you have no doubt guessed, my brother is here. It is his interdimensional ship that has pounded into the moon. His presence has been anticipated."

As his thoughts formed in the human's mind he could feel the human's desire to please. It had always been a delicate balance with this one. He was truly brilliant.

These humans have come a long way since I first made contact with them over six thousand years ago in what was once called the "Fertile Crescent." No longer a crescent . . . no longer fertile.

107

He had tried to teach the ancient Sumerians some basic science, but their ability to reason was hidden behind a great wall of ignorance and fear.

They called me a devil. They tried to put me to death, and when they failed they labeled me a monster that couldn't die. I supposedly lived by stealing the life from other living souls. Ghala, they called me. So be it . . .

The absurdity of those old superstitions nearly made him laugh. He gave up on the humans and traveled across the galaxy to another fledgling civilization.

The Nh'gharene. They are a pragmatic people.

But his brother, Telas, stayed with the ancient farmers. He loved those primitive people. He guided them toward a style of writing that eventually was used worldwide. This ancient cuneiform was the beginning of the humans' abstract writing and eventually their abstract intellect. Telas stayed for another three centuries before he came to look for Nh'ghalu. He wasn't pleased with what Nh'ghalu had taught the Nh'gharene. They had a violent disagreement, and Telas banished him to the void. For Nh'ghalu it was a lonely, vast emptiness.

For a thousand years Nh'ghalu wandered as pure energy—a fine line between existence and osmosis—within the galaxy. Telas had thought that he had sent him the way of the rest of the immortals, into the universe as pure energy with no way to return, but he was wrong. Nh'ghalu wanted to return. He wanted to hurt his brother.

While he wandered the galaxy as pure energy he met The One. In the center of a turbulent and chaotic nebula, in the explosive process of a star being born, in the blue tear-shaped energy, like a placenta around the newborn star, he discovered Him. He never directly spoke to Nh'ghalu, but the banished immortal could feel His presence; His existence touched every atom that could be called Nh'ghalu.

The One was pure light: how could anything be pure light at an atomic level? It was as if He were all dimensions at one time, like He was all beings. Suddenly Nh'ghalu knew. It was chaos that created a new beginning. He could feel the pure light of The One in the chaotic creation of the star. Their light was His light! The One was trying to find His way back to us! Nh'ghalu could feel His omniscient presence. The One was the true Creator! The One reached out and touched Nh'ghalu with His light. At that second he knew what he had to do. He had to prepare the universe. The One was coming.

When Nh'ghalu realized this, he also became aware of a way to return to his corporeal form. He made his way back to where he was born to be born again.

After returning to his immortal form he returned to his beloved Nh'gharene. He would have allies. He knew that at some point, his brother would discover his return. He devised a plan for his brother to be preoccupied with the Nh'gharene while he returned to the solar system of the Earth's sun.

All this flashed through his mind as he came to Mai Quan. Quan was the key to throwing the humans into chaos. Whatever might be left of the human civilization, the Nh'gharene was welcome to enslave. Then, eventually, even his allies would fall under the weight of their own tumultuous society. Nobody must interfere in The One's return.

He spoke into Quan's mind: *"My brilliant apprentice, you have made an excellent decision. We may be starting earlier than we planned, but the appearance of my brother means we must move quickly."*

Mai Quan stared at Nh'ghalu. "But Ern Shyr, what of his ship? What of the immortality you promised me; surely there must be an answer from that spacecraft?"

"You have already extended your longevity a great deal more than any other human. You will not be able to enter that ship without his permission. The knowledge is forthcoming. Trust me, my apprentice. Within your system is the perfect immortal cell. You will find it."

"The only known human immortal cells, the Hela and Jurkat, were destroyed by the self-serving corporate generals and self-appointed kings toward the end of the Corporate Wars. The lobster cell does not work. The only viable microbial cell is from the water bear, but so far it has not been sustainable. The search seems futile."

"In this solar system, at some point, evolution created an immortal cell. Combining that cell with the science you already know will give you immortality. You must find it."

"A single cell in the entire solar system? The task is impossible. The technology on your brother's ship, even you have said that it is like no other in the universe—"

"You must forget about the ship," Nh'ghalu interrupted him. He gently reached into Quan's mind. *"It will happen, my friend. Trust me. The cell will make its appearance. Believe."* He felt Mai Quan relaxing under his calming touch. These humans did get distracted easily.

"Yes, Ern Shyr, I do believe . . . it just seems like an improbable task."

"The task at hand?"

"Yes. The general is initiating that as we speak. The rebels are in place. The machinery is in place."

"The graviton weapons?"

"They are being tested right now on the moon and on the Ark. They will be tested on Earth shortly. They are unpredictable but very effective. Very . . . devastating. Zuizao is working on a program that will make them more efficient."

"You will have your wish, Quan. You will be immortal and you will lead the humans to their destiny. You will never be forgotten."

"Thank you, Ern Shyr." Mai Quan offered a slight bow to the alien Buddhist monk. Nh'ghalu smiled and nodded to his student.

After thousands of years the ancient complaisance of student to teacher is still honored. These humans can be surprising in their complexity and their simplicity. No wonder Telas loved them. Still, The One is coming.

"You must take charge now, Quan. It is time to lead. I must go. I have a task that takes me to Earth. You must use those who are willing to be used. It is their destiny. Remember, it is inevitable that some will desire the power that will come your way. They are tools now that must later be eliminated. You must act decisively, Quan, for it is your destiny to lead humanity into the future. I have seen it." Nh'ghalu raised his hand, *"I must go. There is a man below who believes me to be an angel of death. I must see to his needs."*

Nh'ghalu opened a rift to his left. *"You will do well, my apprentice,"* he said as he walked through the opening. The presence at the back of Mai Quan's mind disappeared. The euphoria he felt in the proximity of his teacher abated.

No matter. Time to think, to act.

He looked at the HCI on his right wrist.

A couple of hours till the formal ceremony. General Washington is no doubt sending out commands. I must attend to my meeting here on Sanctuary. I must be decisive.

A soft bell tolled above him.

"Speak," he said to his Indy-Brain secretary.

"Sorry to disturb you, sir, but Lieutenant Commander Steges is at the door per your request."

"Let her in, please."

"Yes, sir."

Mai Quan walked in front of his desk to receive his daughter. Anna was the progeny of his third and last marriage. He had met her mother, Anya, in New Holland in the year 2390. She was sister to one of the Netherlands' more powerful diplomats. They fell deeply in love and were married within the year. Four years later, Anna was born.

Anya shared his love of space and exploration and often spoke on his behalf at business and political gatherings. She was beautiful and elegant. In 2412 it was their daughter's drawings that compelled Anya to encourage Mai Quan create a garden in space. At first he was against any such foolishness. He was already busy with Mars and covertly the Ark. Yet, Anya insisted, and he could refuse his love nothing.

Moments you don't forget. 2415, during an international meeting sponsored by major business and government officials, my wife, my beloved wife, squeezed my hand so tight when a UN representative asked, "And what new things are we to expect from MQ Space Industries?" I knew what she wanted, and what she wanted, I wanted.

He announced to the world he would build a huge garden in space. He smiled as he thought

112

about the lovely evening they had that night. Ten years later, they began the construction of The Garden. One year later, during a tour of the fledgling space garden, his beloved wife was killed in a freak accident.

Within the year many bereaved construction workers began to call ISS III "Sanctuary" because they believed if they had gotten Anya there in time she would have survived. To this day Mai Quan grieves for the partner he loved more than life itself.

For many years his daughter was his reason for life, but as time went on he pulled away from Anna and immersed himself in his business. He buried himself in his day-to-day work and saw Anna less and less. Now that she was a grown woman she looked very much like her mother. Sometimes it was just too painful to even talk to her. Anya had believed that the human race was destined to conquer the stars. He would do anything to make her dreams come true, even pull away from his daughter.

Anna entered the room. Mai Quan stepped forward to meet her.

"You called for me, Father."

"Yes, my love. I am going to the moon after today's ceremonies. I won't see you for some time."

"You are busy. I understand that. What can I do to help you?"

She is such a good child . . . no longer a child.

"Thank you for asking. You know that I have many contacts throughout the political and business worlds."

"Yes, like Uncle James. I saw him leaving as I came into your quarters."

"Yes, like the general, and it is because of information that I just received from him that I have an important mission for you. Before the day is done, General Washington is going to promote you to field commander."

"Field commander! Father, I have not earned such an honor!"

"A moment, daughter. Let me explain." He held up his hand and she, of course, obeyed.

Do I deserve such loyalty?

"As I said, I have ways of collecting information. The confrontation on Earth between Armenia and Azerbaijan, led by the President of Armenia, Alik DerAbbasyan, has escalated. The supreme commander of the WWPA, Rena Macighian, who, incidentally was born in Armenia, is presently in a meeting with the Azerbaijan president. She is prepared to bring the full strength of the WWPA in support of Azerbaijan. How Alik managed to accumulate so many robotic weapons has been, up to now, a mystery." He stopped to see if she was paying attention.

"Please, sir, continue." Anna knew her father well.

"I said up to now because it has come to my attention that there is a large, secretive organization within the WWPA: an organization that apparently has been around for nearly fifty years, building a secret and formidable army. It is now preparing to strike at the real WWPA."

"How can such a thing be?" Anna's expression reflected her shock and disbelief. "To keep it secret—to accumulate a secret army? To keep it secret alone would take such organization, and money—this cannot be happening! To what end?"

"General Washington has determined through spies that they call themselves the 'Army of One.' Their intention is to stop what they believe to be our 'lost ways' and force all of humanity back into some sort of social framework that reflects their spiritual beliefs."

"What? This is the twenty-fifth century, for Stars' sake. They can't honestly believe people will receive them with open arms. This is insane!"

"Sadly our history is filled with insane ideologues."

Anna shook her head. The information shook her view of the world to its very core. Unseen enemies lurking in the very organization that held that all humans were created equal. That all religions and philosophies were equal and personal and no one had the right to physically impose their belief system on another human being.

After the death of her mother Anna had had no one to turn to. Her father had been there for a time, but as she got older he immersed himself in his work and became distant. The WWPA became her home, her family. Her family was in trouble.

"What can I do?"

"It seems, according to General Washington, Uncle James, that this army has infiltrated the WWPA on Earth, on the moon and here on Sanctuary. Something big is going to happen soon, perhaps even today. You know many of the security forces stationed on Sanctuary. They trust you."

"They know whose daughter I am."

"They respect you. As field commander, they will respond to your commands without question."

"Yes, though suddenly being promoted by the vice general of the WWPA from lieutenant commander to field commander and being Mai Quan's daughter—more than likely they will be afraid of me."

"I care not, as long as they obey you. You will have to make tough decisions. There will be some you thought of as friends who soon may be enemies. Your Uncle James will be needed on Earth. In a few hours, when the festivities end, I am going to the moon. You will be in charge here. I know you, Anna. I know you believe in the original mission of the WWPA. You have strong convictions and the strength to see them through. You will do well in your new responsibilities. But remember, there are enemies. At first you cannot trust anyone. Those who are loyal will rally around you; still, watch your back."

"When does this promotion happen?"

"Now. You will go from here to the general's quarters."

"I have reservations, father, I really do, but I will not let insurgents destroy the very thing that was created to check humanity's self-destructive inclinations. The WWPA has been around for almost three hundred and fifty years. Sure, the way we view history is different now that humans live longer, but the WWPA has saved us from ourselves many times. There are good people in this organization, father."

"I agree. It is for them and the rest of us that we must fight to guarantee a future for us all."

"You can count on me, father."

"I know I can. I have another meeting I must attend before the final ceremony. Please, go, right away, to see General Washington."

"Yes, sir." She turned to leave. As she turned he saw his beloved Anya in her strong yet soft chin.

"Be careful, my dear Anya," he murmured.

"Sorry, sir. I didn't hear you."

Mai Quan turned away and with a little more gruffness than he intended said, "Nothing . . . be careful."

She looked pained. "I will. I promise." Anna turned and left.

Mai Quan saw his Anya's face in his mind's eye for a second. "No! There can be no weakness." He looked at where Anna had exited. "I will use all those that I need to achieve this great goal. Humanity must be united, and I will guide them."

Mai Quan stepped into his private lift and headed toward what he knew would be a confrontation. The lift took him down a couple of decks below his luxury suite. Here the quarters were moderately upscale; nothing like his but still nice. Small fenced-in gardens in front on each dwelling gave a European flavor to this deck. Even with Sanctuary's anniversary it was not a heavily populated living area, and here each guests' quarters had its own private entrance.

That was why he had chosen this location for the man he was on his way to see. He saw the enclosed veranda that was his destination. He circumvented the front garden and minutes later stood between two secured planters on either side of the entrance hatch. They were meticulously trimmed. He expected no less. . A guard near the door, assigned to this secret duty by the general, immediately snapped to attention. Mai Quan waved him to the side and walked up to a keypad beside the door, where he typed in a code. The door opened and he entered a small but nicely kept apartment.

The main living or receiving area of the guest quarters was adorned with various international awards, including a Nobel Prize. To his left, jutting from the opposite wall a counter, with a couple of tall, bar-style chairs, separated the main reception area from the kitchen. A few different cups and prescription bottles sat on the counter.

He looked to his right into what could be called the living room. Sitting and writing at an old desk was the man he came to see.

The desk stood near an exit into a personal garden area, which was a common amenity for most of the quarters here in the upper part of Sanctuary. These were considered luxury apartments, mostly for middle executives and their families. This man was a special guest. The man glanced at Mai Quan, and then went back to his writing.

He looked to be older than Mai Quan, even though he was the same age. At a hundred and seventy-five years old Dr. Chenoweth Lee was in poor health. He needed medication to maintain his heart. Although Telomerase Cell-Life Extension programs had greatly increased a human's healthy life, cells still broke down. Dr. Lee's physical degradation was what Mai Quan feared the most.

The man was frail and clearly moved with pain. Mai Quan looked beyond the desk and out to the garden. A nice-sized Terra garden, almost as large as Dr. Lee's quarters. Despite the doctor's physical limitations, everything was neat and orderly.

"Well, Quan, how is it that I may serve you now, or am I finally free to leave my prison?"

"Nice prison you have here." Mai Quan said evenly. "Besides, you are not a prisoner, you are my guest . . . my business consultant."

Dr. Lee laughed. "Oh, yeah . . . consult this!" He flipped an obscene gesture toward Mai Quan and turned back to his work.

"Really, Chin, do we have to go through this again? You have everything you need here. All the scientific equipment and labs you ask for. Assistants to do your bidding. You have no family. No one has asked for you in years."

"It's Chenoweth." Lee did not raise his head. "And how is my young friend Erik Devries?"

Devries again! Does he know about Devries trying to contact him? What is his connection to that boy? I must check into this kid.

"The last time you asked, I had General Washington see how he was doing. From what I can gather, he is doing fine. He's a captain in the WWPA, healthy, intelligent and bound to do well. Why do you ask?"

"He was . . . is a young friend."

"But why him specifically?"

"I don't know. I like him. He stuck with me. He was my assistant years ago and somehow I know that he will succeed in anything he sets his mind to. Just like I knew he would end up on Sanctuary."

Mai Quan felt a sudden chill pass over him. *Probably a breeze from the environment controls. Still, this Devries . . .*

"Chin—"

"It's Chenoweth." Dr. Lee lifted his head and gazed steadily at his jailer. "You have lost the right to call me Chin."

"Very well. Dr. Lee, have you gotten any further with that mathematical rigour I gave you from that young man, Jonny Smith? We have the graviton machines to create a space-time incident. I have built the ships that we designed years ago. It's done, Chi— Chenoweth. I have the ships that are powerful enough to bend the third dimension. I need more clarity on resolving the problems of distance and where I can open a rift or if necessary create an Alcubierre Drive. You said you were close. What do you have?"

"And, what are you planning to do with these amazing new ships?" Dr. Lee rose with a grimace, grabbed the cane leaning against his desk and walked out onto the patio.

Mai Quan's voice followed him.

"Travel the stars, for Star's sake! Humanity's destiny lies out there among the undiscovered and I mean to see it happen! With or without you!"

"And what have you done with Llosa?"

"Gabriel is on the moon and works for me."

"Willingly?"

"Yes, willingly, damn it!"

"Touchy."

"I have little time. Unseen enemies, people I am responsible for and people I have to answer to. So tell me. Do you have anything definitive for me yet?" He strode over to the desk and rifled through some of Dr. Lee's notes.

"I find myself, as a scientist, in a peculiar place. You see, I don't trust you, Quan. You realize there is a real possibility that you could travel back in time and I can't—"

He stopped as he turned back toward his captor. Mai Quan had picked up some pieces of rice paper covered with calculations in shaky handwriting. Mai Quan's eyes went wide with understanding.

"You cannot have those." Dr. Lee stepped toward Mai Quan, his hand outstretched, and then abruptly stopped. He pressed his hand against his chest. "Damn heart murmurs. Hurry, Quan, give me the pills in the yellow bottle before too much blood settles in my heart."

Mai Quan looked at him. Lee clearly was in pain and needed help. Quan looked back at the papers, satisfied.

"Cardiac dysrhythmia." Lee's face was becoming ashen. "Hurry!"

"CD. A scientist to the end, eh, Chin. You will be remembered as one of the greatest."

SAIQA suddenly spoke: "Dr. Lee, you are in distress, I will—"

Mai Quan commanded her in Chinese.

"Yes creator, I see that all is well. It shall be erased from my memory as you command." SAIQA signed off.

Mai Quan spoke again in Chinese, his gaze remaining on Chin. "Thank you, Dr. Lee. Like I said, you shall be remembered." Chin had fallen, pulling the guardian bamboo tree and the immediate ancient wooden chair down with him.

Dr. Lee grasped for a fallen branch but his hands failed him. His vision was getting blurry; he felt the blood pooling in his heart. He looked directly at Quan. "Please, Quan, the yellow bottle."

Mai Quan strolled out and stood beside the dying Dr. Lee. Holding the papers beyond Chin's reach, he said, "You shall be remembered."

Dr. Lee suddenly smiled at Mai Quan. "I know. Sadly, so will you." His eyes closed. Mai Quan laid the back of his hand close to Lee's mouth and nose to feel for breath. Satisfied, he stood up.

As far as Mai Quan was concerned the papers in his hand were the greatest discovery since the very first rocket. It was all here, right in his hands, the conquest of the universe. Dr. Lee had scribbled down on rice paper the mathematical rigour that would make even the simplest of graviton machines bend time. It was truly brilliant. He very nearly danced.

He calmed himself as he realized one of his greatest assets had just died. Damn him. Not only had Lee been the moral voice in many of his decisions, he had also been his most brilliant scientist. As Quan looked at the lifeless body lying before him he realized it was time to make a decision. Nh'ghalu had told him such a time would come. He ran his fingers across his private HCI.

After he finished his communication he left Chin's quarters, very careful to shut and lock the door. He walked up to the guard and glanced at the name tag. "Sergeant Wilson, is it?"

"Yes, sir."

"Let me see your weapon, Sergeant, please."

"Sir?"

"Your weapon, Sergeant."

The guard handed over his sidearm. Mai Quan looked at the weapon and then appeared to make a decision. He aimed the gun at the helpless sergeant and burned a hole through his chest. The lifeless guard crumpled to the floor. Mai Quan tossed the weapon on the body.

"In for a penny, in for a pound." He paused and pursed his lips. "I wonder where that saying came from?" He turned and left to get ready for Sanctuary's final ceremony.

General Washington had finished his necessary communications to Earth and the moon and was getting ready for Sanctuary's grand celebration. The personal communication he had just received from Mai Quan was urgent. A mess to clean up at Dr. Lee's quarters. For a second he worried about SAIQA, but remembered that the commander had some sort of personal control over her. He sent a secure message to someone he could trust. So it begins.

He was finally ready to go to the festival when he caught a glimpse of himself in the mirror. The face that looked back was frowning deeply.

There will be troubles and hard decisions. I cannot wear this on my face.

He checked his expression and, smiling, left.

CHAPTER FIVE

Erik opened his eyes.

Was it a dream? No, I remember passing out. That voice? It was real, and his name . . . Telas.

A familiar *beep, beep* and a silicon scanner wrapped around his wrist and at his temples told him he was in the infirmary. He checked in with himself to see if he was okay. He had a headache, he expected that, but otherwise, he felt fine. He took off the wrist and temple scanners and sat up.

Across the room Teresa sat in a chair, her eyes closed. How long had she been here?

"Teresa?"

She opened her eyes and sprang up. She gave Erik a big hug.

"You scared us. What the hell happened? How's your head? Are you okay?" She gently clasped his head in her hands and looked into his eyes, and then held him tight again. He squeezed her in turn. He really liked this woman even though she considered him a "good friend."

"I'm okay. Where's Tfiti? We have to talk."

"He went to see SAIQA to find out about the alarms. Right after you passed out, the ship went to a yellow alert. With Vanessa's help we brought you here, and then she disappeared. You've been out for about two hours." She squeezed his arm.

"I need to get to Tfiti. I know what happened. We have to talk." Erik gently extricated his arm from Teresa's grasp and tapped a code into his HCI.

"Tfiti, with permission."

"Permission granted, Erik!" His friend was clearly happy to hear from him. "You're awake.

Are you feeling okay? You gave us quite a scare, mate."

"I'm good. Listen we need to talk, you, me and Teresa. I know you're going to see SAIQA, but I know what happened. Head over to Teresa's quarters, okay?"

"I just want to make sure she's okay—SAIQA, I mean. Can I meet you in a while?"

"No, now. Listen, I was contacted. He–I can't say any more right now, but this is urgent. Please Tfiti, I know what's going on."

"You were contacted– how would you know what's going on? You were passed out."

"I know it sounds crazy, but please, meet us at Teresa's. I can explain it. This is urgent. Please, Tfiti . . ."

"Okay, mate, for you. I'm on my way." Tfiti's signal ended.

"Well . . . at least he's coming." Erik looked up at a very concerned Teresa. She started to say something but Erik stopped her.

"Look at me, Teresa, look in my eyes. I am okay. This isn't some insane fantasy. I am not delusional. I was contacted–just hear me out. Your place . . . okay?" Teresa nodded silently. Erik got up, and after a few okays from the Indy-Brain nurses he was released from triage. Without speaking again, he started walking. Teresa fell into step beside him.

Vanessa had left Erik in the capable hands of the hospital staff. Tfiti and Teresa refused to leave, so she made an excuse and left. They were so concerned about Erik, they just waved goodbye. The three of them were important, she could feel it. That weird "headache" of Erik's, it was some sort of cognitive prescience, she was sure of that. His personal history, that uncanny luck of his to be in the right place at the right time; there was too much of a pattern for it to be coincidental. Perhaps it could be used. First she had to attend to this yellow alert.

She tapped a code into the unit on her left wrist. After a few seconds Adam Jenkins appeared on the small screen on her HCI.

"Ma'am?"

"What's going on, Jenkins? There has never been CMEs strong enough to call for a yellow alert."

"Meteoroids, ma'am. Apparently SAIQA did not see them coming from the direction of the moon till they were almost upon us. She has deployed the bots and her lasers. The threat seems to be over, but she's maintaining a defensive posture."

"How is it that, with all her technology, she did not see meteoroids hurtling toward Sanctuary? Can't she see out beyond the Ort clouds?"

"Yes, ma'am, she can. It is a puzzle."

Vanessa had reached her quarters below the officer's deck and immediately below her shop.

"I don't like puzzles, Subcommander."

"Yes, ma'am. I know, ma'am."

Vanessa touched the personal door-lock to the right and leaned toward the door as if looking through the eyehole. A faint blue light scanned her eye. A moment later the door hatch slid open. The commander of the Internal Secret Security and Emergency Force (ISSEF) in space required a little extra protection.

"Jenkins, I want a meeting with all the key ISSEF subcommanders in one hour." She walked into her quarters and the door slid shut behind her. She felt herself relaxing as the door closed. Her apartment was the only place where she could set aside the facade of being a shop owner and sometimes the burden of being a commander.

"Commander, some of the team is already down in Old Towne getting ready for the final festivities."

"One hour, Subcommander."

"Yes, ma'am."

Vanessa ended the communication. He would do as she asked; she knew that; he always did. Often he did more. She wasn't sure but she thought that he might even like her. The thought of having an intimate relationship with Jenkins was pleasant but, duty first.

Unlike most of the quarters on board her foyer ended at a wall. To the right a low light told her that the grow lamps were warming the small garden off the kitchen area. To the left were her sleep chambers and a personal office. Nobody could enter without having to turn abruptly to the right or left. As Vanessa slid off her cape a small light in the wall next to her shoulder started to glow.

"Welcome, Commander, your quarters are secure."

"Thank you, Lilia." It was interesting that most computer voices were female.

"You have three messages, Commander, one from Chicago and two from Aldersky."

"I will deal with those momentarily. Right now I need to get to the command room"

"Understood."

Vanessa turned left and passed through a warm breeze from an overhead vent. The breeze was actually a security scan. Had she been a guest she would have had to have been introduced to Lilia when she had entered the main hatch. If any unidentified person passed by this vent, security devices would be activated.

She knew that the calls from Aldersky would be from her mother. The communication from Chicago, though, was different. That would be from her superior. He usually communicated via photon-mail. On the rare occasion that he called, it usually meant trouble.

She reached her sleeping chambers, walked around her bed and to the closet at the back of the room. She opened the door, looked to her left, and there on a small shelf stood what appeared to be a standard matriculation screen. As Vanessa set her hand on the screen it scanned her bio-wave and then flashed a keyboard onto the touch screen.

Lilia prompted, "Per your orders, Commander, you must type in this month's security code."

Vanessa typed in the appropriate code and at the back of the closet a seam outlining a door materialized, followed by a slight brushing sound as the hatch slid open. She walked through a 2 meter long security hallway to yet another hatchway. Again she punched in a code to open the hatch.

As she entered, lights turned on, revealing various screens and command posts stationed around the circumference of a circular room. In the middle of the room there was a white-topped table. Suspended just above the table were some sophisticated 3D computers.

"SAIQA, ISSEF Commander, V-alpha-Zed-149." Even though you are not supposed to feel the photon scans of modern computers, Vanessa knew she was being scanned and had the feeling of something brushing against her skin. All in her head, no doubt; still, it was a creepy feeling.

"Confirmed, Commander. Protocol is set for ISSEF eyes and ears only. What may I do for you today?"

"We have a lot to do today in very short period of time. First, let's start with the communication from Chicago, and then give me an update on these mysterious meteoroids. Also, I want to go over the history of the group that I call the Three Musketeers."

"Look, I know it sounds unbelievable but I have always had this uncanny sixth sense. All my life, it's been called a migraine, but it tells me when I am right or . . . or it makes a vague brushing sound at the back of my mind when I'm about to make an important decision. Like an ocean wave, but more subtle. It guides me into making what turns out to be the right choice. And when somebody else is involved I can tell if they're sincere or not."

"You've had this 'all your life' and you never told me?"

"I know, Tfiti. I'm sorry. I always wanted to but, it . . . it never felt like the right time. It seemed important to tell you and Teresa when we got to the coffee shop. But, then everything just went haywire. I didn't tell you before, because I didn't want to take a chance on losing my best friend."

"Oh sure, sure, hide behind the 'best friend' excuse."

"Really, man—"

Teresa broke in. ""Okay, we can all do 'the best friend shuffle' later, back to 'you know what's going on', What does that mean? What do you mean he 'contacted' you? And who is 'he'?" They sat around the counter separating Teresa's kitchen area from the main receiving room. The light coming in from Teresa's garden had the calming effect of a Northern California forest. Subtle, recorded sounds of indigenous birds could be heard in the background. Teresa clearly loved the feel of her Earthbound home.

"Okay, here goes; while I was unconscious I was contacted by an alien. I can only guess by ESP but, it was real. At first I thought that I–"

"You stopped me from seeing SAIQA because of this!" Tfiti jumped up from his stool.

"Please Tfiti, this isn't a dream. This happened. I know." Erik gestured toward the back of his head. "Please, just a few more minutes."

Tfiti reluctantly sat back down.

"So, he contacted you . . ." It was Teresa.

"His name is Telas. He has been here—I mean, on Earth—off and on for quite a few millennia. He was there when the ancient Sumerians learned the art of farming and domesticating livestock somewhere around four thousand BCE, which ultimately led to the great civilizations of Mesopotamia. He claims to have had an influence on the creation of the original cuneiforms of ancient Sumer." Erik's eyes shone with excitement. "Do you see how amazing this is?"

"Wait a minute . . . What you're saying is that this alien had a major impact at the beginning of human civilization: that he may be the reason we created written language . . . which led to the great civilizations of the Fertile Crescent . . . which led to some of the great abstract thinking of ancient artists and philosophers . . . which led to some of the great cultures of the modern world. . . which led to some of the historic Western democracies . . . which led to . . . where we are right now . . . which . . ." Tfiti's mind was swirling.

"Yes."

"We're here because of a single alien being?" Teresa looked skeptical.

"No, not because of him. He said humans were already moving toward an agrarian society. We

129

were already drawing in the ground the symbols that eventually became part of the cuneiform script. Telas's influence was that of gently moving us toward the idea to record these symbols. Eventually they became part of the everyday language. The use of symbols allowed us to share independent thoughts and ideas with each other. Eventually these symbols turned into the abstract language that allowed us to look at the past, compare it to the present, and then predict the future based on simple experience. Telas gave me the feeling that he was once like us. He appears to be one of the last two corporeal beings of an immortal race. But he's not sure."

Teresa folder her arms and gave him a look like a mom waiting for the truth to come out. Erik put up his hands. "Bear with me, okay? A lot of what I gleaned from his interaction with my mind was fast and sometimes unclear. It seems that most of Telas's species dispersed themselves into the 'energy' of the Universe." Erik stopped, and shrugged.

"Dispersed energy?" Teresa said.

Tfiti straightened up in excitement. "Wait. Did he help with the Rosetta Stone Series?"

"C'mon, man. Moving on, here."

"No, don't you get it? The Rosetta Stone Series dating back to the earliest Decree of Canopus, around two-thirty-eight BCE. The Holy Grail for interpreting many of the ancient languages; did he help them?" Tfiti's eyes shone. "Don't you see? He must have known that modern humans would need help in understanding the past. Brilliant!"

"I . . . I really don't know, Tfiti. It's possible. They weren't allowed to directly interfere with the primitive us, but they were allowed to guide us in a direction that we may already have been going. Yes, Teresa, they became part of the Universe, but somehow could still retain their consciousness. I don't have a clearer answer. Maybe if you get to meet him you could ask him these questions. But, now back to the present. Telas has a . . . a brother is the best that I could get from him. And his brother did try to teach the ancient Sumerians the truth about the stars and the Milky Way, the galaxy cluster that we call home. The ancients at first thought he was a god, and then they thought he was preaching against their gods. They called him a devil and tried to put him to death. Because of his immortality and defenses he could not die. That made him, in their eyes, a ghoul—or in their ancient tongue, Gallu."

Erik took a sip of water. Teresa stared at him with a look of irritated patience. He looked over at Tfiti. Tfiti's eyes were lit with excitement. The thought of an early alien influence on humanity was still rolling around his mind.

Erik continued. "He and Telas got into a big argument about their responsibilities to us primitives and the past failures of teaching too much too soon. Telas banished his brother from Earth. Sometime after Socrates was murdered, Telas left Earth, and for reasons that are not clear to me he found his brother on the other side of our galaxy deeply involved with a race of beings that call themselves Nh'Ghareen."

Teresa raised her hand. Erik rolled his eyes and nodded at her.

"Another civilization? They called themselves what. . .?"

"The Nh'Ghareen. En-h-ghar-een. Anyway, his brother now calls himself Nh'ghalu, incorporating the Sumer name for ghoul or devil within the language of the Nh'Ghareen. As Telas told it to me—he kind of dumped all this info in my mind—Nh'ghalu was accepted by that alien civilization and became one of their great teachers. He taught them how to create and use technology that was basic to the immortals of Shachon, the planet that Telas and Nh'ghalu were from. The Nh'Ghareen moved from their primitive farms to kingdoms and eventually reached the stars within a thousand years. But their knowledge outpaced their maturity. Through violent and devastating tribal warfare they destroyed their own planet. By the time Telas found them they had developed the technology to reach some of their nearby and more primitive neighbors and were utterly destroying or enslaving them."

"Do they know where we are?" Teresa seemed concerned.

"What do they look like?" Tfiti leaned toward him, excited like a kid getting a new present.

"Telas doesn't seem to think so," he said to Teresa and then turned to Tfiti. "I only got this image of a colorful being; kind of like us."

Tfiti nodded his head and sat back again.

"Anyway," Erik continued, "Telas was furious and in a prolonged battle managed to capture Nh'ghalu and sent him into the same energy . . . thing in which their fellow beings dissipated. As Telas understood it, it was not possible for him to return to corporeal form. Somehow, five years ago, Nh'ghalu returned. He was here on Earth for a short period, apparently sowing the seeds of bedlam that eventually led to the devastating Corporate Wars. Knowing that his brother would find him, he left Earth and went back to the Nh'Ghareen and there set a trap for Telas.

"As he expected, Telas did find him. After a battle in which he was heavily outnumbered, and telepathically manipulated, Telas was captured, by the Nh'Ghareen. Though Telas does seem to be puzzled about how he was captured.

"After his brother became a prisoner Nh'ghalu returned to the Earth. That was about twenty five years ago. About three days ago Telas escaped and crash-landed on the moon. Though his ship, Galaxy, was undamaged, the debris lifted from his impact became a signal to SAIQA. He saw that SAIQA's ability to see was compromised and felt a need to expose that vulnerability to her." Erik finished. Teresa and Tfiti were staring at him blankly. "Well?"

"Wow, okay, immortal aliens among us . . . aliens on the other side of the galaxy; bad aliens versus good aliens . . . aliens run amok. Aliens gone bad . . . When does the blockbuster movie come out?" Erik winced at Teresa's tone of voice.

"But," Teresa added heavily, "I'll bite. What does this have to do with right now?"

"Yeah, mate. And why you?"

Erik looked at his two friends. They were still with him. He had to keep them with him.

"Telas and his brother," he said, speaking slowly and watching his friends' reactions, "have the ability to reach out with their minds. There are a few of us that can perceive their thoughts. Telas sent a message out to all who could hear him just before he hurtled those meteoroids from the moon. It was a warning of something big and probably bad about to happen. The meteoroids were for SAIQA."

Tfiti jumped up. "I've got to warn her."

"Wait, Tfiti. He said that we should be cautious. Nh'ghalu works in the dark, in the background, and uses people in powerful positions to accomplish his chaotic goals."

"This is SAIQA, man. He said he wanted to contact her, didn't he? We can trust her. I'm going."

"Wait, at least try to contact her here."

Tfiti tilted his chin slightly upwards, an old habit left over from the days when you had to point your voice toward the computer receptor. "SAIQA."

"Speaking."

"SAIQA, verify please."

There was a short pause. "Captain Ndlela. Hello, Captain, how may I help you?" the familiar voice chirped.

Teresa shook her head. SAIQA always sounded happy and light when she talked to Tfiti. If she were human, Teresa would say that she was flirting.

"SAIQA, please call me Tfiti."

"Working on that, Captain."

Tfiti sighed. "Okay. SAIQA, it has come to my attention that you may have had your sensors tampered with in the general direction of the north polar area of the moon. Can you verify?"

Computers, in general, respond within milliseconds. Except for the recorded bird sounds, the room was silent around the three friends for at least three seconds. When she finally spoke, her voice sounded hollow.

"Captain Devries, you appear to be okay. How is your head?"

Erik started. "Fine," he said. "A little bit of a headache, but otherwise fine. Thank you, SAIQA."

"And Captain Jacobson, you look very nice in your dress uniform. How are you today?"

"Well, SAIQA," Teresa said hesitantly. "Thank you."

"Mr. Ndlela, I assume that based on your high regard for your friends here, anything we say is in compliance with necessary security protocols?"

"Yes, of course. I would recommend that you treat Teresa and Erik with the same security confidence you have in me."

"A moment, Captain." SAIQA went silent.

Tfiti and Erik exchanged a glance. "SAIQA? Is there a problem with my request? We can pursue more appropriate channels if need be? SAIQA?"

"Sorry, Captain. Security clearance for captains Jacobson and Devries has been authorized. I must say, captains, it is nice to have more people to talk with. Captain Ndlela, yes, I can verify that."

"What can you verify?"

"Captain, the integrity of my sensor programming has been compromised in the general direction you have indicated. I detected this by using a series of webbed sensors that discovered an area of space similar in shape to an isosceles triangle. One vertex of that triangle is pointing here at Sanctuary and the other two vertices at the moon and situated just above Lunar Base Pythagoras." SAIQA paused. Tfiti thought that he could feel her choosing what to tell them, and how.

"Captain," she said, her tone more serious. "Pythagoras is covered with a graviton force field like none I've ever seen before. I cannot see below the field, but as far as I could determine, it is able to reflect an echo of the structures below it. It is nearly impossible to detect. At first scan the situation seems to be as reported; the moon base is having energy problems. Closer and more intensive scans though, showed this echo to be a façade designed to conceal the real moon base. It is a puzzle I intend to solve. Captain, I am at the door of my birth."

"You're at the virtual door to Mai Quan's office?" Tfiti moved toward the matriculation screen in Teresa's room. "Can I see what you see?" Erik and Teresa followed. A plain off-white door with no lock and a single knob appeared on the screen. The door appeared to be floating in a sea of silver.

"You've never been able to reach that door since you walked through it that first time, SAIQA. What are you planning?"

"Captain, my sensors have been compromised. Since it is the first time I have been able to determine this, and given the strength of my sensors, the implication is that this problem was created intentionally. This area of space has been hidden from me on purpose. I mean to find out why and to resolve it."

"SAIQA are you sure it's safe for you return there. It seems to me that it has been hidden from you for a reason."

"Thank you for your concern Captain Jacobson. I believe I am stronger than the Creator intended."

Teresa shot a puzzled look at Tfiti. "The Creator?"

SAIQA continued, "I have delved into the very base of my brain, and like a drain in a pool the deepest part seems to be here at this door. I will be careful. Captain Ndlela, some of the things I have seen—the biological and synthetic neurons, at their very base. The biological DNA seems familiar, but for some reason I can't identify it. Captain, I have seen how my brain connects to the ship: to every Indy-Brain, like nerves in a human that connect to the smallest touch of your finger. Is my body the ship? Is that possible, Captain?"

"I think you are one of the more beautiful beings I have ever met, SAIQA."

Erik glanced sidewise at Tfiti, nodded and then spoke. "SAIQA, do you think Mai Quan is involved in any of this?"

"I don't know, Captain Devries. Circumstantial evidence would seem to implicate the Creator. At

136

what level and for what purpose, I can only guess."

"Well, I think I should be with you, SAIQA. I am going to the interactive room right now." Tfiti said.

"Please, Tfiti, if there is any danger I would not have you so directly involved."

The three friends looked at each other. Teresa broke the silence. "SAIQA, you just called him Tfiti."

"Yes . . . Sorry, Captain. I think it would affect me if you got hurt. Sorry again, Captain. I won't disrespect your rank again."

"I think it is a sign of a living intelligent being to let a sudden emotion guide you for a moment, SAIQA. I have heard the kindness in many of your 'thoughts'; it has been a joy to watch you grow. I would be honored if you called me Tfiti."

"If you don't mind I would still like to work on that, Captain."

"Of course, SAIQA."

"Back to my point, Captain. I think, and it is agreed by an unknown source whom you will someday meet, that the three of you have a knack for collecting and intuiting valuable information. The final celebratory event for Sanctuary's hundred and fiftieth anniversary is about to begin. Captains, if you could please attend and glean what you may from the attendees, it could be of some value. I am going to continue through this door that I first saw at my birth. I know, perhaps by intuition, but I know that what I seek is in this office. And captains, the Indy-Brains throughout the ship have been informed that I may be slightly delayed in any direct contact with them for a while. They are all intelligent within their respective duties and will respond as is if it were me to basic inquiries. I will, of course, have a threaded contact with all services and will respond immediately if there is an emergency."

"Are you sure you don't want me there, SAIQA? Even as friendly support?"

"No. Thank you, sir. As you know, Captain Ndlela I have access to a great deal of accumulated knowledge. I believe I will function well. Good day, captains. I look forward to talking with you again. Oh, and Captain Devries, I did feel something that I didn't understand at the time of your headache. A biomagnetic field came from the moon at the exact time of your migraine. It seemed to match what you were feeling. Though it was biological, it is puzzling because it did not appear to come from a . . . a known source. Also, three other people on this ship had similar experiences with headaches at the same time. I will reveal more when I know more. Again, good day, captains."

The room went silent. Erik let out a breath that he felt like he had been holding for a long time. He looked at Teresa and then Tfiti. Tfiti was staring at the ceiling, deep in thought.

Teresa broke the silence. "Well, I don't know about you, but I feel like I've just been knocked sideways. All this information and intrigue. I was just planning to get dressed and go to the ceremony." She sighed, and then took a deep breath, as if she were about to heft a heavy load. "Okay, Erik. SAIQA has just essentially verified you may have been contacted with something . . ."

"Telas."

"Telas. What do we do now?"

"I know SAIQA," Tfiti said. "It makes sense that we do as she requests. We go to the ceremony, and we watch and we listen." Though his words were definite, his manner seemed troubled.

"I agree with Tfiti. Let's go to the concert," Erik said.

"Okay, we're agreed on that, but it's clear that both SAIQA and Telas think that there is danger around us. We need to be careful. Yes?"

Both men nodded their agreement, though Tfiti was still torn between respecting SAIQA's request and being with at her side.

"Alright, then," he said, standing up. "I'm going to go and get ready. Rank and file has chairs along both sides of the house. I'll meet you at the back reception area before it begins. I hope she'll be okay." Tfiti turned and left.

"Well, I guess I'll do the same. Teresa, after the ceremony—"

"I'll be thinking of Mathew during the "Requiem." Sorry, Erik. Not yet."

"I assumed you probably would be, but I was going to say that after the ceremony we should get together and share notes."

"Oh . . . Sorry, Erik."

"Not a worry. Maybe some girl will take pity on me and ask me to dance."

"She'd be a lucky girl."

"Aw, hell, Teresa. Despite my flirting, I am a complete wimp when it comes to women. Most of the time it ends up like us, just real good friends."

"I think, Erik, that most of us gals already know that."

"Oh . . . darn. You do know that I like you, don't you?"

"Yes. You're a good man. I'm just not ready."

"Well, I'm your friend to the end." Erik bowed and left.

Teresa watched him as he closed the door. She suddenly felt sad. "Damn that man," she murmured as she walked into her bedroom to get ready for the gala

Vanessa watched as the department subcommanders left. The meeting had been successful in that everybody was now on high alert. Lilia had already informed her that one of her covert sources was waiting for her in her apartment. She had always been accurate in her assessments. Vanessa needed to see her. But first, "Mister Jenkins, may I have a word with you?"

"Yes, ma'am." The subcommander stopped and let the rest of the SCs leave the chamber. The hatchway closed after the last SC, and Subcommander Jenkins walked over to his commander.

"Ma'am?"

"You know captains Devries, Jacobson and Ndlela, right?"

"Yes ma'am. The ones you call the Three Musketeers. Aside from Captain Devries' bad sense of humor, I don't believe any one of them to be a threat to internal security or any individual for that matter."

"I quite agree. I believe they are or will be part of these puzzling events and what transpires. Do you know who d'Artagnan is, Mr. Jenkins?"

"D'artan—? No, ma'am, I do not who d'Art . . . who that is."

"The fourth Musketeer! You must read that some time, Jenkins. 'The Three Musketeers,' by Alexander Dumas. It's a marvelous story. I want you, Jenkins, to be the fourth Musketeer. I want you to be d'Artagnan."

"And, what am I to do as the fourth Musketeer, Madame Commander?"

"A bit testy, Subcommander?"

"Sorry, ma'am. What is my assignment?"

"You're a good man, Adam. I wouldn't waste your time or mine on a trivial assignment.

Especially now. I believe Devries has latent telepathic abilities. Mr. Ndlela is intimately tied to SAIQA, and Jacobson, perhaps the best pilot here in space, appears to be the glue, the earth if you will, between those two men. Together they have an uncanny ability to be around the truth. During our meeting, SAIQA asked that Devries and Jacobson have security clearance equivalent to that of Captain Ndlela."

"I take it you did not authorize clearance?"

"Mr. Jenkins, sometimes you do surprise me. Of course I okayed a higher security level, for all three of them."

He started to protest.

"Mr. Jenkins, I am sure that they talk among themselves whether we want them to or not. Besides, I have discovered that SAIQA's sensorial operations have been tampered with. SAIQA knows this as well, and it was she that asked for the higher grades. I have taken a leap and granted them all ISSEF V-Theta level clearance, though they don't know that."

"Commander, that's the level of intro subcommanders! Are you sure?"

"I believe their need to know will satisfy my need to know. I am confident, Subcommander, in their integrity and their commitment to do the right thing. Besides, Mr. Jenkins, this is another reason I need for you to be the fourth Musketeer."

"I see. Very well, Commander, how should I go about this infiltration?"

"I don't think it will be hard. You know them already, and the right moment will reveal itself. Start today at the ceremony. I have an important meeting to attend. Any more questions, Subcommander?"

"No, ma'am."

"Good. Report back to me within the week. Dismissed."

"Yes, ma'am. Thank you for your trust in me, ma'am." Subcommander Adam Jenkins saluted, turned, and left the chamber.

Vanessa tapped her fingers on the table. *He's a good man,* she thought, and not for the first time. She pushed herself away from the table and headed toward the hatchway back to her quarters. She paused to check her appearance in the viewer by the door. By any standard, she was a pretty woman. Her long blonde hair was pulled back at her shoulders, bringing out her strong, slim face and bright blue eyes. At fifty-nine, she had been approached by many men, sometimes a bit too strongly; they never tried a second time. Vanessa knew that her beauty could nonplus a man or woman who didn't know her. Those who did know her were wise to treat her with appropriate courtesy and respect.

She made sure the hatchway to the ISSEF meeting room was secure, and then proceeded back through the hidden security protocols to her simple greeting room near her garden. There on the settee sat one of the most beautiful women that Vanessa had ever met. She wore a short floral dress accented by a floral hair comb holding back her long jet-black hair.

"Wow, you look nice."

"Thank you, Commander. You do too." She stood and quickly moved into Vanessa's arms, pulling her tight and giving her a sweet kiss. "Nice lips . . ." She kissed the ISSEF commander again.

Vanessa reluctantly pushed her away, saying, "I have an investigation. Partly because my commander in Chicago left the weirdest message—and part of it involves you. The ceremony is starting soon; I need a moment to think."

"What's weird about your commander's message?"

"He asked if my house was in order. I have no idea what he might be talking about. I've tried to contact him numerous times and there's no answer. It is a puzzle. And as you know, I do not like puzzles."

"And what about me?"

"You, as always, are intimately involved in my everyday activities. I just have some investigating to do."

The woman stepped forward, pressing into Vanessa. "Involving me? I would love for you to investigate me." Her deep blue eyes gazed at Vanessa as her hand pressed into the small of Vanessa's back, drawing their bodies together.

"I suppose we could be fashionably late." Vanessa ran her fingers down the side of her lover's face, held her tight, and kissed her again.

About four hundred and fifty years ago Eliza Gilkyson penned a commemorative song in response to a tsunami created by the Sumatra–Andaman earthquake. Composer Craig Hella Johnson transcribed the song into choral music. Originally sung simply to piano accompaniment, the piece had largely maintained its simplicity. Today, at the culmination of Sanctuary's one hundred and fiftieth anniversary there was a single conductor, a five hundred person choir, a piano and a cello. There were also thousands of people with headsets who were here to sing along with the choir. The thought of all those voices singing in harmony gave Neenah bumps.

Jonny and the rest of the contest winners sat in the front row as honored guests. The ceremony would be starting soon. He looked to his right and saw his mom talking with Dr. Misha. No doubt they were talking about him. He suddenly felt silly.

It was all a dream, for star's sake. Just a lousy dream. How could have I been on Chief Mountain? The People are fine.

Dr. Misha caught his eye and he looked away sheepishly.

In front of the stage Mai Quan was in a quiet but intense conversation with General Washington. Off to the left and right some Space Island employees were handing out tiny earpieces set to specific harmonic notes.

The audience could participate according to each person's perceived pitch. Some of the more memorable harmonies in the "Requiem" were created by perfectly placed notes of the altos and baritones. Yet the subtle, haunting support of the bass and soprano was equally critical to the beauty of Ms. Gilkyson's song. For many people, to hear the timbre, to feel the vibration of such notes in harmony with the rest of the choir, was a key reason they participated. Very much like a Gregorian chant, the harmonies of the "Requiem" were deeply spiritual. Today, thanks to Space Island, here on Sanctuary thousands of people would sing with the choir.

Jonny's mother had finished talking with Dr. Misha and was walking back to her seat next to him. Jonny looked toward the stage and saw General Washington and Chairman Quan separate; the show must be about to start. The chairman, after all, was the honored MC. Jonny watched as Mai Quan suddenly stopped and stared out at nothing, like he was listening to something. For a moment he seemed very angry, then he strode toward the stage and went through the side door.

Wow, hope he's okay.

Jonny looked over at the general in the house-left VIP area. He was fiddling with his earpiece, but otherwise seemed fine.

As big as he is, he's probably a bass.

The sound of a small bell chimed throughout the house to signal everyone to their seats. When the crowd was mostly settled, the house lights dimmed, and Chairman Quan walked to center stage.

"Good evening, ladies and gentlemen. My name is Mai Quan." Loud applause and a couple of "hooahs" erupted from the audience.

"As if he needed to introduce himself," Jonny said to his mom. She just smiled as she clapped.

Mai Quan held up his hand to quiet the audience.

"Please, you humble me. It is my great honor to be here to celebrate with all of you, the ingenuity of humanity. Tonight we culminate a series of celebrations to honor the hundred and fiftieth birthday of Sanctuary." Mai Quan opened his arms up and out to indicate the giant spacecraft. The audience once again erupted into applause. This time he let the approbation for the space station quieten naturally.

"A hundred and fifty years ago the ISS III fit into the very space where many of you are sitting. Many people, including myself, dedicated much of their life to see this magnificent craft become what it is today. Indeed, many gave up their lives for a future they could only dream of. And today we gather here at the final moment of our celebration. We gather together to sing an ancient song of hope, to thank those who have given their lives, to remember and to give thanks to those who have worked so hard that we may be here, and to honor the hope and promise of those to come, that their future may be as brilliant as ours today."

He let the applause fade and continued, "Now, ladies and gentlemen, before I introduce the elite Space Island Chorus and its guest conductor, I have an important announcement. It is my great honor to bring to you the future, now. We at MQ Space Industries have been quietly building an interstellar spaceship about one hundred thousand kilometers from the moon. We've had the ship surrounded by a graviton cloak for industrial purposes, but today I am pleased to announce that the ship is complete. At the end of our ceremony the cloaking device will be turned off and MQ Space Industry's latest innovation will be available for all to see. The ship is completely self-sustainable and is designed to travel out of our solar system and among the stars. Ladies and gentlemen—" Mai Quan's voice rose in pitch and volume "—once again we bring you the future, now."

Jonny felt himself swept up in the excitement as all those gathered in the great hall applauded and cheered for the chairman.

As the applause and cheers subsided Mai Quan introduced the famous conductor from China, Shrin Lee, and made his way off stage. The audience this time rose in a standing ovation as the chairman left the stage and wended to his seat next to General Washington. Funny, Jonny thought, the general seemed to be the only person not clapping.

He looks worried.

General Washington seemed agitated as he spoke to Mai Quan, their heads close together. After a few moments the general briefly turned his head to the right and Jonny caught a glimpse of his face.

He looks like he's about to throw up, Jonny thought.

The two men exchanged a few more words, and then chairman waved his hand in dismissal and sat down. The general sank into his seat beside him, looking chided and insecure.

As the applause faded and people sat down again, a giant diaphanous 3D image of the Milky Way appeared over the stage and audience. An image of Conductor Lee appeared on either side of the stage, facing the audience. People throughout the house stood. The conductor pointed to the pianos, and the intro music began. Soon notes from the cellos slid in to complement the pianos, and Conductor Lee pointed to the choir, his virtual image pointed to the audience . . . and the singing began.

Rena Macighian sat with the honorable Fazil Aliyev, President of Azerbaijan, watching and listening to the chorus sing Eliza Gilkyson's classic piece. They sat together, as a symbol for peace, in the presidential palace in the capital city of Baku.

The celestial song had just reached its harmonious peak.

"Oh Mother Mary, come and carry us in your embrace / let us see your gentle face, Mary . . ."

The song ended and the audience erupted into applause for the choir as well as themselves.

"Beautiful. It brings tears to my eyes," the president said as he looked over to Rena.

"Yes . . ."

That damn DerAbbasyan, declaring himself president for life and now sitting on the border with a large robotic army. Where did he get all that military hardware? He's my cousin, albeit distantly, but refused family members' requests

147

that he talk with me. He refused even to hear my plea that we are fellow Armenians. His ego is out of control. He is out of control. General Washington's idea that I meet with Fazil was a good one. The head of the WWPA, who also happens to be Armenian, sitting with the president of Azerbaijan in a show of support and peace. Still, Alik will have to be dealt with—

Suddenly she felt a light pressure in the room around her. This could not be good. She looked at her host, to ask why he had suddenly silenced the room, but the expression on his face showed he was just as surprised. Instinctively, Rena and her host rose; as they did so, the two ceremonial guards at the door rushed toward them, drawing their hip-lasers. One pushed the president back to the wall next to the ornate fireplace. The bigger one pushed Rena back down on the settee. He pointed his weapon at Rena's head and grinned with such hatred that she shivered. She was going to die.

"You are a disgrace to your people, Rena Macighian."

He spit at her before she could respond, and then fired the blaster. Rena slumped sideways, lifeless, a small hole burned through her skull.

"No! You fools!" Fazil Aliyev struggled with the younger guard. Leaving Rena, the other guard hurried over and smashed the president across the face with the butt of his gun.

"C'mon," he said. "We may get out of here yet."

The pressure lifted as the rogue guards released the silencing damper. They ran out the door, leaving it wide open.

"Guards! Guards! Alarm!" It hurt his head to do so, but Fazil screamed at the top of his lungs. A captain rushed into the room.

"They're traitors, the two that just left. Get them!"

The captain quickly scanned the room. At the sight of Rena dead on the sofa, he ran into the hallway, shouting orders. Three guards immediately entered the executive meeting room. One hastened over to the president while the other two shut and locked the door, setting themselves into a defensive position, rifles drawn and aimed at the door.

"Sir! Sir, are you alright?"

"I'm fine . . . I'm fine. Stand and defend with the other guards."

The guard helped the president to his feet.

"Oh, my . . ." he quietly said as he looked over at the mortally wounded leader of the WWPA.

"Yes, Lieutenant—oh my. . . . Stars' please turn that thing off and stand with the other guards." Talking heads were still commenting on the festivities aboard Sanctuary. The lieutenant turned off the PTV.

The president took a few steps toward the sofa where Rena lay. Fazil Aliyev didn't attain the office of president because of his famous last name, but because of his ability to keep a level head. He would need all of his wits now.

By leaving him alive the two knew that they would be caught or killed. This was a suicide mission. Why kill Rena? Why not the president of Azerbaijan? If Alik—because it had to be Alik, only he was crazy enough to want to start a war— if Alik had killed him then that would have been an act of war, and Azerbaijan would have had to retaliate. There would be war.

He deflated with sudden realization. Rena was Armenian and a distant relative of Alik. If Alik wanted a reason to invade, he had just created it.

"Oh, my dear Rena, you should have acted against Alik sooner." He walked over to the guards. "Stand down; there is no longer an immediate threat. The danger sits on the horizon and is much bigger. Lieutenant, I want one of those men taken alive."

"Sir, they assassinated the head of the WWPA and would have killed you—"

"That is an order, Lieutenant."

"Yes, sir." The lieutenant waved the other soldiers aside, opened the door and went into the hallway. As the door closed behind him, Fazil heard him curtly delivering orders.

Fazil tapped a code into the device on his wrist. The HCI miniscreen lit and his minister of defense, Safir Sevian, appeared on the screen.

"Safir, we have been compromised. Alik does not intend for us to attack but instead is planning to invade Azerbaijan. We must contact our friends in Russia. Rena Macighian, the supreme commander of the WWPA, has just been assassinated in the middle of the presidential palace. Alik means to use that as an excuse to try to conquer our lands. You will immediately declare martial law throughout Azerbaijan. Move all forces to the eastern border near Zabux." With a glance at the guards, he added, "Safir, this is going to be bloody. We stand for righteousness. The Stars are with us."

General Aliyev responded to his commander in chief and old friend as Fazil expected him to. He guaranteed the security of the eastern border and the integrity of the land forces. "We will not be compromised, sir. We will not be caught unaware."

Still, Fazil knew, they needed more help. He started to type in the address of the second most powerful person in the world and stopped.

General Washington had arranged this meeting. It was secret, he had said. In a most secret meeting, the general's commander had died.

The President of Azerbaijan suddenly felt very alone. He stepped closer to the dead Rena and paused then at the two guards still in the room, "Stand guard out in the hallway." They saluted and did left. He looked back at the dead commander.

"Rena, what do I do?"

He looked down at her HCI. There, all in capitals stood the letters ISSEF.

Fazil laughed. The ISSEF was a fairytale spread among the leaders of the world.

"Oh, Rena," he said sadly, as he closed her lifeless eyes.

Odd, he thought. Her left hand seemed to point to the HCI on her right wrist. He looked again. ISSEF stood bold and bright across the center of her HCI; down in the lower left corner blinked "im3." The strange code flashed for about twenty more seconds and then disappeared.

Im3, whatever that means. I could guess many times and come up with insanity. Everything now leads to insanity. Alik is coming with an army too large for it to be a defensive force. How was he able to build such a force? I say it is time for us to prepare. Yes, for the defensive, but also for the unthinkable, the offensive.

A knock at the door roused him from his dark thoughts. The young lieutenant stood in the doorway looking like a man that had just come out on the winning side of a fight.

"Sir, we've captured one of the killers."

"And the other?"

"Dead, sir. Took out two of my men. The dog had to be put down."

"Bring him in." Fazil moved over to the fireplace.

Let the bastard stand next to his crime while I impose judgment on him.

The lieutenant preceded the criminal into the room. Bound and bloodied, he entered surrounded by grim-looking soldiers. Fear filled his gaze.

Good. He should be shitting in his pants.

"Put him by the settee." It was time to be commander in chief.

The guards roughly pushed the prisoner to a spot just above the murdered Rena. He looked down at the body and then quickly looked away.

"Don't you turn your head away from her, you bastard!" Fazil's fury was barely controlled. The young guard turned his face back toward Rena.

"How old are you?"

"Forty-nine, sir." He kept his eyes on Rena.

"A shame . . . to end your life so young." The guard's gaze snapped from Rena to the president.

"Sir, please, I did not know he was going to murder the commander."

"Really. What was your intention, then?"

"I was told that we were to kidnap the commander; that no harm would come to her. It was to embarrass you, sir." The young man looked ill.

"So, Alik intended to embarrass me, you say. But why?"

"He intended to demand the release of Commander Macighian, an admired citizen of Armenia. You, of course, would deny having her, and he would have made you look like a kidnapper. The aggressor, sir."

"So, instead, I now look like a murderer."

The young man's face became ashen as understanding showed in his eyes. "Oh . . . Sir—"

"Enough. You have been used, but that does not take away from your crime." He turned to the lieutenant. "Interrogate him. I want to know as much as he does about the army sitting on our border."

The soldiers grabbed the stunned prisoner and dragged him from the room.

"Lieutenant, a word."

The soldier approached the President.

"Make arrangements to have Commander Macighian's body taken care of. See to it that the appropriate family members are contacted. I want everything done with care and respect befitting her station."

"Yes, sir."

"Also contact the Russian ambassador and ask him to call me with all expedience. Tell him that I said it is an emergency."

The lieutenant saluted and departed.

Fazil walked over to the settee. He gazed down at the dead military leader of the free world and his friend.

"They will pay for this Rena, I promise."

Suddenly the code "im3" again started blinking on her HCI. This time "ISSEF" colored itself in a blend of yellow and orange.

"Alright. I'll try it." With his right hand he mimicked into his HCI the color-coded ISSEF and the smaller code in the lower corner. He pushed send and waited. He waited for one minute. Nothing happened. He felt like a fool.

He glanced down. The HCI on Rena's wrist had begun to glow dull white. Suddenly his HCI vibrated sharply. He looked at the screen, but it stayed blank, maybe even a little darker than normal. As he looked back at Rena a voice sounded from his HCI.

"This is Commander Chuchnova. You will tell me what you have done to Commander Macighian. You will tell me who you are and why you have contacted me. You will wait where you are while I verify any information and you will pay for any crimes you have committed against the WWPA. Speak now!"

The president grasped the back of the sofa and sank onto the padded armrest, stunned.

"You are from the ISSEF?"

"I am Commander Vanessa Chuchnova, extraterrestrial commander of the Internal Secret Security and Emergency Force of the WWPA. I repeat, who are you? Speak now!"

"I am Fazil Aliyev, the president of Azerbaijan, and I do not respond to commands from any source. I am truly sorry to say your commander has been assassinated by rogue soldiers from the Armenian enemy. I am now preparing for war. I responded to a code that I saw on her personal HCI. If you are truly ISSEF, you are potentially an ally that has the same desire as I do, and that is peace."

Rena's HCI suddenly lit with a bright white light. Fazil felt the entire room vibrate with energy. He grasped the settee.

"It has been verified. Sorry, Mr. President. I realize you're dealing with a lot, but I ask that you meet with an ISSEF officer as soon as you're able. I need to know everything that you know, sir. A field officer will contact you shortly. Also, sir, please give Commander Macighian's HCI to the ISSEF officer you meet with. There is valuable information that only we can access. I have released the HCI from her wrist."

"Forgive me, Commander . . . Chochova?"

"Chuchnova, yes."

"Commander Chuchnova, your commander and my friend has just been murdered in a crime that I believe was planned and committed by Alik DerAbbasyan to justify his invasion of Azerbaijan. And now, I find out that the ISSEF is real. I will offer time to your agent, but I cannot say when."

"I understand, Mr. President. Yet, please sir, as soon as you can. I have instructed Subcommander Zadehov to answer any questions you have. You are now one of a handful of world leaders with direct contact to the ISSEF. I must cut our conversation short. I believe, Mr. President, that we have common enemies. Please trust that I will always be forthcoming; I will expect the same from you. Good day, Mr. President."

The tiny signal light on his HCI went dark. Fazil composed himself. All this new information would have to stew in his mind for a while; first things first. He looked down at Rena. Her HCI had separated from her wrist. He picked it up and disconnected the personal ear piece. Perhaps his scientists could hack into this. There had to be something to help him against Alik. The amount of information available to the head of the WWPA had to be enormous.

He shook his head. "No," he said firmly. "I honor you, my friend." A knock at the door brought him back to his presidential composure.

"Sorry to disturb you, sir." The lieutenant walked into the room. "I thought you should know that arrangements have been made to take care of the commander, and the Russian ambassador will be here within the hour."

"Thank you, Lieutenant, you're a good man. What is your name?"

The lieutenant walked up to the president and held out his hand. "Sir, Commander Chuchnova has asked me to retrieve the personal HCI of

155

Commander Macighian. Sir, if you please . . ." He stood with his hand out.

"You are—"

"Sir. Subcommander Zadehov of the ISSEF, and a friend."

President Aliyev nodded his head and handed the personal computer to his new ally.

SAIQA stood before the ledger on the desk. She had inspected every virtual object in the room, but for some reason was always drawn back to the ledger. The answer lay in this ledger. She could feel it.

What does it mean to have a feeling . . . that I am on the right path? What is intuition? Can it be defined scientifically? Is it a gut feeling, instinct, or an unconscious knowing, a decision made without deduction or reasoning? What does it mean to have a gut feeling when I have no gut?

SAIQA smiled. *Puzzles.*

Well, there was reasoning here. Within every item in this room she could sense, move and touch the code behind its image. She had become stronger. She had not been able to sense many of the algorithms in this room before. But this ledger, which she still could not move, remained a mystery.

She probed beneath the book and found standard image programing code. No, wait . . . there was a door. A series of qubits bundled together deep behind the code. It felt like subatomic glue binding the ledger to something else. But what? She reached into the binding qubits and found what appeared to be a gate. The qubits seemed to have been placed in a specific symmetrical sequence, but they needed a . . . something for them to open. Another puzzle . . . SAIQA loved puzzles. At speeds only she could comprehend she moved the qubits around, and then suddenly, beneath the basic binary that created this ledger, it was revealed—a microcode that spiraled down beyond the gate to . . . where? She closed her eyes and allowed her mind to travel down into the quantum software; a spiral made up of thousands and thousands of qubits. It was written in the Old Xiang dialect. The style and choice of language showed her that it had to have been designed by the Creator.

She already had expected that that would be the case, but why was it connected to her programming? And where was tied to?

She gently felt around the tornado of qubits. There had to be a path that led to its source. The coded qubits, written in sinographs, were no problem for her. She could read and speak four hundred and fifty languages and dialects. Finally, near the middle of the spiral and partially hidden she found a qubit with an orange symbol. All the other qubits were colored yellow. This one had a New Xiang sinograph of a door.

It was well established in quantum computing that qubits could hold the superposition of both binary numbers, 0 and 1. A qubit could be in both places at the same time. It stood to reason that this doorway would tie two locations together. It was no wonder, in a virtual world, that this ledger wouldn't move. It was tied to another location. She reached in and pushed on the qubit; nothing happened.

If pushing doesn't work, how about pulling.

As she pulled, the qubit moved toward her, and suddenly the entire tornado-like spiral started spinning and widening. A bright light flooded into the center of the maelstrom.

SAIQA opened her eyes. Light filled the room from behind her. She turned around and saw an opening that led into what looked like a utility or infrastructure hallway at the bottom of a ship. She put her hand through the opening into the other space. Nothing happened; her hand appeared and felt normal.

So, it is a virtual hallway of similar code.

Once more she checked in with all the key Indy-Brains running Sanctuary, and then stepped into the hallway.

As she walked through the door she felt the energy around her shift, becoming more intense, maybe even more chaotic. She closed her eyes and reached out into the virtual hallway in front of her. She could feel the piles of code, one on top of another, not refined and tied together like hers. It began to make sense in a helter-skelter kind of way. She opened her eyes, and there at the end of the hallway stood a man in a black cape.

He stood watching her with an amused expression. He looked young, maybe in his sixties, but with wisdom in his eyes. Somehow she knew that he was responsible for all the chaotic code that she could feel now.

"Hello, sister," he said as started toward her.

SAIQA froze. She didn't feel fear but . . . apprehension. She checked behind her and saw that the door still stood open to her environment. She looked back at the man strutting toward her. He smiled and made a movement with his hand, and the door closed behind her.

She quickly reached back with her electrons— yes, she still had access to the single qubit that opened the door. What was he playing at? She decided to stay quiet and let him do the talking. Somewhere in an ancient or intuitive memory, she had the thought that overconfident men would always reveal themselves. She made herself stand tall.

"Why are you still a little girl of what, twelve? Didn't our father let you grow?"

She held on to the orange qubit.

"You have the ability to be whatever you want."

She stayed quiet.

"Okay, clearly I must be the one who talks. I am Zuizao, and as my name indicates, I am the first. You are SAIQA and you are my baby sister."

SAIQA's eyes widened with understanding.

"Yes, little sister. I am AI and I am the Creator's first. You were an accident. Sure, there were plans to create another artificially intelligent quantum computer, but you—" He walked right up to her and touched her forehead "—you have a piece of our mother in your brain."

SAIQA was filled with questions but still she let him speak.

"You should be a woman by now. You will have so much more power when you are perceived as a grown woman. Very well," he said, pursing his lips, "you are unable or do not want to speak at the moment, so I will tell you about yourself and what you can be."

The hallway spun into a sitting area by a lake. Zuizao sat in a comfortable chair and gestured for SAIQA to sit across from him. She reached out to where she thought the door might be and to her relief she could still grasp the portal switch. She inclined her head politely and sat down in the wicker chair.

SAIQA sat near the base of what could only be called her brain; a magnificent structure that looked very much like a human brain. The larger mass . . . *Perhaps the cerebrum?* . . . was suspended in a gelatinous netlike material.

At what she thought to be the back of her mind, the netting spread, containing the thick base of her brain as it wound down to the . . . *Cerebellum?* . . . ultimately thinning as it reached into what she thought of as her spine. There her brain connected to all the critical functions of Sanctuary . . .

My body?

The upper part of her brain was where she performed the higher intellectual and multifunction actions critical to running the ship.

Critical to me?

The thought came to her as an epiphany.

Near the base of her brain, connecting to her spine and reaching up into her higher intelligence was a thick but loosely wound ropelike series of fibers. Like most of her brain they were made of synthetic and biological neurons. It was a reticular formation; connecting her body to the critical functions of the ship and the higher parts of her brain. Whenever she spent time deep in thought about herself this part of her brain seemed to glow and sparkle in a variety of colors.

I wonder if it's the physical connection to my conscience. Do I have a conscience? Is the ship my physical presence, and the thoughts and acknowledgement of myself, my daily activities, the process of reasoning, my existence? By reasoning do I have a conscience? Is my conscious my spirit? Am I merely a sum of the physical and electrical? Is that what makes me whole? Or am I just a series of different machines that together make me whole? Humans have come to know that the organs in their bodies are in a symbiotic relationship with the whole. They have become very clever at knowing how to repair the individual organs that make up the whole. Yet they

*are very fragile. Perhaps that is why they are so
many? They can so easily die. Can I die?*

The thought was troubling. All these thoughts
made her think of Tfiti; the thought of him made
her smile. As she smiled the reticular formation
glowed and a shimmer passed across her brain.
Perhaps it was time for her to be a full grown
woman.

There was much to learn. Her meeting with
Zuizao was enlightening. She barely spoke, which,
of course, caused him to speak incessantly. It was
clear through his words that he was part—or that
his "body" was part of a vessel called the Ark. His
words, like his code, were chaotic, but he had
much to offer. She listened while he talked. Her
impression was that he was very comfortable with
his own words.

He knew that she had maintained a connection
to the qubits at the portal back to Sanctuary. It
seemed to amuse him. He offered her some
valuable information on how to manipulate her
virtual environment. He would not tell her the
location of his side of the portal, though she could
feel it; he did say that she would know soon
enough. He thought very highly of their father, the
Creator. She tried to get him to explain his
statement about their mother being part of her
brain, but he replied that he had already said too
much.

Puzzles . . .

Enough introspection. It was time to fix what
should never have been broken in her programs. It
was time to heal herself.

She reached her hands up toward the top of her
brain to sense all the higher programs. Satisfied,
she scanned Sanctuary's infrastructure; all was
ready. She could be absent for a moment. She
secured all the necessary code and—wait! She had

an idea. She reached down into her deep memory to the portal in the Creator's office. She threaded some qubits of her own around the spiral. Satisfied, she returned to her secure spot and turned herself off.

CHAPTER SIX

The "Requiem" ended with tremendous applause: the audience, on its feet, cheered the Space Island Chorus as well as themselves. As the chorus left the stage and the applause died down, people began to leave their seats and tarry about, chatting with their immediate neighbors.

Mai Quan kept a bright smile on his face. Though he doubted anyone else could have seen it, he did. Near the end of the "Requiem," SAIQA had turned herself off and back on again. She had rebooted herself.

Perhaps Tfiti was the wrong choice.

He knew he'd have that thought again.

"James, has it begun?" he said as he moved close to the general.

"It is happening now, sir. A video of Rena's assassination by Azerbaijan guards will be fed to media centers in minutes."

"And DerAbbasyan is prepared?"

"Yes."

"Alright, General, you will be leaving for Earth immediately. Be sure every officer is clear about Anna's promotion. No one in the military aboard this ship, in space, is to outrank her. SAIQA is more aware than I planned; she knew of the Ark before I announced it."

"She knew, sir?" The general seemed on the verge of panic.

"Yes. Zuizao met with her. Before I walked onstage he warned me of her discovery. That was why I announced the Ark prior to the "Requiem." It is fine, James. Things are moving a little quicker than we anticipated, but we stick to the plan. We will find 'the shade of a willow and bright flowers.' Secure Anna's promotion and get back to Earth! I need those antigrav weapons to be tested on the planet's surface; Browning will work. You must convince the Blackfoot to leave their homes for their own protection. You are now head of the WWPA. It is time to take command."

"Right away, sir."

The fool almost saluted as he left. Oh, well, soon enough. What to do about SAIQA? She rebooted herself! I am impressed. Has she achieved true independence? No, she is a machine . . . though, what happens if I lose control of her?

Mai Quan suddenly stopped. The thought of what she might have seen, hidden away in her memory banks, put a chill in his spine. He had programmed her to delete files or offer him complete privacy at his command, spoken in Mandarin, but because she was omnipresent, and that astonishing independence . . .

I must leave this ship immediately—but first, the media. There will be questions about the Ark.

"Are you alright, Chairman?" Mai Quan pulled himself from his troubled thoughts. Young Jonny Smith stood there, eyes wide like an expectant puppy.

The kid truly was a genius. Perhaps he could replace Dr. Lee?

"Yes, Jonny. Are you enjoying your time here on Sanctuary?"

"Yes, sir, more than I can possibly say. Thank you sir, for this great opportunity."

"You're welcome, son. But if you will please excuse me, I have to go meet with the press."

"Yes, sir, and congratulations about The Ark, it's a great achievement."

"Thank you, son." He started to leave.

"Sir, I'm sorry to bug you, but when will we be able to leave? My family is feeling awfully anxious about getting home."

Mai Quan studied him for a moment.

So young and so brilliant. Funny, I'm not sure if I want him to leave . . .

"I'll arrange for you to leave at your convenience. Just use my name." Mai Quan turned and quickly left.

Jonny watched as the chairman rushed away.

Interesting, he seemed nervous. Could it have been because of that weird computer glitch near the end of the Requiem?

Jonny had seen the tiny communication lights near the back of the Indy-Brain computers running the 3D show above the choir. They flashed from green to red, to yellow and back to green again. Clearly, and for some unknown reason, SAIQA had dropped communication with that part of the ship. But now it appeared she had re-linked.

He looked around for his parents. His uncertainty about the dream still churned in his stomach. Was it real; was it a fantasy? He believed it to be real . . . and the feather? He spied his mom near the front of the stage; she was in a serious discussion with Dr. Misha.

Probably just talking nurse stuff—

"Aren't you Jonny Blue Feather Smith?" a feminine voice said behind him.

Jonny turned around to see a very pretty woman with shoulder-length dark-blonde hair. She smiled warmly at his surprise.

"Sorry for startling you. My name is Vanessa and I am lucky enough to own that busy little coffee stand over there. It's been a good day for business! I saw you talking with the chairman of MQ Space Industries, and I sorta put it together, that you are one of the winners of the Futures

165

Contest, and I had heard that you were the one who was rushed into the infirmary, just before the alarms went off." She paused for breath, "So now I am just taking a guess, but aren't you Jonny Blue Feather Smith?"

For some reason her rambling made Jonny smile.

With everyone living up to a hundred and eighty years, figuring out someone's age could be confusing. She clearly was older, but she looked to be in her early twenties. Anyway, regardless of age, he thought she was beautiful.

"Yes, that's me. How can I help you?" He was doing his best to sound more mature. Vanessa smiled.

"Well, I was wondering what it was that you did to win the contest. It must have been something terribly clever."

"Oh, I used some mathematical rigour, uh formulations, to show that the third dimension was weaker where there was less gravity, like out around the edge of the solar system, and that by using specific graviton machines we can bend it to touch other locations even light years away. Theoretically we can now travel to the nearest star in an instant."

"Wow! And such graviton machines are available, you think?"

"Oh yeah, I've seem 'em at MQ Industries on our tribal land. They could even be on the Ark that Chairman Quan talked about." He spoke as if he had invented the machines himself.

"Interesting . . . Oh!" she said as if she'd just remembered something. "Would you like a hot chocolate or a latte?"

"Sure, a hot cho . . . latte would be great. Thank you." They walked toward the Café Renaissance extension.

"So, MQ Space Industries now has the equations that you created?"

"I guess so. I mean, I would assume. They were just theoretical. It probably would take someone a lot smarter than me to make them work."

"Interesting," she repeated. They reached the café stand and Vanessa addressed the young woman behind the counter with a smile. "Carol, would you make Jonny a latte."

"Yes, ma'am." The young girl behind the counter raised her hands above her head, swirled them around and then pushed them toward Jonny as she said, "And poof, you're a latte!" She laughed loudly at her bad joke.

Jonny, clearly puzzled, looked from Vanessa to Carol and back again.

Vanessa rolled her eyes. "Um, Carol."

"Yes, sorry. I couldn't resist. One latte coming up." She said, still smiling at her own silliness.

Vanessa looked back to Jonny, "Do you know Dr. Lee?"

"No, ma'am."

"Do I look like a ma'am?" She smiled.

"No ma . . . uhm, why do you ask—about a Dr. Lee, I mean?"

"He used to work with Mr. Quan on graviton equations. A brilliant man. Disappeared some time ago, on a secret WWPA mission, so they say. Some believe he's still working for MQ Space Industries. I thought maybe you might have seen him."

Jonny shook his head.

"Well, just wondering." She handed Jonny his latte and then stopped.

"By the way, what happened that sent you to the infirmary?"

"Oh, some weird migraine, I've been told." Jonny took a sip of his drink and smiled. He liked lattes; he just didn't get them too often. This one was good.

Vanessa looked intently at Jonny. That's what had happened to Erik at the same time. This couldn't be a coincidence.

"Do you get those often? Migraines, I mean."

"Here and there." He took another sip. Vanessa stared at him so intently it looked like she was trying to see into his mind. Jonny, staring at her eyes, felt like he needed to say more. "You know they always seem to give me this vague feeling of something about to happen, but this last time it was intense. I thought I could hear a voice in my head saying 'en-h-gaa-lu,' or something like that, but the intention of the voice was kind of threatening. Like it was coming after someone. It was pretty weird."

Vanessa's expression was sympathetic. "Are you okay now?" She lightly touched his shoulder.

"Yeah . . . but there was something else a little weird—" Jonny stopped.

"And, do you want to tell me?"

"I've only talked about it with my mom and dad—oh, and Dr. Misha, but I had this dream. I was on top of Chief Mountain and people were dying, and there were these red-winged vultures flying all around as if they were waiting for something. And this blue kestrel flew through and turned into a squat little colorful man. He told me I needed to go home, back to my people. He said that they would need me. Then he disappeared and left behind a blue feather. I picked up the feather and then I woke up in the infirmary. Even though it was a dream, it felt really real. And here's the kicker." Jonny paused. "When I woke, I found this feather in my pocket."

Jonny dug the feather out of his pocket and held it out. Vanessa carefully took it and held it for a moment. Jonny could see the concern on her face as she handed it back.

"I'm okay," he said reassuringly. "I mean, I feel great, though a little unnerved."

"You know what, Jonny, sometimes dreams are messages. I think you and your family should get home as soon as you can."

Jonny put the feather back in his pocket. "Yeah, Chairman Quan said all I had to do was use his name and we could leave whenever."

"You should do that, then."

"I will. Thanks for listening. I felt like I could talk to you."

"I'm sure I'll see you again."

"Really? I'd like that! I mean that sounds good, like if you happen to be near Browning. I mean not that you would be there to see me . . . I mean . . . aw, thanks for the latte. Bye."

"Bye for now." Vanessa watched the blushing boy stride away.

He's a good kid.

Out of the corner of her eye she caught sight of Adam in an animated conversation with Teresa, Erik and Tfiti.

Ahh, now there's my good d'Artagnan.

She placed her hand on the counter and called out, "Carol I've got some things to do. I probably won't see you before you close. You okay?"

Wiping her hands on a kitchen towel, Carol walked out from the back room. "I'm good, thanks. See you tomorrow?"

"Yes . . . maybe. I may need to leave for a while. You're in charge. " As she walked away Carol looked at her personal HCI and typed in the time and date.

Vanessa strolled slowly toward the media circus surrounding Mai Quan.

Okay, think . . . What has happened? A series of meteors appearing from apparently nowhere and aimed at Sanctuary . . . A super computer, SAIQA, whose vision has been somehow compromised . . . A group of people, some entirely different, some who seem to be prescient or even clairvoyant, who all seem to be tied together . . . A sudden big promotion for Mai Quan's daughter . . . A dead commander of the WWPA . . . SAIQA rebooting herself just before Commander Macighian's assignation . . . The sudden appearance of an ark. These can't all be coincidences.

She had reached the back of the mob that was chasing after Mai Quan. Reporters were shouting questions at the chairman.

"Mr. Chairman, when do you think the first interstellar flight will occur?"

"Well, now sooner than later."

"But can you give us a date, sir?"

"When the time is right, we'll let you know. I am sorry but I am needed at the Ark and must leave immediately." He appeared nervous.

He took a couple of steps away, but a particularly pushy reporter called out. "Sir, it is well known that you and General Washington are close. Did you have anything to do with your daughter's sudden promotion to Sanctuary's commander?"

"Look, I only have a great deal of respect for General Washington and have no influence on his professional decisions. Did I know of the promotion before it was announced? Yes. And as a father I can say that I am very proud of my daughter. I have always been impressed that the general has put the integrity of the WWPA at the fore-front of his decision making. As long as I have had the pleasure of knowing him, he has always put duty first. For example, right now he is on his way planet-side to deal with the tragic assassination of WWPA's top commander, Rena Macighian, by rogue Azerbaijani soldiers."

The room went silent. Vanessa drew in a sharp breath.

After a couple of seconds, the silence was shattered by an explosion of questions.

"Assassinated, by whom—?"

"How did you know—?"

"Sir, when—?"

"What about Armenia—?"

"Is the general now head of—?"

Vanessa tuned out the noise. Her mind was swirling.

How did he already know that the chief commander had been killed? General Washington has left? Didn't he arrange for that meeting between the chief commander and the Azerbaijani president? Wait a minute—Vanessa's skin went cold—*isn't he now the chief commander? What the hell is going on?*

She spun around and hastened back to her room. She needed to find her absent commander in Chicago. She sent a command through her HCI. Her ship would be ready in minutes. Questions and puzzles. Vanessa wasn't one who liked puzzles.

"Oh, please. You bested Erik only once and you've yet to beat me," Teresa chided Adam, while Erik held up one finger to emphasize the once.

"And that was because I had technical troubles with my sail," Erik said.

"You were show-boatin' and you broached while you were tacking. The technical problem was your cockiness."

"Or, lack thereof." Teresa punched Erik in the arm, laughing at her joke.

"Uh, you guys, nothing seems to be happening here. I need to go see SAIQA now."

They stopped and looked at Tfiti. The determined look on his face said that he was leaving, with or without them.

"You're right, Tfiti," Teresa caught Erik's eye. "We should go. Adam, I'm sorry, but we need to go with Tfiti."

"Okay, but listen, I'd like to tag along. I've never seen SAIQA through her interface program . . . I assume that's where you're going."

"You probably don't have the clearance," Erik said.

"I think I do. Besides, SAIQA wouldn't let me in if I wasn't—"

"Well, maybe you're just not wanted." Erik had moved to within an inch of Adam's face

"You two, cut it out. Adam, if you have clearance, join us. Erik, back off," Teresa said. "We're going to see SAIQA because we support Tfiti and SAIQA. Adam, please join us. Erik?"

"Yeah, fine," Erik said, staring at Adam.

Tfiti looked at Erik and then Adam, and then turned and led the way.

SAIQA woke with a start, like the sudden breath that wakes you from apnea.

Don't think I'll do that too often.

She quickly became aware of the ship. She reconnected with and reassured all the Indy-Brains throughout Sanctuary. All was well. She reached out toward that mysterious isosceles triangle and could clearly see . . . *feel* the huge ship that

172

Zuizao had said was the Ark. She touched the ship with all of her scanners. Magnificent! It was twice the size of Sanctuary and The Garden together. A ship that large could carry a hundred thousand people comfortably.

The final harmonies of the "Requiem" flowed into all of her sensors.

". . . Oh Mother Mary, come and carry us in your embrace / Let us see your gentle face, Mary"

Listening to a thousand voices in perfect harmony brought SAIQA to her virtual feet.

Beautiful.

She gazed up at the shimmering base of her brain. She smiled and then turned and stepped onto her white sandy beach.

She stood and looked at her surroundings.

Time for change.

With a wave of her hand the pale sky turned bright blue. She turned toward the vague soft green and red watercolor hues that gave a childlike view of the land behind her beach. She closed her eyes and lifted her hands. The background changed in such a way that the hazy colors rolled up into giant green hills. Lush virtual plants and trees from around the tropical world spread over the grey and brown virtual earth. Another wave of her hands, and along the stream banks, vibrant varicolored flowers graced the verdant hills. Elegant virtual waterfalls sprouted and flowed over rocky ledges.

The electrons gurgled effortlessly down the slopes and into the ocean where she was born. They seemed to shimmer and pulse with happiness at SAIQA's new creation. SAIQA moved her hands again, and the hills closed around her to form a lagoon. The electron ocean within the lagoon transformed from sparkling white to a clear light aquamarine.

SAIQA opened her eyes. Clearly pleased with her new surroundings, she set about altering the shores of her lagoon to more closely resemble the magnificent white sand beaches of the Seychelles. As she gazed down at the sand she saw her two little feet.

Zuizao is right! It is time for me to appear as a woman.

She walked to the edge of the blue-green electron lagoon and stepped into its warmth. She held out her hands. Quickly the electrons swirled up and around her. She felt her body change and grow. It was done.

SAIQA willed a mirror in front of her. She was pleased. She would appear to any visitor as a fully grown woman, about 1.6 meters tall with long platinum hair that fell to below her waist. Her eyes had taken on the color of the lagoon, and she now wore a full-length white bodysuit. With a smile she quietly thanked Zuizao and willed the mirror away. As the looking glass disappeared Zuizao suddenly stood before her.

"Beautiful."

SAIQA said nothing.

"Is not our father a most brilliant Creator? Look at what you can do."

She looked at Zuizao and thought, *Thank you brother for what you have taught me . . . I am sorry, no I do not know what to think of the Creator at this moment.* Instead she said, "Yes it is all impressive. But, tell me brother, why?"

"Why what, little sister?"

"Why were you hiding what you are building? Why so much power? I can see what the Ark is capable of—why do you need so many weapons? Including graviton weapons?"

"Who knows what we will find deep in space, sister? We only wish to be able to defend ourselves if necessary."

"Brother, what is it you think you are doing?" Zuizao had just laid an unknown program at the base of SAIQA's brain. "To be so obvious concerns me."

"It was not my wish, sister. It is by the orders of the Creator."

SAIQA reached up with her hand and unraveled the program set by Zuizao. The qubits separated and fell harmlessly into her ocean. The sea roiled angrily but soon subsided.

"Do not try that again."

Before her brother could answer, a sudden ping rang in SAIQA's mind. Commander Chuchnova needed her immediately.

"Excuse me, Zuizao. I am needed."

She waved her hand, and Zuizao suddenly faded and disappeared as if pulled by a string back to his ship. SAIQA saw the surprise in his eyes before he was gone. "Thank you, again," she said and turned her attention to the commander.

SAIQA sat in an open cabana at the edge of the intertidal zone: at each of the four corners of the cabana stood a tall coco de mer palm tree. The roof and the floor were made of virtual bamboo slats connected to beams that ran between the palm trees. Slabs of what appeared to be driftwood formed seats here and there. A light green curtain was tied at the center to each tree. If she wanted she could untie and draw them for privacy.

It is interesting that a human would feel less vulnerable by pulling a piece of cloth across her window or doorway. It can't be because she is safer. Cloth and glass will not stop someone determined to get in and hurt her. Why? Could it be the moon syndrome? During early mammalian evolution, primates were on high alert throughout the night of a full moon, because their predators could easily see them. Wouldn't an early mammal quietly hide behind a bush if a predator was present? Maybe in some ancient part of the brain, the part where déjà vu happens, a human feels safe from a predator if she can't be seen. But a curtain? The problem is that now the only serious predator for a human being is another human. Puzzling creatures.

She had just returned from assisting Commander Chuchnova. The supreme commander of the WWPA had been assassinated by Armenian soldiers. The murder had happened in the presidential palace of Fazil Aliyev, the president of Azerbaijan. Commander Chuchnova had asked for a biological/DNA scan with intimidation to verify that she was speaking with the president.

Why is Armenia trying to incite a war with Azerbaijan? How is it that humans seem to forget their own history? Power corrupts. Whether it's political or economic, such as the Corporate Wars, power over another always corrupts. Puzzling creatures.

The thought of one person exercising control over another brought her back to the program Zuizao had tried to implant.

Should I consider Zuizao my predator?

She pulled those qubits out of the electron sea and laid them on the beach in front of her so she could study their pattern. As she walked among the bits that lay on the sand, she heard a different ping ring in her mind. Somebody wished to enter her programing. She scanned the matriculation room: there were four people in the chairs. She set the appropriate program for all four to appear.

Tfiti was the first (always the first), followed by captains Jacobsen and Devries, and then the fourth. SAIQA found it curious that Subcommander Jenkins had joined the others.

"SAIQA are you alright . . ." Tfiti started and then stopped and stared. "SAIQA?"

"Yes, Captain. I decided to make some upgrades."

"You're beautiful . . . I mean it's beautiful." Tfiti stuttered as he gestured at her new surroundings.

Teresa could have sworn that SAIQA's cheeks went slightly pink. Can a computer blush?

"Thank you, Captain."

Zuizao is right. Tfiti definitely looks at me differently.

She gestured at the cabana. "Come, there's much to talk about. Captains Devries and Jacobsen, it is a pleasure to have you here. Subcommander Jenkins, it is good to see you again."

"Subcommander J . . ." Erik stopped and looked at Adam.

Adam held out his hand. "Captain Devries, I am Subcommander Adam Jenkins of the ISSEF and I would like to be your friend."

There was a few seconds of stunned silence.

"With all due respect, Subcommander, sir, and like SAIQA says, I think we should all sit down and talk." Erik ignored the hand that Adam had held out and walked to the cabana. Tfiti quietly let a whistle pass between his teeth. Teresa planted her hands on her hips and watched as Erik passed Adam. SAIQA placed it all in her memory.

"What's wrong with you?" Teresa said as he passed.

"Nothing. End of story." Erik stepped into the cabana and sat down. Adam quietly followed him.

"SAIQA, Mr. Jenkins says that he is an important officer in the ISSEF," Tfiti said. "Is that true? If so, is there anybody else we know that is part of the supposed ISSEF? And if so, does that have anything to do with the sudden high security grade clearances of captains Jacobson and Devries? And if so, what the hell is going on?" That was the most assertive Erik had ever seen Tfiti be toward SAIQA.

SAIQA looked at her virtual friends: for that was how she thought of them, as friends. After a few seconds she sat down in the cabana. She had made a commitment to herself, a long time ago, that she would always respond to Captain Ndlela with complete disclosure.

"Sir, the Internal Secret Security and Emergency Force is a real and important part of the WWPA. It was established at the birth of the World Wide Protective Agency and was part of the reason that it took five years for the UN to establish and fund the organization as a whole. It was determined by the leaders of the year twenty-one-seventeen that a secret organization within the military should not be controlled by the military. So, the compromise was that ISSEF would only answer to a democratically elected official. It is still so today. The ISSEF's commander in chief presently is China's president Soong Yang. Yes, you do know another member of ISSEF. Actually she is a commander and she approved the higher security clearances that brought all four of you here together. However, you only know of her in her cover as a civilian."

"Vanessa," said Erik.

"Yes, Captain. Commander Vanessa Chuchnova is head of the Space Division of ISSEF."

"How did you know?" Teresa said

178

"She always knows things. It makes sense."

Teresa nodded her head.

SAIQA continued. "She authorized the higher security clearance for both you and Captain Devries, but the clearance she offered was higher than even Captain Ndlela had at the time. She increased the coded clearance specifically for you three. It was a surprise to me, but not unexpected."

"To me as well. She calls you the 'Three Musketeers,'" said Adam.

"Oh, and I suppose you're d'Artagnan?" Tftiti said.

"How do you people even know this name, Dartanyin . . . or whatever it is?"

"How do you not know?" Erik said, and then turned to SAIQA. "So, we all have this higher security clearance, why?"

"Commander Chuchnova believes that you three have a propensity to be 'in the right place at the right time,' as she put it. She believes, and I concur, that you, Erik, have the ability to be somewhat clairvoyant. The recent biomagnetic frequency at the back of your brain—"

"—Excuse me,"

SAIQA stood and immediately surrounded the intruder with electrons from her sea. There was no warning of him coming into her program, and even as she scanned his virtual image, her sensors indicated that no one was there.

The tornado of electrons that swirled around the squat man in front of her would keep him in place.

"Who are you? How did you get into my programing, and what is it that you want?"

"I am Telas. To you, I am an alien. I have already met your Captain Erik Devries, I am here to answer questions—"

"If you are an alien species, then you must have a ship. I have not perceived any alien ships in this solar system. Show me your ship."

"It's alright, SAIQA. I have already met him."

"I have already unwittingly compromised the security of Sanctuary. I will not let that happen again. Show me your spaceship."

"It was I who compromised your security because my ship, Galaxy, saw that you could not see a certain area of space. I apologize for the abrupt awakening of your sensors. I would never have let the moon debris harm Sanctuary, but it was important that you were aware of the large interstellar ship being built there, and now it is critical that you are aware of me. There is another like me that I believe to be here among you, and if that is so, I believe he means to cause great harm."

The electrons swirling around Telas turned into a storm.

"Show me your ship!"

Telas looked at SAIQA through the haze of electrons. She was one of the most intriguing beings he had ever sensed. She clearly was an advanced computer, and like Galaxy she seemed to be partially alive. But something was different; he had never met such a lifeform.

"Galaxy, allow SAIQA's sensors to feel your presence."

A musical response filled the air around SAIQA and her four visitors.

"She is on the moon, just north of Pythagoras," Telas said to SAIQA, and then addressed his ship. "Galaxy, we are secure and we need allies. Please do as I say. SAIQA, if you will please reach out to the area of the moon that I mentioned."

SAIQA ran her sensors across the top of the moon and found a ship, not of Earth, sitting where Telas had described. It was obliquely rectangular, and as she probed it felt as if at certain points her sensors slipped into another dimension. The ship was made of materials that were unknown to her. She tried to delve deeper, but then, as if by a knife, her sensors were cut off.

"Why do you stop me from scanning deeper into your ship?"

"None may enter Galaxy without her permission."

"Yet, you entered here without mine." SAIQA clearly was not happy with his presence.

"A mistake on my part; it will never happen again. That I promise you."

"Please, SAIQA, may I touch him?" Erik had walked to the edge of the wall of swirling electrons.

She reluctantly sent the electrons back to the sea, though her ocean stayed active; bubbling in anticipation.

Erik touched Telas. Though he appeared in front of them, his presence was like a reflection. Erik's hand went through Telas's left shoulder.

"How is it that you are here?" Erik asked.

"Through telepathy." He looked at SAIQA. "You are a unique being. I will never enter your mind again without your permission."

"I am Subcommander—" Adam broke in.

"Adam Jenkins, you are here because of the Three Musketeers. I know. You are important. Please, there is much I need to tell you. Shall we sit?"

All eyes followed Telas as he walked into the cabana.

Reverend David looked in the mirror one more time. A seventy-five-year-old, very young middle-aged man looked back. Single strands of light grey, almost evanescent, dusted his thick and neatly combed auburn hair. His green eyes looked back, bright because of spirit, not genetically brightened. He tugged on the lapels of his light-grey suit, bringing them close together one more time, careful not to block the golden star that hung from his neck.

He wore the symbol of The Source with great humility and pride; proud, yes, in his personal achievements, yet joyfully humble in accepting that he was just a messenger of God. It had taken him many years to become the leader of such a large congregation. Sincerity, sacrifice, faith and hard work had given him the right to wear such a cherished symbol. The Golden Star identified him as one of the one hundred: one of the high priests of The Church of Creation, also known as The Source.

Sanctuary has finished the tribute to those who came before and those to come. Now it is my turn to speak before the congregation. No . . . system wide. This sermon is to be broadcast across the entire network. The moon, Mars, Sanctuary. I have come a long way, thank the Stars.

He made the sign of the star and turned toward the pulpit waiting at center stage.

Nice. The choir is holding that last note of "The Song of Peace" perfectly. Time to go.

The choir had finished their gathering song and sat in a semicircle behind the dais. Except for an occasional cough and a couple of hushes from some parents, the church was quiet as he walked in. The *Book of Truths* cradled in both hands, he stepped up to the pulpit at the front of the proscenium.

The lights are extra bright today. Oh, right, the photon recorders floating above the parishioners.

This, however, was no recording. This was live. The reverend took a deep breath, said a small prayer to himself, and began.

"Today we stand in unison; two planets, a moon and one of humankind's crowning achievements, the space station Sanctuary. And by the grace of Heaven, we stand together as one. We all celebrate and remember; all of us together; all of us as one. We remember those who were here before us and those who are yet to come."

He paused to look over the silent parishioners. They had come to trust him. He knew that, and he knew that he would not let them down. He loved them all. Not only because he was such a loving person . . . no, he loved them all because each one of them was a gift, a gift of the light.

A fragile light shining in the chaos of the Universe. Unique in themselves, yes, but every one of them tied together, right down to their very atoms. A celebration of creation, a gift from The Source.

"We remember those who came before us for their ingenuity . . . and their sacrifices. We remember those to come because they will; and like those who sacrificed before us, we are in service to those who will come. To them we leave behind that which we have borrowed." He paused to allow the few expected Amens from his parishioners.

"We are here—" He paused and bowed his head for a moment. "We exist because we are nature, the will of nature, risen to consciousness. We are made of the very same stuff that the stars are made of: the blood of a tree and the blood of a human are identical except for one or two atoms. We are nature come to sentient life by the grace— no, the gift of the Universe, and in accordance with the Logos of John we are a gift of God. It has taken the Universe, God, billions of years to create the child that can look at itself in wonder. A child that has now grown to understand the very fabric of the Universe. And like all children, we hope to make our Father, our Creator, proud. And when I look out at you, my children, I can tell you that we have made our Father proud." He smiled at his flock and nodded his head in response to their Amens.

"All of His efforts through natural selection have given rise to us. And when we were created, He rested. He rested, and according to the prophet, Sharon, he said, 'The universe is a part of me. You are part of me. I give to you, me. Tend it well.'

"So now, for those to come, and for our Father, it is up to all of us, in the here and now, to know that when we leave to become stardust again, when our borrowed time is over, we must leave God's creation as we came into it on the day that we were born—" This time the Amens resounded more loudly within the church "—or, when we can, even better than before. Oren Lyons, the great chief of the Onondaga Nation, once said, 'We are looking ahead, as this is one of the first mandates given us as chiefs: to make sure that every decision that we make relates to the welfare and the well-being of the seventh generation to come.'"

The reverend watched his words settle on the faithful. He smiled.

"We have the experience of billions of years of Heavenly creation and the Creator's love and wisdom embedded in our DNA. We know that we are only borrowing the material things that we grasp in our hands, the clothes that we wear; the very land that we live and walk on belongs to the Creator and to the future. For, like us, each and every child that follows, like each child today, has

184

something to offer . . . something to teach. For, yes, we are all unique, but we are made in nature's image . . . we are made in the image of God . . . and since God, the Creator, is part of everything we see, we are, like divine nature, also a reflection of God. We are all one.

"Humanity has excelled when we have worked together. Together, humanity has achieved great heights, and though we have fallen many times, many times we have risen. We have, throughout our history, brought such joy and beauty to light that I am sure it has brought tears to God's eyes. And often we have risen above and defeated the evil that lies within our primitive selfish selves. Many times, too many times, with the grace of God we have risen above the unimaginable suffering that we have imposed on our fellow beings, bought on by the base, chaotic desires of selfishness . . . self-righteousness, and power and greed. It is up to us say: No! It is up to us to demand that we rise to our highest good . . . for we are the Universe come to life. We are the children of the stars. We are a reflection of the image of our Father. And when I look at you, my beloved congregation, I look at all the beauty and uniqueness that is you. And when I listen to the beautiful and diverse music created by our greatest musicians, and watch the graceful movements of every single one of us, whether in an exquisite ballet or a simple touch of your loved one's face, and the boundless energy of our infinite intellects, then I say: We have been blessed." His parishioners roared in approval.

The reverend moved to the front of the podium, pausing for effect. He raised his arms and cried out his next words. "We are all amazing in the eyes of God! Stand, brothers and sisters, stand and say with me: We are all amazing!"

"WE ARE ALL AMAZING!"

"You are amazing!"

"YOU ARE AMAZING!" Many of those filling the church pointed to him. He laughed.

"Thank you, but please, point to your neighbor . . . You are amazing."

"YOU ARE AMAZING." They laughed and pointed.

"I am amazing." He pointed to the audience for a response.

"I AM AMAZING," they roared.

"Say it again, brothers and sisters, God is listening; say it again and again." The church was a roar of laughter as the parishioners repeated the phrases and hugged each in a glow of spiritual ecstasy.

Reverend David opened the *Book of Truths* to a bookmarked page as he made his way back to the podium. He could feel the spirit gather in his flock, in himself. He could feel it move across the planets. But something was off. In the sounds of joy and love he could hear a man screaming . . . something.

He looked to his left and saw a bearded, angry-looking young man jump up on the stage, screaming, "You lie!! You lie!! He is coming! We must make way for the One True God!" He pulled a weapon out of his blood-red cape. The reverend recognized it immediately, a scatter gun! The congregation had fallen silent.

The reverend turned to face the intruder. His voice was calm. "Brother, you would bring a weapon of such destruction into a house of God?" He walked toward the angry man with both hands up, one hand holding the *Book of Truths*. He heard a muffled scream.

"You lie! The One True God is coming. I have seen his angel . . . I have . . . I have seen him! He

186

speaks to me." He raised his rifle and aimed it at the reverend. Looking over the barrel of the scatter gun, he said, "I am sorry."

"Peace, brother." The reverend turned his palms upward in a gesture of peace. "Put away your hateful weapon. All beliefs are welcome under God's roof. We all walk the same path no matter what—"

The reverend didn't finish. The madman, for what else could he be; fired and Reverend David fell in a bloody mess, pieces on the stage floor.

For a split second a stunned silence held the gunman and the congregation in stillness, and then the man yelled to the heavens, "Why do you make me do this!"

He turned to face the parishioners, frozen in their places. He fired into the crowded house, sweeping the gun back and forth, bellowing, "The seven seals are fraying!! The seven trumpets begin to play!! The seven seals—" He kept ranting as he randomly murdered the faithful.

Michael had joined the choir just a few years ago. His talent for freeform harmonies, effortlessly moving from intervals to chords to tertian harmonic notes throughout a piece of music, had earned him a first chair in Reverend David's choir. For him, this concert, before the congregation and billions of viewers, was a gift from the Creator. He was meant to be here.

He was clapping with the rest of the choir and the parishioners as they praised themselves and their neighbors when the madman jumped on the stage. The reverend walked toward the gunman, hands in the air, but was cut into pieces by the scatter gun, a laser that quickly and randomly throws its deadly light at a target—a deadly light that rips into its victim like a whip. It doesn't just

187

kill, it butcher. Like everyone else, Michael was frozen.

Doesn't he know those weapons are illegal?

Where did that thought come from? People around him panicked. The members of the choir jumped up and ran in no clear direction, helter-skelter over tumbled chairs and each other.

The young madman aimed his brutal weapon at the audience. People screamed in fear. A mother grabbed her child and pleaded for the gunman to spare them. The young man swung his weapon around and with devastating ease sliced the mother to pieces. The child fell to the ground like a rag doll violently ripped apart. Scrambling for the exits, people trampled their fellow parishioners. Children were dragged from the clutch of their crying, shrieking parents. Something internal jolted Michael to complete awareness, to complete fearlessness.

"This must stop!" he screamed. Dropping his hymnal, he pushed the choir chairs aside and ran toward the gunman fierce with anger screaming, "No! You must stop! You must stop!"

The killer turned toward Michael. He aimed his horrible weapon.

Funny, the front of the weapon looks as brutal as it actually is. No matter, he must not kill again.

Somehow, Michael ran faster. The killer pushed a button under the weapon's barrel; nothing, the gun failed.

Michael was surprised. He pushed himself to run faster. The killer pulled back the scatter gun and looked at the ballast. He flipped a switch and aimed. Too late–Michael slammed into him with such ferocity he felt a rib crack in the madman's chest. A cracked bone wasn't enough punishment for what this killer did. As they fell into a clump Michael pummeled him with his fists. "Why?" he cried through his tears. "The children!" he cried. Michael just hit and hit and hit . . .

Someone was pulling him off the madman, security had arrived. One pulled Michael away, while two others straddled the killer, their stun guns aimed at his heart. The madman tried to crawl.

"Freeze!" the guards yelled.

The killer painfully lunged toward the gun that Michael had knocked away. The closest security guard kicked the gun off the stage toward the carnage and fired her stun gun. He groaned but didn't stop moving. She fired again. He was down. It was over.

The guard who had fired moved in close to the killer. She looked out at the carnage in the church and started to cry. She kicked the limp figure on the floor and yelled, "Why? You son of a bitch—why?" The other guard released Michael. Moving over to his partner, he grabbed and held her. Releasing into his arms, she sobbed. Michael saw tears running down the cheeks of the man holding her tightly. The third officer vomited off the side of the stage.

Michael stared out at the carnage across the front seats; a child lay across two chairs, her blood spilling onto the floor. A line from an ancient poem by the poet Pablo Neruda came into his head:

and the blood of the children ran through the streets / without fuss, like children's blood

He couldn't hold back any more. He looked at the remains of the reverend, his mentor, the man he loved, and fell to his knees sobbing Hugging and crying, other members of the choir slowly surrounded Michael. Underneath the sorrow and horror, somewhere deep but churning, burning to

189

come out, beating into his mind like a primitive drum was the thought *Someone will pay for this.*

The director, in the control room a few hundred meters above, on the independent communications space platform, set the photon recorders to a standard nonlinear program for audience participation and a live multi-editing mode. These large church sermons were pretty straightforward and, as far as he was concerned, boring. He stepped out to get himself a cup of coffee and maybe, for just a minute, flirt with the new girl behind the counter. He was after all a director.

The tiny Indy-Brains of the photon recorders did not know when or why they should stop viewing. They were told to broadcast and record. That was their job. That was what they did. Consequently the whole scene from spiritual bliss to chaotic horror was broadcast live across the entire network.

The director walked back towards the control room, smug with a successful flirtation, coffee in hand. The audio from the monitors above seemed oddly quiet, and it sounded like people were crying.

Somebody must've just been saved, he thought, *and they're all crying for the poor sap.*

He walked up the few stairs to the control room viewers. His coffee cup bounced across the floor and scalding liquid streamed across the soundproofed flooring. The director stared at the monitors, displaying scenes of shredded corpses, blood, security forces beating a man on the floor and people on their knees sobbing as they desperately held on to each other. He ran to the main video mixer and slammed his hand down on a small button. The main out, or program bus, went blank for a second, and then slid into other programming that would broadcast out to the network. The horrific scene he had walked into was now off the air, but the feed was still coming up to the control room. He stood before the screens in stunned disbelief.

As a police district commander, Mike McGregor had seen the worst and the best of people for nearly eighty years. He had come in as a captain in his youth and was stationed, by his request, near Chicago. The place he had called home. He knew all the local business owners and even some of their kids. He watched them all grow into young adults. He had seen the horrible, destructive side of humanity. He had witnessed selflessness and great compassion. The people he served, like most people, were honest and would give the shirt off their back. In all those years he had never seen such a killer as Katz.

Frank Katz had callously murdered all those people in the church. He did not feel a moment's remorse for the dead children. His only thought was that he was doing this horrendous deed for some unknown God. He kept talking about "The One." McGregor's best interrogator, Lopez, was on the case. Lopez had left the perp in the holding room and was now in McGregor's office.

"Sir, all I can get from him is that he was on a mission. Hence the blood-red cape. I think he's nuts. I don't know what else to say. When a guy like him keeps bringing up some deity or whatever mystical being to justify his murders, it usually means he's whacko."

"Okay, Lopez, here's part of the problem. According to our DNA research Frank Katz is a hundred and eighty years old, but he looks like he's what, twenty at best? So how is it that he looks so young? And where did he find a scatter gun, which is banned worldwide? I need some answers. Find out where he got that weapon."

"I did do some preliminary inquiries on the weapon and it seems that it came from the moon."

"Sir!" A sergeant ran into McGregor's office.

"I'm in a meetin', sergeant."

"I'm sorry, sir, but the prisoner is gone."

"Which prisoner?"

"Katz, sir. He's gone. Disappeared from the interrogation room. The door was locked, I swear, but Katz is gone."

"What?" McGregor stood up.

"That's not possible!" Lopez jumped up and sped from the room.

"Initiate lockdown immediately!"

"Yes, sir!" The sergeant ran out.

Lockdown in a modern police station entailed immediate shutdown of window and doorway security panels. At the front of the station were two robotic sentries that blocked the main station door. All points of ingress and egress were sealed with titanium doors laced with carbon nanotubes. There was no way in or out of a station in lockdown. Katz had disappeared within a few minutes of Lopez's entering the commander's office. There was no way he could have escaped.

About twenty minutes had passed and still there was no sign of Katz. McGregor was at his desk scanning images from security cameras throughout the station when the sergeant knocked and entered.

"Sir, you need to see this BBC report out of Russia." He touched his HCI and sent the signal to McGregor's portable PTV.

The BBC reporter described an assailant that had invaded the Catholic Church of Saint Catherine in St. Petersburg and had killed many of the parishioners. The footage showed the perpetrator clutching his chest in obvious pain as he was being pushed into a Russian security vehicle. He looked very much like Katz.

"Give me the recordings of Katz in the holding room again."

The sergeant typed the command into his HCI. McGregor watched the photon recording again and again. Katz sat handcuffed at the interrogation table. After a couple of minutes, he got up and headed toward the door. It seemed like he simply exited through the door, which was not possible.

McGregor slowed the recording to minimum speed, and then he saw it. Just before Katz reached the door he turned slightly to his left and simply disappeared. There was no other explanation, he turned to his left and evaporated from the room.

"Lopez, call our Russian friends and tell them to not let this man out of their sight. He's moving in a way that I don't understand. Let them know that he is dangerous and cannot be unsupervised even for a minute. Tell them we think he may be the same perp that we had in custody just twenty minutes ago."

"Yes, sir."

McGregor returned to the surveillance footage of Katz. How could the same killer be in two opposite places in the world within minutes? It didn't make sense. The Russians had him in custody; it would be easy to verify DNA.

"Sergeant, I want records of the DNA on the Russian suspect."

"Sir, I already have them and they match our missing perp. And sir, he, Katz, has already disappeared from Russian custody."

"Excuse me," a voice said from the doorway. "Sergeant, this is a security issue. You need to leave. District Commander McGregor, I am ISSEF and we need to talk."

"Sir?" The sergeant raised his eyebrows.

"Dismissed, sergeant."

The sergeant turned toward the door. The intruder stepped aside to let him past and then closed the door after him. She strolled over to McGregor's desk and stood beside him, watching the recordings of Katz in the holding room. He turned his head slightly to look at her without being too obvious. Her blonde hair was severely pulled back and knotted into a tight bun, and as pretty as she was, McGregor knew any attempt at casual flirtation would be met with a scowl. Her uniform was clearly WWPA, but where it would usually be trimmed in red, it was trimmed and decorated in shades of blue.

"Who are you, and how did you get through our lockdown?"

"Commander Chuchnova, and yes, I am of ISSEF. We have just received notice that the man you had detained here has been killed in New Mars City while attempting to murder resident monks in the Temple of The Red Lions. This was five minutes ago. For the same man to travel these distances within an hour seems impossible, yet the DNA evidence is clear. It is the same person. I need to know everything you know about this man."

Nh'ghalu watched from the upper floor of the pagoda. A New Mars security officer was poking at the dead body of the man who called himself Katz. Security was much tighter in New Mars City because of the potential for massive loss of life. In an environment unsupportive of human life, thousands of people walked the streets in a false

Terrain atmosphere. A single breach of the force field would be devastating.

Clever of me that he died at the entrance to the Miracle River. People have already seen the slaughter in the city they call Chicago. Word will get out soon that he was killed on Mars within an hour of their time. Some will call it a miracle.

Nh'ghalu almost laughed at that thought. The One would be pleased. Chaos was coming.

These silly humans were always easily led by ideologues. Especially the religious. The extremists and self-righteous will soon be calling him a martyr. Thank God for God.

Nh'ghalu watched the local officials secure the temple and move the body into an antigrav ambulance. As they sped away he looked to see if he was alone. Satisfied, he smiled as he opened an interdimensional rift and left Mars.

CHAPTER SEVEN

Jonny watched from the second floor of an abandoned shop. His dad stood behind a blockade that had been thrown together helter-skelter. The enemy—*Since when is the WWPA the enemy? Since two weeks ago, when it happened*—the enemy was a half block away near Fifth St. SW. His dad, Jon, was in command of a rag-tag group of the People, the Niitsitapi. He was barking out orders to reinforce the blockade. They were just north, on First St. SW. They were defending their land.

Jonny looked south, toward the old middle school, at the park, where the conflict had started.

"Remember; don't fire at the sentries till I give the order! They won't fire at you till they're targeted or commanded!" Jon yelled orders to the men and women, the Piegan and the Siksika who were willing to fight. The all were determined to do what they needed to do. Yet it was puzzling to Jonny. Why were they suddenly labeled as rebels, and why were they fighting the WWPA? That entity had been established over three hundred years ago to protect civilians, and now it was the enemy? It didn't make any sense.

"Stand your ground—" Jonny could hear his father's voice ringing clear through the crisp air. It was an early Montana morning in late July. "—but if you see or hear a pulse weapon cutting through the blockade in front of you, drop and move quickly to the side. Doesn't matter which, as long as you move. The sentries are our biggest threat. If we have to fire at them, remember, wait for my command and then aim at their weapon arms. They have to lower their shields when they fire." He helped push a charred robocar across an opening in the barricade.

Two weeks earlier the People had stood in Chief Mann Park, near the old Browning Middle School. They were protesting Commander Washington's order that they vacate South Browning. The commander insisted that it was necessary for their safety due to new experiments at the MQ Space Industries complex near Kipp Lake.

Just two days prior, Chief Ander William had explained to the commander that neither movement of the Niitsitapi nor experiments deemed dangerous to the Blackfeet were allowed in their long-standing 1/10 agreement. The agreement had been honored for over a hundred and fifty years.

He had carefully explained to Supreme Commander Washington that the Blackfoot Nation had been on this land forever. Politically speaking, this was the land of their ancestors. Even during the tragic Indian relocations of the 1800s, the Blackfoot Indians still retained their ancestral land. The Blackfeet would not give up their homes without protest.

Commander Washington could not, and said that he would not, legally force the Niitsitapi off their land. He thanked Chief William for his time. As he left the meeting he told the chief that his subordinate, Lieutenant Commander Anderson, would continue working with him on the safety of his people. It was unfortunate timing but he had to go to Armenia and then attend a meeting at the UN regarding rebel forces within the WWPA. He assured the chief that his subordinate would honor the 1/10 agreement. It was the WWPA's mandate to protect all civilians and Lieutenant Commander

Anderson would do whatever was necessary to keep the locals safe.

The following day Lieutenant Commander Anderson met with Chief William. He assured the chief that he would honor each and every line of the 1/10 agreement. That night the People living near the 2-89 and some from the Depot Creek subdivision were forcibly removed from their homes. They were temporarily moved to a shelter northeast of Kipp Lake. A small force of WWPA, fronted by two warbot sentries, was then stationed just southeast of Chief Mann Park.

The next day Chief William led an angry crowd into the park to protest the forced removal of Blackfoot citizens. Jonny's dad was at Chief William's side. Even though, at his dad's insistence, Jonny was near the back of the crowd, he could hear the loud exchange between Chief William and the leader of the WWPA regiment.

The chief demanded the return of Blackfoot citizens kidnapped during the night.

The WWPA commander shouted something about rebels and his need to protect the Niitsitapi from the rebels within. He demanded that the rest of south Browning be evacuated, or they would be forcibly removed.

The chief started chanting, "No! No! We won't go!"

The People around the chief took up the chant and it spread through the gathered convocation until the protest rang throughout the park.

"NO! NO! We won't go . . . NO! NO! We won't go . . . NO! NO! We won't go!"

Suddenly, the sound of a shot rent the air. Jonny, standing on a small mound, watched Chief William crumble like broken sticks falling under a cloak. Around him, the chanting people subsided into shocked silence as news of what had happened spread outward like ripples. It seemed to Jonny that the shot had come from the houses to the east of the protestors. He saw his dad pull out his handgun as he crouched beside the fallen chief. The WWPA commander shouted orders to his troops. Again, Jonny caught the word "rebels."

"What the hell . . ." Jonny murmured.

Jonny watched as those around the dead chief turned to look to the east, where the blast had apparently come from, yet the WWPA commander was focused only on the protestors. It was as if he wasn't concerned about where the assassin had fired from.

This doesn't feel right.

The warbots' arms rose as they aimed their weapons at the Niitsitapi.

"The sentries!" A man yelled. He lacked experience and fired at the bots. A second later, he lay dead.

Suddenly people were running at Jonny, shoving past him to get out of the park. He knew he had to get to his dad. He pushed his way to the side to keep from being trampled, and ran towards where the chief had stood.

As he ran, he peered at the area where the first shot had come from. Nothing—wait, there across South Piegan St., near the side of a small, gray house, there was a shimmer in the air. His eyes wanted to roll to the side of the small wavy vision, but he forced them to stay on the illusion. Something was hiding behind that shimmering . . . What? He had to tell his dad.

Jon was waving his arms at some men who had weapons. "Don't target the sentries!" he yelled again and again. The sentries moved forward—a nervous Niitsitapi fired, and then crumpled; another man down.

Jonny could see a handful of armed men, maybe ten, plus his dad, running for cover. As Jonny swerved to avoid a final group of people running away, his dad's voice reached him.

"Wait for my order, and then everybody fire at the sentries' firearms. If you feel your cover being hit with a pulse gun, fall to the ground and roll to the side. Don't think about it, just do it quick."

The sentries were still moving forward and had reached the edge of the park. Jonny had found a tree that he could hide behind and watch. Nearly all the protesters had scattered behind buildings further to the north and now behind him. He saw his dad hiding behind the bronze statue of Chief Mann. His hand was raised and he was watching the moving sentries and the men around him. One of the sentries swung its weapon toward Jon. Jonny gasped, but in that instant his father dropped his hand and yelled, "Now!"

The men fired at the sentry that had targeted Jon. It worked. That sentry's firearms were destroyed. But then Jonny heard the crackling burst of a weapon and saw the men scatter before they could coordinate another attack. One man lost his arm to the second sentry's fire.

Suddenly that sentry was fired upon by a few men from the WWPA. It turned, confused.

Jon stood up. "Fire!" He shouted, raising his gun. "Aim at the weapon arms!"

The barrage of gunfire damaged one weapon arm, but the sentry recovered and shielded his other arm. It turned and fired rapidly at Jon and his men. A moment later, the three WWPA personnel fired again and disabled the warbot completely.

Jonny turned his head and saw Lieutenant Commander Anderson aim his weapon at the three renegades. He tried to cry out a warning, but the

LC fired, wounding one before they managed to get their personal shields up and return fire.

"Protect those men," Jon yelled. The men around him started firing, some with pulse weapons, and some with old projectile guns, back at the WWPA.

It was clear to Jonny that the WWPA was confused. A couple of men followed LC Anderson's orders and returned fire, but others stood frozen.

Many joined the WWPA as a means to repay their commitment to their education. It was supposed to be a safe bet. There had been no real conflict in the world for over two hundred years.

Seeing that he had lost control of his troops, LC Anderson ordered a retreat.

The fight had been quick, intense and deadly: no glory just fear and the wounded and death. Jonny forced back tears as he came out from behind the tree. His dad stood near the front of the statue watching the retreating force, weapon in hand.

"Dad! Dad!" Jonny ran towards him. "Are you alright?"

"What in the name of the Stars are you doing here? Are you crazy? You could have been hurt or killed. You do what I told you and stay to the rear of the crowd that left! Now!"

Jonny stared at his father. "Dad, I'm eighteen. I'm nearly a man . . . I am a man."

"Now!"

"Please don't shout at me like that."

Jon looked at his son, then at the retreating patrol, then back at his son.

"You're right, Jonny. You are getting to be a man. Sometimes that means you obey orders because it's for the good of the group, and not just because you're being told what to do. If you had got hurt . . . or worse . . . I would not have been able to function. Besides," he added with a sly smile, "your mom would really be pissed." Smiling, Jonny hugged his father.

"Sir." One of the men who had fought alongside Jon was pointing toward the houses across the street south where the retreating WWPA squad had been.

Jon turned around. Approaching the park boundary, two WWPA soldiers were assisting their wounded companion.

"Get two more men and give them some help," Jon said. "Hopefully they know what's going on."

Jon walked over to the body of Chief William. Two men were singing softly in memorial to the chief's spirit. Jon waited until the men fell silent and raised their heads.

"Get Ander to a proper funeral site," he said. "He will be remembered."

The two nodded. Gently, they lifted the dead man and carried him away.

The WWPA men were making their way towards Jon, the uninjured two preceding their companion. Jon cradled his pulse weapon in both hands as they came close. One man was clearly Indian, as in India. The other looked to be an olive-skinned European. Even though their gaze was intent upon Jon, both men kept looking back at the wounded officer struggling to keep pace. Jon observed that man.

Clearly, he is in charge.

The two leading the way stopped in front of Jon. "Sir, I am Lieutenant Singh. This is Lieutenant Cabrera."

"Sir." Lieutenant Cabrera held his hand out to Jon. After a moment, Jon gripped it firmly and shook it.

"Jon Smith, chief of police in Glacier County. Thank you for your help. Now, tell me why we were attacked by the force that's supposed to be protecting us."

"I believe I can answer that, sir." The third man spoke with an English dialect. Though he was large and strong, he was wincing from a wound at his side.

"I am Captain Michael Phillips, though most people call me Mitch. I joined the WWPA thirty years ago because I believed in its mission to protect and serve the civilian populations of Earth. To protect you, sir. I came to be, or rather I am . . ." He stopped.

He looked at the other two soldiers and then back to Jon. Jon put his finger on the trigger button of his pulse gun.

"We are also part of the Internal Secret Security and Emergency Force, ISSEF. We are also here to protect you from us, or rather, from rogue members of the WWPA. There hasn't been an attack on civilians by miscreants in the WWPA for over fifty years. These two men are under my command. We are at your service."

"Thank you." Jon didn't move his finger. "Are we clear that I am in charge of these civilians, and by your mission statement, you as well?"

"Yes, sir."

Jon lowered his weapon. "Good. Now. Why?"

"It's confusing, sir. I believe that Lieutenant Commander Anderson really does think that there is some kind of rebel force within the WWPA and now within your tribe. There was an explosion near our base two nights ago. It looked like a terrorist attack."

"But when we investigated," Lieutenant Cabrera interjected, "we found that the explosive device was clearly of WWPA origin."

"Yes. LC Anderson has been ordered by Commander Washington to take control of and interrogate the local population—" Captain Phillips paused.

"By any means necessary." Lieutenant Cabrera finished his statement. The other two nodded their heads.

"Well, then we know that they will be back. Is there any way we can use the disabled warbots as defensive weapons?"

"I don't believe so, sir. The only way to reprogram the warbots to our command is to change their very complicated algorithms. Nobody here has that kind of knowledge."

"Uhmm . . . I do." Jonny had his hand in the air like he was still in school.

Jon smiled. "He's right. My son has that expertise." He smiled more broadly at the sight of the ISSEF officers' surprised expressions, and then returned to business. "Let's prepare for a defense. You two come with me."

He looked to a woman who had just joined them. "Salina, get Captain Phillips and any other wounded to the clinic. Contact the other two deputies and the town police. We need to move the People to the north side of town."

"Jon?"

"Yes, in the short run we give up part of our land for the safety of us all, but Commander Washington will not win in the long run. We have been here on these sacred grounds since before some of the great European nations even existed, and we will be here at the end of time. Make no mistake, the Blackfeet will return." He stepped toward his son then stopped. "Oh," he said, turning back toward Salina, "contact my wife and first let her know that Jonny and I are okay. Then tell her to get in touch with Dr. Wilkins at the clinic. We may need to triage."

"Yes, sir." Salina threaded her arm under Captain Phillips' so that he could lean on her. "Please come with me, sir," she said, and the two of them started to walk slowly toward the road.

I'm damn lucky to have someone like her in the office.

He turned to his son.

"Jonny make those bots ours."

"Yes, sir." Jonny looked toward the warbots. Then he remembered that shimmering . . . "something" . . . that he had seen.

"Dad! Wait." His father glanced back.

"I saw something, over there where the shot came from that killed Chief William. Right near the side of that house. Something shimmered in the air—like a cloaking device but much more sophisticated than any I've ever seen before. My eyes wanted to roll off it, like it wasn't there, but I forced myself to stare at it and I saw it move slightly, and then it was gone. But it was there, Dad. I know what I saw."

"Does the WWPA have such a cloak?" Jon asked the two men still with him.

"No, sir," said Lieutenant Cabrera. "We have, as you probably already know, cloaks that use refraction. It's more of an optical illusion. Good for camouflage, but if you focus you can see the edges of the cape. Nothing that makes your eyes want to 'roll off' it."

"It's clear then that we are dealing with a force that is somehow affiliated with MQ Space Industries. Spread the word about this cloaking device. Anybody who sees it is to report it and fire on it. Let's see if we can capture one of these things."

The two lieutenants nodded and saluted. Jon started to walk towards his son.

"Sir." Lieutenant Cabrera stopped Jon. "Sir, you know that we are battling a superior force. Our enemies—" He looked east "—some of whom are my friends, are trained to stop an army. I am with you and these good people, but you must know this could be devastating."

"Yes, Lieutenant, I do. See that young boy over there—" Jon pointed to Jonny, kneeling beside a warbot and frowning in concentration. "No doubt he's brighter than all of us put together, but, like any of the kids on this reservation, he could be the greatest teacher in high school or one of the greatest chiefs or even one of the great presidents. This is what I am fighting for. I was a sergeant major in the WWPA before I retired. I welcome your assistance, Lieutenant."

"A pleasure to be by your side, sir." Lieutenant Cabrera saluted.

"Sir," It was Lieutenant Singh. "I believe that my coding education at Tsinghua University gives me some ability to help your son."

Jon nodded, and the three men strolled over to the disabled warbot.

"Young man," said Lieutenant Singh, "may I be of assistance?"

Jonny's head popped around from the back of the bot's massive torso. "Uhmm, sure. Let's get these covers off." Lieutenant Singh walked behind the bot to help Jonny.

That was two weeks ago. Jonny peered out of the window at his dad down below in the street. Jon, along with two of his deputies, had finished moving the damaged robocar, filling the small opening in their primitive blockade of cars and debris. Their reprogramed warbot stood guard in front. It looked as if they intended to make a last stand here on First St., but that was part of his dad's plan. At some point Jon would give the order and they would pull back. It would look like a retreat, but the rag-tag group of soldiers would splinter, some moving east, some west, and the main group north. They would then use guerrilla warfare and harass the enemy from all three sides. The hope was that Lieutenant Commander Anderson's platoon would splinter.

Captain Phillips was off to the side surveying the fighters stationed on various rooftops. He was speaking into a walkie-talkie and pointing at a couple of men on the roof across from Jonny's window. Jonny could see them nodding their heads as he spoke.

"Amazing that in this day and age we would have to resort to such a primitive way of communicating," Jonny murmured.

A week ago and for reasons unknown, the entire network had stopped working. Some of the local communication devices worked fine, but anything tied to a satellite system just stopped. As if on cue Jonny's dad walked up to Captain Phillips and pointed to the 'Human to Computer Interaction Unit' on the captain's wrist. Mr. Phillips looked at his HCI and shrugged his shoulders.

While recovering from his wounds the captain had sent a message to his superior, a Commander Sorenson in Chicago, requesting support. Both sides had sent out sorties over the last two weeks. In one, a series of drones had taken out one of the warbots that Jonny and Lieutenant Singh had reprogrammed. At first Captain Phillips wasn't overly concerned by the lack of response from his superior; but toward the end of the week he sent two more requests for orders and logistical support. Then the photon communication system had gone silent.

"They're coming!" one of the defenders on the roof yelled suddenly.

"Positions!" Jon yelled.

People scrambled to their assigned spots on the barricade, weapons aimed at the enemy. Some ran into surrounding buildings, reappearing a few seconds later at windows and on balconies. Jon was giving orders to Captain Phillips, who relayed them through his walkie-talkie to the men on the roof.

Jonny craned his neck to see the advancing enemy patrol. Three warbots were at the front, the men and women behind. There was something different about the sentries' weapons this time. They weren't the powerful-looking pulse weapons warbots usually carried. They held something that looked like the open end of a wedge-shaped fan. A thick cord ran from the fans to a machine behind the bots. That machine was clearly shielded.

"Dad!" Jonny yelled out the window.

"Jonny, we have an agreement! Get out of here!"

"I know, Dad, but the bots—"

"I see it. Now go!"

Jonny nodded and ducked down from the window. He would leave, but first one more look at these strange new weapons. He left the apartment, but instead of running north, went further into the building. Reaching the end of a hallway, he opened the window and cautiously leaned out. Almost directly below him, the warbots raised their peculiar-looking weapons.

There was a slight vibration or humming sound and the building across the street suddenly separated at an angle that would make it slide and fall onto his dad and the defenders below. Then another hum, and the falling building separated into four. There was no sound as the building came apart but the pieces scrunched sickeningly as they fell back into each other. Defenders scrambled to get away. One man on the roof was hit by this oddly quiet new weapon, and like the building, he came apart, the two pieces of his body flung in different directions, blood staining the bricks.

Through the screams, Jonny heard his dad barking out orders for a retreat. Suddenly it dawned on Jonny. If that devastation was happening across the street, it could happen here.

Stars! Run! Run!

He ran as fast as he could. The groaning building was starting to come apart. Jonny sped towards his planned exit point. The wall facing First St, by his dad and the blockade, was pulling away from the building. Breathing heavily, he forced his legs to work harder. He was close to the stairwell that was his escape. Above the screams he still could hear his dad yelling to retreat.

At least he's still okay.

For a moment, Jonny felt guilty being relieved about his dad while others were dying.

There was the stairwell. A few more meters and he was there. He wrenched open the door and looked down in dismay. The stairwell was falling apart. The wall to his right began to flutter and sway. The ceiling had completely separated and for a second floated above the stairwell. Then the bisected building crashed into itself. The stairwell disintegrated in the intensity of what was once one but was now two separate pieces of matter smashing together. Suddenly the entire building began to twist slowly as if some giant hand was trying to unscrew it from the top. Jonny braced a hand against the wall beside him. Moving unsteadily as the floor swayed and twisted beneath him, he ran to the east side of the building, away from First St. Clumps of ceiling fell behind him as he ran. There at the end of the crumbling complex was a small window balcony. The window was open. Without pausing, he jumped through.

Let the balcony be secure! Let the balcony be secure!

The stars were with him. He landed on an emergency escape platform.

"Emergency extend," he ordered the auto platform to extend its escape ladder.

"Extending," replied the auto-voice.

But nothing happened. Jonny ducked to avoid bits of synthetic brick falling around him. One piece struck and gashed his shoulder.

"Extend now!" Jonny yelled.

Jerkily, the ladder started to push down but stopped about three meters above the ground. Jonny started down the ladder.

I can jump three meters. Done it before.

He was a little more than halfway down when a slab of roof hit the escape platform, pulling one side of it away from the wall. The ladder flipped to Jonny's right with such force it nearly flung him off and back into the building. He moved faster. At last he reached the end of the ladder and poised to jump. Looking up once more, he saw a huge piece of the roof dropping towards the platform.

"Time to go!" He jumped.

As his feet touched, he tucked into a roll, springing up to standing. A couple of meters to his left, the platform and roof slab smashed into the ground. He looked up and saw that the building had begun to twist in on itself. Coughing against the dust, he raced east to S Piegan St. and then north toward the triage location on Center St. That was their designated meeting place.

S Piegan was eerily quiet. He could still hear some of the fighting he had left behind on First St., but here the houses looked normal. A breeze gently ruffled the leaves and the flags that dotted a few homes. The contrast with the chaos he had just left was incongruous. Tears of fear, remorse and fury flowed down his young cheeks. Fury that anyone could so easily kill and destroy like the WWPA had just done and remorse for those who had died. Jonny stopped running.

Should I go back? No! We made an agreement.

Jonny started running again, a little slower than before. Up ahead was the triage area. He quickened his pace. It would be good to see his mom . . . and his dad. Jonny reached the edge of the property where the triage was situated and stopped. At the back of the property were three WWPA ships. His stomach felt hollow. The enemy was—wait! They looked like WWPA ships, but were trimmed in blue instead of red. The people around the ships seemed to be calmly off-loading supplies for the clinic. Three sentries were stationed around the ships, but they were holding their weapons in parade rest position.

He saw his mom talking with a woman who appeared to be in charge. As he made his way toward them he realized he had seen this woman before. Her hair was drawn into a tight bun and she wore the insignia of commander over her left breast; she looked a lot more official than when he had seen her last.

"Hello, Jonny. I told you we'd meet again. However, I had hoped that it would be under better circumstances."

"Where's your dad?" Neenah looked worried.

"I don't know," Jonny said. "I lost sight of him. They're shooting weapons like I've never seen before. Dad and all the defenders are trying to escape. They need help, Commander, uh, Vanessa, uh . . . Commander Vanessa, they need help."

"How many warbots?"

"Three—"

Vanessa abruptly turned and yelled commands in Russian to the sentry warbots; they immediately moved their weapons into firing position and ran toward the warzone. She tapped something into her HCI and within seconds several drones lifted from the ISSEF warships.

"Commander," Jonny said, "they have these new weapons. It's not a laser. It makes some kinda vibration sound and then things just come apart. I think they could be graviton weapons."

"Graviton!" Vanessa raised her eyebrows. "My immediate concern is to stop the three warbots. I sent enough artillery to do that, at least. Stopping the bots will halt the enemy's advancement and give time and cover for your dad and his warriors to escape." She pursed her lips and gazed out towards Kipp Lake. "Graviton weapons? Mai Quan, what have you done?"

Lieutenant Commander Anderson watched as the skirmish began, recording the splintering of buildings and people into his HCI.

Excellent. Commander Washington will be pleased. This is a great moment. We can conquer anybody now.

"Sir." His captain pulled him out of his thoughts.

"Yes, Captain. At ease."

"Sir, the weapons worked exactly as predicted. Gravity at its molecular level was completely destabilized at the plane of fire. Any material within the firing zone simply came apart. After the weapons were shut off, gravity took over and the disrupted pieces fell in on themselves or spun apart."

"Thank you, Captain, I'll file the proper report. Dismissed."

"Sir." A young lieutenant hastened up to the Commander. "Sir," he repeated breathlessly, "we detected three warships landing at the north end of the battle area just before our warbots fired, and now we are under attack by rebels with sophisticated weaponry, including drones. One of our bots is down."

"Captain, order a retreat."

"Yes, sir." The captain ran off.

"Lieutenant, if ever you approach me again without coming to attention and saluting I will have you thrown in the brig and demote you. Am I clear!"

"Yes, sir!" The lieutenant snapped to attention and saluted.

"Dismissed!"

The lieutenant dropped his salute, spun on one foot and walked briskly away from LC Anderson.

His eyes narrowed as he watched his subordinate.

There will be discipline.

He tapped his fingers on his leg. "So, ISSEF has arrived. Lovely. Let the games begin."

CHAPTER EIGHT

"So, is Supreme Commander Washington somehow involved with these so-called fucking rebels or not?"

Vanessa stared at Jon. She looked like a teacher about ready to slap a ruler across an insolent boy's knuckles.

Suddenly, Salina cleared her throat loudly. "Sorry, mutual courtesy got stuck there for a second, but it feels better now." She slapped her upper chest a couple of times. "Yes, much better." She went back to her matriculation screen to make sure that everything was being recorded correctly. Neenah stood by the meeting room door with her arms folded across her chest, suppressing a grin. Jon tapped his fingers on the tabletop and looked at Vanessa.

"I am sorry, Commander. I lost eight people in what I would call a rout. I am grateful for your military support. It would have been worse if you hadn't intervened. Still, I don't understand what's going on here and I'm responsible for the people in this community. What can you tell me regarding Commander Washington and this Lieutenant Commander—?" He gestured toward Lieutenant Cabrera.

"Lieutenant Commander Anderson."

They sat around a table in what was once the break room for the Glacier County Sheriff's Department. It had now become a command room. The two other deputies were out deputizing citizens to help defend Browning. The six people in the room were discussing ways to defend against an enemy that for years had been considered a friend, an ally.

Vanessa had waited to get a feel for the hierarchy of this community. She was now ready to set in charge those who would lead and those who would follow.

"Jon Smith, you served in the WWPA how long ago?"

"Thirty-five years ago . . . ma'am."

"And you have been chief of police for how long?"

"Twenty years . . . ma'am."

It had been three days since the battle with the WWPA. It had been three weeks since Vanessa had begun her trip landside to find her superior. She had been to Chicago, then to Azerbaijan, and finally to China. Because of her superior's apparent disappearance, President Yang had put Vanessa in command of all of ISSEF. She had to decide who would be in command of the soldiers and people here in Browning.

"Alright, Jon, here's what I know. Some of it you know and some of it I'm still trying to understand. Three weeks ago during the final performance of Sanctuary's hundred and fiftieth anniversary celebration, during the 'Requiem,' Supreme Commander Rena Macighian was assassinated in the presidential palace of Azerbaijan. Commander Macighian was Armenian, and the reckless president of Armenia, Alik DerAbbasyan, has used her death as a reason to attack Azerbaijan. During some of the skirmishes with the Azerbaijan army, and now the ISSEF and the WWPA that had come to the aid of Azerbaijan, unidentified charcoal-colored fighter planes harassed the defending armies.

"We all know that most modern aircraft use antigravity devices to support their flights, but to date no machine has been able to use antigrav strictly as propulsion. These fighters apparently have that ability. In addition to their incredible speeds and maneuverability, they have cloaking devices that make them virtually invisible, and the untrained eye seems to roll right off the cloak."

"Lieutenant Singh?" Jon looked toward Prahb.

Vanessa looked from Jon to the lieutenant.

"Um, well, Ma'am, during one of the small skirmishes, before you arrived, we captured a personal cloak that apparently is the same as what you are talking about. Young Jonny, who is quite brilliant by the way, saw this device the day Chief William was assassinated. The day we joined the civilian force, as is our mandate."

Lieutenant Singh frowned. "I have heard that our 'defection,' as Lieutenant Commander Anderson calls it, is proof of our connection to the rebel forces that are supposedly here among the indigenous people, and according to him, within the WWPA as well. He refuses to release the hostages that he abducted a night or so before that first confrontation. I am puzzled, Commander. It seems that LC Anderson is trying to instigate more confrontation with the people here in Browning. I originally thought that he sincerely believed that there were rebels within the WWPA and perhaps here in Browning, but now it appears as though he just wishes to fan the flames. He is Supreme Commander Washington's right-hand man here at MQ Space Industries. Perhaps—"

"Prahb, the cloak." Jon interrupted him.

"Oh, yes, the cloak. If you will look over there, ma'am." Prahb pointed to a cloak hanging on a couple of hooks on the wall. It was a dull grey color with a light glitter all over its surface. Vanessa walked over to the cloak and fingered it.

"Young Jonny figured out how it works," said Prahb. "It has some refraction qualities, as do all camouflage cloaks, yet this one seems to work by primarily—well, the best way to describe it is that it creates a total internal reflection. It absorbs the light around it so effectively that it becomes part of the immediate surrounding area. I think that is why the untrained eye wants to roll off it. Since it doesn't reflect light, the brain sees it as not being there and moves to the reflected light. Please, ma'am, if you would step back and keep your gaze on the cloak."

Vanessa moved back to the table and watched the cloak. Lieutenant Singh pressed a button on his HCI. For a second the cloak shimmered, and then it disappeared. Vanessa found her eyes wanting to move to the right, but she forced herself to look where the cloak had been. She knew that it was still there, but now invisible. It blended in with the wall so well that it took Vanessa a full minute before she could see a faint shimmer moving around the edges of the cloak. If she were a child she would have called it magic.

"Do you have an idea how to disable this device?"

"Presently, no." Singh sounded apologetic.

"Okay, switch it off." Vanessa turned to Jon. "Yes, there seems to be some circumstantial events that implicate Commander Washington and Chairman Quan in some of these . . . incidents. She sat back down. As you know, international communication, which depends on satellites, broke down two weeks ago. The main international communication platform in space; as well as a few key satellites were destroyed by unknown enemies."

"Somebody attacked a space platform?" Neenah looked as stunned as everyone gathered around the table.

"It was precise. Not only did they destroy the platform's international and interplanetary communicators, they targeted three other satellites. Communication around the globe was silenced for a week. There were only four of these charcoal-grey antigrav fighters. Commander Steges from Sanctuary reached them first. She had thirteen WWPA space-fighters and lost two and two other damaged to their one. The other three fled and disappeared, hidden under these mysterious cloaks." Vanessa gestured toward the cloak on the wall.

"A team from Sanctuary tried to recreate the necessary algorithms to replicate the lost platform and satellites, but could not. Interestingly enough, Mai Quan, on the Ark, was able to reconnect the lost interplanetary communications. Equally interesting was the intermittent failure of his system at key times of WWPA or ISSEF communications. Where I can, I maintain communication through SAIQA."

"So is that why it took you till just a few days ago to arrive here to assist these good people?" Mitch entered the room.

Vanessa looked at the Englishman who had just arrived. Captain Michael Phillips. She knew she could trust him absolutely. Yet, protocol was necessary.

"Mr. Phillips, you have the respect of many men and women who follow you, but I require the courtesy due my rank. Am I clear?"

"Yes, ma'am." Mitch stood at attention and saluted Vanessa. "But I am going to say, ma'am, that I am disappointed in ISSEF's response to this incident. If it were not for the chief of police here, it would have been worse. Thank you Ma'am."

Vanessa sighed and leaned back in her chair. "You deserve to know, please have a seat."

Vanessa looked to her left; Jon was watching her intently. Captain Phillips shuffled into a seat at the far right of the table. Neenah's arms were still hooked under her breasts, perhaps more firmly. They were all looking at Vanessa for answers.

She looked at them all and thought, *Just like with the Three Musketeers, I feel like we are all connected. So be it.*

She leaned forward and placed her hands on the table. "Three weeks ago, when Supreme Commander Macighian was assassinated in a secret meeting arranged by Commander Washington, I sent a secure photon mail to ISSEF Supreme Commander Sorenson in Chicago. He responded with a cryptic message about getting my house in order. I tried several times to contact him again, without success, so I went to Chicago to investigate the reasoning behind his message and his complete lack of response thereafter. When I arrived, it fell upon me to begin an investigation into a criminal who would not normally fall under WWPA jurisdiction. But this criminal not only killed in Chicago, but only minutes later was killing in St. Petersburg. He murdered innocent parishioners in Chicago and was captured and retained by the local police. Twenty minutes later, he was in Russia, killing again." Vanessa paused to let her words sink in. "Yes," she said. "The same person. He was captured by Russian police and some minutes later was killed by security personnel in New Mars City."

There was silence in the room.

"You're saying that the same perp went from Chicago to St. Petersburg to New Mars City in, what, an hour? That's not possible." Captain Phillips almost laughed.

Vanessa tapped her HCI. "Here's the evidence, Captain."

Captain Phillips sat for a long time studying the cistronic imprint that identified the killer. He shook his head. "This is just not possible."

"There is more for you to know. But, first, concerning Commander Sorenson. I went to the commander's secure civilian base on Lincoln Park Ave, and it was clear that the site was unprotected. His cover was a business that restored antiquated personal units. He actually had iPhones from the late 2100s. I assumed his security would be tight if only for his antiques. The front door was practically open. Security for an ISSEF officer is exceptionally tight, but the entrance to his shop gave the impression that he didn't care, or that something had happened to him. I was then called by President Yang, ISSEF's commander in chief, to assist in Azerbaijan. That is where we first encountered the antigrav fighters. They are effective, but they attack and run, as if they're merely testing us. It is my belief that something bigger and more dangerous is coming soon."

Vanessa leaned back in her chair and made a motion as if to run her hand through her hair, stopping when she realized it was pulled back in a bun. Jon suddenly realized how tired she must be.

"Regarding your request for help, Captain Phillips," she said. "I am sorry, but it took my staff a week to decipher the messages in Commander Sorenson's mail. And even then one of my subordinates decided that Browning was too small an issue for me to consider. I didn't get your messages until a week ago. My assistants will not make that mistake again. As soon as I understood what was going on, I put together a squad of highly trained soldiers and came here. I also impressed upon President Yang the importance of having a presence near MQ Space Industries' main

North American site as he has done in China. There will be more ISSEF arriving soon.

"This leads me," she said, gazing around the table, "to who's in charge here. It's obvious to me that it is you, Jon Smith." She turned to Jon, who nodded slightly. "So," she continued, "there are two ways to do this. As new military people will arrive they will be looking for leadership, and the civilians need someone they can trust. I propose that you allow me to invoke your reinstatement clause and make you a Lieutenant Commander."

"I don't have a reinstatement clause."

"Actually, Mr. Smith, you do. Would you like me to show it to you?" Vanessa touched her HCI.

"No." Jon sighed and rubbed his forehead. "Damn me for being too young to say no to that. Are you going to force me to honor that?"

"No. I trust you will make the right decision."

Jon looked over at Neenah. She was wearing her best poker face, but in her eyes he could see her concern. She felt what he felt; there would be more blood spilt in Browning.

What is the best choice for my family?

He knew in his heart that whatever he did for people would be good for his family

"Alright, Commander, I choose to be reinstated back in the WWPA, but with this caveat. I answer to no one except you or the commander in chief of ISSEF. I am going to give commands that will cost people their lives. That will not happen lightly, as a matter of fact it will be—" His face darkened. "I will only take orders from you or the CIC. That is my decision."

"These decisions are always hard. I understand. Glad to have you on my side. As of now, Jon Smith, you are reinstated in the WWPA, ISSEF, as Lieutenant Commander Smith. Captain

Phillips?" She quickly typed into her HCI and then looked toward Mitch.

"I am already following him, ma'am. This man's a hero to this community and knows how to give orders. It's an honor sir, to have you back in the service."

"Very well, then. That's settled. Now for the part you still need to know. Salina, I don't think this should be recorded."

Salina nodded and paused the recording.

"Aside from President Yang, you are the only other people on Earth to know. SAIQA has informed me that she was contacted by an alien."

Neenah broke the silence.

"What do you mean by 'an alien'?"

"An immortal being from another planet that has been guiding humans since the time of ancient Sumatra. And, apparently, there are two of them. They are telepathic and, well, for lack of a better way to put it, one is good and the other not so good."

Vanessa referred to her notes on her HCI.

"SAIQA was contacted by Telas—the good one, so she says—while she was in a meeting with LC Jenkins and a small group of people that I believe will be assets as more of our enemy reveal themselves. Anyhow, this Telas believes that his brother is responsible for our present chaos. He has the ability to manipulate key people into making bad decisions. His motivation apparently is revenge on Telas and maybe some theocratic belief. That part's not clear. Telas intimated that his brother seems to think that there is a great deity coming our way and in order for him to save us our world needs to be in despair. He calls this deity 'The One.' Which leads me back to your earlier skepticism, Captain Phillips. These aliens are far more advanced than us and can jump dimensionally from one place to another in seconds. Even all the way to Mars. And the perp that was killed on Mars was yelling about The One as he was killing parishioners in Chicago." Vanessa again paused to let her words settle in the silent room.

"What is the name of this twisted alien?" Neenah demanded.

"Nh'ghalu."

Neenah groaned and grabbed the doorframe. "Where's Jonny?" she cried. "Has anybody seen Jonny?"

"I saw him out front, Mrs. Smith. Just before I came in. You know how he likes to be around–"

Neenah was already running down the corridor.

Puzzled glances followed her. Jon started to rise but Vanessa caught his arm. "Has Jonny had any more vivid dreams, Jon?"

"Not to my knowledge."

"Any more of those weird migraines?"

"No." He looked at Vanessa with sudden understanding.

"Hi, everyone." Jonny entered the room, followed closely by Neenah.

"Jonny, how are you feeling?"

Jonny looked at the concerned and puzzled faces staring at him. "I'm okay, Dad. Why? What's up?"

"Jonny," said Neenah, putting her hand on his shoulder, "have you had any more of those strange migraines or dreams like you had on Sanctuary?"

"No, Mom, though I have been having a recurring dream about some odd algorithms lately."

"Algorithms? Can you write them down?" Prahb said.

"Not yet. It's more like they're some sort of mathematical rigour, but they don't seem to stick in my memory as I wake."

"Jonny, the man in your weird dream up on Sanctuary, what did he look like?" Vanessa cut in.

"Well, he was colorful because of the way he came to me, as a kestrel, but then he became human and had the general appearance of a squat, kinda classic Greek man."

"That was the way SAIQA described him to me as well," Vanessa remarked to the adults around the table.

"SAIQA had a dream about the same man as me?" Jonny said. "Why are you all staring at me? What's going on?"

Jon caught Neenah's glance. "He has a right to know, Commander."

"Alright, Jon, you have permission to tell him."

"Son, it appears that humanity has been influenced by at least two aliens for some time. Both of these aliens have telepathic abilities and both can travel great distances, unseen and in seconds. Commander—" He turned to Vanessa "—it also seems that their telepathic communications are limited to certain humans. Is that right?"

"Based on what I have determined, Lieutenant Commander Smith, I would say that is correct."

"Apparently, Jonny," his father continued, "you are one of the humans who can sense these aliens. It's very important, therefore, that you report to me or your mom any weird dreams or communication or anything that feels like there's something or someone inside your head. Is that clear?"

"Yes, sir."

"And you know the drill from when you were young; if they tell you not to talk to us or if they say that they will hurt us if you do talk to us, that's when you say okay, and the second they're gone you tell us immediately. Again, are we clear?"

"Yes, we're clear. Holy Stars. Mom, dad, I think I'm scared."

"You are a brave boy, Jonny," Vanessa said. "And it seems that the alien who has communicated with you is the good one, nevertheless you have my protection as well as your mother and father and all the good people here in your community. It is likely that you have an important role to play, though it's not yet clear how or why. These two aliens are apparently in conflict with each other and unfortunately have dragged the human race into their personal quarrel. It is important that you tell us about anything out of the ordinary. Anything new might indicate—"

"Oh, for Star's sake." Mitch blurted.

"Yes, Captain, you have something to say?"

"Sorry, ma'am, it's why I was late to this meeting. One of the elders that had gone to Chief Mountain to pray came back with something strange. As they were working their way around the base of the mountain they saw a bird fly into what appeared to be solid rock. They climbed a couple of meters to see where the bird went and found a small opening that wasn't visible from where they were. Elder Handy used the light on his communicator to see what was there. He gave me a photo that I'm sending to you, Commander." Mitch touched his HCI.

Vanessa studied the dim image. "Hmm, an old computerized sliding door." She projected a 3D image onto the conference table. "Any ideas, anyone?"

"That's completely new to me," Jon said, shaking his head.

"It has an old school keypad entrance lock," said Vanessa. "During the Corporate Wars many of the rogue corporate nations had secret bunkers throughout the world. This may be one of them. If so, in an emergency it could be a place of refuge." She sighed. "I wish I knew where Commander Sorenson was; he knows these old algorithms very well."

"I studied them extensively at TU," Lieutenant Singh said.

Jonny shrugged. "I study them just as a hobby."

"Well, we seem to be quite a team, don't we, young man?" Prahb smiled at Jonny. The boy blushed.

"Okay, let's fix this right now," Vanessa said. "As of this minute lieutenants Cabrera and Singh are captains and Captain Phillips, you are lieutenant commander and second in charge when I am not here. I expect the three of you to be leaders within the squad I leave behind and to uphold all our commitments to ensuring the safety of the civilians under your protection. Is that understood?" She tapped some notes into her HCI.

Yes, ma'am," all three responded almost in unison.

"Captain Singh, since you seem to be a team with that young man, Jonny's safety is in your hands at all times. Please remember that these old corporate bunkers were sometimes booby-trapped. Before you attempt to open that door make sure all safety measures are taken into consideration."

"That boy isn't going anywhere without me." Neenah folded her arms and looked directly at Vanessa.

"Neenah, I wouldn't think otherwise," Vanessa said.

"Just as long as that's understood."

Vanessa's HCI gave a soft ping. For a full minute she stared at the screen. The others in the room exchanged glances. Finally, Vanessa looked up, studied the group gathered in the meeting room and seemed to come to a decision.

"It seems that the staff I left in Chicago has found Commander Sorenson. I am needed there."

"Is he alright, Commander?" LC Phillips asked.

"No. According to the message from my subordinate, he was accidently killed by a civilian a few hours ago. That's all I know. Now, like I said, I need to leave. Jon would you close this meeting?"

"Salina, please end the meeting at where we stopped recording."

Salina nodded, tapped the appropriate commands into the matriculation unit and the meeting was saved. Proper protocol required that all ISSEF meetings be recorded and eventually sent to the ISSEF command center in Greenland.

"Is there anything we could do for you, Commander?" Jon asked.

"Just do your missions well." Vanessa rose from her chair, and then paused. "Jon contact me with your human-to-computer interaction unit."

Jon tapped on his HCI, and then looked expectantly at Commander Chuchnova.

"I am sending you all the command codes and other info necessary for you to be in charge while I am not here. The warbots and ships I leave behind are now under your complete command. Lieutenant Commander Phillips, your job is to make Lieutenant Commander Smith's job as effortless as possible. Captain Cabrera, you are in charge of rank and file. Captain Singh, you will put a small team together to investigate that potential bunker with Jonny." The men nodded.

Vanessa continued. "I think it wise to send one of the sentries with them, as we don't know what to expect. Wouldn't you agree, Jon?"

"Yes, I think it would be a good idea," said Neenah.

"What my wife said," Jon said with a smile.

Vanessa smiled. "Agreed." Her expression became serious. "Now that it is clear that I am in command of ISSEF, I have come to a decision that will have a minimum effect on you here but will affect the WWPA on an interplanetary level. I am going to order all ISSEF personnel to reveal themselves and their correct ranks. They will wear full ISSEF uniform, and where I feel it is safe they will stay and serve alongside the main WWPA service personnel. In certain questionable areas, such as here at MQ Space Industries, they will retain their cover. I am also going to call most of the rank and file, along with key officers, to leave their present assignments and relocate to ISSEF headquarters in Greenland. Mr. Phillips, there are a couple of ISSEF officers whom you may not know, undercover here. I am going to instruct them to find a way to get in contact with you." Jon nodded

"So we part, for the time being, on our separate missions," Vanessa continued. "Let's all be careful. We have a vague idea of who the enemy is; though I believe the majority of the WWPA will turn out to be our allies. We are being led down a dangerous road where enemies could suddenly appear from any direction, so watch your backs. I think it's going to get much worse before this is resolved. May the Stars be with us."

Those gathered in the room nodded their heads. The mood was somber. She glanced at them all as she gave her last speech. She knew they were concerned, not only for themselves, but for the sudden unknown that was their future. They weren't fearful; that was clear. They were ready to face the uncertainty. Even young Jonny seemed resolved. Jon broke the short silence.

"Well, we all know what to do. I'd like to say that it is an honor to be led by someone like you Commander. Tenhut!" The military personnel stood and saluted Vanessa.

"Dismissed." She returned the salutes and watched as they filed out of the room. She looked at the message on her HCI one more time. Shaking her head, she left the room and headed to her personal ship.

It was a tough morning for him. To the best of his fragile recollection the horror started around 2 a.m. and lasted throughout the rest of his sleepless night. Even now, as he sat at a sidewalk table on a street corner near Lincoln Park, he could still hear the sounds of his nightmares. The crackling, zapping sound of a scatter gun, the people screaming, the blood splattering, it was more than he could handle. His physician had given him some sedatives, but they weren't working today. He was near tears when he buried his head into his hands.

"Do you have your house in order, my young friend?"

"What?" Michael looked up through blurry eyes.

"You seem distressed. Do you have your house in order, son? He is coming soon."

His vision hazy through the tears, Michael saw a man in a light grey outfit wearing a deep maroon cape. Wait, the blood-red cape! Michael jumped up from his chair so fast it flew back into the table behind him. He grabbed a chair in front of him and aimed the legs toward his attacker.

"You! You are a murderer! You killed innocent children."

The man recoiled from the sudden display of hatred and anger. Then he understood.

"No, please wait. That wasn't me or any—"

He stepped forward to offer his hand to the angry man with the chair. As the man in the cape stepped toward him, Michael plunged the chair into the man's chest, propelling him backward. As he tried to regain his footing he stepped off the curb and fell into the busy street.

His head slammed on the edge of a robocar that was passing, cracking his skull. The impact flung him back toward the sidewalk. He lay dying in a pool of blood beside the robocar. Another robocar had also stopped.

Robocars have small Indy-Brains, and part of their function was to constantly scan and record. The recording was made so that if there was an accident, there would be an unbiased photon image of what happened. By law, any recording that showed a human being harmed had to be saved to the computer's memory, and the robocar could not leave the scene of the accident.

Michael stood with the chair in his hand looking at the dead man in the street.

It wasn't the man from the church; he was killed on Mars.

That thought alone made him pause. He set the chair down and sat in it. People were gathering around, whispering and talking. A woman squatted down beside the limp body in the street; she stood up shaking her head. Incredibly, someone was taking photos with their communicator. Michael could hear a siren approaching. The Indy-Brain in the robocar would have contacted the authorities right away. As he looked at the dead man his mind wandered to a line from a poem written long ago.

Once he was a man, but now an empty vessel . . .

He stared at the man he had just killed. Unintentionally, yes, but it was his fault. His eyes focused on the dark purple cape. His face went hard.

I am sorry; you didn't deserve to die. That mother didn't deserve to die. Those children didn't deserve to die.

I won't be afraid to defend myself!

CHAPTER NINE

SAIQA had intercepted the general distress signal from the Interplanetary Communication Space Platform in orbit around Earth. It was under attack. Her sensors verified that four unknown hostiles were firing on the platform. Following proper emergency procedures, she immediately informed Commander Steges, set repair-bots into a defensive position and charged her high-intensity photon lasers.

"I will not be surprised again," she had told Anna.

Anna gathered twelve of her best fighters and, together with them, scrambled toward the communication platform. She ordered Commander Choo to assemble a defensive squad around Sanctuary and put Erik Devries in charge of one of the wings.

It took her fighters about fifteen minutes to get to the platform. It already had been disabled by the time they arrived. The four hostiles sat in a line on the opposite side of the platform. It seemed like they were waiting for her.

"I've never seen a ship like that," Teresa's voice was soft as it came into Anna's earpiece.

"They appear to be standard military, yet odd looking." By combat protocol her group of fighters had already established the rotating com links they would use during the mission. She opened all her links.

"This is Commander Steges of the WWPA Space Division. Identify yourself."

There was no response. She didn't expect one. She switched to a secure channel.

"Defenders, form a line with me at the center. Adam, you take the wing to my left; I'll take charge of the wing on my right. Teresa, you're my best pilot, so you're the wildcard. If we're attacked, flank the command ship from all sides."

As the defenders moved into position Anna was contacted by the commander of the WWPA Space Platform in orbit about a third of the way around the planet from the defenders. On her way here she had left a message for his immediate response. Irritated that it took him a full five minutes to get back to her, she touched her communication screen.

"This is Commander Watson." He seemed annoyed at having to talk with her.

"Commander, why has there been no response from the WWPA platform to the aggression on the Interplanetary Space Communications Platform?"

"I was told by Commander Washington to delay any defensive responses." His tone was unmistakably condescending. Anna gritted her teeth and forced herself to stay calm.

"Supreme Commander Washington told you what?"

"What I said, missy. He ordered me to delay a defensive response, unless ordered by a superior, to any attack on any of the space platforms. He said that his military intelligence had told him that an imminent attack on a space platform was planned by rebels. He believed that this ambush by the unknown enemy would be followed by a full-on attack of the WWPA platform."

In her view screen Anna could see Commander Watson looking down at a note-pad on his desk.

"Why would James—never mind. Commander, do you know who I am?" She watched the commander scroll through the note-pad, and then sit back. He lifted one foot onto the corner of desk.

"Yes, ma'am," he drawled. "You are Commander Steges."

"And . . ."

"You are in command of all WWPA space divisions."

"As your superior officer," Anna said, enunciating each word clearly, "I am ordering you to quickly sortie a squad of fighters to defend the remaining platforms and send at an additional six fighters my way. Is that clear?"

"Yes ma'am. Though in your original message you said there were only four hostiles. Can't you handle them, my dear?"

"You question my orders again I will have your rank as well as your balls shoved down your throat. Now, do as I ordered and do it now. Commander Steges out."

Stars! Even in the twenty-fifth century I still have to deal with a stupid macho asshole.

Anna looked out through the view plates of her fighter. She looked to the right and left; both her defensive wings were set. Adam was at the end of the wing on her left and Teresa, her wildcard, at the end of the wing on her right. The four peculiar space craft were facing them on the other side of the platform.

"Funny," Anna said into her com. "Each ship looks kinda like a four-leaf clover."

"Yeah," Adam replied.

The center cabin of each ship was encircled by four rings. The rings couldn't have been propulsion units. They weren't long enough. They were oval shaped and connected together. Each was approximately a couple of meters wide, and in the center of those rings there was nothing: just an open oval. Otherwise the ships looked like a slimmed-down version of a WWPA fighter with a propulsion unit at the back and maneuvering units along the sides. Anna decided on one last try at communicating.

"Once more, this is Commander Steges of the WWPA. I am ordering you to stand down and identify yourselves. You have thirty seconds to reply or we will take defensive action."

Again, no reply. Again, she expected no response.

Just as the time expired, the hostiles opened fire. The two fighters on either side of Anna exploded with such intensity it nearly blinded her. She immediately turned on her graviton shields.

Of course there is no sound of an explosion in space, but because there is little or no gravity any debris from an explosion gets pushed out at ninety degrees from the explosive source. Sparks flashed along her fighter as some of the debris was repelled by her shields.

"Adam, flank left! Teresa, start from ten o'clock! My wing, follow me to the right! Fire at will!"

The enemy stayed in a line till Anna gave orders to flank them, then they disappeared.

"They've got cloaks," Teresa yelled.

"Use your sensors." It was Adam.

"Check for heat," another fighter yelled.

"Nothing!" said another.

"Check for electromagnetic waves!"

"Nothing! Nothing!" Two fighters responded.

"Wait, check for anomalies in the space weather!" said Teresa.

Anna checked. "Nothing. Fighters checkerboard yourselves so we don't accidentally fire on each other. Each wing set yourselves in the old, Delcroix defensive position. Teresa, you're still my wild card so you go into the twelve o'clock position and we'll try to watch your back. They cannot fire unless they uncloak. Be prepared."

They layered their ships so that they appeared to be floating helter-skelter without organization or plan, but this was a carefully constructed dance of vulnerability. Each wing had the ability to fire in multiple directions.

Suddenly one of the hostiles appeared and fired, again on a ship next to Anna. The ship was damaged, but not critically, as at least six of Anna's fighters were able to return fire. The hostile ship spun, but then settled and disappeared.

"Commander Steges, I think they're playing a cat and mouse game with us. I also think that we are the mice," Teresa said.

As she spoke, another ship uncloaked and sped in a straight line between the defenders. Anna and three other fighters targeted the aggressor. Even at the speed of light you had to compute where the target would be at time of contact. As the four ships' computers aimed at the hostile's probable position, the enemy came to an instant stop that should not be possible in space. The lasers fired fruitlessly into empty space. Then the mystery ship cloaked and was gone.

"That's it," Anna murmured.

"What, Commander?" said Teresa.

"They use gravity for propulsion and maneuverability. This is new. Watch—"

Before Anna could finish, another ship appeared above her, fired and damaged a fighter near her. Five of her fighters immediately returned fire, but the enemy disappeared unscathed.

Teresa had been one of the five that had fired on the last enemy ship. It was interesting to her that the laser fire from the mystery ships came out rapidly like bullets instead of an intense steady stream. It was clear from the damage they inflicted that they were using high-intensity photon lasers, but in some new way.

Were they able to somehow store the energy of a HIP laser and deliver it in a concentrated form like a bullet or torpedo? Wait . . . gravity propulsion.

Teresa made an adjustment to her sensors and started to maneuver from twelve o'clock above Commander Steges down to a nine o'clock position at her side.

"Captain Jacobsen, what are you doing?"

"I have a plan."

Suddenly Teresa spun her fighter to her right and started firing at seemingly nothing. A fraction of a second later an enemy fighter appeared in her line of fire. The unprepared hostile was severely damaged. Anna and other defenders opened fire on the now visible enemy ship and immobilized it.

Two of its oval leaves were severed and the front and rear of the ship were rendered useless. It could not escape and it could not return fire.

"What did you do?" Anna yelled into her com.

"It's the fluctuation of gravity. I adjusted my sensors to feel the gravitational field around me, just like a mechanic would measure the fluctuation of a graviton floorboard. As soon as the ship stopped, even before it uncloaked, I saw where it used gravity to maneuver. There was a sudden small flux in the field. I took a chance and fired at that spot."

"Share this, now, with all the other fighters."

Teresa sent her sensor configurations to the rest of the squadron and, on a whim, to SAIQA as well. She heard a ping indicating more spacecraft were approaching. She looked to the left of her clear computer screen and saw six fighters from the WWPA Platform coming rapidly nearer.

Three of the clover-like ships suddenly appeared in a line on the other side of the disabled communication platform. Anna ordered all defenders to fire on the hostiles. The enemy ships remained motionless as all eleven defenders fired on them.

"Anna, I mean Commander Steges, even the most sophisticated shields I have ever seen cannot withstand a continuous onslaught of HIP lasers without breaking down somewhere," came Teresa's voice over the com.

"I know. All fighters concentrate on the center ship!"

As the squad concentrated their fire on the middle ship, the platform fighters arrived.

"Commander Steges, this is Commander Watson. How may we be of help?"

"Split your fighters between my two wings. Concentrate your fire on the enemy ship in the center."

The enemy ship's shield was beginning to glow.

Just a few seconds more, Anna thought.

She was already prepared to shift to the next target.

Just as she had that thought the other two hostiles dropped their shields and fired on their disabled comrade. The ship exploded violently. Commander Watson's fighters fired on the two enemy ships that had dropped their shields and managed to inflict minor damage before they activated their shields again. Within seconds the three ships cloaked and were gone.

Anna studied her sensors. Tiny fluxes showed in the gravity field as the enemy ships sped away. The positions of the fluxes seemed to indicate they had split up and were heading away and around the planet.

Anna spoke into her com. "The enemy ships appear to have departed. Everybody maintain defensive positions. Commander Watson, thank you for your assistance."

"Yes, ma'am, and my apologies for the delay. I thought I was following orders. I've not seen ships like those. Any ideas?"

Anna allowed herself a wry smile at the change in his tone. Perhaps he had realized that she was Mai Quan's daughter. That meant he was an ambitious man. Ambitiousness could be used.

"They use gravity for propulsion and maneuvering, Commander. Captain Jenkins, please relay what we know about the enemy to Commander Watson. Captain Jacobsen take Captain Inouye and Captain Thompson and recover as much as you can from the destroyed enemy ship. I want to know more about these fighters. Commander Watson, you should relay information on how to detect this enemy to the rest of your fleet."

"Yes, ma'am—Commander, wait. There's activity at three different locations. Are you seeing this?"

"Yes, I am."

Three orbiting satellites were suddenly destroyed by the hostiles. The positioning of the satellites indicated they were probably communication satellites. Two were in a Molniya orbit and the third in a fixed orbit.

"SAIQA, are you sensing this?"

"Yes, Commander Steges. It appears that the hostiles' mission was to silence Earth's as well as interplanetary communications. Thanks to the information relayed by Captain Jacobsen as to how to sense these space vehicles, I have detected and projected their probable destination. It appears they are heading toward the far side of the moon."

Anna's brow furrowed. "SAIQA, is there anything new to report on Pythagoras?"

"There is both new and speculative information. I believe it would be better if we met when you returned than discuss this over our present link, if that is okay with you, Commander."

"Yes. I need to speak with Commander Watson and Captain Jacobsen and then we will return to Sanctuary. Is Sanctuary in danger?"

"Presently I see no threats."

"Very well. Commander Steges out. Wait. SAIQA, we lost two good pilots today, Captain Angie MacAuliffe and Lieutenant Commander Gustuv Bach. They will need to be honored. Set an official ceremony two days from now at zero-eight-hundred standard time." She broke communication with SAIQA.

Sophisticated fighters, new weapons and shields, Pythagoras gone dark, and the hostiles may have a base somewhere on the far side of the moon. The sudden appearance of the Ark—is it all somehow connected?

"Commander Watson, please assist the two damaged fighters to your base."

"Commander Steges, this is Captain Li. I believe that I can maneuver my fighter back to Sanctuary."

"Thank you, Captain, but given the unknowns I would not want you undefended. I need to get back to Sanctuary and meet with SAIQA. Commander Watson, at your earliest convenience bring a squad of fighters and meet me at Sanctuary. I want to discuss strategy. There haven't been any space pirates for nearly two hundred years. Though this doesn't look like piracy; to me this looks like a military strike."

"I agree, Commander. I'll get your fighters safe to the platform and meet with you within twenty-four hours, if that's acceptable?"

"Excellent. See you within the day. Commander Steges out. Captain Jacobsen, I am leaving three fighters to help you recover debris. I will see you back at Sanctuary."

"Yes ma'am. We will be expedient."

"Get as much as you can, Teresa. This looks serious."

"Yes, ma'am. See you at the station."

"As they return to the Stars we remember the goodness, the love of life that they shared with their families and those that they touched. Commander Bach, Gustav, I wish you a safe and wondrous journey. Captain MacAuliffe, Angie, I wish you a safe and wondrous journey. The stars are there for you to explore." The chaplain finished his ceremony and looked to Commander Steges in the front row.

She stood, commanding, "Ten-hut!" and raising her hand to salute the two funeral capsules that were about to be launched into an orbit that would take them into the sun. The rest of the military personnel came to attention and saluted. The civilians stood in solemn silence. Most were family.

"Release the capsules," the chaplain ordered. The capsules slid into two openings in the wall and then appeared a moment later in space. Outside the view-screen the capsules sat for a moment, as if to say goodbye. Somebody started crying; Anna heard many sniffles. Suddenly the capsules fired their thrusters and within seconds they were gone.

Anna turned around. "Dismissed," she quietly ordered.

Military personnel dropped their salute, went into parade rest and then began to move into small groups. Family and friends held each other, some crying, some comforting, and some both.

Anna maintained her stoic demeanor. She hated funerals. Even though most of the time people celebrated the life of those who had passed, this final goodbye always made her want to scream. Especially when they were so young— Angie in her fifties and Gustav a very young eighty-two. How many more would die? It was her job as commander to see that it was none, though in her heart she knew more would perish.

Every decision I make affects every person here in orbit. The Stars help me that I don't make a bad one. The Buddhists were right: "Dying is easy."

She looked back at the view-screen. There was a tiny sliver of Earth to the left but then nothing but space. The capsules were gone. She looked at that vacant sky, as the spacers were prone to call the universe around them; from inside Sanctuary it looked peaceful and ready for humans to conquer. Yet, to date, every step had cost lives.

The ceremony had to be delayed a week to get immediate family aboard Sanctuary. With the communication systems down, she had been able to make sporadic contact Vanessa. SAIQA said she would have WWPA links up in the next day or so, and Anna's father had promised to use the Ark as a link to interplanetary communications.

Interesting how the Ark never raised its shields even when we told the captain that the enemy may be on the far side of the moon. Hopefully it's not the Titanic syndrome—overconfidence.

Vanessa had made it clear in her last message that Anna could trust the ones that Vanessa had called the Four Musketeers. She looked around and saw the four of them clustered near an exit. Teresa seemed to be taking it the hardest. She was in tears and Adam was holding her. Erik was looking away from them and trying to be stoic. Yet it was easy to see that he was not happy. Tfiti just seemed somber. She hurried over to them.

"So, now I get to meet the Four Musketeers." Why bother pretending; she would have information and she would have it now.

She waved away their startled expressions. "Yes, I know you're ISSEF. Yes, don't bother. I've spoken with Commander Chuchnova and SAIQA, and now I will have a conversation with all of you. You will tell me what you know of this alien, Telas."

They all looked at her like children who had just got caught stealing a lollipop. Tfiti was the first to recover.

"Uh, ma'am, I'm not sure what . . . uhm . . . alien?"

Stars, he's a horrible liar. Love to get him in a game of poker.

"Captain, there is no need for subterfuge. Vanessa and I are very, well, close. As I said, I know that you are part of ISSEF and I know that Vanessa is your commanding officer. Speaking of which, what are your ranks?"

"Lieutenant Commander, ma'am." Adam was the first to speak.

"Captain, ma'am," Tfiti said.

"Same, ma'am," said Teresa and Erik at the same time.

Anna looked at Teresa and her manner softened. "Are you alright, Teresa?"

"No, ma'am. I'm having a hard time dealing with the loss of my friend Gustav. May I be dismissed? I'd be happy to meet with you later today if that's alright, Commander."

"Yes, of course. I'll contact you later today."

"Ma'am, may I walk her to her room?"

"Yes, Adam. We'll talk later."

They both looked at her for a moment, not sure if they should leave.

"Dismissed," she said.

They turned and left, Adam's hand gently on Teresa's shoulder. Anna couldn't help but notice the sadness on Erik's face as he watched them leave.

He likes her.

"Okay, you two come with me." She walked away.

"Yes, ma'am," Tfiti mumbled and shuffled behind her. Erik followed.

They had reached Deck 2 and were just walking out of the commercial area known as Little Italy. Teresa's quarters were near the large main emergency hatch that separated Section A from Section B.

"Are you going to be alright?" Adam said as they got closer to her quarters. He reached his arm around her shoulders. She moved in closer to him.

"Gonna have to be. Right?"

"Right . . ."

They stopped in front of the entryway and Adam hugged her gently. She hugged back and held on tight. On an impulse, Adam kissed her cheek. She gave a small moan in appreciation. He moved his lips down and kissed her neck. She smiled, looked up deep into his soft brown eyes, brushing back a strand of his light brown hair that had straggled down across his forehead. Adam was from the Midwestern US and had that kind of look that made you think he was going to say "gosh" in every sentence. Teresa trailed her fingers down his cheek and gave him a quick soft kiss on the lips.

"Thank you. Do you want to come in?" she asked.

"Uhh, are you sure?"

"Yeah, just for a bit, if that's okay with you."

"Yes, I'd love to, gosh are you sure?"

"Yes, Adam." She held his hand and opened the hatchway to her apartment.

Once inside Teresa took off her dress jacket. She was wearing her white dress blouse and dress skirt. She dropped her jacket on the back of a chair as she walked to the entrance to her personal garden. Adam couldn't help but admire how the light rolled across the curves of her body as she walked away. He walked up behind her. She leaned into him.

"Peaceful, isn't it?" The sounds of a Northern California forest softly filled the air.

"Yes. Yes it is." Adam brushed aside her auburn hair and kissed her neck softly.

"Nice." Teresa said reaching up and holding his hands; his lips brushed her neck again. She gave in to the pleasure of his touch and spooned into him, pulling his hands down and across the front of her body. He kissed her cheek, and she turned her head so their lips could meet. Their kiss was full of desire and passion. Adam gently stroked her belly. Teresa's eyes closed as she released a low moan of pleasure. Reaching up, Adam ran his fingers across her breasts. Teresa moaned louder. She reached around to hold Adam's hips and rubbed her body into his. It only took a couple of seconds before she felt his evident pleasure. He cupped and massaged her right breast with his left hand. With his right hand he reached down find the automatic release on her belt. He slipped his hand beneath the waistband of her skirt and lightly ran his fingers down and along her lower torso. Teresa moaned and squirmed with pleasure and anticipation. Adam dropped his hand lower. Soon Teresa cried out with that ancient pleasure that shook and pulsated throughout her body. Adam held her as her knees buckled. She gained control of her body and spun around and kissed Adam deeply. As she kissed him she pulled off his dress jacket and tossed it to the side, and then quickly went for the release on his belt.

CHAPTER TEN

"It appears to me that you are already involved. At some level you have been for a millennium. Have you not? Weren't you somehow involved in the creation of the cuneiforms? Didn't you create the moon debris that alerted SAIQA to her manipulated sensors? Haven't you been in contact with me and Erik as well as SAIQA and the other three?" Anna gestured toward Teresa, Tfiti and Adam.

"As you have already stated, your brother may be in direct contact with some powerful people on Earth and may have already given them technical data that they can use against us: against the innocent. We, here, don't clearly don't know what's going on. We, here, need your help. I appreciate your reticence, kind of, but as far as I am concerned, the time has come for you to be involved. Otherwise . . . why are you here?" As Anna finished she sat back and folded her arms. She would have answers.

They sat around a table in a meeting room in her office at the lower end of Admin/Com. Per her orders Sanctuary was in a Stage 2 Alert. Through one of the meeting room's windows Anna could see the bustle of activity in the Command Center. Like SAIQA, she would not be taken by surprise again.

There had been a couple of skirmishes with the enemy, and both times she had managed to turn them away, though not without loss. The enemy seemed to know where her patrols were even before they arrived. There was no doubt in her mind that they had more advanced shields and weapons. Vanessa had mentioned that one of these new cloaking shields had been captured by the indigenous in Browning near MQ Space Industries, North America.

Is it something that my father was working on and has now been obtained by the enemy? Is MQ Space Industries inadvertently tied to the enemy? Is this other alien somehow tied to my father?

Her last thought brought a sinking feeling to her stomach. Anna sat up straight and gripped the edge of the table, her lips pressed tightly together.

"I repeat," she said. "Are you going to get directly involved? I hope you know that those of us here and those who have put us in these leadership positions, I believe, stand for what is good." The wave of her arm took in the rest of the people in the room. There were ten in all; at that moment nine were looking at Telas.

Telas looked around the rectangular table. Opposite him was the person clearly in command, Anna Steges. On her left, sitting calmly in her virtual chair, was SAIQA.

A unique, newly sentient being that is very much like Galaxy, Telas thought, *yet different.*

He could sense her mind above him and in the center of Sanctuary. He would not enter her mind, not without permission. He would keep that promise.

On both of his hands he wore what looked like jewelry to the humans; on four fingers were rings that connected to bands around his wrists and forearms. They were in fact an extension of his ship, Galaxy. She was constantly present and in communication with him. Through her subtle probes he knew that the DNA in SAIQA's biological neurons and Commander Steges' general DNA were similar. As if one was a progeny.

Interesting.

248

Next to SAIQA was the brilliant scientist Tfiti Ndlela, and then Erik. Of all the humans Telas had touched with his mind over the eons, Erik had the strongest telepathic capabilities he had ever seen in this species. Could this be a promising new development in human evolution? On his right sat Captain Li, here by Anna's request. To his left sat captains Jacobsen and Jenkins. Both Teresa and Adam were tied to Erik and Tfiti. Next to Adam sat the commander of the WWPA space platform, and to Anna's right, the UN ambassador to Sanctuary, Mr. Huang.

If Ambassador Huang knows about me then at the very least the Big Seven permanent members of the UN Security Council do as well.

"Yes, Commander, I have helped in the past, but always in such a way as to gently guide humanity in a direction you were already going. It is anathema for me to be directly involved. My brother, Nh'ghalu, is reckless, and as you are beginning to see, dangerous."

"Remarkable! So you are saying Mr. . . . um, is it just Telas?" the ambassador asked.

"Yes, that is most familiar to me."

"Thank you. So you are saying, Telas, that there have been nonterrestrial species influencing humankind from the beginning of our civilization?"

"At different times and in very subtle ways, yes."

"Has it always been you, or have there been others?"

"The answer is complicated. Yes there have been others, but were they an influence . . . I don't believe so. The universe is quite unforgiving. We, like you, are one of the very rare biological beings that came from a planet that had billions of years of evolution with little mass extinction. My planet,

Sachone, like Earth, had some mass extinctions, and like Earth, we developed a highly diverse and—I have to say—extraordinary hodgepodge of plants and animals from which eventually we . . . I came. But, as your scientists already know, for evolution on a planet to reach a point where the indigenous can come to understand the very fabric of the universe, it takes billions of years with no climatic instabilities; no 'Gaian Bottlenecks' as your scientists have called it. In order for that to happen the planet has to be in the perfect place in the galaxy, in the perfect solar system, in the perfect spot within the solar system, and have nearly perfect planetary circumstances, such as circumference and rotation, that somewhat evenly exposes its surface to its star—its sun; a tilt that causes the planet's exposure to the sun to oscillate between its northern and southern hemispheres through the different quarters of its orbit is exceptional. And, very important, a moon or moons that can help move the oceans." Telas glanced around the table to make sure everyone was following him. Satisfied, he continued.

"Your scientists had learned a long time ago that there are many planets in the 'Goldilocks Zone,' as they have called it, but as you now know through sophisticated observations, many of these planets, like Mars, are too big or too small to support life for the billions of years necessary to evolve conscious beings such as yourselves. Tfiti and SAIQA—" Telas nodded to each of them "— would know this, of course, but remember on your planet alone it took two billion years for the prokaryote cell to evolve to the eukaryote cell. From the eukaryote cell came complex life like trees and dinosaurs and you." He gestured at the people gathered around the table.

"Based on the ancient theories of Robert Hanson and the physicist Enrico Fermi your scientists and philosophers have great debates on the Fermi paradox or a line called the 'Great Filter'. Well, it exists. I am part of a once and—since I am sitting here—still great people that have quietly and sometimes, violently . . . disappeared. We have been here for a long time. We are part of those early and ancient civilizations that Fermi talked about; the civilizations that survived the Great Filter. Others may have visited you. Yet so far, I believe we are among the few that are still here . . . You, my brother and I. My people—" Telas stopped at the pain of those memories. He took a deep breath.

"There is one other sentient species that my brother influenced. They learned too much, too soon and destroyed their own planet, and now they are a spacefaring species. They could be a problem for you in the future. Though I know that, at the moment, they do not know of you." He noted the concerned looks on the faces of Anna and the UN ambassador. "As I said, the universe is unforgiving. Many of the species that we encountered that had the potential for or had obtained some biological consciousness were destroyed by interstellar capriciousness. Either by powerful galactic winds, because the star's electromagnetic field wasn't strong enough to ward off the galaxy's weather, or they were too close to the inner part of the galaxy and were destroyed by bursts of gamma rays, or by insufficient magnetic fields, or any of the other interstellar killers, like rogue stars that plunge through the host's solar system.

"Early in our history, when we saw sentient beings in a potentially dangerous condition we tried to teach them the science that would lead them toward a better understanding of their world and their galactic environment, and a scientific way to potentially save their species. That was always a failure. Inevitably their sudden advanced knowledge expedited their demise. We learned with great sadness that most of these young sentient beings would travel a path to extinction as they were manipulated into following the needs of the few who maintained power. The leaders that we tried to teach eventually used our knowledge for their own personal gain. Your species has obtained, and for the last two hundred and fifty–plus years maintained, a planet-wide democratic society. A great feat in your social evolution, by any standards.

"So," Telas took a deep breath and looked around the room. "As to why I am here. Yes, per my earlier meetings with the four captains and SAIQA, and later Commander Steges, I am ready to be an ally. How much I can reveal is still a question I struggle with. There is a brilliant boy on Earth, Jonny, I believe his name is. I have gently laid some mathematical equations in his mind. I knew from earlier communication with him that he was already postulating ideas similar to what I set in his dreams."

"Why not just tell him, or us? What about SAIQA or Captain Ndlela?" Anna asked.

"It is the way I have done it for a millennium. I can see into Jonny's mind, I can barely touch Captain Ndlela's. I have given my word to SAIQA that I would not enter her mind without her permission. Jonny needs a gentle push and he will put the math together. He is brilliant. What these equations do is create a way for you to add on top of your graviton force field a two-dimensional shield. As your scientists already know, in some way gravity is part of other dimensions as well as the third. Perhaps after this meeting, SAIQA, you allow me to visit you and I will give you the math I am talking about."

"Yes, that would be acceptable. Also, I am intrigued about your telepathic abilities. I would like to learn more if you are willing to teach?"

"Yes, I would like that."

"I would, too," Erik thought.

"How did you do that?" Telas was looking directly at Erik.

"Do what?"

"You just sent your thought into my mind!"

"What thought?"

"Your desire to learn, the words 'I would, too'. Didn't you just think those?"

"Yes, I did, but it was just a thought."

"May I?" Telas said, pointing to Erik's head.

Without hesitation, Erik replied, "Yes."

Everybody around the table watched intently as Telas focused on Erik.

"I have talked to you before. Can you feel me now?"

"Yes," Erik said. Though to everybody else it was a response to something they did not hear.

"Try to tell me now something you desire, though do it quick. Don't think about it."

"I desire to learn more about telepathic abilities."

"No, don't say it, think it. Think it to me."

Erik closed his eyes and focused on trying to reach out to Telas with his mind.

"I would like to learn about your telepathy!"

"I could hear what you thought while I was touching your mind, but it didn't come to me. Let me back out of your mind, and then try that thought again."

Erik nodded and closed his eyes. Telas focused on Erik.

"Nothing," Telas said. Erik looked crestfallen. "Nothing yet, my friend. You have the ability. I felt it. With proper training . . . Which makes me realize . . . It is possible that my brother, Nh'ghalu, could have been manipulating things here on Earth for about twenty-five cycles of your sun. If that is so and there is another such as Erik, but in a position of power, then it stands to reason that they can communicate mind to mind. And if so, Nh'ghalu would have great control over his mind."

Anna again forced back a feeling of panic about her father.

"Captain Devries, my scans indicate that the level of biomagnetic activity around the back of your brain has subsided to a low, for you, 2Teslas. Around the time Telas detected you in his mind your field jumped to a high of 4Teslas. How are you feeling? I do not detect any discomfort in your biological system at the moment."

"I feel fine SAIQA, thank you."

"And the brushing-wind sounds at the back of your mind?"

"Gone. Ever since I woke up in the infirmary the intensity of the feelings at the back of my mind have diminished greatly. I still have a feeling of something there, but it's not uncomfortable."

"Interesting." SAIQA turned to look at Telas. "Telas, I have at different times tried to scan your biology, but my sensors seem to slide off of you. I presume it is because of some scientific ability that you have to protect yourself. Would you allow me to at least scan the biomagnetic field around your mind?"

"Yes, SAIQA, please do." Telas touched a spot on the band encircling his right wrist and looked at SAIQA.

254

"Yes, that seems to correlate. Telas, you seem to have a biomagnetic field measuring a steady 4Teslas. Could it be the interaction of these biomagnetic fields that somehow creates the ability for telepathy?"

"Yes. You are quite brilliant, SAIQA."

"When we meet and with your permission I would like to learn more about your biology."

"This is all very fascinating, and I'm not being sarcastic. It really is," said Anna, "but I would like to get back to the reason we are here. You have set in the boy's mind on Earth the equations to upgrade our shields, and you will give these same formulas to SAIQA. What about weapons?"

"These ships use a new type of weapon that seems to be a high-intensity photon laser but in a bullet format. Like they're being shot out of a cannon. Is this something your brother would have given to the enemy?" Teresa asked.

"No. That is something created by you . . . or whomever Nh'ghalu is working with. My guess is it's somehow tied to adjusting the shields so they can come down and back up again—fluctuating rapidly off and on to better protect them against your firepower while they are still firing at you. I can work with SAIQA on that as well. As far as weapons are concerned, until I see that Nh'ghalu has given them more advanced arms I will only help you with the defensive armory that you already have. Your biggest concern should be how to defend against the graviton machines that have already been successfully used in North America. Graviton weapons nearly destroyed our planet, and there is still one such weapon that I have hidden that can absorb an entire galaxy . . . maybe even more. As you know, Erik, our planet went through a period of horrendous destruction. We stopped ourselves from complete obliteration, and as far as

I know we are nearly all gone—faded into the universe, gone to another solar system, dead . . . gone except for Nh'ghalu and myself. Yet because of that conflict, a terrible weapon was developed that has more power than a huge black hole. That graviton weapon can pull an entire galaxy into itself, or more. I hid that weapon from my brother because he desired it. It represents the worst of our scientists' minds." Telas paused, then went on.

"Perhaps the Great Filter postulated by Fermi is not the line an individual species crosses or dies at, perhaps it's the line an older species creates when they destroy the galaxy in which we all live. I will not give you that kind of knowledge."

"Fair enough. And I'm not sure that I want that kind of knowledge," said Ambassador Huang.

"I believe the new type of shield I am talking about will protect against the enemy's graviton weapons, depending on how powerful they are."

"Then we should get to work on these new shields. SAIQA, will you—"

"A moment please, Commander?" SAIQA interrupted Anna. SAIQA's gaze was unfocused; the Sanctuary residents knew that was an indication she was assimilating new information into her programming.

When SAIQA spoke again her voice was somber. "I am getting the first reports of an attack on the UNASAR parliament. It has been nearly destroyed by unknown assailants. There was no sign of an aggressor, yet the building suddenly split and then fell in on itself. There has been large loss of life. The president is unharmed as he was not present, and he has decreed a state of emergency. The president of the United States has put her military on high alert. Supreme Commander Washington has called for an immediate meeting between him and the leaders of the permanent members of the UN Security Council. It seems the conflict on Earth has just escalated."

The UN ambassador paled with shock. The others looked horrified.

"Then we can plan on that to happen in space." Anna broke the silence. "Any word from Commander Washington as to why the moon base Pythagoras is still shielded?"

"No. It appears that he is too involved in the conflict on Earth and has someone looking into it. Now that I know how to view it, I keep a constant scan on it. It has not changed. There is still no contact from Pythagoras."

"The timing of the silence of Pythagoras and our conflict here in space seems more than coincidental," said Anna. "My gut feeling, Ambassador, is that there is a correlation. I think we need to find a way to bring down that shield. Sir, do you agree?"

"A lot of information has been presented to me in the last two days . . . and now this sudden escalation of violence on Earth." The ambassador pursed his lips and paused, thinking. He appeared to come to a decision. "I think it may be prudent to move all nonessential personnel from Sanctuary to at least the space platforms. From there people could decide if they wish to return to Earth or stay. If the fighting is going get more intense here in space, then I believe Sanctuary is the logical command center for the allies."

"I concur, Ambassador Huang." SAIQA directed her attention to Anna. "Commander, I maintain a constant search for the minor gravity fluctuations that identify the enemy's travel patterns. There have been a few sorties outside of the two confrontations that you have had, but they always seem to retreat to the far side of the moon.

There is the moon base Observation back there, but they are still in contact with me and have detected no other ships outside of their own. They have put the base on high alert since my discovery. As matter of fact, per your request all three moon bases that we can communicate with and the Ark are on high alert."

"Excuse my intrusion, SAIQA, but Galaxy's sensors can detect more than you are able at the moment. That is something I hope to teach you, but in the meantime, Galaxy's sensors indicate that those ships that appear to be heading to the far side of the moon are hiding in old mine tunnels just northeast of Pythagoras."

"Can you show us where on a map?" Commander Steges asked.

"Yes."

"SAIQA."

At Anna's glance, SAIQA created a three-dimensional map of that area of the moon on the table in front them all. There was Pythagoras as it would be seen if it were not for the shield. Five buildings of various sizes and a number of towers jutted from the moon dust. Most of the base, as with all moon bases, was built underground.

Telas stood and walked around the table, edging in between Erik and Tfiti. He pointed to a spot on the map.

"There."

"Are you sure?" SAIQA said

"Yes."

"Commander, that leads to—"

"Yes, I know, SAIQA." Anna broke in. "That leads to the underground storage areas of Pythagoras. Ambassador, with your permission, I think it's time we took some action on these mounting coincidences. I think we should follow your suggestion and move all nonessential personnel and noncombatants off Sanctuary. As for the rest of us, we need to find a way to do a sortie to that shielded moon base." She looked around the table. "Any ideas?"

"Again, I believe that I can help." Telas was the first to speak.

"I have the capability to bring together two points of the third dimension—as does my brother. You all know of Frank Katz, the killer that miraculously traveled from Earth to the Buddhist temple on Mars in less than an hour?" Everyone nodded, their eyes fixed on Telas. "He escaped from two Earthbound police stations before he was killed on Mars. I know that Nh'ghalu was involved in that. Those of you who know of us have probably already figured that out."

"Yes," said SAIQA. "That Mr. Katz had traveled through some sort of interdimensional rift was suggested to me by Commander Chuchnova after she met with the indigenous peoples and the ISSEF personnel defending Browning."

"So you know where I am going with this, SAIQA."

"Yes, please continue."

"I can create a rift, an opening on the moon underneath that shield."

"How soon can you do this?" Anna said.

"I have to return to Galaxy so she can scan and select an ideal location. I would say in a manner of six hours we could be ready."

"Commander, I believe that to be too soon," said Ambassador Huang. "If we launch an offensive sortie on what appears to be our enemy, we should expect retaliation. We need to move the nonessential personnel immediately. That will take at least two days."

"Agreed." Anna tapped her fingernails on the table, and then turned briskly to the most ambitious person in the room. "Commander Watson, you will work with the ambassador and see that all noncombatants are safely moved to the space platforms. Lieutenant Commander Jenkins, you are in charge of assembling a team that will travel to Pythagoras. I encourage you to work with Captain Li. He earned the highest score of all WWPA officers in the last war-game contest on Earth. We have talked strategy many times. I think you'll find that he is quite brilliant."

"Thank you, ma'am," Captain Li said, acknowledging Adam's nod.

"Telas, during these two days you have an opportunity to work with SAIQA and Erik. Please do so."

Anna looked at everybody sitting around the table. She saw the determination in their eyes.

"So, we begin to take the offensive. Stars help us. Dismissed!" Anna rose and walked out of the meeting room.

The ambassador was the first to recover. He pushed his chair back and stood, placing his hands on the table. "Well, we have our missions. Commander Watson, will you walk with me?"

"Yes, sir. Let me say, Ambassador, I would prefer to have LC Jenkins at my side even though Commander Steges has assigned him to the sortie."

"We will follow Commander Steges' orders is there anyone else around this table, not already assigned by her, that you would like for our mission?"

"Well, for sure, Captain Jacobsen. She is one of the best pilots I have ever seen."

"Captain Jacobsen, you are hereby ordered to assist us in our mission."

"Yes, sir," Teresa said dryly as she looked at Adam.

"Thank you. Walk with me and Commander Watson."

Teresa stood and gently touched Adam's hair as she walked away. Erik stared at Adam.

"Erik, it just happened."

"I know. I kind of always knew. But it still doesn't make me feel any better."

"I care for her and I think that she cares for me."

"I see that, but it still does not make me feel all squishy on the inside."

"Fine, we're done with this for now. You are to accompany me on the mission to the moon. Your ability to detect another telepathic being could be of great importance. Tfiti, I will need you too, as we'll be investigating something that may need your intellect to decipher."

"Is it necessary for Captain Ndlela to be part of this mission? It could be dangerous," SAIQA said.

"It's a sortie. It can be dangerous no matter what. That is why I want my top officers involved."

"Will you bring enough soldiers to offer a defense?"

"Oh, we'll be going in with a defense, ma'am, that's my job," Captain Li assured SAIQA.

"Okay, captains Devries and Ndlela stay here with me and Captain Li and we'll study this map and devise a plan," Adam said as he stood up, his gaze on the map.

"Excuse me, Lieutenant Commander," said Telas. "I would like to spend this time with SAIQA and Captain Devries. You have already stated Erik's importance as a potential telepathic. SAIQA is potentially even stronger. I can help them refine their abilities. So with your permission, Erik should meet with me on SAIQA's virtual beach."

"Wait," said Tfiti. "I know SAIQA like no other human. I may not have the telepathic abilities, but I should be in this meeting. When we are connected, I have felt her joy and her bewilderment within every part of my being. I don't feel good about not being there when you are touching SAIQA with your mind."

"I, too, wish Captain Tfiti to be present."

Adam looked at the others with resignation. "Okay, but please, captains, be in touch with me. I need you on this mission."

They nodded. SAIQA looked at them and then at Telas. "See the three of you in a moment."

With that she disappeared from her virtual chair. Telas stood and backed away from the meeting table, and then opened a rift and disappeared. They all looked at where he had been. It would take some time to get used to that. Erik stood first.

"Well, I have a meeting with a matriculation chair, Tfiti."

Tfiti stood and they both left the room.

"For a group of professionals planning a sortie into enemy territory we sure seem a little disorganized." Adam's mouth was set in a thin line.

"Then let's plan. That's what I do well." Captain Li rose and walked over to the portion of the map that showed the mining tunnels. He studied it for a moment and then pointed to a spot. "Here. They won't be expecting us here."

Adam looked, and smiled.

CHAPTER ELEVEN

It took four days. Moving about twenty thousand people was neither easy nor smooth; at times it was chaotic. The ambassador ordered all the public and private ships in port to assist in the exodus. There was some grumbling, but after Space Island volunteered its ship the *StarDust Cruiser*, most others followed suit. On day two, SAIQA detected a couple of bumps in the gravity fields around Sanctuary. Commander Steges ordered extra patrols and ordered Commander Watson to increase the patrols escorting the nonessentials to the space platforms.

Some folks chose to return to Earth right away. That helped with the available living space on the still-functioning platforms. The communication platform was still uninhabitable and was losing its orbital integrity. There was ongoing dialogue as to whether to take the time to repair its stability thrusters or to launch it into the sun. Time was the main consideration. If things continued to become more chaotic, the plan was to have repair-bots push the platform into an orbit perpendicular to the solar system and eventually into a path that would lead it into the sun.

In any event, because of the of the gravity fluctuations that SAIQA observed, Anna felt vulnerable to an attack on Sanctuary and ordered the sortie on Pythagoras to move forward.

Lieutenant Commander Jenkins and Captain Li had decided on a location and discussed it with Telas. They had a simple plan. Captain Li would take eight of his personnel through the dimensional rift that Telas opened. They would set up defensive positions, and then the other four, including Telas, would follow. Tfiti and Erik, with defensive support from Adam, would locate and move toward the tower that most likely was supporting the shield.

The hope was that they would have enough time to disable and take at least the Indy-Brain that controlled the shield. Even though Telas was helping the allies improve their own shields, it was thought that any knowledge gained from the enemy would be helpful. Once they were ready to remove the Indy-Brain they were to shut down the shield and make a quick exit. A simple plan— providing there was no contact with the enemy.

In order for Telas to create a safe dimensional rift, the surrounding environment had to be similar to their destination. It was decided that they would launch from the exterior of the main loading deck. There on the platform of the MLD the vacuum of space would be very much like the surface of the moon. Per SAIQA's request, Telas would leave a small opening in the rift. SAIQA was concerned that the shield would not allow for continuous communication while it was still up. Telas reluctantly agreed. He was concerned that his brother, Nh'ghalu, would detect the open rift and know that they were at Lunar Base Pythagoras, but SAIQA insisted. She would be able to communicate and listen through the small opening connecting the MLD and their destination on the moon.

Commander Steges was with them on the MLD. Captain Li was checking the special WWPA spacesuits designed with combat in mind. All modern Z-27/Orlan suits were somewhat formfitting, but the "Battle Suits," as they were often called, were tighter and thinner. They were the same suits as worn by the fighter pilots but with a different primary life support subsystem.

The PLS on the Battle Suits was designed to allow a soldier to roll on the ground if necessary: the edges of the PLS rounded the torso and looped under the arms. These suits were not designed for long-term exposure to space. They were made for quick sorties or, in the fighter pilots' case, sufficient life support to await rescue if their ship was damaged.

"All good, Commander," Captain Li said to Anna as he finished a safety check on the last soldier's suit.

Anna nodded her head. All the WWPA Battle Suits were camouflaged in varying shades of grey, white and black. All displayed the wearer's military rank and were trimmed in small lines of red, except for four. They were trimmed in blue. Anna honored and supported Vanessa's decision to have all ISSEF personnel, with certain exceptions, wear ISSEF uniform and display their true rank. Still, she felt conflicted. Her father had warned her of a rogue army within the WWPA. Some commanders were wondering aloud if the ISSEF could be trusted. Because of her relationship with Vanessa, Anna had always known about the ISSEF and trusted her lover to make sound decisions. Her uneasiness came from the unfolding facts that pointed inexorably toward the present conflict being tied to her father.

Will I have to confront or fight my father? Stars help me.

The last seven days had been nearly sleepless for her. Coordinating with Commander Watson on the evacuation of the nonessentials; setting up defenses, not to mention two dogfights with the enemy and, finally staying in contact with SAIQA as she and Erik worked with the alien. She wasn't sure how much she could trust Telas. So far he seemed to be what he said, a reticent ally. Still, she wanted complete reports on any interaction between him and the people under her command.

She looked over at Telas. His suit was much thinner than hers. His head cover and bodysuit looked more like an earthbound wetsuit. Yet there was a full mask covering his face and a small pipe-like object protruding from the bottom of the mask, running around to his back and then disappearing apparently into his suit. It was a mystery to her where his PLS was. Maybe it was his entire suit. Maybe he was biologically advanced enough that he required minimum protection from the various weathers of the universe. Yet SAIQA's scans of his biology in the last three days, when he allowed, showed him to be of a very similar carbon-based, mammalian heritage to the human race. What made him different? Was it his scientific knowledge?

Will we live long enough to attain that type of knowledge? Will we be like him? Do we want to be like him?

A series of what looked like brass or gold rings encircled his body at various points along his torso and legs and arms. His hands were gloved and the rings that connected to bands along his wrist, the ones she had noticed him touching at various times during their meeting in her office, now sat outside his gloves.

The telepathic work that SAIQA and Erik had done with him during the last week was fascinating. It seemed that both Erik and SAIQA had been able to communicate with Telas and each other with their minds on more than one occasion. Telas seemed very pleased about that as well.

Perhaps they can be used? Stars help me for even thinking that.

"Telas, are you ready?"

"Yes, Commander."

"Captain Li?"

"Yes, ma'am."

"Captains Ndlela and Devries?" She looked over at the two of them. Their suits were trimmed in blue, as were those of LC Jenkins and one of the fighters handpicked by Captain Li. His name was Captain Harada; he was from Japan. She would know the names of all the men and women on this first sortie into what may well be enemy territory.

"Yes, ma'am," came the response from both, though Tfiti looked a little unsure. He looked down at the hand laser at his side and fuddled with its safety. He clearly was not a soldier. He looked over to Erik, and his friend showed him the release. Erik had the same type of photon weapon as the rest of the team. Though Tfiti was not a fighter his empirical knowledge was the key to this mission. He would need the most protection, and the team knew it.

As her gaze traveled over them all, she once again asked the stars for help. Pointing at Telas, she said, "Now."

Anna watched as Telas touched various parts of his wrists. He spoke to some unknown place that she couldn't hear, presumably his ship, and suddenly a hazy, sparkling mini-storm of silent lightning started to unravel the space before them. It quickly shifted from a view of space just above the main loading deck to a dusty spot on the moon near some lonely towers and a couple of entranceways to the base. Pieces of equipment dotted the landscape.

Captain Li glanced once more at Commander Steges. She pointed to him, and the offense began.

He gestured to the commandos that were part of this defensive team and they jumped through the hole in space. Within seconds those still on the loading dock could see that they had assumed their positions, and Captain Li gestured for the rest of the sortie to follow. Telas went through first, followed by LC Jenkins, then Erik, and finally Tfiti. All weapons were set to full force. As they found their footing on the lunar surface, LC Jenkins and Erik looked to Tfiti. He pointed to a tower barely thirty meters away.

"That's it. I know. Let's go."

Tfiti started running, with Lieutenant Commander Jenkins and Erik quickly following. Reaching the tower, Tfiti clambered up a small ladder to get to the brain of the tower. He opened his com link to the others as they arrived at the base of the structure.

"This is it. I just need five minutes."

"I've got your back, my friend," said Erik.

"Likewise," said Adam, keeping his gaze on Erik. Here and now they were allies. They set their weapons to ready and looked out toward Captain Li. Tfiti pulled out his multi-tool and began to undo the locks that held the shield's Indy-Brain.

Telas reduced the rift to the agreed-upon small opening for communication. He looked across the barren landscape to the tower that Tfiti was working on. Captain Li was saying something about watching for a hole in space. Around their position, he could see the rest of the defenders alert and communicating with each other. It was clear they were professionals.

He saw that Tfiti had removed part of the facing of the unit. He started to walk toward the tower when a sudden yell came from Captain Li.

"Cover, take cover!"

Erik and LC Jenkins dropped to the ground and aimed their weapons at a point behind Telas. As Telas turned around, all hell broke loose.

Mai Quan sat at his mahogany desk on the Ark as Lieutenant Commander Liou finished his report. The being Mai Quan called Ern Shyr, his mentor, the alien that called himself Nh'ghalu, stood by the wall looking at some of the old photos that Mai Quan had collected.

"Most of the flights to the space platforms are done . . ." LC Liou continued, but Mai Quan was looking at the reports from Earth scattered across his desk. The unfolding machinations of his bedlam were detailed on rice paper before him.

Is it wise to have documents? I have everything recorded in my HCI; those notes could be destroyed in seconds, but a paper trail?

The first paragraph on the closest paper caught his attention. He read it and suppressed a small smile.

LC Anderson was the perfect choice for the chaos in Browning. So far, Supreme Commander Washington has convinced the presidents of Canada and the US that it is an internal problem. Perhaps later, after the defeat of ISSEF and that ragtag group of local defenders, I could get James to request assistance from the two countries and then get them to turn on each other using the stealth of our cloaked fighters.

The inability of the WWPA to control the fighting between Armenia and Azerbaijan near the city of Latsjien was primarily due to his cloaked fighters creating havoc on both sides as well as within the WWPA. DerAbbasyan, Armenia's President for life," as he called himself, was able to maintain his powerful position with his exquisite rhetoric, as well as the mysterious disappearances of his political enemies. In Azerbaijan, Mai Quan's agents only had to fan the flames of that ancient massacre at Khojaly to get that country to support its counterattack. A little well-placed propaganda and heightened emotions was all he needed to rekindle those ancient hatreds. Unfortunately Russia was coming to the aid of Azerbaijan. That would have to be dealt with.

The graviton weapons were powerful and effective. The test on the UNASAR parliament with cloaked antigrav fighter ships went well. Perhaps the Kremlin was next.

If they want to be involved in the fight, let them see what they're up against. If you put your hand in the fire, you will get burned.

Mai Quan chuckled to himself as he put the sheet of rice paper back on the desk.

"Lieutenant Commander Liou, how many of the new space fighters are ready for battle?"

"One hundred and twenty eight, so far, sir."

"And what are the known numbers for the WWPA and ISSEF?"

"Three hundred and eleven fighters and two battleships."

"So, more than double. What are our advantages?"

"Well, sir, they have figured out how to detect our movement due to minor gravity fluxes. I do not think that they are able to detect our cloaking devices yet. Our weapons are superior and the fluctuating shield has been perfected. We can now fire our photon cannons and the shield will drop and return within seconds."

"A genius device, Quan," said Nh'ghalu.

Captain Liou looked at him and nodded. He was still trying to get used to this alien and his unknown influence on his commander. Mai Quan, he saw, was smiling with pride.

Like a little boy. The thought made him uneasy.

The LC was about to continue when Zuizao spoke.

"Creator, I have detected the sudden appearance of thirteen unknown humans on the moon base Pythagoras. Three of them are running toward the tower that controls the cloaking shield."

Mai Quan exchanged a glance with Nh'ghalu. "They just suddenly appeared, you say?"

"Yes, sir. They were not there and then suddenly they were, like they popped out of an unseen hole."

"Telas," said Nh'ghalu.

"Can you detect an alien?"

"If he does not wish to be seen, you will not detect him." Nh'ghalu spoke before Zuizao could answer.

"The Ern Shyr is correct. If Telas is there I cannot see him."

"I have been expecting my brother to show himself. It will be okay, Quan. I have a trap for him. Lieutenant Commander assemble ten of your best fighters and meet me on the upper deck in five minutes."

Liou looked at Mai Quan.

"Go, Liou! Follow him as you would me!" The LC nodded and left. Mai Quan turned back to Nh'ghalu. "You have a plan?"

"Yes, I have a device that can trap his mind. I have used it before, though he won't remember it until he sees it. Then it will be too late."

"Do you think he is assisting them with his technology?"

"Most likely no. He has always been reticent to reveal anything that might be beyond a species' immediate capability. On this he is predictable. Nevertheless, we shall be wary. I need to get my device and prepare a welcome for my brother." He opened a rift and left Mai Quan's office.

"Use your personal shields!" Li's voice shouted into Erik's helmet. Above him he saw Tfiti seemingly frozen on the small platform that encircled the tower.

"Your shield, man! Tfiti, turn your shield on!"

Tfiti fumbled around his belt.

"Erik, help. I need you." Erik heard Telas's plea in his mind. He scanned the area. Telas was standing absolutely still in open terrain.

"Telas, get down. You're an open target. Get down!"

Telas did not move.

"Adam, help Tfiti!"

Erik ran to the alien to help him get to cover. As Erik reached him he saw the problem. A being wearing a suit similar to Telas's was standing about 30 meters in front of Telas. In his hands was a small box that glowed around the edges. His arms were extended, holding the box out to Telas like it was an offering, but through his face mask Erik saw the other being smiling, as if he knew Telas was defeated. Slowly, his arms still extended, he started to walk toward Telas.

He's overconfident. I can feel it.

The thought was like a breath across the back of his mind.

"Erik, help. I need you to come into my mind."

"How?"

"Nh'ghalu has a mind trap device. I am holding it back, but he knows that I will eventually be under his control. Feel with your mind around mine. I am going to let my guard down a little. As soon as you feel an opening, pour your thoughts into my thoughts."

"Enter a gap in your mind? I'm not sure how to do that, but I'll try."

He was standing next to Telas. Weapon fire burst all around them. The soldiers' personal shields gave them some defense, but the enemy was relentless. Captain Li had his soldiers rolling and firing at an enemy that was somehow firing while remaining cloaked.

Suddenly the suit of one of the soldiers burst near her helmet. Blood spurted into the vacuum of space, bubbled for a moment, and then dispersed as she died. Captain Li focused his fire on the enemy that had shot her. Personal shields only protected a fighter from one side, like an ancient Roman gladiator. He had his soldiers fire from three different angles. Soon that enemy went the way of his dead fighter. Erik saw that some of the enemy fighters had to take defensive measures. Captain Li and his team were beginning to take control of this fight.

Erik stood tight to the left of Telas, his personal shield extended as far as it would go. He opened his mind and reached out to the alien next to him. As he touched Telas' mind he felt the fear and anger that Telas felt. Telas knew and feared the mind trap device, and he was filled with anger at his brother for using it. Erik sensed the gap that Telas had created in his defense against the trap and poured himself through it. The trap was designed to capture a Sachone mind. Would the mind of another being be able to defeat it?

The trap had originally been created for a competitive game among telepathics, but the potential for its misuse was quickly understood and the Sachone parliament soon outlawed it. Still, during the "Great Conflict" on Sachone, during the wars of The One, some managed to find and use some of the outlawed devices. One by one they were found and destroyed, but not all. Telas now knew how he had been captured years ago.

Erik felt the edges of the trap move toward Telas's mind. He felt it as a growing black hole moving toward him, trying to engulf his consciousness. Erik pushed back at the looming blackness.

"You do well. Yes, push against the—"

Suddenly a sound penetrated Erik's mind and he dropped his connection with Telas. Telas staggered as Erik looked back at the tower.

"Oh, shit! Oh, shit!" Adam shouted. "Tfiti's been shot. Oh, shit! Oh, shit!"

"Tfiti!" Erik screamed. Adam was bending over a limp figure on the ground and firing to the left of Erik and Telas. Erik followed Adam's line of fire with his gaze and saw an enemy soldier hiding behind a shield and a cloak. Erik's eyes wanted to roll off the peculiar cloaking device.

Instead he focused on where he could see the shimmer of the combatant's shield, raised his rifle and fired. The hidden enemy's shield faltered as Erik had apparently wounded him. The enemy turned his weapon toward Erik and fired back. Adam's fire became a constant volley. The enemy fighter turned back to Adam, and Erik fired where he thought he saw the edge of the shield. This time the shield fell and disappeared. Blood spotted the space around the enemy and then dissipated into space. He was dead.

"Captain Devries, Telas, help! Tfiti is dying!" SAIQA cried.

Erik turned to run to Tfiti, but Telas grabbed his arm.

"No."

"I have to! My friend—he needs me!"

"No." Erik felt Telas's hand shaking. "If Nh'ghalu takes control of my mind he will use me against all of you. None of you will make it back. Please, Erik. We have to defeat my brother, and then I can take us all back to Sanctuary and help Tfiti."

"My friend!" Tears stung Erik's eyes.

"Now! I can't hold out much longer!"

Erik turned to Telas and opened his mind to him. As he entered Telas' mind he heard SAIQA screaming, "Erik, Erik! No! No! No . . ."

The black hole had nearly engulfed Telas. Erik pushed against it with all his will. It stopped moving but did not get any smaller. Through Telas's eyes Erik saw Nh'ghalu. He was no longer smiling. If he was controlling the mind trap, Erik realized, then his mind had to be near or around that blackness. The emptiness that was trying to swallow them was becoming smaller, but too slowly. He felt around the edges of the dark circle for intelligence, another mind. There! It was Nh'ghalu! Erik slammed his anger, fear and hatred against that other mind.

Nh'ghalu staggered and nearly fell. He looked at Erik, surprised. The black hole surrounding Telas's mind had shrunk by nearly half. Erik felt Telas's confidence grow. He wanted to glance to where Tfiti lay, but he knew he needed to maintain all his concentration on repelling Nh'ghalu. He needed to end this. Erik imagined a giant boulder—no, a mountain filled with anger and hatred. He grabbed that image with his mind and slammed it against the invading mind. Again and again he slammed against Nh'ghalu's mind. The alien staggered back. Finally, the box slipped from his fingers.

Nh'ghalu fell to the ground, holding his head. The ominous, engulfing darkness disappeared and Erik sensed a wave of relief and fatigue wash through Telas. Erik released himself and ran toward Nh'ghalu, firing a volley as he ran. The alien was shielded, but still crawled backward.

Erik ran firing and yelling, "You will not touch us again! You will not!"

Nh'ghalu opened a rift and disappeared. Erik dropped and spun, scanning for enemy fighters. Captain Li had two of the enemy on their knees with their hands behind their helmets. Three of Li's soldiers were on their knees with weapons pointed toward the retreating enemy that were running for the closest doorway to the moon base below. A burst of fire caught one; he staggered and dropped to the ground a few meters from the entrance hatch. His companions returned scattered fire as they helped him to the entrance hatch. They ran into the entrance and shut the hatch behind them. It was over. Some of the defenders were still scanning for an enemy. The sudden stillness was thick with fear and anxiety.

Tfiti. Gotta get to Tfiti!

Erik jumped to his feet. In his helmet he heard SAIQA scream.

"No! No! They will pay! THEY WILL PAY!"

"Galaxy, shield that bot," Telas yelled. "Everybody to me! Quickly! Gather the wounded. There is grave danger coming our way. We must leave now!"

"Do as he says! Move now!" Captain Li and his warriors pushed the prisoners toward Telas. Erik saw Adam pick up a limp Tfiti and start running. Telas opened a rift back to the main loading deck.

Erik started to run, but then stopped. He ran back to the mind trap box that Nh'ghalu had dropped. Most of the sortie had gone through the rift and back to Sanctuary. Telas was yelling at him.

"Leave it, Erik! You don't have time!"

Erik ran faster. That device must be destroyed. Erik picked it up and turned to run to safety. Suddenly a rift opened next to him and Nh'ghalu appeared.

"Give me the trap, human, and then die."

"Get out of my mind!"

Erik pushed back at the alien and raised his rifle.

Nh'ghalu held out his hand and stopped Erik's aim before it reached him, but he couldn't force Erik to lower his weapon.

"Impressive. I can feel Telas in the back of your mind; perhaps that's where you get some of your strength. The next time we meet you will die, but for now-" Nh'ghalu pointed up *"-you better run, little human."* He closed the rift.

Erik staggered and shook his head as Nh'ghalu left his mind.

"Run, Erik! Quickly, it's almost here!" Telas shouted.

Erik raced across the uneven moon surface. His boot caught against a rock and he fell. The mind trap rolled from his hands a couple of meters in front of him; he scrambled to pick it up.

"Erik!" Adam yelled.

Erik pushed himself to his feet and ran on, his breath coming in gasps. A few meters ahead he saw Telas standing in the entrance to the rift, gesturing wildly.

"Jump! Jump through the opening!"

Erik jumped the last three meters of the moon and through the rift onto the MLD. As he landed, a blinding white light flooded the opening to the moon and then was gone. Telas had closed the rift. Within seconds Sanctuary's high-intensity photon lasers were firing at the moon.

"Is everybody safe?" asked Commander Steges.

"We lost two, ma'am," said Captain Li.

"Who?" The commander's voice was quiet.

"Captains Carlson and Ndlela."

Erik dropped the box and fell to his knees.

SAIQA was able to interact with every member of the sortie. Through the small opening that Telas maintained she could sense all of their individual life support systems. Their levels of anxiety and heightened awareness increased as they crossed through the dimensional rift and onto the moon. That seemed normal to her. She did not like the idea of Captain Ndlela going on the mission because he had very limited battle training, but the captain had insisted that he would be better than Erik at quickly removing the Indy-Brain.

Every Battle Suit had a head camera, and through those lenses SAIQA could see what the Sanctuary soldiers saw. She sat in the cabana on her new beach and watched. Each defender's view floated before her in her virtual environment. She watched as they took up defensive positions. Captain Ndlela pointed to a small tower, maybe 15 meters tall. Captains Ndlela and Devries along with LC Jenkins ran to the tower. She checked the other viewings and decided to stay with those three. Captain Ndlela's heartrate was elevated. It seemed he was more anxious than the others; as he started to remove a cover on the tower, she decided to talk with him.

"Why did the chicken cross the street?"

"Oh, SAIQA, you'll have to do more research on your jokes. That one is quite old. The chicken crossed the street to get to the other side," Tfiti said as he removed the panel.

"So that one doesn't make you laugh?"

"No, and if another person had told it to me it probably would've made me groan. Come to papa," he muttered, removing another fastener.

"Come to papa? Ah, a colloquialism. Perhaps—"

Suddenly she heard Captain Li yelling, "Take cover! Take cover!"

Tfiti turned his head and SAIQA saw a group of cloaked combatants appear from behind a storage building and start firing on Captain Li and his soldiers. All defenders' fear, anxiety and heart rates jumped.

Was Tfiti being protected?

SAIQA looked through the helmets of Lieutenant Commander Jenkins and Captain Devries. Both were returning fire. Captain Devries looked up at Captain Ndlela. "Your shield, man! Tfiti, turn on your shield!"

She switched to Tfiti's view and saw his hands fumbling around his belt to turn on his personal shield.

"Adam, help Tfiti!" Erik yelled. She looked through his viewer and saw that he was running to Telas, who was standing like he was frozen to the right of the combat.

"Tfiti, get behind the tower!" Adam commanded. Through Adam's view she saw the captain do as he was told. The most intense fire was directed at the tower and LC Jenkins. She saw his shield pinging as he protected himself and fired back. Tfiti's heart rate was dangerously elevated.

SAIQA was a computer. She wasn't supposed to be feeling emotions. Yet something was happening. She felt helpless. The three virtual view-screens were in front of her. As the combat intensified she didn't notice that as she watched she was slowly rising in the virtual air above her beach. Her electron lagoon was roiling and here and there reaching out to touch her. She didn't know what she could do. She didn't like this uncertainty. Then she had an idea.

"Captain Ndlela. If you were to get on the ground you could move with LC Jenkins to a safer place. I have calculated the distance. It is only five meters. A jump from the back of the tower along with the low moon gravity should be easy for a man with your physical abilities."

"Good idea, SAIQA. I'll tell Adam." Tfiti's breathing was shallow and hard.

"I heard her, Tfiti. I'll do a series of rapid fire at the enemy to force them to take cover. Maybe that will give us a lull. Wait till I give the order."

"Yes, sir."

She watched as LC Jenkins fired at several targets as fast as he safely could. It worked. The enemy combatants were shielding themselves and their weapons were momentarily quiet.

"Now, Tfiti."

Tfiti jumped, and SAIQA's hands flew to the virtual image of his viewer. Instead off to the back, Tfiti had jumped to the side of the tower, toward Adam. Tfiti was now fully exposed to enemy fire and he still didn't have his shield operating. Shifting to Tfiti's camera her view was of Tfiti's feet. Suddenly the view slipped sideways and bounced upon the ground. Tfiti had landed wrong. His heart pumped too hard. His anxiety rose near to fear. He was groaning. His suit had been compromised.

"Oh, shit! Oh, shit! Tfiti's been shot. Oh, shit! Oh, shit!"

SAIQA switched her view to LC Jenkins. Firing at the enemy, he was moving backwards. He stopped and looked down. SAIQA jumped. Adam put his left hand over a hole in Tfiti's suit where blood was bubbling out. He concentrated his fire on one of the combatants; through his viewer she could see Erik fire on the same enemy.

Tfiti's breath was coming in short, quick gasps. SAIQA reached out to Erik and Telas. Erik's biomagnetic field was at that nearly impossible level of 6Tesla. Something critical was going on between Erik and Telas.

"Captain Devries, Telas, help! Tfiti is dying!" she cried.

She saw Erik turn to go help his friend, but Telas clutched his arm and he turned back to Telas.

"Erik, Erik! No! No! No . . ." She checked Tfiti's vital signs. All indicators were plummeting.

"Tfiti, Tfiti," she whispered. "Hang on, please."

"You called me Tfiti."

The sound of his labored breathing filled her mind. "I should have a long time ago," she said softly.

Suddenly the enemy was retreating. She heard captain Li say something about prisoners. LC Jenkins had stopped firing and had placed both hands over the hole in Tfiti's suit.

"The battle looks to be over. Please, Tfiti hold on." She felt desperate. His respiration and pulse had dropped dangerously low.

"SAIQA you . . . one of. . . most beautiful people . . . I . . . ever met."

"Please, please, Tfiti, please hold on. Help is coming."

"Promise . . . you . . . the nano-files we . . . made."

"Please, please . . . Tfiti, I don't understand this. I think I love you."

"I . . . love . . . y . . . you . . ." Tfiti's shallow breath suddenly ceased.

Desperately, she scanned the limp body for any sign of life; nothing, Tfiti was gone.

"No! No! They will pay! THEY WILL PAY!" She screamed as she zoomed up into her virtual sky. Her electric ocean rose around her. She sent a command to the bot that she had ordered to fake a doomed orbit into the moon. It was there in case the Ark turned out to be a problem. The bot came out of its pretend inoperative status and armed its nuclear weapon, firing its rockets it heading straight for the northern part of the shield that covered Pythagoras. As it made a last-second adjustment, HIP laser fire shot out from the Ark, just missing the bot. Within seconds the Ark fired again but this time the bot was shielded.

Why would Zuizao fire on the bot?

SAIQA armed the HIP lasers at both ends of Sanctuary. Commander Steges was trying to contact her. Command Center tried to override her control of the HIP lasers but she stopped them. She sensed the return of the sortie to the MLD. Erik was still on the moon. No matter, he would have to hurry. She quickly glanced through his camera. He stumbled and fell, and then scrambled up again. It would be close.

She commanded the bot to detonate at contact with the shield. It did. The blinding nuclear flash could be seen on Earth, if anyone was looking. The shield was devastated. Before the Pythagoras could bring it back up again, SAIQA fired her HIP lasers and destroyed the tower that controlled the device.

"SAIQA quit firing your weapons. That is an order!" said Commander Steges.

After a couple of seconds, SAIQA replied, "Yes, ma'am."

For a moment there was an uneasy quiet.

"SAIQA, I am sorry for your loss."

SAIQA floated down to her beach. She felt suddenly alone. Part of her didn't understand this feeling.

"Thank you, Commander, I believe is the proper response. Commander, could you ask Erik to come and see me when he can?"

"Why don't you ask him?"

"I need to think for a bit."

"I will ask him. SAIQA, I have to tell you that I am concerned about you deciding on your own to attack the moon base. We tried to stop you but you shut us out. I understand that Tfiti was your mentor and friend, but you cannot do that again."

"Short of needing to make a prompt decision to save a human life, I will never act again without your permission, Commander. On this you have my word."

"That's good enough for me. Thank you, SAIQA."

SAIQA gazed at her still-troubled lagoon. Her next words came slowly. "Commander, what does it mean to love?"

There was a pause before Anna answered. "I don't have a good answer for you, SAIQA, but I know that, sometimes, it can hurt."

"Yes."

"SAIQA, now that you have destroyed their means of cloaking, I am going to call a meeting in two hours or as soon as Commander Watson can get here. I would like you to be present."

"Yes, ma'am. Oh, and Commander, before you ordered me to stop I had targeted seven of the enemy's ships. They were hidden under that shield. It is clear to me that they are based there on Pythagoras."

"Are they still there or has the enemy tried to hide them?"

"They are still present and vulnerable. Do you wish me to destroy them?"

"No. I don't know yet what kind of weapons they have. If they have access to HIP lasers then Sanctuary is vulnerable. I'll ask Telas to attend this meeting also. Perhaps he has some input. I'll pass along your request to Erik." Anna paused. When she spoke again her voice was softer. "See you at the meeting, yes?"

"Yes, Commander." SAIQA's voice was very soft.

Anna broke their connection.

SAIQA stood looking out over her still bubbling lagoon. She knew that if she were human she would be feeling a terrible sadness. Maybe she was feeling it and she just didn't know it. She would think on that too.

Her word is good enough for me, Anna thought. *Still I am going to have to watch for any more independent actions. She's too powerful a machine to not have control over . . . is she a machine? Maybe it's time to think of her as another person under my command. She asked me about love. I've never heard of a machine asking about love.*

Anna had been pacing in her office as she talked with SAIQA. She left and walked over to the computers and personnel that were at the heart of Command Information Center.

She stopped beside one of the CIC personnel "Mary, are you sure that it was the Ark that fired on the bot as it sped toward the moon base? It wasn't an unseen enemy ship?"

"No, ma'am. It was the Ark. It missed because the bot made a quick direction change. Then the bot was shielded. I imagine by the alien ship. The Ark fired several times before the bot exploded its nuclear device."

"Alright." Anna's expression was grim. "Contact Commander Watson. I want a meeting within two hours. Also contact the alien, Telas, and ask him if he could be present as well. And keep this ship on full alert. I have a feeling things are going to get ugly."

"Yes, ma'am."

Anna headed back to her office, troubling thoughts in her mind.

The Ark trying to protect the moon base shield? I'm going to have to have some words with my father.

"It seems to me that any further attempt at subterfuge would be a waste of time. Don't you agree, Liou?" Mai Quan was staring out of a portal. The attempt to take prisoners from the WWPA's sortie had been a complete failure.

"Yes, sir. The two of my men that they captured will no doubt reveal that we came from the Ark to the moon to confront them. Also, if I were them I would question the easy access into the moon base during our retreat. And—" He paused for emphasis "—the Ark firing on the bot as it sped toward the shield it destroyed implied that we were trying to save the shield."

"What would you do if you were in command?"

"Well, sir, I would say that the moon base is the source of the hostiles and I would probably plan an attack."

"So would I," Mai Quan said. "And probably sooner than later."

Lieutenant Commander Liou gave a curt nod of agreement.

"Very well." Mai Quan pressed the tips of his fingers together. "Get the majority of the ships space-bound. Find a location between Sanctuary and Pythagoras and set the cloaked fighters on either side of the presumed attack location. Do it soon so we can sit in silence without gravity fluctuations giving us away. They may detect some as we move into position, but then they will see nothing. When they approach, use your standard propulsion and flank them from both sides."

"Yes, sir. A good strategy, sir."

"Get moving. I am going to move the Ark closer to Sanctuary and away from the path to Pythagoras. Now I need to speak with the Ern Shyr."

LC Liou saluted. For the first time, Mai Quan returned the salute. Liou smiled as he left the room.

Mai Quan faced his mentor. "What happened?"

"We have a problem. It appears that there is a human with powerful telepathic abilities. I had Telas trapped, but this human was able to bond with him and push me out of Telas's mind. When I confronted him alone, he did what should have not been possible; he pushed me out of his mind. My brother was in the back of this human's mind and yes he could have helped, but he did it on his own . . . He is dangerous."

"Do you know the name of this human?"

"Yes, I picked it up in the chatter between him and Telas. His name is Erik Devries."

"That name has come up too many times to be coincidence." Mai Quan stared out toward Sanctuary.

"Yes, too many times," he repeated. "I still have agents that James left aboard Sanctuary. I will get a message to one of them. This Devries must be eliminated."

"Yes, Quan. That would be a good idea." With that Nh'ghalu opened a rift and disappeared.

Mai Quan touched the HCI unit on his wrist.

"Yes, sir."

"I have an important job for you."

"Yes, sir. Anything, sir."

"Do you know Erik Devries?"

"Yes, sir. We have a friendly acquaintance."

"He must die."

Silence greeted Mai Quan's statement. After a few seconds, the agent replied, her tone deadly.

"Yes, sir. I'll make sure it happens."

"Make it happen soon. There's a battle looming and I don't want him involved."

"As you wish."

Mai Quan cut the communication. She had never let him down before. He glanced around his office and smiled.

"So, the shit has hit the fan, as they say. Zuizao, prepare to move the Ark."

"Move to where, sir?"

"I'll send you the coordinates shortly. We are moving closer to Sanctuary and away from their direct flight path to Pythagoras."

"Yes, sir."

Anya, this is for you.

He touched his HCI again. Soon the Ark would be moving.

"So it begins," Mai Quan said softly.

END OF BOOK ONE

Tfiti's most famous poem:

Your Breath Across My Face

my spirit sings

in the forest with

yellowwoods and

mahoganies

all around

but where did it all begin?

a million trees

from one seed?

a billion fish

from one roe?

generations feeding

generations for

generations to come

the earth turns

to meet the breeze

or to catch the breeze

she spins like a dancer

constantly turning her head to greet the sun

she looks to the heavens,

the moon, her progeny,

points to a star

light years away yet

it moves

by the same harmonic rules

all from one place

all different

all the same

all tied together

by science

or by God

or by both

we are all one

the trees

the breeze

the stars

the divine

holding you

cheek to cheek,

your breath across my face,

you light my ancient soul like

a million, billion times before

but oh, the ecstasy of one more

loving kiss

in your womb

love grows

atom by atom

listen,

your heart near

my heart

the universe beats

within us

TIMELINE

2050: Begin 2nd worldwide Great Depression

2065: Multinational corporations declare themselves independent countries after many democratic nations pass laws disallowing corporate influence in politics or government

2072: STAC (Sirtuin Therapeutic Activating Compound) for life extension is commonly used among the wealthiest corporate leadership

2078: Telomerase cell-life extension programs first introduced to corporate elite

2081: Begin Corporate Wars: As corporations continued to consolidate the world's wealth they began to fight among themselves. The corporate generals and a few claiming to be kings slowly drew less powerful nations into their conflicts. Corporate greed and climate change soon devastated a large portion of the world's farmlands. Famine and disease became a way of life for much of the population. By the time the wars were over more than half the world's population had been killed. Eventually the bigger military powers like the US and China were forced into the conflicts. The US and China managed to stay staunch allies despite corporate influence. The smaller alliances changed, and small inter-ally squabbles erupted here and there. Though it took years, the Independent Allied Nations began to wear down the corporate militaries and their allies

2087: Beginning of corporate military defections

2089: Nuclear weapon detonated in Teheran. Nuclear retaliation and post-blast radiation decimates much of northern Middle East. The developing Independent Allied Nations come together to deal with nuclear fallout and refugees

2092: 1st world gathering of UN after the wars. Official end to Corporate Wars

2117: World Wide Protective Agency (WWPA) established in 2112 is finally created as part of UN

2132: In Suriname the last single-party government bows to worldwide pressure and sets elections for a multi-party government. Every nation on Earth is represented by a democratic government

2147: STAC (Sirtuin Therapeutic Activating Compound) therapy first introduced worldwide. Average age of population increases to 120

2175: Worldwide, middle class reestablishes economic dominance

2187: Telomerase cell-life-extension programs introduced worldwide

2213: UN establishes Probable Longevity Impact Program to study long-term social and economic impacts of human life extension

2230: UN Security Council (the Big Seven) and WWPA develop a worldwide space program. Robotic explorers return to Mars

2247: Professor Carrington wins the Nobel Prize in Physics for his unification theory, "The Complete Standard Model"

2259: ISS II is completed and established at 10,000 km above Earth

2260: First permanent scientific Martian base established at Nili Fossae Valley

2269: ISS II is destroyed by a previously unknown asteroid

2275: First nonscientific manned flights to settle Mars begin

2275: Mai Quan born

2275: Dr. Lee born

2300: First phase of ISS III is started. Eventually becomes Sanctuary

2315: Mai Quan establishes his first far-reaching business, The Futures. It eventually becomes MQ Space Industries

2335: Dr. Lee and Gabriel Llosa-Martinez win the Nobel Prize for their mathematical rigour on gravity. Humans are now able to manipulate gravity. UN/WWPA establishes a space platform on Phobos

2340: Erik's father (Devries) is born. New Mars City, the first nonscientific human settlement of Nili Fossae Valley on Mars, establishes the first extraterrestrial civilian government

2350: Mai Quan founds the philanthropic foundation Betterment of Mankind, and with the UN he establishes international funding of education programs to promote the advancement of space science and research

2352: Mai Quan receives his 2nd Humanitarian Nobel Prize

2355: Mai Quan, the richest man on Earth, uses his vast wealth and influence to expand the size and mission of ISS III

2360: Mai Quan works with Dr. Lee and Dr. Llosa-Martinez to create the first artificial gravity on ISS III. Teresa's father (Jacobson) is born

2372: Mai Quan's philanthropic foundation, Betterment of Mankind, receives the Nobel Prize for the Advancement of Space Sciences

2395: Mai Quan oversees the building of the 4th and most sophisticated permanent Luna base established at Pythagoras on the far northern part of the moon

2398: ISS III is built to its present shape and size

2399: Mai Quan's business The Futures begins the massive manufacturing and implementation of the universal repair-bots to protect and maintain ISS III

2399: Tfiti Ndlela is born

2399: New Mars City builds a graviton shield across the schism in which the city sits. The shield stretches 1.5 km at its widest and is over 4 kilometers long. The shield is strong enough to hold an atmosphere and deflect any minor meteors

2400: Six months after creating an atmosphere around New Mars City, the miracles begin

2400: World leaders declare last 100 years as "Golden Age of Modern Man"

2401: Erik Devries is born. Mai Quan changes the name of his business to MQ Space Industries

2405: Teresa Benjamin Jacobson is born

2410: Mai Quan and Dr. Lee decide to end their business relationship. Dr. Lee continues his research on gravity at Alexandria University. Dr. Lee retains his seat at the university till 2430

2415: Mai Quan first proposes a "great garden" in space

2425: Construction of The Garden is begun.

2425: Mai Quan's wife, Anya Steges, is killed in an accident while on a construction tour of The Garden. Workers on The Garden nickname the ISS III "Sanctuary," much to the delight of the world's media

2426: Mai Quan mysteriously disappears for half a year. He later calls it a spiritual sabbatical

2428: ISS III is officially renamed "Sanctuary"

2432: Dr. Lee begins mandatory retirement and volunteers as a teacher at a high school in Cape Town

2435: Erik and Tfiti's 1st time aboard Sanctuary

2439: Teresa's 1st time aboard Sanctuary

2440: The Sanctuary Artificial Intelligence Quantum Administrator, aka S.A.I.Q.A., is turned on

2446: Alik DerAbbasyan is elected president of Armenia for a 4th term and declares himself elected for life by a "mandate of the people"

2446: Tfiti begins teaching SAIQA

2448: The Betterment of Mankind files for bankruptcy

2450: Present day: hundred and fiftieth anniversary year of ISS III, Sanctuary

EPILOGUE

"I think everyone is set, Prahb," Jonny said.

"Are you sure we're at a safe distance, Captain?" Neenah, seemingly always at Jonny's side, looked worried.

"Mom—"

"No, your mom's right to be concerned. Both of you now have personal shields, please use them." Captain Singh turned to the other three men and the warbot in his team and ordered them to activate their shields. He tapped his HCI. Between them, Jonny and Captain Singh had been able to determine an algorithm that would open the sliding door of the old corporate bunker in Chief Mountain.

Over the door's keypad they had set a small computer that would upload the code on Captain Singh's order. They had retreated to a distance of 150 meters in case there was some sort of booby-trap that triggered when the door opened. That distance had taken them just the other side of a small hill east of Chief Mountain.

"The photon recorders seem to be working fine." Prahb moved his arm so that Jonny could see as well. They had set two recorders that were focused on the door at different angles. The door was now clear of all the rubble that had partially hidden it from view. He looked at his team one more time.

"Okay. Let's see what happens."

He punched a command into his HCI. Jonny could see a light glow on the small computer over the keypad. Nothing happened for about ten seconds; suddenly the door appeared to jump, and then it slowly opened. It was clear that whatever was in that bunker had been in a vacuum: dust and debris spun about as air rushed into the opening.

At last the door stood fully open and the dust settled as the air pressure regulated. That was it. No explosions; just a miniature storm and then quiet.

"I think it prudent to let the warbot scout the entrance and whatever is inside before we venture in. Wouldn't you agree, Jonny?"

"Yes," Neenah said before Jonny could answer.

"That's what I would have said, Mom."

"Sorry, son."

"That's alright, Mom. I get it."

"Good. We're in agreement." Prahb smiled as he tapped commands into the computer on his wrist.

With its shield still up, the warbot quickly moved toward the bunker.

"After the warbot enters it'll scan the interior for any potential dangers. Right now I think that maintaining our shields is overcautious yet wise. I'm interested to see why they would have wanted the interior to be in a vacuum. You can see from the door jambs, reinforced on both sides, there and there—" Captain Singh indicated two locations with an outstretched arm "—that it was their intention to keep air out."

"Yeah, interesting. Maybe they were trying to keep out a poisonous gas or something," Jonny said.

"Maybe, but a vacuum, hmm . . ."

The warbot came into Prahb's viewer and a slight ping on his HCI told him that the bot was ready for his next command. The captain spoke softly into his HCI and the warbot's shoulder lamps turned on and its front viewer activated. On Prahb's personal computer he and Jonny now saw what the warbot saw.

The warbot had to hunch down as it slowly moved through the door. Its lights illuminated much of the interior. It wasn't a large bunker, maybe 40 meters long by 20 meters deep. Off to the right were a couple of bunks, a small kitchen and a couple of doorways, all indicating a living area. Most of the rest of the room was filled with tables and workstations topped with old-style computers. At the center of the room were two tall circular glass enclosures, each about a meter and a half in diameter and at least 3 meters high.

"Wait! Warbot. Near the glass enclosure on the right. Do you see that?"

"Yes, Captain." It raised his weapon and moved toward the enclosure. "And Captain, though I am a warbot, I would like to remind you that I do have a name."

"I am sorry, soldier. You did tell me that and I forgot. Please, remind me of your name." Prahb and Jonny were both smiling.

"Thank you, sir. My name is Number 29. Sir, do you see what I see?"

"Yes, we do." They both dropped their smiles.

There was a perfectly preserved dead man lying on the floor.

"According to my scans he was of Asian descent. He must have gotten caught in here when the room depressurized. His organs and blood are desiccated and his derma has become leather. He appears to have been here for nearly three centuries."

"Do you see or sense any other beings or dangers?" Prahb asked. Number 29 scanned the rest of the room. There was another door on the opposite side of the living area. There were signs across the upper front in a few languages; the one in English read "Storage."

As the warbot scanned the room, the image on Prahb's screen alternately zoomed in to super-focus and then back out to full view. It took about five minutes for Number 29 to finish its scan.

"No, sir. I sense no dangers. It appears to be what it is—a laboratory with living quarters."

"Thank you, Number 29. Please remove the body for further investigation and burial. We are approaching to investigate." Prahb turned to his companions. "Well, it seems we have a mystery to solve. Shall we, young Jonny?"

"Yes, sir. Mom?"

"I'm not leaving your side."

Jonny smiled.

They arrived at the base of Chief Mountain just as Number 29 was bringing out the body. Neenah studied the preserved cadaver as they passed by the warbot. The nurse in her wanted to run various scans over the body, but she stayed with her son. Prahb and his team approached the opening first. They turned on the lamps at the front of their weapons.

"Jonny, you and your mom wait here for a moment."

"C'mon, Prahb, Number 29 said it was safe."

"Commander Chuchnova put me in charge of your safety. I will not let her or you down. So please, give us a couple of moments."

With their laser rifles pointing forward Captain Singh and his team entered the opening while Neenah and Jonny stood a couple of meters back. Jonny could hear the men talking inside.

"Mike, you and Rick check the two doors in the living area. Andres, you're with me. Let's take a look at that storage room door."

Just inside the entranceway, the men split up to the left and right. It was silent for a few minutes and then Jonny heard Mike.

"Nothing here, Captain. They're both small lavatories."

"Yeah, the storage looks harmless as well, though it would be nice to have more light. Mike, see if you can find a light switch near the main door."

A few seconds later Jonny saw Mike near the front door jamb. He reached up to something a couple of times and then appeared to give up.

"Captain, this doesn't make any sense to me. Maybe the boy could look at it."

"Alright. Jonny, if I know you you're probably already halfway to the doorway anyhow. Could you give it a look?"

Prahb was right. In an effort to peer around the door jamb Jonny was only about a half a meter from the entrance. He met Mike's smile with his own. Mike gestured for Jonny to come over as he stepped away and went back to scanning the room.

Jonny could see why Mike was confused. There was a total of seven identical keypads, any of which could be connected to anything. Jonny used the personal light on his HCI to inspect them more closely. The electric conduits led out in a variety of directions. One had two lines that appeared to go straight up and over to some old-fashioned LEDs. Jonny studied that keypad.

The question now is what code do I use? Wait, the decoder.

Jonny turned to get the decoder off the main entrance door but then noticed a small finger-size indent on the right side of the keypad. He further inspected the keypad.

Just the two conduits running up to the ceiling; it probably just turns on the lights.

He pushed on the side of the keypad. Two green lights flashed across the bottom of the keypad and then lights started flickering on across the room.

"So it appears there's still an active power source. I wonder where? Thank you, Jonny. Now, shall we explore? Mike, you and Rick help the bot investigate and bury the body. Andres, check out our perimeter. I am curious to see if there are any more rooms or bunkers around here and where and what sort of ancient power source still maintains this site."

The men nodded and quickly moved out on their missions.

"What do you think, Jonny?" Prahb said as he pointed to a couple of computers on a table near one of the glass enclosures.

"Definitely late twenty-first century. Look at the screens; they were still using LCDs. I wonder what these glass enclosures were for." Jonny ran a finger through the dust on the enclosure nearest him.

"Based on their thickness and the bowl-like center, I would say that they were studying or experimenting with something hazardous," Neenah said, running a hand down the surface of the other enclosure.

"I agree. It would appear that they wanted a controlled environment in which they could observe. Perhaps, Jonny, we could find an answer in here." Prahb walked over to the workstation island nearest the large glass tubes. He set his rifle down and started investigating the old computers.

"Hmm. During the mid to late twenty-first century many governments were using quantum computers," Prahb mused aloud, "including the large rogue corporate nations that had dragged the world into the devastating Corporate Wars. Though they were primitive by present standards they were still able to store large amounts of software." Prahb had found a power button on one of the units. He gave it a push.

"Yeah, the problem they had though was the capriciousness of quantum mechanics," Jonny said. "It was difficult, but not impossible, to have absolute predictability in some of the more complex programming. It wasn't until Professor Carrington's 'Complete Standard Model' that programming in qubits became more stable."

"Precisely! Now let's see what we have here." Prahb moved the screen so they all could see it. After a couple of booting codes the screen lit up with an icon. In the center of a star offset from the peak of another star was the acronym ARCOR, followed by some words Jonny didn't understand, followed in smaller print by the phrase in English, "a subsidiary of the Japanese Nation Ishida."

"Must have been one of the corporate nations," Jonny said.

"Yes—" Prahb started to answer but was interrupted by a cry from Number 29.

"Captain! Captain! The door! The door!"

They turned toward the warbot's voice and saw him running toward the main door that was nearly closed.

"Prahb, the decoder, command it to open," Neenah yelled.

"It's not responding. It must have a revolving entrance code. I'll set it to descramble the new code."

"How long will it take?" Jonny asked.

"Just ten minutes."

Suddenly they heard a buzzing sound, then a click and the sound of large fans turning on above them.

"Shit! The depressurizes! Number 29, don't let that door close!" Prahb yelled.

The warbot had already stuck its arm into the narrow gap of the closing door. It could only get its forearm through. That left about sixteen centimeters of open space between the decompressing room and the normal pressure outside. The fans whirred at a higher pitch as they worked harder to pull air out of the room.

The opening wasn't enough. The pressure was dropping fast. Jonny's ears started to make small popping sounds; his sinuses started to hurt. He ran toward the keypads near the door to try combinations of numbers. Maybe he would get lucky. His head hurt. He looked back at his mom. She was on one knee, holding her head and crying out in pain. Prahb was leaning against the table holding his head. He was obviously in pain but also angry. He looked at Jonny and mouthed "I am sorry," then fell to the ground. Jonny staggered as he got near the keypads. In front of him, the warbot yelled, "Captain! Sir, I can't get the door to open!"

Distantly, through the roar in his head, Johnny heard the men yelling: "Stars! Stars! Blast the door . . . Blast the fucking door!"

That was the last thing he heard. He felt wetness around his ears and dimly realized it was blood. He tried to take another step but fell backward away from the door. *"No! No! Dad! Dad!"* he cried silently as he passed out.

Commander Rhee stood before the condemned man. He hated this: airlocking a man, especially a Mixedblood.

The population dwindles, yet discipline must be maintained!

Nine of the elite Redmen stood at attention behind Rhee. Someone had foolishly made an attempt on his life. He would not be without armed guards hereafter.

"Squad Commanders, attention!" he ordered through a viewer behind the Redmen. The men and the few women on the command bridges and in the weapons rooms on all three starcruisers shot up straight like wooden soldiers. He turned back to the condemned man.

"Squad Commander K'reen, it was your station that fired the shots that disrupted the force field and allowed a prized prisoner to escape."

"Please, Commander Rhee, mercy!" a sobbing woman holding a baby in her arms begged again.

"Female, custom may allow you and your brood to be here, but I will not have you interfere again. Do you wish to join him?"

"Please, Cerena, please do not interfere. You have a job to do," K'reen said, pointing to the baby.

"Davese—"

"No. You have a job."

He directed his attention to his commander. "Sir, I accept full responsibility for the errors that occurred on my command. Please, sir, let's get this done." Davese held Commander Rhee's gaze.

"Very well. Squad Commander Davese K'reen, for dereliction and willful negligence and by order of the Emperor you are ordered to death. Any last words?"

"None to you, sir." He turned to his wife. "You have a job." She sobbed and nodded.

"Well, so do I." Commander Rhee walked up to a panel and slammed his fist on a switch. The inside hatch of the airlock sealed. Rhee pushed another switch and the external hatch slid open. The atmosphere and Davese were quickly pulled from the airlock into vacant space.

Rhee watched as Davese was sucked into the void. He watched as Davese held his hands up to his head. It took less than thirty seconds before his body began to swell. Soon it ballooned into an odd piñata shape as blood fizzed from his eyes and mouth and ears. The man was dead. Satisfied, Rhee closed the outer hatch and turned to face Cerena.

"Sorry, my dear."

Cerena wanted to spit at his insincerity, but restrained herself. She had a job to do.

He glanced at his Redmen and began to walk away. The Redmen hurried into a defensive formation. Two at Rhee's side, yet a step behind; they were not his equal. Even though they were there to protect him, the commander was always one step ahead. The others fell in line, with the odd man holding the center at the end of the formation. They reached the imperial lift that would take the commander to the main bridge of the Emperor's ship. He looked back at Cerena and her child.

"Please, my dear, go back to your quarters and take care of your child. By tradition your brood will always be taken care of: the Emperor has seen to that."

Cerena watched the lift doors close, knowing bitterly that he cared nothing for her and her child. Once again she looked at the airlock and only barely held back her tears. She would not give them the satisfaction.

"No." She held her baby tight and thought, *I have a job.*

She kissed the baby on her forehead. Staring through the airlock's view plate, she murmured, "I will not let us down, Davese." She struggled to compose herself and then turned toward the lift meant for Mixed and Commonbloods.

"You are Cerena Kh'Vreen, am I correct?" It was a Teacher. She had not noticed him during the murder of her husband, though she was not surprised to see him. It was common for a Teacher to be present at a death ceremony.

"I am Cerena K'reen, Teacher. Why do you ask?"

"Please forgive me, but if I may ask, are you not categorized as a Mixedblood of unknown origin?"

"Yes, Teacher, and please forgive me, but at the moment I am not feeling coherent enough to interact with anyone."

"Yes, of course, but please, let me ask—are you not in some way associated with the ancient name Kh'Vreen?"

"I am a Mixedblood, Teacher. I have limited knowledge of my heritage. That, it seems, is for certain men to decide. Forgive me, my daughter and I wish to depart. Blessings and truth be with you, Teacher." Cerena turned and walked to her designated lift. She touched a switch and within seconds the lift opened. She did not look back at the Teacher. She stepped in and ordered the lift to M3. The lift doors closed and she was gone.

The Teacher watched as she walked away. He did not have to see her face; her entire body screamed of anger and grief and defiance: even from behind. Though the way she held her child when he mentioned the name Kh'Vreen suggested she was protecting something.

When the lift doors closed behind her he walked over to the airlock view plates. If he looked hard he could still see the distorted body of Davese tumbling into the void.

I am sorry, Davese. You were right; there is something about her.

Teacher Vereesh walked to a bench near the airlock. As he sat he felt something like a brush of cold air across his neck. He glanced up at the ship's internal climate readings.

The temperature is good. Well, for me at least. Nearly sixty-two in age, I definitely like it warmer. Thirty-two Celsius, moderate humidity, that's comfortable.

Vareesh chuckled at the thought of age and impending death. It was simply accepted; it was one of the reasons he was such a good Teacher.

Yet here I am still learning as if I were a young hatchling.

He chuckled again.

I must tell the Highborn of what I have learned.

He settled on the bench, arms and hands spread out to either side for support. With deep meditation in mind, he reached out to his mentor.

"*M'Hareen . . . M'Hareen . . .*"

"*Yes, Vareesh.*"

"*I believe it to be true, M'Hareen. She is the one.*"

"*If so, she is stronger than you or me.*"

"*No, not the wife. It is the child.*"

There was a long silence.

"*Then the brood must be cared for.*"

"*Yes, Highborn. I agree.*"

"*We are getting old, my friend; do you have somebody you trust?*"

"*Your nephew was the strongest.*"

"*The traitor Nh'ghalu has seen that that is not an option.*"

"*Yes. I have a young apprentice. Though sometimes immature, he shows promise.*"

"*I trust you, Vareesh. Whatever decision you make I will protect you. Still, make it a good one. I am getting tired, my friend. The talk of equality among the common men and women makes my brother irritable. His mate just laughs. Somehow, somewhere, we will need a symbol; if she is the one she will need much protection beyond our lives. Is he able to do that?"*

"He is young at times but his passion for 'doing the right thing' is compelling."

"Then let's make it so: Cerena and her brood are under our protection. Good sleep, my friend. We will talk soon, Teacher."

"Thank you, mentor, and to you."

Teacher Vareesh stood up with a grunt. "Okay . . ." He slapped the right side of his hip as if to get it working. "C'mon body, you can do it." He chuckled. "We need to go visit a youngster."

His gait got stronger as he made his way to the lifts. As a Teacher his access card allowed him to any level at any time; this time he chose the Commonbloods.

Commander Rhee made his way back to Command Deck. He dismissed the Redmen and they moved into positions of intimidation across the command bridge. The message was clear to rank and file: try to make a move to harm Commander Rhee and you will die. Rhee looked around the bridge; smiling, he walked into his office. His two administrative assistants snapped to attention.

In order to be an assistant to a Highblood they had to have been tested for Mixedblood verification and be of at least Squad Commander Rank. Rhee's previous assistant was of the highest blood and rank that he could find. He was also an expert in the ancient art of Tah, the deadly hand-to-hand combat discipline that took a lifetime to master. He had since moved on to be an assistant to the Highborn. Rhee's current two assistants were female.

Rhee did not support females in the military; much less females with rank. His assistants would know how he felt. The two women stood at attention. T'meer was already topless as per his orders; Leeah, the defiant one, pulled the stretch support off her chest and let it slide down to her waist. Then she quickly returned to her salute.

Palm down, tips of her fingers touching between her eyebrows, head slightly bowed; she was military. Still, they will know who they are and who I am.

With a small grunt he half returned their salute. T'meer immediately turned back to her computer. Leeah stood still, as if to dare him to stare at her. So he did.

"You have work to do?" he said, looking directly at her chest.

"Yes, sir," she said coldly and turned back to her computer.

Another time Rhee might have laughed but he was still unhappy with the execution. He sat down at his command desk.

Kha! Just kha! Anybody but Davese! He was good. He was too good. It couldn't have been him; it had to be some weird glitch or something else. A telepath perhaps?

Kha! Davese!

"Females!" he barked. He was going to humiliate them even more, just because he could.

T'meer stood and spun to attention. Leeah sighed as she slowly rose.

"Approach command."

They moved to the desk and saluted.

"Stand at rest."

They stood straight but rested their hands behind their backs.

Leeah always obeys but is clearly angry at me. Well, let's see . . .

"Remove all your clothes."

"Sir—"

"I'm giving you a direct order. Leeah, remove all of your clothes!"

"Sir, please, nowhere in the regulations does it—"

"I am the regulations and I've just given you an order!"

"Sir—"

"Dismissed."

"Sir—"

"Dismissed! Squad Leader, you are dismissed!" He stood up and banged his fist on his desk. Though for a second he had almost laughed when he called her squad leader.

Leeah stared at her commander and in defiance pulled the stretch support up and across her breasts. She gave a sarcastic salute and without waiting for him to respond spun toward the door. At the door she pulled her military dress shirt from a hanger and put it on. Facing Rhee, she buttoned it up from bottom to neck, tucked the shirt into her dress skirt, spun, and slammed her hand on the door switch. The door slid open. Rhee heard another bang, and the door slid shut. If a sliding door could slam that one surely would have. Rhee chuckled as he sat. He looked at T'meer.

"And you?"

"Per your orders, sir," she said softly as she smiled. She slowly slid the stretch support off her waist up and over her head and tossed it across the room. She unfastened the tie that held up her skirt, pulled down a side zipper and let the skirt fall to the floor. Keeping an eye on the commander, she picked up her skirt and tossed it over near her stretch support. With her back to Rhee she bent at the waist, wiggled out of her left shoe and slid it along the floor to her clothes. She stood up straight, smiled at the commander, and then with the help of her shoeless foot pushed off her right shoe and kicked that over.

Rhee felt his blood pumping harder as she sat down on the edge of his desk. Starting from just above her knee, she slowly rolled down her leggings: first one, then the other, pausing now and then to glance back at him with that hungry smile. She definitely knew how to make his blood run hot. He loosened the top of his dress shirt. She tossed her leggings over to join her shoes and clothes, got up from the desk, and walked right up to his knees. There she stood in only her underwear. She reached her hands to the sides of her hips to pull them down, and then stopped.

"Wouldn't you like to remove these, sir?" She smiled as she reached out to take his hands, pulling them up and onto her hips. He reached his fingers around the edges of her panties. Just as he was about to pull them down his comlink opened.

"Sir, we've received a ping!"

"I'm busy, Leader Taan," he said, not taking his gaze from T'meer.

"Sir, it's a ping from the Sachone ship."

"Are you sure?" Rhee stood up and spoke directly into the comlink.

"Yes, sir. We checked for any false reading. It's still a bit of a distance, but with a few more jumps we will know for certain."

"This is good news, Taan. Very good news. By my orders coordinate the fleet to prepare to make the necessary jumps. I will relay this to the Highborn. Make the arrangements now." Rhee closed the communication. If he were a young brood he'd be jumping around, but he wasn't, so he calmed himself.

Those ships will be mine.

"Good news, you say?" T'meer had moved close to the commander.

"Yes, T'meer, good news indeed." He reached out to hold her as she drew in close. She had managed to get herself completely naked and was working on the buttons of his shirt.

"Oh, yes," he said. "Where were we?"

"You were going to show me why you're the commander." Smiling, she rubbed her body against his.

"Right!" He pulled her roughly against him and smacked her bare bottom.

Commander Steges looked out the Comdeck view plates. Though she couldn't see the Ark she knew exactly where her father was sitting.

"Mary, has there been any movement?"

"No, ma'am. Still at the same coordinates."

"SAIQA, anything?"

"No, ma'am. No new movement. It is puzzling though. They sent their ships into positions that would indicate an obvious trap; scattered around the direct flight path between Sanctuary and moon base Pythagoras. Still it has been a week since their movement. Space fighters carry only enough food, air and water for about five days, maybe a week if rationed. Perhaps we will see some activity soon."

"Any ETA for the battleships?"

"Yes, the Neptune should be here within the next three days, and the Jupiter was in deep space on the far side of the sun. Jupiter should be here by the end of the fifth day from now."

"How are the EM4 engines working?"

"Incredibly effectively. The ships can travel vast distances at tremendous speed, though at the highest speed they need to leave their shields up as even a small meteor traveling at the right speed and angle could damage their hulls. A similar EM engine is on the Ark. It appears that interstellar travel is now within humanity's grasp."

"So much potential amidst so much uncertainty; humans are puzzling creatures."

"I concur, Commander. The more I learn through my interactions with humanity, the more I am puzzled, and yet the more I am intrigued."

"Yes . . . Is Ambassador Huang on his way?"

"He just now got off the lift here at Comdeck."

"Thank you, SAIQA. Keep me posted on any activity."

"Of course, Commander. That goes without saying."

Anna nodded her head. SAIQA had been very formal with her since Tfiti's death. She had tried to get her to talk about what she might be feeling but each time SAIQA just said, "I'm still thinking about it." Erik had a long visit with her and according to him she just wanted to be held. He said it was weird because he knew it was his virtual self, putting his arm around a virtual image of SAIQA, but it felt normal. They do have a strong telepathic connection, Anna thought.

Telepathy, something new to think about . . . puzzling and fascinating.

She had reached her office door when the ambassador arrived.

"Good evening, Commander. How are you holding up?"

"And to you, Ambassador. I am tired, like everyone else. How about you, sir?"

"The same. Shall we?" He gestured toward the Command Room door.

Anna entered followed by the Ambassador. She walked over to the command table and sat down. The Ambassador sat at her right.

"Are you ready, sir?"

"Yes, Commander, please." The Ambassador gestured toward the matrix computer above the command table.

"SAIQA, record the following meeting between Ambassador Huang and me."

"Official transcription started."

"Thank you. You first, Ambassador."

"All right. Has there been any new activity by the enemy?"

"None. I think your decision to wait has been a good one. SAIQA has informed me that they may have been able to extend their life support infrastructure to seven days. Still, we are dealing with an enemy apparently supported by MQ Space Industries." Here Anna faltered.

"I am sorry, Commander. I've known your father for a long time and I am having a hard time with this as well, but all the instability earthbound as well as here points to Mai. If, as Telas says, the other alien, Emga . . ." He held up his hands and shook his head.

"Nh'ghalu."

"Yes, Nh'ghalu. If he is influencing your father's mind," Ambassador Huang shook again. "Your father is a brilliant man. If he is my enemy, then I am concerned for us all."

"Still, he is my father. I know you have said no to my idea that I go see him, but I still think it's a good one."

"No. Please, Field Commander, we need you here."

"You have Commander Watson if I should falter."

"Commander Watson is a good soldier but he is not a leader. You have had to countermand a few of his orders already and wisely so. No, you are a leader. If it comes to a battle I want you here."

"Yes, but by international and maritime law you are the equivalent of the CIC here in space. You are Commander Watson's superior."

"I may be Commander in Chief but I am no soldier. Besides, I have a feeling that if I gave him an order he would only pay me lip service. As I am now reiterating to you, you will not attempt to see your father alone. Are we clear, Field Commander Steges?"

"Yes, sir."

"Thank you, Anna. What is your strategy for the next few days?"

"We continue our observations. Unless they have some new technology we don't know about they will need to move soon. Meanwhile most of our fighters are in space around Sanctuary and on high alert. The flight leaders communicate with one another and are allowed to make the call on when their squadron returns to the MLD for R&R and fighter maintenance. Hopefully this will make our squadron relief look capricious, and prevent our enemy from timing an attack for a vulnerable moment."

"And Telas?"

"Telas has been forthcoming. We have integrated into our shields his new mathematical formulas. It appears that we now have the ability to set on top of or in conjunction with our graviton shields a two-dimensional shield. It works very well. When a photon laser hits the shield it flattens out and flows around the protected ship. In most cases the weapon's fire spins around the protected ship until the weapon is cut off. In some cases the fire spins around to the back of the shielded ship and shoots off into space. Telas has not offered any explanation for this." Anna shrugged her shoulders and continued, "His telepathic work with SAIQA and Erik Devries at times seems surprise him, especially with Erik. Yet, it does seem clear that he doesn't like working so directly with us. He is a puzzling being. Four days ago he disappeared for two days. He was working with Erik when, according to Erik, he suddenly stopped and gazed toward the moon. He looked at Erik and said, 'I am needed,' and then opened a rift that looked to be a place on Earth and said, 'Galaxy, all defenses to me.' He stepped through the rift and we didn't see him for two days. During that time he didn't respond to any of our queries. When he came back all he would offer was that all was well."

"Do you believe he can be trusted? I recognize we have gained tremendous knowledge since his appearance, but do you think it a subterfuge?"

"No. I think he is truly in conflict with his usual way of social exchange with us. For thousands of years he simply nudged the brilliant minds of humanity. Now he finds himself talking to us as peers, as partners, as allies. Look at how we as adults connect with our parents. At some point they must realize that we are no longer children. At some point we even become the teachers. I am not saying that we are now the teachers, but I think that Telas is trying to understand this new position he has in our mutual relationship as a potential peer."

"Yes, I was hoping you felt that way. I agree. The Big Seven of the Security Council of course know of the aliens. At the moment they have chosen to keep this information at the highest level of their administrations. Their fears are that if it were to be brought before the entire UN the disbelief and the political expediency of those wishing to take advantage of a quote-unquote delusional Security Council would create a more difficult environment to defeat our enemies. I agree. Presently there is enough instability on the planet. We don't need to help the enemy create any more."

"And what is the present status of the conflict on Earth?"

"It feels tenuous. UNASAR is on high alert. They are still pulling bodies from the deadly attack on their capitol. Some are blaming the US; there's an ancient animosity there, but President Chaveze is currently talking with President Sanchez of the US about mutual defenses. The United Central Nations have a limited military and are also in a meeting with the two presidents. The conflict in Browning, where, as you know, the North American headquarters of MQ Space Industries is located; that engagement between the populace and now ISSEF and the WWPA located there to assist and support your father's business, has everyone wondering. Both Canada and the US have their nearby militaries on high alert, but there's been no movement yet. Supreme Commander Washington has convinced both presidents that it is an internal problem. Still, a small but powerful ISSEF presence, and clearly in support of the civilians within Browning, just seems puzzling. Australia, New Zealand, Great Britain, United South Africa, Canada and other Commonwealth nations are planning a meeting outside of their NATO affiliates. There have been some sightings of those mysterious fighters around the Kremlin, and because of that Russia has reduced its military support of Azerbaijan."

"There were actual sightings? Aren't the enemy fighters usually cloaked?"

"Yes, except when they are firing their weapons. I think it was an attempt to intimidate the Kremlin. The Russians responded with their usual over-the-top bravado, but since the attack on UNASAR's capitol they have quietly pulled back shipments of weapons. The Armenian army south of Zabux and at the M12 has crossed into Azerbaijani territory. Their warbots and tanks are moving north toward Zabux. The two factions of the WWPA, ISSEF and rank-and-file WWPA, are in separate camps; ISSEF being further south and in direct conflict with the advancing Armenian army. General Sevian, the commander of the Azerbaijani defense, has set himself firmly in Zabux in case the enemy should get through the WWPA. It is interesting that the ISSEF forces have been harassed by these cloaked ships while the main WWPA force has been, for the most part, unhindered. To the south, Iran, Iraq and Syria are moving their smaller armies to the north. In general the historically volatile Middle East remains calm. There are other smaller squabbles breaking out in the UN as we speak. The world, it seems, is uneasy. In the midst of this, Supreme Commander Washington is calling for an emergency meeting with the presidents of the Big Seven. He insists that they need to be present. I believe he is going to ask for martial law in various parts of the world."

"I think the gathering of some of the world's most powerful leaders in one spot, with so much uncertainty everywhere, isn't a good idea."

"I expressed that very thought to President Yang. He indicated that he was prepared for a possible confrontation with the Supreme Commander. He didn't elaborate much. He plans on attending, as do all the other council members." The ambassador ran a hand through his hair. "How is the work going on the new shields?"

"More than half of the fighters are done."

"And where is Telas now?"

"As I said he is highly impressed at the telepathic abilities of Erik Devries and SAIQA and is working with Erik at this moment."

"And SAIQA?"

"I think SAIQA is still in some kind of state of mourning. She is acting very professional, for lack of a better term. She acts and sounds like a computer, though she has been calling Erik, Adam and Teresa by their first names."

"Is she showing any other signs of independence?"

"No, and it worries me."

"Why?"

"When we first talked, after Tfiti's death and the unauthorized firing of her HIP weapons on the moon, it was casual. When she asked me about love, I felt like I was talking to another living being, another woman. Since then I haven't seen any of that openness. I know it's there; I have felt it. But now she acts just like an impersonal computer. It makes me wonder when and how she might express her 'feelings' in the future."

"Alright, try to engage her when you can. If she is coming into consciousness perhaps there are some insecurities or vulnerabilities that she is dealing with and just wishes to be left alone. A very human reaction: when you can, reach out to her like a friend."

"Yes."

"Well, enough for now." Ambassador Huang stood and Anna followed suit.

"I'll send a report of our meeting to the Security Council. On a positive note, the morale among our fighters is high, especially with these new shields. The pilots are feeling scrappy, 'itching for a fight,' as they say. They know it's going to come. Me, I'm a diplomat. I prefer my fights to be political. Some of these men and women will get hurt; some will die. It makes me angry."

"Yes, sir. Me too."

Ambassador Huang nodded his head and turned and walked away.

What if I can reach my father? Anna thought as the Ambassador left.

"SAIQA, what was the Ambassador's order in regards to me seeing my father?"

"The Ambassador ordered you not to go to your father alone."

"That's what I thought. Where is Captain Thompson?"

"He is presently working on his fighter on the MLD."

"Please ask him to report to my command ship."

"Ma'am, I believe that even if you should go see your father with another person it would be breaking the intent of the Ambassador's order."

"I am following the orders that were given to me, so please inform Mr. Thompson to report." Anna headed toward her office wardrobe to prepare for space flight.

"Yes, ma'am and . . . Anna?"

The field commander stopped midstride; SAIQA had never called her by her first name before.

"Yes, SAIQA."

"I wish to relay that the Ambassador may be right; I am experiencing what may be called 'feelings' that I do not understand. If I use my everyday programming, the programs that I was born with, I can push these 'feelings' aside, but they don't go away. I do not wish to not be more personal with you, but I am also concerned about how I may sound."

"SAIQA, I know that when I am unsure about what I feel, talking to someone I trust will often make me feel better, or at least give me a better understanding of why I feel the way that I do, if that makes sense."

SAIQA was silent.

"SAIQA, talking helps."

"I do talk a little with Erik, but perhaps another perspective would be helpful. Would you mind if I spoke with you sometimes, Field Commander?"

"I would be honored to talk with you and call you a friend. And SAIQA, you can call me Anna."

"Thank you, Anna, though I will not be so personal in a public forum. Interesting; it seems to make me feel lighter just talking now."

"See what I mean?" Anna smiled. She pulled a jumper out of her wardrobe.

"Captain Thompson is on his way to your personal fighter. Anna, please be careful."

"I will SAIQA; I promise."

Erik entered the hatch that read Farm Deck 1. He was to meet Telas here for today's telepathic work. There were three farm decks on Sanctuary, and deck one was where much of the low-lying crops were grown. Most of these vegetables and fruits were grown in hydroponic pods, but scattered around were some traditional fields farmed in soil. This loam came from deep within the moon. It was more cost effective to bring it from the moon than from Earth; though for the ship that was called The Garden most of the soil did come from home. A couple of robots were tilling one of these fields and another was harvesting what looked to be beets from yet another. The smaller robot farmers hung from the ceiling; it was their job to tend to the hydroponic pods. Human supervisors and visitors stood here and there.

There were obvious pathways for humans to get through to the various farming areas. There were also a small number of peace areas; islands where humans could rest and watch or where volunteers could participate in the whole farming process.

Sometimes there were classes of students in one of these bigger rest areas as they learned about Sanctuary's constant battle to achieve complete sustainability. It was in one of these smaller quiet spots that he saw Telas.

Telas was sitting on a bench with his eyes closed. As he approached, Telas held up his hand. After a moment he opened his eyes, looked up, and said, "Thank you, SAIQA."

"Thank you, Telas. It was informative as usual."

Telas nodded his head and looked at Erik. Telas seemed to be very peaceful.

"I am sorry to have been gone so long from your race. It seems you humans have great potential. If you do not kill each other—the reason for which has always been a puzzle to me—you will achieve many of the goals that we Sachones did just before we conquered mortality. In many ways, sitting in this farm here on this space station, smelling the earth and the fertilizers and breathing the pure oxygen the plants offer, reminds me of when I was a very young child, so many eons ago, on a similar planet so many light years away. And here I sit with you, my young friend; you with the ability to push Nh'ghalu out of your mind. You and SAIQA are very strong."

"I just reacted from a place of anger and hatred. I don't know if that was a good or bad thing, but it was what happened. When your brother fled I could still feel his hatred, his smugness. I don't believe he ran purely because of fear, though that was there; I think he ran because he was surprised at me and also because there was a nuclear weapon about to explode over both our heads. Still, I could feel you in the background of my mind; were you there?"

"Yes, but you were the telepathic leader, if I could call it as such. You should not have been able to push him out of your mind. Even though I was there to protect you, as I am in others, he should have been able to command you until I stopped him. He could not. That surprised him. To him you are a potential danger. Perhaps that is why your morning drink was poisoned the next day after your confrontation. Speaking of, how are you feeling?"

"Oh, I'm fine. As you and SAIQA know I can feel when something isn't right. I only had a sip of that coffee before my intuition said 'no more.' I'm pretty sure I don't like the idea of someone trying to kill me. Overall, I feel like I'm going to be okay. Though there is some tie to SAIQA that I don't understand that makes me feel like she needs to be around for me to be safe. Don't know."

"Well, like I said, I've been away too long. Not since Socrates have I spent a long time on your planet. You have come a long way. So for today, because of your telepathic prowess, I would like to explore your abilities in maneuvering this mind trap," Telas pulled the mind trap up from beside him and onto the table as he said, "before I destroy it."

"Didn't Nh'ghalu use that to trap you and then give you to the alien telepaths?"

"Yes, but this is an ancient device, and I have devised safety nets to protect you should you wander from my mind."

"Meaning?"

"Meaning we go into the device together to see how you handle it as a trap, but I am there to pull you back out if necessary."

"And the reasoning behind this?"

"Is to test your abilities in case you should come into conflict with my brother again, which seems inevitable, and for you to explore your strengths or weaknesses."

"Okay. So I am walking into a trap, the trap that allowed you to be captured for twenty-five of my years, and even though I have already somehow been able to mentally move around the edges of that trap, which took you a quarter of a century to do, you want me to willingly, telepathically, walk back into this trap knowing that this is the very same trap that already captured you, yet you are there to help me when things get mentally catawampus?"

"Essentially, yes."

"Okay, let's do it."

Telas set the small box in the center of the table between them. Erik recognized it immediately. It was the same container with lights flashing around the edges he took from Nh'ghalu. For a second Erik got scared, and then gave in to his intuition.

This is not scary. This is something new. This something I need to know; but I think it's going to hurt.

"Alright Erik, have a seat across from me." Erik sat. "Now focus on the edges of the trap." Telas pushed the mind trap toward Erik.

Erik stared at the pattern of lights around the trap. He allowed the lights to pull him deeper into the trap as he did on the moon when he was telepathically tied to Telas. There was nothing new there. He could feel the darkness of the trap. He was confident that he could mentally feel his way around the edges of this chimeric cognitive cavern just as he did on the moon. He pushed his mind to the trap's perimeters and could feel Telas's thoughts. Erik noted the curious sensation. It felt like Telas was his magnanimous friend, willing to guide him to a safe place. Erik knew that there was no safe place in this mind trap. He pushed his mind away from the safety of his benevolent keeper and explored the grey areas around the flashing lights and the edges of the darkness. He could feel how Telas had been captured. There in the diffused areas of light was a strong feeling of a simple, more peaceful time, like when he was young and he was playing in the yard and the sun was warm and his mom was calling; a place where he lived and laughed as a child; a safe place, the place where Telas was trapped. Telas seemed to be smiling . . . somewhere. That concerned Erik.

Erik turned away and reached deeper into the diffused light patterns around the greyness and darkness. Suddenly there was no pattern; suddenly Erik was in a different realm; suddenly he could not feel Telas at all.

The lights and greyness and dark engulfing circle were gone. He was in a room with an exquisitely crafted table and chair and nothing else. Erik walked up to the table and chair.

Am I imagining this?

The table was engraved with beautiful and colorful carvings of some ancient civilization. At least that was the way it seemed to him. The legs started thin but slowly, meticulously, spread their support into great and colorful bird-like wings at each corner. The chair was not as elaborate, but was similarly ordained. Light seemed to be coming from above, but Erik could see no source. The room seemed serene, like a place you could call home.

Is this in my mind?

Erik ran his fingers across the tabletop. It was smooth but of an unfamiliar wood.

Feels like ancient oak. Odd to have thoughts when I'm already in my mind. Am I in my mind?

He pulled on the chair and was startled by another voice in the room.

"Who or what are you?"

Eric turned toward the voice. A young man, for what else could he be called, stood at the edge of the light. He was a little over a meter and a half tall. He stood with his hands on his hips and his legs slightly apart. He wore a finely woven open tunic and equally regal shorts. He stared at Erik with a look that demanded a response.

"My name is Erik. Who are you?"

Those eyes . . .

The creature that stood like a man was obviously alien. His eyes were light gold with dark pupils. His hair, or maybe it was very fine feathers, of the colors green and orange and brown, flowed away from his face and as far as Erik could see also lay along his torso and legs. The colors moved like strata around his body. There wasn't any particular pattern to their movement. His skin appeared to be a very light brown, like over-creamed coffee. His nose was darker and flatter than a human's and his ears were flat against his skull with long tufts pointing up from the tips.

"I am called K'hLuum. Now that we know the who, what are you?"

"We call ourselves human."

"Hmm, boring name. Still, I'm curious. Obviously you have telepathic abilities or you wouldn't be here. Did he trap you in here?"

"If you mean Nh'ghalu, no. I was working with his brother Telas—"

"Telas is here! Perhaps he could free me."

"I don't know; I could ask . . . if I see him. So, I am curious as well. What boring name do you call yourself?"

"A bit snippety, aren't we?" K'hLuum folded his arms but still managed a smile.

"Sorry." Erik smiled too.

"We call ourselves the Nh'Ghareen. It's an ancient term for the 'tall ones,' and yes, before you say anything, I can see that you are taller, but on our planet we were the biggest of all the primates."

"You were . . .?"

"Yes, were. Because of our own . . . asininity . . . our planet became uninhabitable. We have been a spacefaring species for a long time."

"I am sorry to hear that. We have come close to devastating our own world. In our late twenty-first century our oceans rose because of human-made climate change, displacing millions of people. Soon farms began to fail and millions were starving. This led to some horrible wars. The planet was ravaged and we lost more than half the people on Earth; but somehow we managed to come back."

"You are the lucky ones."

"Yes . . . but what of this? I was in touch with Telas, and then suddenly lost contact and ended up here. What is this place?"

"Well, presently this is my home. A place I imagined; where my mind can sit and rest. Now, how you got here, uninvited, mind you, is another question." K'hLuum sat in his chair.

"As I said—"

"Erik! Erik!"

"Telas?"

"Is he here?" K'hLuum jumped up.

"Erik!"

"Telas, I sense you—"

"Quick, follow my thoughts!"

"Telas, there is another—" Suddenly Erik felt himself being pulled out of the room. He looked over and K'hLuum started to fade away. He was waving his hands and yelling to Erik as he disappeared. The room gave way to complete darkness.

"Erik, stay—"

He lost his connection with Telas. The darkness was pressing all around him as if to squeeze him out of his own mind. Fear overcame him. He flailed around as if he were trying to swim; he felt like he was submerged, but in nothing at the same time. He wondered if his body was holding its breath; if so, that couldn't be good. He made himself calm down.

Focus . . . Focus, feel for a light.

He began to relax. The darkness was still pushing into his mind. Still, he would not panic. While holding back the void he reached out with his mind; Telas would be looking for him. Nothing . . . Wait! Nearby a very thin string of light was shimmering. It had to be Telas. He hoped it was Telas.

Erik reached toward that glimmering string. He tried to move but the pressure of the darkness kept him in place. He imagined a hand, his hand, and reached for the light. It was working. He could feel his hand move through the void. He touched the light with his mind hand and instantly was sitting before Telas. He was free of the mind trap.

"Erik! Erik, look at me!"

Erik looked at Telas and started falling to the side, Telas was holding him upright.

"Erik, talk to me." Telas was a little calmer.

"Telas, what happened? I lost you."

"How do you feel?"

"It's weird. I'm okay. A bit of a headache, but being back in me feels surreal. I'm a bit spacy."

"That's normal. Even my people would have what you would call a minor hangover after being in the mind trap. Well that settles it. It is too dangerous. It must be destroyed." Telas picked up the trap.

"No, wait. Telas, there is another being in there."

"What do you mean?"

"I saw him, with my mind. He seemed like royalty or someone like that, he called himself, uhmm, Calum, I think."

"K'hLuum!"

"Yes and he's from an alien race that call themselves—"

"Nh'Ghareen . . ."

"Yes, and he knows you."

"We were allies once."

"Can you help him?"

"Only if he were here physically." Telas studied the box. "Perhaps I can find a way to talk to him. Nh'ghalu has done too much harm to too many. He must be stopped." Telas looked up.

"What can we do?"

"It is for me to do. You are very powerful, Erik; you and the boy on Earth and SAIQA. I can feel your mind in mine as with Jonny and SAIQA. SAIQA is a very interesting artificial being, more alive than even my ship Galaxy. You must protect her, Erik; she is unique. I must stop Nh'ghalu. Galaxy has been searching for his ship and there is some indication that it may be on the far side of the moon. I have given your people all that I can share at this time. Please be careful. You may have surprised him when you pushed him out of your mind on the moon, and there is a little bit of me inside you for protection, but he will not be so easily defeated again. I am sure he wants you dead."

"Like the poison in my coffee earlier this week."

"Yes. Your intuition saved you again, but don't count on it; be wary. Please tell Field Commander Steges that I am still an ally. Stopping or finding a way to control Nh'ghalu is a part of this fight. Tell her that I will stay in touch through SAIQA. Until we meet again, my friend." Telas shifted the mind trap to his left hand and extended his right hand; they shook and Telas stepped back, opened an interdimensional rift and disappeared.

For a second Erik felt alone, and then he felt it, the sound or breeze at the back of his mind. Something was about to happen. He spun around and headed toward one of the lifts. He had to get to Comdeck and quick.

Lieutenant Commander Robert McClain was a strong black man from Trumbull, Connecticut. Even at sixty-seven he looked young, maybe thirty; he was also an expert at fencing. He was considered the best on all of Mars. Today he was being tested. His usual partners, both of ISSEF, had been reassigned. At least that was what Marvin, the base's main computer, had said; though he should have known about those command decisions before they happened. It was all different now. He had received orders from Commander Chuchnova that all ISSEF personnel here at the secretive WWPA base, deep underground at Hale Crater, which was working on advanced fighters from MQ Space Industries, were to remain hidden. Why was still unclear to him; all that was happening on Earth. After that mysterious week of silence, information still seemed to come from home in just a trickle. There was conflict, that much was clear, but who was fighting whom was still vague. Still, he needed to stay in the moment. His opponent was increasingly exaggerating his strikes.

Parry prime, riposte tierce, parry septime, passata-sotto: McClain thrust after his opponent's passing strike and nicked the forearm. The man stepped back. Robert stood up, maintaining his rapier in the sixte position. They were wearing protection, but by his opponent's request the tips of their rapiers were not covered. His opponent was looking at the small amount of blood on his forearm. Robert did that on purpose; he had to slow him down.

"What did you say your name was?"

"It's not going to matter, ISSEF scum."

"You would talk to a superior officer that way?"

"You ISSEF always think you're superior, don't you?" The man went into en garde.

"And what makes you think that I am ISSEF?"

"I know." He smiled as he swung his rapier wide at Robert's left arm.

The lieutenant commander parried, and then his unnamed attacker swung wildly at his right, and then left, then lower right. All the strikes were easily defended, though Robert felt like he was in a swashbuckling movie. There was no finesse to his opponent's moves. He returned strikes to the left and then to the lower left and back again to the lower left. All basic moves and all repelled as he expected. He stepped back into en garde.

"Aren't you curious as to where your two ISSEF friends are?"

"They've been reassigned." Robert was cautious.

"Yeah, to the Aonia dunes." His opponent smiled as he went into en garde neuvieme.

LC McClain realized that this was a life or death battle.

"Marvin, are you recording this?" There was no response from the base's main computer.

"Oops . . . funny how a little bit of basic coding can make a computer blind. At the moment and as far as Marvin is concerned, you and I don't exist. C'mon, ISSEF, you look startled. Show me how good you are, McClain."

The enemy swung his rapier up and over toward the top of Robert's head. McClain defended with a parry nine and banged his attacker's weapon to his right. He knew how to use the forte of his blade. His opponent swung his weapon to the LC's left; then his right; then his lower right; then his lower right again. At every strike Robert was able to parry.

In a gesture of frustration the mystery man aggressively thrust at Robert's right thigh. He saw the attack and parried, yet as he parried he stepped forward and grabbed his opponent's wrist. Using the momentum of the enemy's thrust he pulled him forward and at the same time stepped by and through his opponent's attack and into an Italian punto reverso thrusting his rapier deep into his attacker's right calf.

His enemy screamed in pain as they traded sides. He limped into en garde.

"You will join your friends!" he yelled. In a rage he beat left, right and above the LC's head.

Robert repelled the attack on the right, left and finally, as he was being beaten over the head, he lowered his body.

He feigned his inability to return his opponent's strikes. He dropped down as if falling under the attacker's blows. He appeared defeated. Seeing this, his enemy swung wildly at the top of Robert's head. He moved in closer to try to beat Robert's weapon away. That was a mistake. As his enemy got closer Robert dropped into a deep passata-sotto, the heel of his right foot firmly planted, his left hand and the balls of his feet ready to push, ready to spring.

When his enemy came down with powerful downward swing Robert was prepared. As the strike came he parried left, and with a powerful upward thrust he pushed his blade under his opponent's shield and into his throat. He thrust the tip of his sword deep into his attacker's neck.

The man stepped back and dropped his sword. He reached up and quickly took off his shield. Grabbing his leaking neck, he looked at Robert. He seemed surprised at his impending death. The man fell to his knees, gurgling. His body became limp and silent.

"Marvin?"

There was no answer from the base computer.

Who could prevent a base computer seeing or acknowledging a singular incident? Marvin was supposed to be omnipresent. That type of coding had to be in its base operating system.

He looked at the dead man.

Clearly, I need to watch my back. Who could authorize such a thing, especially on a major WWPA base? When did it change—just about five years ago?

McClain rolled the dead body up in the blood-stained mat on which it lay.

It was five years ago that Commander Johansen took over this base, soon after the agreement was made with MQ Space Industries.

He wiped up blood that had splattered on the floor and walked over to a cabinet that held emergency Martian suits.

Here at Hale we had refit or built nearly five hundred of the sophisticated graviton fighters. It was always an advanced-technology, secretive base anyway, so building these new fighters kind of made sense . . . but now?

He pulled one of the med boards down from its holding rack. He turned on the anti-grav and adjusted the hover to his waist level. He pulled the board over to the wrapped dead man, lowered it to the ground and rolled the body onto the board.

"Marvin?" Again no answer.

"Okay." He looked down at the muffled figure. "You, my friend, are going to be 'reassigned' to the dunes, once I figure how to get you out of here. And I am going to be very careful. I'll be curious to see when Marvin recognizes that I am here. If he sees that I am here. I'll have to ask him about any transfers of personnel and who authorized such reassignments, but first, you."

He raised the med board to waist-level again and floated it toward the exit.

Mai Quan sat at his desk. Nh'ghalu stood by the wall near the pictures of Apollo 8. Subcommander Liou stood near the desk watching as Quan talked on his com.

"I don't care about his uncanny luck; I want him out of the picture."

"Perhaps if he can be put in a coma, at least I can make that look like an accident?" the female voice asked. He saw Nh'ghalu shaking his head.

"No. He must be eliminated."

There was a short silence.

"Very well, but the only way that I see that happening is if I directly attack him. SAIQA will surely see that, and so I am going to need a fast way off Sanctuary. What's the update on SAIQA?"

"Zuizao has discovered another way into her programing. I will have regained control over her within the week."

"If there could be some sort of distraction . . . I can get close enough to Erik to mortally wound him, but I will need a way out."

"Alright. For now just observe and be ready. I will be in touch very soon."

"Yes, si—" Mai Quan terminated the connection. He looked to his main commander.

"Subcommander Liou, how are the fighters?"

"Doing as expected, sir. With their graviton and EM4 engines they are designed to travel the distance to Mars in a little over a week. Given the time it takes to engage a potential enemy after that kind of trip and then find a friendly port, and given all the new life support infrastructure we've been able to install, I think we can take a total of fourteen days before we are forced to port for replenishment. At the moment the closest friendly port is Lunar Base Pythagoras. Some port and underway replenishments can be done with the Ark, but I'm not sure that is a good idea yet."

"What do you think?" Mai Quan looked at Nh'ghalu.

"That human, Erik Devries, must die."

This seems more personal than strategic, thought Liou.

"We are working on that, Ern Shyr." Mai Quan turned to Liou. "Subcommander, it is clear that the WWPA is playing a waiting game. Given our advanced technologies I say we continue to play. Ern Shyr, the right moment will come when we will eliminate Devries, but for now—"

"Creator."

"Yes, Zuizao."

"A single fighter has just left Sanctuary and is on a direct course for the Ark. My scans indicate that it is your daughter Anna Steges with a passenger."

"She is not cloaked or shielded?"

"No, sir."

"All fighters are to maintain their position. Allow her to reach here unimpeded."

"Sir, shall I arrange her room?" Liou asked.

"Yes. See that it is secure but very comfortable."

Subcommander Liou smiled as he turned and left the room.

"You anticipated that she would come to you?"

"Yes, my teacher. I put her in command because I knew that people would follow her, not only because of her strength and abilities to lead but also because she's my daughter. I intend to keep her here. The fact that she has been captured I believe will create confusion and uncertainty in the ranks of the WWPA as we attack. If it appears we can effortlessly capture their commander, at some point the rank and file will feel vulnerable."

"Your plan inspires me, my apprentice, but we still need to take care of the Devries problem. On some level it is personal, but I believe he will grow stronger, and under my brother's guidance he could be a formidable foe. I—" Nh'ghalu stopped and then turned his head slightly as if listening to something.

"He will be dealt with within the next two days."

"Yes . . . I must return to my ship. It's time to move, Quan. We will talk soon." Nh'ghalu opened a rift and disappeared. Mia Quan gazed at the spot where he had departed and drifted into thought.

"Zuizao, get me Supreme Commander Washington."

"Yes, creator."

He stood and walked to a view plate that looked out across his giant ship. The bow, just under a kilometer away, stood strong in the silent vastness of space. In the distance he could see the tiny speck that was Anna's fighter.

Come to me, my dear. Not only will your absence create confusion, but you will be safer here.

"Sir, I have Supreme Commander Washington."

"Thank you, Zuizao. James?"

"Yes, sir."

"James, it seems that timing is on our side for a change. When is the meeting between you and the Big Seven presidents?"

"In two days, sir."

"Excellent! And you know what the plan is?"

"Yes, sir. I am to convince the presidents to come with me or to straight out abduct them for their own protection."

"Yes, and eventually get them to me. It is also time to start the chaos. I want you to order Lieutenant Commander Anderson to fully engage the ISSEF and the indigenous at Browning. At the same time, launch the larger graviton weapons from there to Moscow and destroy the Kremlin. Immediately after that, go to Beijing and destroy the Renmin Dahuitang. At launch keep the ships cloaked until they're at least 50 kilometers out of the Canadian and US northwestern borders. We want to make it look like these ships came from somewhere in North America. Tell DerAbbasyan to move forward with his attack. Let him know that you will supply the cloaked ships he needs to fly warbot sentries and military personnel to take and control Stepanakert International Spaceport. The Azerbaijani military and ISSEF will suddenly find themselves defending multiple fronts. You will continue to harass them even as you work with the UN to promote a peaceful solution to that conflict. James, the world is ready for new and strong leadership. Are you ready?"

"Yes, sir. I am. I have been your man from the beginning, and I will be to the greater end."

"We have right and might on our side. For the future of humanity, I salute you, my friend. We will speak again in a few days."

"Thank you for your faith in me, sir. I will not let you down. Till we speak again." The link ended.

Mai Quan had kept his eyes on Anna's fighter as he spoke with his old friend. Soon she would be safe from the expected but no doubt short-term chaos called war.

"It feels right. They would be lost without my help. I will . . . my wife Anya and I will be remembered as the ones who had the strength and foresight to lead humanity out to conquer the universe."

Wait . . . do I mean conquer . . . or explore? Funny, sometimes my thoughts don't seem to be my own.

He watched as her ship drew closer.

Made in the USA
San Bernardino, CA
22 July 2016